Taking Heart
and
Daisy's War

Rowena Summers is a pseudonym for Jean Saunders. She began her career as a magazine writer, and has published over 600 short stories and some 80 novels. Ex-chairman of the Romantic Novelists' Association, she lectures at writers' groups in both the UK and USA, appearing frequently on radio and TV. She lives in north Somerset and is married with three grown-up children.

Taking Heart
and
Daisy's War

Rowena Summers

Pan Books

Taking Heart first published 2000 by Severn House Publishers Ltd
Daisy's War first published 2001 by Severn House Publishers Ltd

This omnibus edition published 2002 by Pan Books
an imprint of Pan Macmillan Ltd
Pan Macmillan, 20 New Wharf Road, London N1 9RR
Basingstoke and Oxford
Associated companies throughout the world
www.panmacmillan.com

ISBN 0 405 00280 8

Taking Heart

One

As the family gathered in the sitting-room of the tall Bristol house that Sunday afternoon, Quentin Caldwell looked at his three daughters with immense satisfaction and pride. There were none who could touch them for beauty as well as brains – and that was rare enough. Women were not supposed to have any intelligence at all, or if they did, they were not supposed to show it. He prided himself that they got the brains from himself, while the looks were all down to his beautiful wife.

At the thought, his composure slipped a little. Frances was so frail and delicate now, her smile alarmingly vacant as she quietly hummed a ditty from the far-off days when she had danced on the stage in front of royalty. Quentin knew she was still there in her dreams.

Such royalty, too, he mused. So many changes, in so short a time. The sad death of the old king had plunged the country into mourning, followed by excitement over whether the dashing Prince of Wales would be crowned Edward the Seventh, or give way to his passion for Mrs Simpson. And then there had been the uproar and scandal when he abdicated and the new and hesitant George the Sixth had been crowned.

Such momentous matters of state – and the wild speculation surrounding them – could put the modest affairs of people like themselves into a different perspective. But only temporarily. Only until whole livelihoods were turned upside-down, and someone had the unpleasant task of relaying the news to his family as gently as possible. And to Quentin the family had always meant everything.

"Why so gloomy, Father?" his eldest and best-beloved daughter Imogen asked him with a smile. "It's such a lovely day; tell us what's so important so that we can all go out and enjoy it."

1

"I wanted Baz to be here first," Quentin said with a frown. "The boy has no sense of time."

"You won't tear him away from his old boats on a day like this," eighteen-year-old Elsie chipped in. "He'll happily spend all his spare time chatting with the ferrymen on the river, and nothing's going to change that."

Imogen hoped Elsie's words wouldn't upset their father. His shop was his pride, and despite having three vivacious daughters he hoped and expected that his son Baz would eventually take it over and carry on the family tradition. But Imogen was all too well aware that at nearly fifteen, and with schooldays behind him, Baz had definite ideas of his own. The lure of the fast-flowing river Avon and the old salts, who passed on tales of adventure that went back into history, had captured his imagination far more than the idea of working in a clothing and haberdashery shop. They all knew it, even if their father refused to acknowledge it.

"Anyway," Daisy said, precocious at sixteen, and tossing back the russet curls that were her current vanity, "whatever the news is, it can't be anything *too* terrible!"

Her father said nothing.

Imogen felt a sharp stab of fear, and knew the truth of the old saying of a goose walking over her grave. She was more perceptive than her sisters and, seeing her mother drifting off into a world of her own as she gazed unseeingly out of the window as if to shut out everything else, she knew that something was terribly wrong.

It wasn't her mother, was it . . . ? But something was going to affect them all, and Imogen felt the strongest instinct to put her arms around all of them and protect them from whatever it was.

As the door burst open, she turned with a feeling of relief as her strapping young brother breezed into the room. He was closely followed by five-year-old Teddy, inevitably still trailing his blanket behind him.

Teddy's traumatic birth had caused the mental and physical affliction that had gradually turned their mother into the frail creature she was now. To his credit, their father had never blamed the boy, but nor did he give him the attention he deserved, with the result that Imogen and her sisters had initially lavished far more affection on Teddy than was good for him, and Quentin told them more than once that they were in danger of turning the child into a monster.

"So you've decided to join us, have you?" Quentin said to Baz now.

The fact that he spoke so mildly and didn't censure him added to Imogen's sense of impending disaster. She couldn't shake it off. Moments before, it seemed, the midsummer day had been so blue and sunny. It still was, and yet to her it was as if a big dark cloud had obscured the sun, though she couldn't say why.

"Take the child to the nursery, Imogen," her father went on, before Baz could make any sparky reply. "No, wait," he added, as Frances's incessant humming grew louder. "Your mother had better go too. It's time for her nap, anyway. Ring for Miss Lindsey to see to them both."

Imogen pressed the bell at once, thinking it heartbreaking that her once so-beautiful mother should be reduced to the status of a child with needs as simple as Teddy's. But she knew it was true. When the doctor had stated plainly and bluntly that Frances's mental state was declining rapidly into some kind of dreamland, the nurse-companion had become very necessary for both of them.

More than any of the others, Imogen remembered her mother as she had once been, enchanting them with her dancing at Christmas time and on birthdays, and entertaining them at the piano in the sweet voice that Daisy had inherited. Frances was softly singing a half-remembered song from those lost days now, but the mumbling words were no more than a parody of the lyrics she had once known so well.

Quentin swiftly crossed to his wife and drew her away from the window.

"It's time to stop that now, Frances," he said, his voice more husky than before.

"Stop what, my dear?"

He squeezed her hand before raising it to his lips. It was an old-fashioned, loving gesture that tugged at Imogen's heart, and from the way her sisters averted their eyes, she knew they felt it too.

"Your singing is purer than a nightingale's, my love,"

3

Quentin went on gently. "But perhaps you could treat us to it another time."

She nodded happily, and crossed her small delicate hands together, as demure as a nun. She was so thin now, her limbs so brittle that they almost seemed in danger of breaking if anyone hugged her too tightly. It was a relief when the nurse-companion came to take her and the complaining Teddy away.

"Well, thank goodness he's gone," Baz said feelingly. "He clings to me like glue lately."

"That's because you're his hero," Daisy said with a giggle. "You should be flattered, brother dear!"

"Well, I'm not," Baz retorted. "I don't care to be seen with an infant tagging along at my heels all the time. My friends will think I'm a milksop."

"Seeing that most of your friends are those burly riverside fellows, and that you can keep up with them with your banter *and* your fists from all I hear, I doubt that there's any danger of that," his father said crisply. "But now that we're all here, it's time to get down to business. I wanted you all here together for a very special reason."

He looked round at them again, knowing he was about to shatter their world, and thinking that he would give anything he owned to spare them what was to come.

His lovely girls were like three beautiful butterflies in their summer frocks, their complexions as fresh and clear as their mother's ever had been, the three pairs of doe-soft brown eyes looking at him with expectancy and curiosity. Especially Imogen, his Immy. He knew she must have a shrewd idea that they weren't meeting just to spend a Sunday afternoon together.

They were all growing up so fast. Even Baz was almost a man – and showed such assurance, he had to admit. The boy was lounging against the window now, his attention still drawn to far below the crowded hillside street where they lived, across the great seafaring city of Bristol, to the river whose whiff could be sensed even up here. And no matter how tainted or rank it was, it still seemed as pure as the finest wine to his son.

"Please come and sit down, Baz," he said abruptly. "I need everyone's full attention."

Baz flopped into an armchair, his thoughts diverted from how soon he could broach the subject of working for one of the ferrymen instead of continuing behind the shop counter, which in his opinion was no occupation for a young man. Let the girls do it, he thought loftily. They seemed to enjoy it well enough, especially when any of the young men of the town brought their mamas in to browse for their fripperies.

Daisy wasn't averse to flirting with them, flashing her big eyes at them and pushing out her small bosom as far as it would go. Baz sniggered to himself, feeling a tug in his loins at the thought. Not with regard to his *sister*, of course, but remembering some of the tales the sailors told him about the women in every port, and the games they got up to.

Elsie wasn't interested in flirting, as far as he knew, though you never knew much about what Elsie was thinking. And Immy was already secretly courting a young man. He knew, even if no one else did.

He'd followed them one day and seen how Morgan Raine had pushed his laughing sister down into the hollow on the grassy hill above their street and covered her mouth with kisses. She hadn't objected either, and he doubted that their father would be pleased to know of it. It was a little piece of information Baz was keeping up his sleeve in case he should ever need it.

"Are you actually *with* us, Baz?" he heard his father say more sharply, and he pulled his thoughts back to the sitting-room where everyone was looking at him now. He felt his face redden, thankful that they couldn't see into his mind.

"I'm sorry, Father. I'm all yours," he said quickly.

Daisy giggled and he glared at her. But some of Immy's anxiety was starting to transmit to all of them now, and she glared back at him.

Their father cleared his throat, picked up a pile of papers from a side table and shuffled them.

"I've had several lengthy discussions with our accountant, my dears. I won't bother you with all the details, but since Immy has been dealing with the business side of the shop lately, she can go through the figures later and see that what I'm about to tell you cannot be changed."

5

"Why should Immy understand things any better than the rest of us?" Baz said at once.

"Because you've never shown the slightest interest in figures, and it's a little late to start now."

Baz's face reddened still more, even though he knew the slight was true. He was a dunce when it came to figures; his skills were more practical.

"Listen to what Father has to say, Baz." His oldest sister turned on him. "What do you do to earn your keep, anyway? You're always down at the river—"

"I don't have to do anything to earn my keep yet!" Baz whipped back. "That's what fathers are for!"

As Elsie gasped and Daisy's hands flew to her mouth, their normally tolerant father lunged at him.

"You insufferable young prig! You'll be eating those words before this meeting's finished."

"If it ever gets started," Baz muttered, crimson now, and knowing he'd gone too far.

"Then let me start it at once by telling you that you will very soon have to think about earning your keep, my boy, because we are in serious financial trouble."

"What!" Imogen gasped. "But we can't be."

"Daddy, that can't be true," Elsie said uneasily. "The shop has always done good business – and still does, surely."

"Caldwell's Supplies – or 'the shop', as you all persist in calling it – will not continue to do the business that will keep us all in the same standard of living we've always enjoyed for much longer."

"What does that mean, exactly?" Daisy said, nervous now as the nightmare prospect of having to be a penny-pincher like the people who lived in hovels along the riverside suddenly dawned on her.

"Well, I don't see how there can be any problem," Baz put in, determined to show that he was sufficiently involved in the business to know what was what. "There's never a shortage of customers and we've always been on good terms with our regulars, so I don't see—"

"That's the trouble. You never see what's not right beneath your nose," Quentin retorted. "If it doesn't smell of fish, or have two oars and a few fathoms of water beneath it, you don't want to know, do you?"

"Well, I know it suits the girls, but I never wanted to stand behind a shop counter for the rest of my life," Baz retorted, too wound up now to mind what he was saying. "Any ignorant female could do that!"

"Well, thank you!" Daisy said indignantly. "You've got a nerve, Baz Caldwell. I'd say any idiot could row a boat and ferry a few paying passengers from one side of the river to the other. Where's the skill in *that*?"

"Will you please calm down?" Quentin begged as their voices rose. "We're not going to get anywhere if we all shout at one another. I want no squabbling, and I need to tell you what's to be done."

"Is it all cut and dried then, Father?" Imogen asked.

"There was no choice," he answered, his voice as flat as if someone had stamped on it.

In the small silence that followed, Elsie, normally the quietest of them all, spoke more assertively than usual.

"Won't you please tell us what's happened, Daddy? Nobody's fatally ill, or going to die, are they?"

They all looked at him as her words fell away, their thoughts immediately flying to their mother. As if he knew at once where their anxieties would lie, he shook his head.

"Nobody's ill or going to die, my loves," he said more gently. "But we're going to have to make a change in our circumstances."

"But *why*?" Elsie persisted, for once taking charge of the questioning, since the others seemed to have been temporarily silenced. "What's happened?"

"What's happened – is Preston's Emporium."

As they stared at him, he gave a resigned sigh. And to Imogen's eyes, he seemed to shrink physically from the larger-than-life figure they all knew.

"You'll all have heard of the name," he said at last.

"Of course," said Immy. "It's been mentioned enough in the retail circular. Its owners seem to have bought up half the north, if you believe their boastfulness."

"Believe it, darling," Quentin said heavily.

"You're not saying they want to buy out our lease, are you,

Father?" Imogen asked quickly, when no one else seemed willing to put the thought into words.

"They buy out whatever and wherever they want to, apparently. And now they're coming south to build on their little empire."

"But they're a northern company," Baz burst out, wanting to prove that he knew at least something about the retail trade. "They've never opened shops in the south before, have they? It must be a mistake."

"It's no mistake. We're only leaseholders of the property, and Preston's are intending to buy out the entire row of shops and turn it into another Emporium, which will establish them in Bristol."

"Well, why can't we just open another shop somewhere else?" Daisy said at once.

Quentin chewed his lip. "I'm afraid that's not possible, my love. It pains me to have to tell my children of our financial situation, but in recent years we've had to take far more out of the business than has been coming in. And then there were the riots last year, when we had to replace all the broken windows and the shop front, and restock after the looting."

Immy guessed where the other expenses were coming from. Their mother's medical bills were heavy, and so was the salary for the nurse-companion who looked after her and Teddy. She ached that her father was obliged to explain all this to them.

"What does the landlord have to say about it?"

"A verbal apology, followed by a letter of explanation," her father said, suddenly bitter. "But since he'll make a killing from Preston's, I suppose you can't blame him."

"Well, I think it stinks," Baz said passionately.

"Do you, Baz?" his father queried with the glimmer of a smile. "That's the most encouraging thing I've heard you say yet about Caldwell's Supplies."

"It won't be that any longer, will it?" Elsie said sadly. "*We* won't be Caldwell's Supplies any longer, will we? It will be Preston's. Will we have to work for them now?"

"Well, *I* won't," Baz raged.

"None of us will," Quentin said carefully. "But I'm afraid you haven't heard the worst of it yet. We have been living on

8

credit for some time, and there are simply too many debts for us to continue living in this house."

"*What!*"

He couldn't have said which of his children spoke first, since the sound seemed to be a collective cry that tore at his heart. He was a proud man who had always provided for his family, and never had he felt such a failure as he did at that moment.

Immy's throat was tight, but she knew she spoke for all of them. "Father, you can't mean it. It will break Mother's heart if we have to leave here."

"There are other houses, my dear. Other parts of the world that are just as beautiful as Bristol. Look how your Aunt Rose and Uncle Bertie have settled in Weston-super-Mare. You've all enjoyed visiting them at the seaside."

"You're not suggesting we go and live in Weston-super-Mare, are you?" Baz said at once. "I won't go, anyway."

"I'm not suggesting it," Quentin reassured him. "I'm merely pointing out that a house is just a house. It's the people inside it who make it a home."

"But there's no place where Mother will feel as comfortable as she does under Doctor Wolfe's care," Elsie pointed out, her voice catching.

Daisy went to her father and put her arms around him, pleading with him. "Daddy, please don't say we have to leave here. I couldn't bear it."

"You'll find young men to flirt with wherever you go, ninny," Baz said, lashing out in his bewilderment.

Daisy ignored him, but Immy too felt her heart sink. Leaving Bristol would mean leaving Morgan Raine, and she was still only on the brink of love, and learning what it meant to feel like a grown-up woman from the more experienced Morgan.

She wouldn't have known what to expect if she hadn't discovered the slim booklet inside a brown envelope in Baz's bedroom one day recently, detailing the kind of intimate information best kept out of childish heads. He had sworn it had been loaned to him by a boy from his old school, and she had demanded he give it back at once.

Before she'd confronted Baz, however, she had taken a sneaking look through the pages herself, and been astonished and embarrassed at what she had learned, since sex education didn't enter the Caldwell household.

Her father would probably deny that physical intimacy had ever taken place between himself and his wife, Imogen thought, trying to diffuse her heightened senses with some cynical amusement. As if all the children had been virgin births. She immediately felt her heartbeat quicken uneasily at the unconscious blasphemy of such a thought. But it was true that the frank details of how love could be expressed between a man and a woman was simply something she could never have asked her mother about, even when Frances had been sensible enough to answer them.

So Imogen had been left as ignorant as Baz and the rest of them, until Morgan Raine had begun to enlighten her about what their vicar would undoubtedly call the sins of the flesh – which didn't seem at all sinful to Imogen, and were deliciously intoxicating to the senses.

As the memories threatened to make her head go dizzy, she forced her mind back to the present, and what was happening here in this room today.

What Elsie had said was true. Her mother relied heavily on the family doctor for her welfare. She trusted him, and a less caring physician would have suggested long ago that Frances Caldwell's mind was wandering so rapidly that she would be better off with specialist care in an institution.

None of them dared say it, of course. But they must all realise now that whatever debts had been incurred during recent months, much of it must be due to the medical bills, and to Miss Lindsey's exorbitant salary, as the nurse-companion their father insisted that their mother needed.

"Father, if the worst comes to the worst—" Imogen began, hardly knowing what she intended to say, but knowing she had to say something to take away the greyness of his face.

"It's already here, my love."

But Imogen was nothing if not practical and quick-thinking. If a thing could not be saved, then you had to think of something else to take its place. A compromise that was half as good, or even better.

The shock of losing the business seemed inevitable, and was a trauma they would all have to deal with, but it was receding a little in her mind now, and being taken over by her reaction to her father's decision about the house.

"I agree with Elsie and Daisy that Mother will hate having to leave here, and it's surely the last thing we want. There's a way out of that, if you would only consider it."

"If you're a miracle worker, my dear, then let's hear it," he said without any conviction.

"Why couldn't we take in paying guests? It's a perfectly respectable situation, and the house is large enough."

The reaction was instant. "*Lodgers*, you mean? Have strangers living in the house, and have to share the bathroom and your mother's kitchen with them, and finding them underfoot every time we turned around? Your mother would hate it, and I certainly won't have strangers treating her like an – an – imbecile, because of her odd ways!"

He suddenly choked, and she was the one now to put her arms around him and hug him.

"Daddy, please don't dismiss it out of hand," she said quietly. "This part of Bristol is familiar to Mother, and it's about the only thing that is now. Sometimes she seems hardly aware of us these days, and she behaves towards us as if *we're* the strangers."

She knew he didn't like what he was hearing, but she plunged on. "As for her kitchen – well, I know you like to think that on Cook's afternoon off Mother does a little baking herself, but Miss Lindsey can't be her eyes and ears all the time, and one of these days I think Mother will either gas herself or set the house on fire!"

She spoke recklessly, but she should have known his response to any censure of his adored wife. He shook her off, his eyes flashing angrily – but before he could say anything Baz had put in his spoke.

"It's not such a bad idea, Father. You'd need to know the people had good pedigrees, of course, but I daresay Immy would see to that, since she's so good at organising."

"Of course I would," Imogen replied, not rising to his bait. She was just thankful to have an ally, however unlikely – and however much Baz was acting in his own interest, of course, she added silently. Baz wouldn't want to move too far away from his beloved river.

"We'd have to interview them to see that they had impeccable references," she went on, improvising quickly. "They would be elderly ladies or gentlemen with means, or respectable couples, or even theatrical people from the Old Vic. I'm sure that would please Mother. It would make her feel that she still had a toe in the door of her old life."

She held her breath as her words sank into her father's brain – and her own. The idea had quickly taken hold of her, and she couldn't see anything wrong with it. Sometimes the best ideas were the ones that came spontaneously. Her mother used to say it was as if fate was giving you a little prod in the right direction, and like Frances, Imogen was a great believer in fate.

As for the shop . . . well, they all knew that the shop was the fulfilment of their father's ambition, not theirs. Baz wanted to be out of it altogether, and she suspected Daisy had always had secret hankerings to follow a stage career. There were always auditions being held at the Hippodrome and the Old Vic, and who knew where her pretty sister might go if she got the chance?

Elsie was clever at hat-making, and took orders from many of the well-to-do ladies who frequented the shop. She could surely pursue that idea. Then there was herself . . . What was for her? What did she really want out of life?

She felt a sudden small thrill of excitement in her veins. Her young man, Morgan, worked in the print shop of a local newspaper: and perhaps she too could find some kind of work to do with journalism. It must be exciting to interview people, to attend dramatic events and report back to the newspaper, and to see your name in print.

More realistically, she knew that was most unlikely to happen. Young ladies didn't usually become proper journalists – but she had learned shorthand in order to take down customers' orders speedily, and she could type on her father's old black typewriter, so perhaps she could start off in a lowly department and work her way up. Maybe.

"This needs a good deal of thinking about."

She heard her father speak as if from a great distance, and she realised she had been totally wrapped up in her own thoughts for the last few minutes, dreaming of an ambition she'd never known she possessed. Until now. Until the chance had come to break out from a family business, and follow dreams of her own.

Guilt immediately flooded through her mind. How could she be so ungrateful, when their father had provided a loving home and a comfortable living for all of them – until now? But until now, none of them had even thought of breaking away. Except Baz, of course – and she had no real idea of what her sisters might be thinking, come to that.

She wouldn't know, until they left the room and had a chance to talk about it among themselves.

"Perhaps we all need to go away and think about things," she said helpfully.

To her surprise, her father was nodding thoughtfully, looking a mite less harassed than before. Bringing bad news out into the open always helped. It was a trouble shared, and all that rot, Immy thought. Even if you didn't always want to have to share it . . .

"If I'm to take this scheme of yours seriously, Immy," he said slowly, "there are a few other things to consider. In normal circumstances I wouldn't dream of dispensing with your mother's companion. But there'll be no need to keep her on when the shop goes, because none of you will be working there. Your younger sisters can help with the household chores, and you can take over Miss Lindsey's duties—"

Imogen gave a loud cry as all her fleeting, half-formed dreams of independence melted away in an instant.

"You could also teach Teddy his letters and numbers until he goes to school," her father went on blandly.

"Father, you can't mean that," she gasped. "I'll be little more than a housemaid!"

"And so will we," Daisy cried. "How will we ever meet young men, if we're stuck indoors all day with old people and boring lodgers?"

"Is that all you think of caring for your mother?"

"I didn't mean Mother," Daisy said, scarlet-faced. "I meant the strangers Immy wants to fill the house with!"

"You were all for it just now," Imogen snapped.

"Well, I'm not any more," Daisy sulked.

"And neither am I," said Elsie.

13

Baz snorted. "Well, I can't see anything wrong with it."

"You wouldn't!" Daisy rounded on him, all spiky curls and bristling temper. "You won't be here all day. You'll be out on your precious ferry-boats with those dreadful men you call your friends, all smelling of fish and the river—"

They suddenly realised that their father was laughing softly as the four of them wrangled.

"Daisy, my love, you do my heart good. You're such a terrible snob, and no one will ever get the better of you!"

"All the same, Father," Immy said quickly, deciding to leave the uncertain question of her own future for the moment, "I think you're wrong to think about getting rid of Miss Lindsey. Mother does need professional help. Sometimes she wanders out of the house alone when Miss Lindsey's taking her nap, and we've had to search for her to bring her back."

His mood changed like quicksilver.

"*What*? Why haven't I been told this before? That incompetent woman must be dismissed, and without references."

"She's not incompetent. She's just exhausted from the worry of trying to keep Mother safe," Immy told him.

"Well, she obviously hasn't succeeded if she lets her go wandering about the city," he snapped.

He swallowed convulsively. The house wasn't too far from the river, and the thought of where Frances might end up was suddenly all too graphic in his mind.

But he was determined not to give way to an emotional breakdown in front of his children. He waved them away and told them to leave him to think.

"And you might all do a deal of thinking as well," he added. "We all have to make sacrifices in this world, and it's never too early for you to discover it. Life has been easy for you until now, but only a fool or an optimist believes it will always be so."

14

Two

The four of them walked down to the river, where they usually did their thinking. Fishing boats and larger vessels jostled for position in the harbour, and sailors of every nationality jawed among themselves on the waterfront.

The aroma of fetid ale rose from the gutters, and the riverside women eyed the foursome with varying degrees of interest. It wasn't the most salubrious place to take a walk, and in the heat of the July sun, the stink was high – but none of the Caldwell family noticed it.

"It's not fair," Daisy burst out at last. "Daddy should never have let things get as bad as they have."

"None of it was his fault," Immy said, defending him at once. "You talk about being fair, but he couldn't have stopped Preston's Emporium bidding for the row of shops. He couldn't prevent the riots, either. Think about his feelings for a minute, Daisy, and not so much about your own."

"But he shouldn't have got into so much debt. Mother—"

"Are you saying he shouldn't have hired Miss Lindsey to care for Mother?" Elsie returned at once.

Imogen interrupted. "I'm sure we all agree that Mother should have *someone* caring for her, but Miss Lindsey must be a terrible drain on Father. She instructs Cook to buy all sorts of exotic food for Mother's delicate stomach, and then there's the ridiculous dress allowance she requested because of the way Mother upsets things over her precious clothes. She behaves more like the lady of the house than Mother herself."

"Well, at least you need have no fears that Daddy's thinking of installing her as a paramour should anything happen to Mother," Elsie said primly. "He's made it patently obvious that he can't stand her airs and graces, and only tolerates her because Mother relies on her so much."

15

"But that's just it, isn't it? Mother adores her, and Miss Lindsey knows it,' Immy muttered. "How is she going to react when Father gets rid of her?"

"What's a paramour?" Baz asked. He had been too enmeshed in his own thoughts to pay much heed to what the others were saying, but his attention was caught by the erotic sound of the word.

"None of your business,' Imogen said smartly, with a warning look at the others as they started laughing. "Anyway, why don't you go and find something to do, Baz? I'm sure all this serious talk is boring you," she added sarcastically.

"No, it's not."

"*Go!*" she said. "And I may just agree to have a game of draughts with you after tea."

Seeing that he always won, it was enough of a bribe, and after a few minutes she saw him talking animatedly with the old fishermen on the quay. Baz would find his feet, no matter what happened, she thought fleetingly.

She turned to her sisters as they sat down on one of the benches on the waterfont.

"Daddy wouldn't have to sell the car, would he?" Daisy said suddenly, aghast at the thought. "It would be such a let-down. I don't think I could bear to be poor—"

"You really are impossible sometimes, Daisy," Immy told her sharply. "There are plenty of people poorer than us, and in any case we all have feet – and bicycles. But selling the car would be the last thing Father would do, I'm sure. Mother does so enjoy being taken out for rides."

As Daisy fell silent at the rebuke, Immy went on determinedly, "So what do you think about the idea of taking in paying guests? I only said it on the spur of the moment, but the more I think about it, the more it makes sense."

"I'm not sure, Immy," Elsie said dubiously. "If Daddy's idea is to move into a smaller house, I assume he wants to dismiss the housekeeper and cut Cook's hours. If we take in paying guests, we'll probably end up employing more people than we do now."

"Unless Immy takes over all the household duties," Daisy said slyly. "As well as looking after Mother and Teddy too, of course. She could get paid a proper salary then. What do you say to that, Immy?"

Immy gave another smart reply. "Definitely not! I'll help Father all I can, but I've no intention of doing everything. You two will have to do your share."

She felt a pang of regret at the thought. It was all a far cry from her little dream of joining the newspaper trade. The charm of working beside Morgan hadn't escaped her; there would be a legitimate reason for seeing him every single day, instead of at snatched, secret moments.

When they weren't kissing and cuddling, he sometimes told her about the excitement of working in the newspaper office. It wasn't all local stuff, he'd say loftily. They got wind of troubles in Europe long before the ordinary public, and in his opinion they were heading for war.

It was then that Immy shivered. She preferred the love-talk and the kissing and cuddling to when Morgan got all pompous and serious. She *much* preferred it to any talk of war . . . although there were murmurings of it everywhere, and strong disapproval of the way Mr Hitler was becoming such a dictator. But Europe and its problems seemed very far away when you had never in your life travelled further than twenty miles or so to the coast of the Bristol Channel.

"Well, I didn't want to work in a shop all my life anyway. I shall look for a proper job now," Daisy declared, lifting her chin defiantly.

"Oh, yes? Doing what, darling?" Elsie asked her in amusement. "All you *know* is serving behind a shop counter."

"I might see if there's any work at one of the theatres. They must need somebody to make tea or paint scenery or be a prompt. I might even offer to be an unpaid understudy – just for a short time – until I'm discovered and they realise they've got a second Sarah Bernhardt right under their noses!" she added, as theatrically as could be.

The other two laughed at her nonsense. But if anybody had the guts to pull her socks up and do exactly what she intended, Daisy did, thought Immy.

"Of course, failing that, I might just go and ask Preston's to give me a job," she went on casually, testing the water for a reaction.

"Oh no you don't!" Immy snapped. "It would be like slapping Father in the face. You hear me, Daisy?"

Elsie agreed. "Immy's right. We all have to stick together. If Daddy decides to go ahead with the paying-guest idea, and if we have to do some of the work for some of the time, that's what we'll have to do."

"Hooray!" Immy put in, pleasantly surprised that Elsie should feel strongly enough to take a stand.

Suddenly they became aware that they were the objects of attention from a small group of swaggering seamen from one of the container ships that regularly came into the city docks to unload goods and materials. The men stood squarely in front of them, blotting out the sunlight and grinning down at them.

"Now that's what I call a sight for sore eyes, ain't it, lads? Three beauties with hair like fire, and as lush a trio of peaches as I ever did see."

"True enough, Sven. And just ripe for the plucking," one of his companions said with a snigger.

The first accent wasn't English. Like the second it was coarse and guttural, and Imogen seethed at the way the men laughed at their own joke, looking her and her sisters over as if they were prime specimens of cod on fishmonger Lacey's marble slab.

She heard Daisy give a nervous giggle, and knew that given half a chance her sister would react to these louts and start up a conversation that would soon degenerate. There was something wild about Daisy that needed to be curbed . . .

Just listen to yourself! Immy thought in disgust. Thinking like a maiden aunt, when she was only a month off her twentieth birthday.

"And where are you three beauties going on a fine day like this?" the second man leered. "If you're looking for company, petals, we've got a couple of hours to spare."

But Elsie too had had enough of these oafs and was already standing up, brushing down the skirt of her cotton dress and tossing back her hair as defiantly as Daisy ever did.

"It's time we went," she said firmly. "Come on, Daisy. Come *on*!" she added as her sister lingered.

They heard the catcalls of the men behind them, but took no notice as they linked arms and strode off along the waterfront.

They had no idea where Baz had gone; he considered himself too old now to be seen for too long in the company of his sisters.

"Don't take any notice," Immy instructed as the whistles followed them. "They've got too much time on their hands, and there are other girls for what they want."

"What *do* they want, Immy?" Daisy said, far too innocently.

"You'll find out when you're old enough and not before."

"Don't treat me like a baby! When I'm rich and famous—"

The words brought Immy up short. "Oh, please, spare us the theatricals! There are far more important things to think about – like how we're going to persuade Father not to give up the house, for a start."

And how could we have forgotten, even for a minute!

"You really are set on this paying-guest idea, aren't you, Immy?" Elsie said. "But I must admit I'm a bit squeamish at the thought of sharing a bathroom with strangers."

"There's always the old privy at the bottom of the yard, if you're so fussy."

"It wouldn't worry me," Daisy said airily. "When Mother was on the stage I know she shared rooms with all sorts of other people. It's what theatrical folk do."

She stopped abruptly as the image of her once lovely mother surged into her mind. In the box of mementoes Frances had hoarded there were posters of her in her spangly costumes, and theatre programmes with her name quite prominent. As a young child Daisy had been enchanted by the images, and pictured herself doing exactly what her mother had done – singing and dancing to the crowds and receiving their applause. She had thought then that it was glamorous and exciting, and she still did.

She felt Immy's hand on her arm, squeezing it tight.

"We all feel sad for Mother," Imogen said quietly. "But nothing can change what's happened, and we all have to go on and do the best we can, don't we?"

"I suppose so," said Daisy, blinking back the sudden blurring in her eyes.

"And right now we have to be strong for Father's sake. He must have felt terrible when he first realised how bad things were, and even if this doesn't work, just giving him the idea of doing something positive will revive his spirits."

"You're always so wise, Immy," Elsie said approvingly.

"Oh Elsie, for pity's sake don't make me sound like a saint," Imogen replied, irritated rather than pleased at this reaction. "I'm just thinking practically, that's all. None of us wants to leave the house, and anything's better than having to decamp down to Weston to move in with Aunt Rose and Uncle Bertie, isn't it?"

Daisy giggled. "You'd better not let Daddy hear you say that about his dear sister. I thought you liked them!"

"Of course I like them. But the thought of all of us cramped into that house of theirs doesn't thrill me."

"The beach is nice, though," Elsie said reflectively. "All that lovely sand – and the donkey rides for Teddy—"

"And all that mud when the tide goes out," Daisy added.

"Maybe if the worst comes to the worst and we *are* obliged to move to a smaller place, we should consider living there. Mother's always been very fond of Aunt Rose. Perhaps we could even open a tea-room on the seafront," Elsie went on, determined not to let her sister be the only one with ideas. "What do you say, Immy?"

Daisy squealed before she could answer. "It's a perfectly horrid idea! It's all right in the summer, but in the winter there's nothing to do. I don't want to live in the sticks, so don't you dare suggest it!"

But Immy was no longer listening to either of them. By now they had walked back from the waterfront towards the city, intending to join the folk who paraded about the town on Sunday afternoons. They headed towards the marketplace at Welsh Back, where the boats from Wales traditionally brought their goods for sale. But not today, of course. On Sundays the marketplace was washed clean, empty of fish and produce, and was a meeting place for young men and their lady friends.

And strolling along one of the alleyways leading off it, a young man was leaning towards a pretty young girl with hair the colour of corn, his arm loosely around her waist as she laughed up into his face. Moments later they had turned a corner and were out of sight.

"What's wrong, Immy?" Elsie said, suddenly aware of her

sister's quickened breathing and painfully flushed face. "Have you seen someone you know?"

"No – I don't know . . . I thought I had, but I'm sure I was mistaken," she said, trying desperately not to stammer.

She tried desperately to believe it had not been Morgan. *Her* Morgan, with the persuasive, silvery Welsh tongue, who had taught her the ways of love, and who could not possibly betray her like that . . .

She swallowed convulsively. It couldn't have been him. It was a trick of the light. Or perhaps everyone she saw resembled him simply because she longed to see him so much. Perhaps she heard an echo of him in every other man's voice because she longed to hear him whispering in her ear.

It was a known fact, according to a book she had read, that the mind could play strange tricks, conjuring up the beloved's face even when it was impossible for him to be in the place where you imagined it. Or something. It was why widows often imagined they saw their dead husbands smiling at them from the foot of their beds, when it was no more than an illusion borne out of loneliness and grief. She found herself reciting the ponderous words in her head as she tried to bolster up her confidence and belief in her beloved.

"You do look a bit odd, Immy." She heard Daisy's voice penetrate her whirling thoughts. "Perhaps we should go home and see if Daddy's had anymore thoughts on your idea."

Imogen tried to remember how disastrous their family situation was, but for the life of her, her own prospects kept getting in the way. Or, more likely, the lack of them. Morgan had never said anything about marriage, but she had assumed it was what he intended eventually, when her father decided she was old enough. Now she wasn't so sure.

She would rather think of *anything* but the sickening thought that Morgan was actually seeing someone else. But she couldn't divert her thoughts from the image uppermost in her mind, especially remembering how he had teasingly hinted that he was going to give her a very special gift for her birthday.

"It will have to be something fairly insignificant," she had teased him back. "I can't show off anything too brazenly, since my family don't know anything about you!"

It had been their lovely secret, and she had imagined a ring, or a locket, or some other token of love. Now, the idea of any gift at all seemed like a mockery. And she knew she must find out for sure if she had really seen him.

She couldn't bear to doubt him like this. Like her father, it had always been her way to face trouble head on. She stopped walking suddenly.

"I've just remembered that I said I might call on Helen Church this afternoon. It had quite slipped my mind with all that Father told us. She hasn't been well lately, so you two go on home and I'll be back at teatime."

"I don't know why you bother with her," Daisy said. "She's such a simpleton, and her brother's always bragging about joining the army, as if he's going to conquer the world if another war comes. I'm sure he *wants* it to happen just so he can become a hero!"

"I bother about her because she's my friend. And James Church has his head screwed on properly, Daisy. There's plenty of talk about another war in some circles."

"Well, I don't want to hear it," Daisy said. "Cook has too many gory tales to tell about the last one for anybody daft enough to listen to them."

"Don't waste your breath arguing with her, Immy," Elsie advised. "You go and visit Helen, and give her my love."

Immy watched them go, bright in their summer frocks, Elsie no doubt admonishing Daisy about her flippant attitude to anything serious. But that was Daisy, Immy thought, with a rush of affection for her youngest sister. And maybe it was no bad thing to be able to flit through life.

Her thoughts switched at once, knowing she was only going to make a token visit to her friend Helen, confined to bed with a sore throat for the past week.

Her first mission was to speed through the streets leading away from Welsh Back to see if she could catch another glimpse of Morgan and the girl he was with. Because, she realised as her heart gave an uncomfortable little leap, she was becoming more and more certain that she hadn't been mistaken at all.

Helen Church was sitting in the small summerhouse in her scented back garden when her mother called out that she had a visitor. She looked up from the book she was reading, and her pretty face creased into a delighted smile as she saw her friend Imogen coming towards her. She stretched out her manicured hand in welcome.

"Immy, how lovely! I've been so out of touch since I've had this wretched sore throat. I think everyone was too afraid of catching it to come near me."

"I'm sure that's not true," Immy said with a laugh. "But are you quite well now? And should you be outside?"

"Oh, pooh, of course I should! It's summer, isn't it? Come and sit with me, and when Mother's brought us out some lemonade, you can tell me all your news."

Her mother was nothing if not predictable, and minutes later a jug of fresh lemonade and two glasses were duly delivered on a tray, and Mrs Church was warmly enquiring after Immy's mother.

"As well as is reasonable to expect, Mrs Church. We can't really hope for more," Immy replied non-comittally, praying that she wouldn't continue with questions about the family. She wasn't ready yet to confide in anyone except Helen about how bad things were looking. Helen was the one who shared her secrets. The only one who knew anything about Morgan.

Immy had begun to realise that the shock of her father's news hadn't fully sunk in yet, and the vague plans for the future were no more than clutching at straws to try to make things seem less horrendous than they were.

Besides, Helen's family was more well to do than her own, she thought uneasily. Mrs Church was a distant relative of the nobility, however far down the scale – and Immy wasn't too sure how she would feel about her daughter's best friend contemplating taking in lodgers.

Being in trade was perfectly respectable nowadays, of course, especially when it was a family affair, but being obliged to take in lodgers was entirely different . . . and until this very moment, it had never occurred to her before.

"So are you going to tell me what's wrong, Immy darling?" she heard Helen's voice say gently, when her mother had left them alone. "I can see there's something troubling you. It's not – you haven't had a falling-out with MR, have you?"

She always used his initials, since it made the secret they shared seem more delicious.

"I almost wish it was something as simple as that," Immy muttered. "A falling-out can always be put right. In fact it only has a *little* bit to do with him."

"*What*, then? Goodness, don't keep me in suspense, Immy! What's happened to upset you? Has he said something – or done something?"

"No, and I dare say I'm just being silly. I imagined I saw him walking out with someone else earlier this afternoon, that's all. I'm still not sure if it was him, but it makes my stomach churn whenever I think of it."

"Well, you goose, you'll just have to ask him, won't you? But from the way you talk about him, I can't imagine he thinks of any other girl but you. I'm sure it wasn't him you saw."

"Perhaps you're right. I certainly *want* to believe it."

Immy took a long draught of lemonade, her eyes clouded, still certain it *had* been Morgan she had seen, and not at all sure how you went about tackling a young man to find out if he was two-timing you. That was the current expression used by all the Hollywood film stars, wasn't it? Two-timing. It sounded glamorous and sophisticated enough on the silver screen, but in real life it was just sordid and ugly.

And in a moment, it seemed, the sight of Morgan – if it had been him, for she had been unable to catch up with the couple and confirm her suspicion – had turned her from her usual confident, practical self, with a far more romantic and sensual streak than anyone else knew, into a mass of insecurity.

"So what else is it?" Helen persisted. "Immy, I hate to see you looking so unhappy. Is your mother worse – or has that idiot Baz rattled your father again with his talk of going to sea, or whatever his latest idea is?"

"We're losing the shop," Immy said abruptly.

Helen sat back, pushing a hand through her fashionably waved fair hair. A look that was almost bewilderment widened her blue eyes.

Like her mother, she was involved in charity work and committees, and had no need for a regular job. Her father, Gordon Church, was a prominent solicitor, and her brother James, just down from university, had a well mapped-out career in the army ahead of him. They were a world away from a family business in haberdashery, and Immy had never felt it more acutely than she did at that moment.

"What do you mean, you're losing the shop? Where is it going, then?" Helen asked, with an feeble attempt at humour.

"It's serious, Helen, and please keep all that I'm about to tell you to yourself, at least for the time being."

"I'm sorry, darling. And of course I'll say nothing. But I don't understand, so please won't you explain?" Helen asked more humbly.

Imogen drew a deep breath, knowing she had to say it all in a rush, because if she didn't she would probably dissolve into tears. "A big northern company is buying out the entire row of shops, and since we're only leaseholders of Caldwell's Supplies we don't have a say in it. Apparently we're in some kind of debt as well, and my father wants us to move to a smaller house, but we all know how Mother would hate it and that it would upset her terribly, so I've suggested we take in paying guests, and my father's mulling over the idea right now, and I know you'll think it's an awful thing to have to do—"

"Why on earth should I?" Helen's voice held genuine astonishment and more than a hint of indignation. "Do you think I'm such a snob, Immy? I think it's a brave and beautiful thing to suggest, and your father should be very proud to have a daughter like you who can turn thoughts of disaster into hope the way you always do."

"Good Lord, do I?" Immy said with a wobbly smile. "I told Elsie not to make me sound like a saint, and now you're doing it too."

"Well, there you are then. We all think the world of you – and so does MR, I'm sure."

"Perhaps," Immy said, plunging farther into depression, and wishing she'd never said anything at all. But she'd had to tell someone or burst. And Helen was her dearest friend, the one she could rely on to support her in whatever she did.

"You won't think badly of me if I have to kowtow to strangers living in the house, then?" she went on, demeaning herself still more.

"Immy, the day you kowtow to anyone will be the day the moon turns blue," Helen said. "And as for the other matter –

well, if MR turns out to be a rat, you can always marry James, and then we'll truly be sisters, won't we?"

Immy laughed hesitantly – for the first time in ages, it seemed. "I'm sure James wouldn't want to marry *me*!"

"Wouldn't he? Oh, well, I've got my own thoughts on that," Helen said airily. "But you can test the water for yourself. He's due home from seeing his pals any time now."

Immy felt a momentary panic at this new idea on top of all her other worries. "I'd better go, then. I don't want him to see me looking such a mess."

"You look perfectly lovely. And for goodness' sake, sit down again. I've never seen you so jumpy, and I'm sure you need to calm down before you go home and face the family."

Immy bit her lip. Helen was always calm, but then she had nothing in her life to ruffle her. Everything went along swimmingly, and no doubt in time she would make a wonderful marriage to a wonderful man and they would go on to have wonderful, well-behaved children . . .

"Immy Caldwell, if I'm not mistaken! By all that's wonderful, it's good to see you!"

Immy began laughing again as James Church swept into sight, tall and handsome, fair haired and blue eyed like his sister. She laughed up into his eyes, and felt her heart miss a small beat as she saw the warmth of his expression. She hadn't seen him for some months, and he had broadened in that time. If she hadn't been so head over heels in love with Morgan . . .

"It's good to see you too, James. How goes it?"

"Very well," he said, sprawling easily on another chair. "I'm joining my regiment in a month's time, and the outlook is exciting, if you know what I mean."

Helen groaned. "Don't start him on the topic of war, Immy. He's convinced it's coming, and we're never going to hear the end of it from him."

"Of course it's coming," he told her. "Why do you think the ARP service was formed last year if the government doesn't expect air raids in the future? And now they've ordered a thousand new Spitfire fighters to be built. They're not going to waste taxpayers' money on war machines unless they expect them to be used."

"Stop it, James. You're making me nervous," Helen said.

"So you should be. If Hitler decides to ride roughshod over Europe, we'll all be involved. We can't let him get away with it. Even you, my sweet, will find yourself having to buckle down and do some war work, even if it's only dispensing tea and sympathy at a military canteen."

"I'd be capable of more than that! Not that I think it will happen – and neither do you, do you, Immy?"

"We-ell, I suppose there has to be a reason why people are starting to move out of London to the country, and the wireless reports are always so gloomy," Imogen admitted, shivering.

"Oh, *them*!" Helen dismissed them scathingly. "Those wireless people would have you believe we were all going to be bombed in our beds at any minute."

"Or in our shelters. I know my father's starting to think they might need to build them," Immy pointed out, half wishing this conversation hadn't got so serious, but thankful it had taken her mind off her own troubles for the moment.

"There speaks a girl with foresight," James said approvingly. "So what will you do in the war, Immy? I rather fancy you as a nurse, soothing my fevered brow."

She grimaced. "Now you are tempting fate – and you shouldn't do it. I'm not sure I could be a nurse, anyway."

Helen had obviously been thinking about people from London being sent to the country for safety.

"We'd be quite safe here, though, wouldn't we? I mean, we're such a long way away from London. I'm sure life would go on just the same for us."

"Helen, sweetie, sometimes I think you live in a world of your own. If you bothered to read the newspapers you would know that the government is taking Hitler's threat very seriously indeed. If – *when* – war comes, life will never be the same again for any of us, and this will be a war of the air far more than the last one was. I'd say Bristol will be a prime target for bombing, with the docks and the aircraft industry. Nowhere will be safe this time."

Helen jumped up, her eyes full of distress now.

"You're being horrid and you're frightening us, James. Immy and I aren't going to listen to any more of it. We're

27

going indoors to play some gramophone records and leave you to your beastly old war fantasies."

"All right. But they're not fantasies, Helen, and pretty soon you'll have to believe it."

He caught hold of Immy's hand as she made to follow her friend. "You know I wouldn't scare you for the world, Immy. But I believe in being realistic, and I thought you would understand."

"I do," she said. "I think I'm beginning to understand only too well."

Before this afternoon she had never contemplated Bristol becoming such a target. And here, today, on this beautiful August afternoon, she didn't want to visualise the skies darkening with enemy planes. It was hard to imagine an enemy coming out of the blue, intent on killing people, or even that Germans could be their enemies again. The war to end all wars was long over . . . but perhaps clinging to such a belief was no more than living in a kind of fool's paradise.

She stayed a while longer, since Helen was clearly upset at James's predictions, and when she left she promised to come again the following week and report progress.

"And you be sure to tackle MR if you have any real doubts," Helen whispered as they said their goodbyes. "But I honestly don't think you've anything to worry about there, darling. I hope things go well on the family front, though"

They hugged one another, and Immy made her way back home, thinking how breezily life went by for Helen. She had never consciously envied her, but right then she thought it must be lovely not to have to worry a jot about money.

Until this afternoon, when it all seemed in danger of disappearing, it had simply never occurred to her to wonder how her father had ever managed to support a family and a large house with domestic staff all these years. But it occurred to her now.

Three

Imogen's mind was full of questions she had never thought about before, because there had been no need to question anything. Five years ago, when Teddy had been born and her mother had been so near to death after his traumatic birth, she had been only fourteen, and the others had been even younger. They were well-loved children who had been brought up with the old values of being seen and not heard, especially where adult matters were concerned.

But she was no longer a child, she thought resentfully. She would be twenty in a month's time, and she had already known another kind of love, however innocent compared with some of the sizzling kisses seen at the picture houses.

She bit her lip, remembering how Helen had once asked her, wide-eyed, if they had gone *all the way* . . . and she had answered crossly that of course they hadn't. Only a *little* bit of the way in reality, and it had seemed daring and a bit frightening when Morgan had begged to be allowed to slide his hand inside her blouse, and she had hesitantly agreed with red-faced embarrassment and a throbbing heart.

Nice girls didn't go all the way. *Really* nice girls never allowed more than a kiss and a cuddle, despite what the more racy and glamorous stars of the silver screen might imply.

But today, thoughts of Morgan slipped in and out of her mind with less comfort than usual, and she applied herself to the more puzzling matter of how the family had survived even this long if things were so bad.

She racked her brains and vaguely recalled a conversation from long ago, when her mother had still been drawing in the audiences at the theatre, and Aunt Rose and Uncle Bertie had come to visit. She had crept to the top of the stairs in her nightgown as she heard the raised voices.

"You should curb it now, Quentin. Her place is at home looking after these children, not showing off her body to all and sundry. We all love her dearly, you know that, but it's not a seemly occupation for a wife and mother."

"I'd like to remind you that Frances is my wife, Rose. If she chooses to pursue her career and I agree to it, then it's our business, and nobody else's."

Imogen had heard her aunt's eloquent sniff. "Oh, well, of course, if she's bringing in the money—"

"That's not the reason, and you know it, Rose. I won't have you belittling me. Not that it's anything to do with you, but all our money is invested to support the business. With Father's legacy, I've put as much into it as Frances has, so I won't hear another thing about it."

Imogen hadn't heard anything more about it either, and it was a conversation she had virtually forgotten. Money had never been a topic of discussion. It had just been there, as necessary as wallpaper, but with no need for it to be mentioned.

But now perhaps it should be. Her heart skipped a beat, wondering what her father's reaction would be if she were to tackle him. It wasn't a daughter's place . . . but if she had been a son, no doubt he would have confided in her. Baz was far too young and scatterbrained to be told the facts, but she was not.

She walked up the hill to Vicarage Street, where they lived, seeing the tall houses through different eyes now. She loved their house, and so did her father. He had been born there, and so had all his children. It was cruel that they need even think of leaving it, Immy thought fiercely, especially on the whim of some greedy northern shopkeepers.

She found her father in his study, sitting motionless at his desk and staring into space. Her heart turned over, unable to bear seeing him like this.

"Daddy, won't you take me into your confidence?" she blurted out, with a catch in her throat.

He gave her a vague smile, ignoring her question. "Do you know how rarely you call me that, Immy?"

She took the bull by the horns. "That's not because I think any less of you. You know I love you and I always will. But I'm grown up now, and I think I deserve to know what's happening to us. I'll bet you've told Aunt Rose," she said with sudden intuition.

Quentin sighed. "I've always respected her opinion, even if I haven't always acted on it. I wanted her advice about sending Mother and Teddy to stay with her and Bertie, and since she always has to know every detail, it all came out about the possibility of selling the house."

"But *why*? It belongs to us, doesn't it? I know your parents left it to you, and surely there can't be so many debts that we can't continue to live here – and even start another small business somewhere else when Preston's takes over."

He sighed. "We can't afford to keep paying the people who are dependent on us, Immy. As for starting another shop, I simply can't invest money that may not be returned. Why Preston's even want to move down here in such troubled times, Lord only knows."

"I hadn't thought of that. Why would they want to move their business south, if what everybody says about another war is true?" She felt a glimmer of hope as her thoughts went off in a different direction. "So perhaps all the rumours mean nothing at all. At least we should be optimistic about that!"

She was trying to cheer him up, to emphasise the fact that she hated the entire Preston clan, whatever their intentions. She hated them with a passion for destroying her life. But, she realised, her father was looking at her sorrowfully now.

"Darling Immy, your loyalty is commendable, but I fear it's not Preston's who have ruined us. It's your father's ineptitude with money and bad investments, and you have no idea how it pains me to admit it to my child."

"I'm *not* a child," Immy almost wept. "Please confide in me, Daddy. I want to help."

"By suggesting that we take in lodgers, you mean?"

"Yes, if it means keeping us all together, and keeping the house we love. What's so wrong with it? Are we so proud that we can't change direction if needs must?"

He said nothing for a few minutes. "You've a wise head on young shoulders, Immy—"

She stamped her feet in annoyance. "Oh, how I wish people would stop telling me that! I'm being practical, that's all. I'm thinking of Mother, and all of us. I want to stay in Bristol, and so do the others, Daisy and Baz especially. We certainly don't want to move down to Weston and live with Aunt Rose!"

"Would that be so awful?"

She stared at him. "I suppose you're thinking about that old war again. I sometimes think men are obsessed with the idea. James Church was prattling on about it earlier today. I think he *wants* another war!"

"I doubt that, but having been in the last lot, I can see his reasoning, darling. If he's set on joining the army, as you say, then he'll want to justify himself. You don't become a soldier to twiddle your thumbs and go on endless parades."

"We're getting off the point, aren't we?" Immy said, even though she knew she had started it. "Are we going to think about my guest-house idea or not?"

She was taking the initiative far more than ever before, but in a weird way she felt more like the parent, and he the child right now. He looked so uncertain, so beaten, and she had to do all she could to bring back the smile to his face.

"We'll think about it," he said. "But I still think your mother will be best off in the country, and Teddy too. And since it upsets you, I won't mention the reason why."

"And Miss Lindsey? Does she have to go?"

"She has already packed her bags and gone," Quentin said.

Immy was astonished. But, like herself she supposed, when her father made up his mind, he acted on it.

"You might as well hear the rest of it", he continued. "I didn't want to tell you all the bad news in one fell swoop, but Preston's people will be moving down here very soon, and we have to be out of the shop in a month."

"My birthday will be very eventful this year, then, won't it?" Immy said bitterly.

"You'll still have your birthday tea and your aunt and uncle will come as usual. It will be a good time to discuss the future. For now I propose putting up sale posters in the shop next week to sell off the stock. Until we finally close, one or other of you girls will have to stay at home to look after your mother. You may draw up a rota as you wish."

"You *have* been doing some forward planning, then!" But

she was more relieved than angry, because at least it seemed he was thinking more positively than before.

"Darling girl, do you think I would have wished all this to happen?" he said suddenly. "I don't intend to tell you the details, but I trusted people to deal with our investments, and it all went wrong. But at least we still have each other. As long as we still have the family, we'll be all right."

She ran around the desk and threw her arms around him.

"Of course we do. We always will, and that's what makes us strong, isn't it?"

Considering she felt as helpless a baby, she wasn't at all sure of her own words, but she felt his answering hug, and knew she had said the right thing. Then they both jumped, startled, as the door opened and Frances wandered in.

"I can't find Miss Lindsey anywhere," she complained. "She always reads to Teddy and me before teatime, and he's getting very cross."

Quentin spoke steadily, knowing that lies would be kinder. "Remember I told you about Miss Lindsey's sister who's very ill, my love? I'm afraid Miss Lindsey has had to go and look after her, and she may have to stay for quite a while."

"Will she?" said Frances, staring. "What will happen to Teddy and me, then?"

Immy felt her heart wrench. Where was all the vibrant passion her mother had displayed on the stage, the reaching out to the audiences that had made them adore her so much? Until that moment she hadn't realised quite how introverted Frances had become, with all the self-centredness of the semi-invalid. But perhaps it was better so. Teddy would display the tantrums, but not her mother.

"I'll come and read to you both, Mother," she said swiftly. "Would you like that?"

"Would you, dear?" Frances said in delight. "How lovely!"

Without a backward glance at her father, Immy took her mother's hand and guided her out of the study and upstairs to the nursery, where Teddy sat on a stool glowering.

"Where's Lindy?" he said, using his own name for the nurse-companion.

Immy answered him brightly, knowing what to expect.

"She's had to go away for a while, Teddy, so I'm going to read to you and Mother today."

"I don't want you! I want Lindy!" he shouted, kicking out just as Immy neared to him, searing her shins.

"You little brat," she hissed at him. "You'll have me and like it." She would not normally have spoken to harshly, but the events of today had stretched her patience to breaking point.

"Tell her, Mama," he shrieked, clutching at Frances's skirt. He was a beautiful child, but right now Immy thought him the work of the devil.

But Frances seemed quite unconcerned as Teddy clutched at her skirt. She pulled him on to her lap on her rocking chair and hummed softly, crooning to him and smoothing the hair from his angry little forehead.

"Hush now, baby," she told him. "We'll listen to Immy's story and then we'll have some tea."

They were like something out of a fairy story themselves, thought Immy. *And who knows what's to become of them . . . ?* She turned away, her thoughts in torment, and opened the book Miss Lindsey had been reading to them.

Elsie Caldwell was the quiet one of the family, but that didn't mean she wasn't deep. She had little patience with Daisy's wild ideas; she knew enough to keep her thoughts to herself until she felt the need to speak out.

Daisy's reckless ambition to follow in her mother's footsteps would almost certainly come to nothing in Elsie's opinion, and when it did, she would be ready to lend a sympathetic ear. But performing on the stage in front of masses of strangers, and risking their displeasure if they didn't like you, was completely alien to Elsie's nature.

She much preferred to remain behind the scenes in whatever she did. She was quite happy to spend her time in the back room of the shop with her needle and her sewing machine and her flat iron, and take in the repairs and produce the neat stitching for which she was praised.

She was happiest when a lady brought in a hat that needed renovating, or bought some silks and buckram from the shop with only a vague idea of a hat to be made for a special occasion, leaving Elsie herself to design and produce it. She had a skill that she didn't want to abandon, and the events of the afternoon had made her think more seriously about it than ever before.

"What are you thinking about, Elsie?" she heard Daisy say crossly, as they sat on their deckchairs underneath the apple tree in the small back garden. "Nobody talks to me. Immy's disappeared to see that friend of hers, and you look as if you're somewhere in dreamland."

"Immy came back a while ago. And if I look as if I'm in dreamland, it's because I am. We'll all have to pull our weight in the future, so I'm thinking about what to do, and not considering silly ideas, either."

"You all think I'm silly, don't you?"

"No, we don't. Just young and a bit headstrong at times, perhaps." Before Daisy could snap back at her, Elsie put her hand over her sister's and squeezed it. "We all have to be sensible now, Daisy, and take what Daddy told us seriously."

"Yes, ma'am," Daisy muttered. "So what great plan have you got in mind?"

Elsie took a deep breath. "Even if Daddy agrees to this guest-house idea and we have to do our bit, I don't see why I can't continue with my sewing. I can still take in repairs, and I can still make hats, but I'll be doing it at home."

"Good Lord! And do you really think people will trail all the way up here to bring a torn jacket to be mended, or to ask you to create a Sunday hat?"

"Why not? They know my work."

"But they don't know Vicarage Street! Caldwell's Supplies is in the city, not in a hotchpotch of houses."

"Then I'll have to advertise," Elsie said, determined not to be defeated. "I'll get somebody to print me some leaflets and we'll put them on the shop counter, and I'll distribute some to houses and shops as well."

"We don't know anybody who can print leaflets."

"I do," a voice said behind them.

They turned at once, not having heard Imogen come out to the garden, exhausted after reading for an hour, and having Teddy fall asleep in the middle of it. Frances was dozing as well now, however, and she was glad of a welcome breath of fresh air.

"Did you hear what we were talking about?" Elsie asked.

"Yes, and I think it's a splendid idea. But you're quite right. You will need to advertise, otherwise people won't know you intend to continue with your sewing."

"Who do you know then, Immy?" Daisy said curiously.

"A young man who works in the print room of the local newspaper," Immy said evenly. "I only know him slightly, but I'm sure if I asked him he'd be able to do some leaflets for a reasonable fee."

"Is he your young man?" Daisy said immediately. "If he is, I'll bet Daddy doesn't know anything about it."

"He's just someone I met," Immy retorted, feeling an absolute traitor to the love of her life, but with no intention of letting this bright-eyed little madam know anything about Morgan. Not yet, anyway.

"Will he do it, do you think?" Elsie said. "I couldn't afford to pay much, but it would take ages to do them by hand myself, and it would be far more professional if they were printed. Unless you'd care to type them all out, Immy?"

She shook her head. "That would take ages too. I'll have to ask my friend the next time I see him. I think Father will have a job for you to do soon, though, Elsie. He wants some posters for the shop window to say we're having a sale" – she swallowed before she went on, because it still seemed so unreal – "and that the shop will be closing at the end of September."

"*What*? So soon?" Elsie and Daisy exclaimed simultaneously.

"I'm afraid so. I don't know any more details; you'll have to discuss the design of the poster with him, Elsie."

"I'll do it now," she said, already considering the way it should appear in order to attract customers. Despite her dismay she knew they all had to move on, and it was becoming increasingly obvious that the change to their lives was to be swift.

"Who's your young man, Immy?" Daisy enquired when Elsie had left them.

"Nobody you know, and he's not my young man. Why don't you go and help Cook get tea ready? We all have to pull our weight now, so you might as well get used to it, Daisy."

Her sister scowled, as belligerent as Teddy, but since Immy had sat down on the vacant deck-chair and closed her eyes against the sun's glare, Daisy knew she would get nothing more out of her, and she went indoors, banging the door behind her.

By now Immy was more concerned with what she was going to say to Morgan than bothering about Daisy's flashes of temper. The shock of seeing him with his arm so blatantly around another girl in the middle of town on a Sunday afternoon was receding a little now, and she was persuading herself that it probably hadn't been him at all.

She didn't *want* to believe it had been him, and the moment she confronted him and put it into words, the more real it would become. It wasn't like her to take the coward's way out . . . but this time, she thought weakly, just this once, it might be the more prudent way.

Besides, what would she do if he denied it? She would have to believe him, of course, but it would put a blight on their relationship, because he would think she didn't trust him. And if he admitted it, it would all be over anyway.

Because of their close, rather cloistered family life, Immy had never had a young man before, and she didn't know the right way to handle this situation at all. If she dared, she would write to one of those "Aunt Em" pages in one of the women's magazines and ask for advice.

But she couldn't have a formal letter sent back to the house without questions being asked, and she might have to wait weeks or months for a reply to appear in print. And she didn't have that kind of patience. Better not to know at all, she decided, than to be disillusioned.

She only saw Morgan on Wednesday afternoons when the shop closed for half a day, and it seemed an age to wait. Before then, her father had been in further consultation with the accountant and the landlord, and had meetings with people they didn't know, whose outcome he kept to himself. They still hadn't come to any decision about the house.

Everyone had become so gloomy over the last few days, and with the sale posters in the shop window now, customers were asking questions they hardly knew how to answer. At home, Teddy was at his worst, and their mother's incessant humming and lack of concern about the presence of her so-called "dearest companion" had begun to unnerve them all.

If Frances could be so uncaring about Miss Lindsey, would she feel any more loss when parted from any of her family? It was an alarming thought, and one which underlined her rapid decline. Was keeping this house so important after all? It was only a building. Immy began to wish she had never mentioned the paying guests at all.

Early on Tuesday evening they received an unexpected visit from Quentin's sister and brother-in-law. Their battered old Morris car drew up in the road outside the house soon after they had all finished tea.

By the time the rest of them had washed their hands and assembled in the sitting-room for the obligatory quizzing, the couple were ensconced with Frances and Teddy. They were clearly desperate to give up trying to make intelligent conversation with either of them, however.

Baz had disappeared as soon as the shop closed. He still wasn't home, and Immy knew her father would have words with him when he deigned to join them.

"We've come to stay for a night or two – if you'll have us, Quentin – and to try to make sense of what's happening," Rose announced, after a brief kiss on her brother's cheek.

Immy glanced at her sisters. It was just as she had suspected: even before they had been given the news, Aunt Rose and Uncle Bertie had been acquainted with it. Treating them like children, she fumed, when they had every right to know first . . .

"If my mother had seen me frown like that, Imogen," she heard Aunt Rose say tartly, "she would have told me my face would stay like it."

Well, yours didn't, Immy said silently, praying she hadn't spoken the words aloud as she forced a smile to her lips.

"How are you, Aunt Rose?" she said dutifully.

"Well enough, my girl, or would be, if I didn't have all of you to worry about."

Immy glanced at Elsie again, sitting there with her eyes

downcast. Elsie didn't say much, but privately they all thought Aunt Rose a bit of a tartar. They knew very well how deeply she cared for them all, however.

"Did you bring me anything, Auntie?" Teddy said, young enough to be oblivious to undercurrents.

His aunt laughed. "Now what could I possibly bring a lovely boy like you?"

"Weston rock," he said hopefully, at which Uncle Bertie guffawed as if he'd said something terribly witty, and produced a paper bag containing five pink sticks of rock, like a conjurer bringing them out of a hat.

They all said thank you, although none of the girls cared for the stuff any more. It was only the boys who thought it a treat. Privately, Immy thought it was nasty, and sticky, and just what you expected from a seaside town noted for its donkey rides and ice-cream stands. Not that she had ever minded *those*, she thought, remembering their childhood outings to the sea.

"So what have you decided to do about the house?" Bertie added his weight to his wife's question.

They were both in their fifties, rotund and grey haired, each as bickeringly argumentative as the other, simply because it was their way. And since they were childless, they had taken it upon themselves to be pseudo-caretakers of this large family.

"Take in paying guests, probably," Quentin said, having no stomach for a lengthy discussion when he was tired, and ignoring the gasps of his three daughters.

"Sensible," Rose said. "I wouldn't want to see our parents' house sold to any old Tom, Dick or Harry."

"I thought you'd object, Aunt Rose," Immy said.

"Did you? Then perhaps you don't know me as well as you thought you did, girl. There's ample room here to take in at least three or four, though I suggest you advertise carefully for suitable guests."

"Where's the other boy?" Uncle Bertie said suddenly.

As if on cue, Baz sidled into the room, mumbling apologies for being late. He stayed at the back of the room, perched on a chair, as if preferring to make himself invisible, which was unusual in itself.

"Immy knows somebody who can print leaflets," Daisy said slyly. "He's going to advertise Elsie's hat-making."

Immy felt her face go as hot as fire, and Elsie rounded on her sister at once.

"Nothing's been decided yet—"

"What's all this?" Quentin said.

Elsie spoke quickly. "I thought I'd be able to carry on with my sewing at home, once we give up the shop. That is all right, isn't it?"

"It's admirable, Elsie," he told her. "And who is this person who's going to print the leaflets, Immy?"

"I haven't approached him yet," Immy said, wishing Daisy to Kingdom Come for putting her in this position. "It's just someone I met who's in the printing business."

"A decent fellow, I hope," Aunt Rose said.

From the back of the room Baz gave a sudden snigger, and everyone turned to look at him. Immy's eyes widened imperceptibly. What did the little snitch know? And more importantly, what would he tell?

"Do you have something to say, Baz?" his father enquired.

He shook his head and Immy breathed more easily. She wouldn't put anything past him. He was becoming far too big for his boots . . . Even as the words entered her head, she found herself looking at his feet, and at the footwear he polished on Quentin's orders every night before he went to bed, the same as they all did.

Today Baz's boots were scuffed and muddy, no matter how he tried to hide them beneath his chair. And when she looked at him more keenly, she could see there were bruises on his cheek that were just starting to discolour. They had all been so wrapped up in the discussion of the moment, and Aunt Rose's domineering presence, that none of them had noticed it before. And from the look of him, Baz was desperately hoping no one would notice it now, and wishing he hadn't brought attention to himself. But it was too late.

"Good Lord, look at the boy! Have you been fighting and disgracing the family name?" Aunt Rose demanded.

Quentin stared at his son hard. His family was his pride and joy, and although it was his right to censure and chastise them when the need arose, he objected strongly to anyone else doing it – especially his sister, who had no idea what it was like

40

to bring up a family at all. But this matter clearly needed investigating.

"Out with it, Baz. What do you mean by coming home looking like a hooligan?"

Baz nervously wiped the back of his hand across his nose, and they all saw saw the faint trickle of blood on his sleeve.

"He's running wild," Aunt Rose snapped. "Look at him. A fine state he'll be in tomorrow behind the shop counter. The customers will think they've come to a zoo."

Big and boisterous as he was, Baz knew better than to defy his father, at least most of the time. But right now, he felt as small as a pea. And his aunt, whom he'd always thought had a soft spot for him, was glaring at him.

He jumped up from his chair, his hands clenched at his sides, no matter how it stretched the skin of his knuckles and made them smart where they had connected with a couple of the young thugs at the waterfront.

"I don't want to stand behind a stupid shop counter tomorrow, or any other day, if you must know," he shouted in a rage. "I'm fed up with being called a sissy. Old Enoch Bray has offered me a job on his ferry-boat if I want it, and I've said yes, so there!"

All fourteen years and eight stone of him was bristle and fire at that moment. His eyes burned with the tears he wouldn't shed, his ribs ached from the kicks he'd endured and his cheeks felt stiff and swollen from where those illiterate bastards had jeered at him and punched him. Well, he wasn't having any more of it. He was as good as them – *better* than them – and it was because he thought that way that he'd got into the fight in the first place.

He waited for the explosion. Instead he heard a slow hand-clap, and gaped in astonishment at his Uncle Bertie.

"I always thought it a namby-pamby job for a young man with your abilities," he said. "I reckon you could go far as a boxer, boy."

Baz flinched as his father voiced a rare expletive beneath his breath.

"I don't want to be a stupid boxer," he almost shrieked. "I just want to be a ferryman and work on the river."

"You might as well let the boy do what he wants, Quentin,"

Rose put in. "He's obviously not cut out to be a shopkeeper. I always told you so."

Quentin threw up his hands. "Has my entire family now decided to dictate to me what's right?"

"Well, you don't seem to be making too good a job of overseeing things, do you?" Rose – the only one who dared to voice the words – remarked.

Her words stunned them all into momentary silence. The girls looked nervous and anxious, and in the corner of the room, Teddy was snivelling, sucking on his stick of rock and plastering it all over Frances's frock. She didn't seem to notice, however, and continued to smile at them all and hum beneath her breath.

Bertie cleared his throat. "Why don't we get down to brass tacks instead of all this arguing?"

"That's rich, coming from you," Quentin snarled.

Bertie went on as if he hadn't spoken. "What we've actually come here to say, Quentin, is that we'd like to take Teddy off your hands for a while. No ifs or buts. If this house is to be overrun with strangers the child will be lost in the crush."

"No child of mine would ever be treated in that way!"

"Listen to what Bertie says, Quentin, dear," Rose said, her hand on his arm, her voice softer than usual. "We all know that Frances can't go on like this for ever, and sooner or later you'll need to do what Doctor Wolfe says, and send her somewhere where she can be properly looked after. You have your affairs to sort out, and the rest of the children are growing up fast, but Teddy is still a baby."

"I'm not a baby!" he shouted, burying his face in Frances's skirt again.

"We know you're not, old chap," Bertie said, kneeling beside him now so that they were on the same eye level. "But Auntie Rose and me don't have any children, so we'd like to borrow you for a while. You and me could go for walks on the beach every day, and we could go fishing in the river. We're going to buy a dog, and you could think of a name for him. He could be your dog if you lived with us, Teddy. What do you say?"

I'd say you should have been a diplomat, thought Immy.

Four

I mogen had longed for and dreaded the thought of Wednesday in equal measure. The grassy hill where she and Morgan always met wasn't far above Vicarage Street, though well away from the tell-tale windows of any houses.

She was as eager as ever to see him, but today was different. There were so many things she had to tell him, yet so much more that she couldn't bear to say.

As always, her heartbeat quickened when she saw him approach, though today it was thumping to a different rhythm.

"How's my best girl?" he said in his lilting Welsh voice, his arms reaching out to encircle her slim waist while he pressed his mouth possessively on to hers.

She breathed in the freshness of soap on his skin, and no matter how hard she tried to not let it affect her, she felt her eyes mist over. His *best* girl? When she had so hoped and prayed and believed that she was his *only* girl? But they were just words, she told herself. They meant nothing.

Nevertheless, she couldn't help standing stiffly in his arms. She normally melted into them, and he sensed the difference at once. He held her away from him, his dark eyes puzzled, his black curly hair ruffled by the small breeze on the hilltop.

"What's wrong, sweetie?"

She blurted it out at once. "We're losing the shop."

"I know."

She stared up at him. "You *know*? How do you know?"

"It's news. Preston's Emporium have instructed us to place advertisements in the newspaper in a couple of weeks' time. The whole row of little shops will be closed for the week, while Preston's move in their stock and erect new shop signs. It's the way big business works, see? It will be an impressive

43

place when it's all under one banner, and it'll put that corner of Bristol on the map."

She felt betrayed by his words and the enthusiasm with which he spoke them. Calling their shop a *little* shop, when her father had worked so hard to build it up! Her face burned with humiliation. He was being so insensitive! Didn't he know what this was doing to them? Was he so blind that he couldn't see how this must be affecting her whole family? The shop was their livelihood!

"Anyway, we don't want to waste time talking about old shops, do we?" Morgan went on, oblivious to her churning thoughts. "Let's find our special place and have a cuddle and make the most of the afternoon."

She swallowed hard. "Can't you appreciate my feelings about what's happening?"

He shrugged. "It's making a packet for your old man, I dare say, so I can't see why it's such a bad thing . . . Oh, come on, darling, don't be so touchy."

"*Touchy*! I'm devastated, if you must know. And not that it's any of your business, but we don't actually *own* the shop. I don't know the details, and I wouldn't tell you if I did, but my father's upset, and none of us knows what's happening any more. We're even thinking of taking in *lodgers*" – she emphasised the less attractive name, since she was starting to feel so wretched – "and we'll all have to do something else, and my little brother's probably going to live with my aunt and uncle at the seaside—"

"Taking in lodgers, eh? Well, how about me, for a start? I could come creeping to your room at night . . ."

As Immy pushed him violently away, he began to get angry.

"Oh, for God's sake, Immy, I'm only teasing. Put a smile on your face, can't you? You know I can't stand seeing you glum like this."

"I know that. You expect me to be always sweet and responsive, don't you? Is that how you like all your young ladies to be, Morgan?"

She was breathing heavily now, and so was he.

"What do you mean by that?"

"I saw you out walking on Sunday afternoon, in Welsh Back," she accused. "It *was* you, wasn't it?"

Her teeth were threatening to chatter, but she wouldn't give him the satisfaction of letting him see how upset she was. Because of course it had been him, and she had always known it, no matter how much she had tried to deny it.

He didn't deny it either. "What if it was? She's a work colleague, that's all. I do have other friends, Immy, and so should you. You shouldn't always be clinging to those sisters of yours and never see anybody else."

"I have other friends too, thank you. And do you always walk around town in broad daylight with your arm around a work colleague?" she went on, seemingly unable to stop.

"I didn't know you could be such a shrew, Imogen."

"I'm not," she said, choked. "I just thought I was your girl, that's all."

"You are," he said, putting his arms around her again. "Really you are. Catherine's just somebody at work."

"I see. And if you'd *happened* to meet me on Sunday afternoon, would you have told her I was just somebody who works in a shop on Blackboy Hill?"

"Probably. Since you're the one who's been insisting all this time that we keep things secret, what else would you have had me say? You're the one who says we can only see each other one afternoon a week, and hell's teeth, Immy, I'm not a monk!"

He certainly wasn't. Even now, she could feel herself weakening as his fingers stroked the soft inner flesh of her arms. He was slowly leading her to their favourite hollow, pulling her gently down beside him, and his kiss was very tender on her lips. And she did love him . . . didn't she?

"You know what those damn cobbles are like on those soft-soled shoes you ladies wear," he was whispering now. "Catherine was in danger of tripping, and you must have caught sight of me when I was trying to keep her upright, that's all. I'd only bumped into her by accident, anyway."

Oh, he was so plausible – and Immy truly didn't want to lose him . . . not when everything else in her life seemed to be slipping away. Foolish or not, at least she could still hold on to this . . .

It suddenly dawned on her that his hand had slid around to the front of her bodice, and was fondling the soft mound of her breast.

She captured it there for a moment longer, pressing it tightly to her in what was virtually a gesture of goodbye – except that he didn't know it – before wrenching it away.

"All right, but I'm not having any more of that today," she said in a clipped voice. "If you truly think anything of me, Morgan, you'll listen to me, because I've got something important to ask of you."

"Fire away," he said, his eyes narrowing.

She remembered her dream, and was tempted to ask him if he could get her a typing position with the newspaper, so that she could work beside him. But even as she thought it, she knew she no longer wanted it. Not if the pretty Catherine also worked there. She would have to face her suspicions of them every single day, and listen to his glib Welsh tongue telling her more lies.

Almost without noticing it, her feelings for him cooled several degrees at the thought. She *didn't* believe his story. She knew him for what he was, a charming flirt. Hadn't he charmed her in the first place? And did it really matter, when she had known in her heart of hearts that he was never going to be the marrying kind? Which was the only thing that really made a girl feel respectable.

"My sister Elsie is going to continue working at home," she said abruptly. "She's the clever one in the family as far as sewing is concerned, and she wants to advertise her skills. She needs some printed leaflets, Morgan, and I wondered if you could arrange to have them done for her. I've brought a rough idea to show you the wording she wants."

She fumbled in her bag for the piece of paper, not wanting him to guess how deflated she felt now at the way this day had deteriorated into a business arrangement, instead of returning the excitement of a clandestine meeting between lovers.

To her surprise, however, she was a little relieved as well. She had always sensed that Morgan's needs were going to become more demanding, and she had no intention of ever giving in to him. The residents of Vicarage Street were still shocked at the way a young girl in the vicinity had allowed herself to be seduced by a man. The young woman and her child had now been condemned to life in a lunatic asylum. It had happened at least ten years ago and it still caused whispers and condemnation for the disgrace it had brought to her family.

Immy shivered. Nothing on earth would induce her to behave in such a way until she had a wedding ring on her finger. She thought she had been in love, but now she was just as sure that she wasn't. Not the steadfast kind of love her parents had, anyway, nor that of Aunt Rose and Uncle Bertie, whose marriage, despite their sometimes entertaining and blistering arguments, was rock solid.

"This wouldn't be any trouble," Morgan was saying now as he glanced at the piece of paper with Elsie's outlined wording. "I couldn't do it for nothing, of course—"

"Oh, we'd expect to pay you for your trouble, naturally," Immy said drily, thinking how grasping he sounded. "We couldn't afford much, though."

"You could always pay me in kind, sweetie," he said with a grin, and she squirmed away from him.

She had always liked his special endearment for her, but not any more. It grated on her, and she wondered how she could ever have let herself fall for his smooth talking.

"No, I couldn't," she snapped. "And I don't think I want to see you again – except to arrange this business."

"Is this all because you saw me talking innocently to another girl? I didn't think you could be so narrow minded, but perhaps it's just as well I found out now!"

"Perhaps it is," she said, aware that her heart should be breaking, and knowing that actually it wasn't. It was almost a guilty feeling – and one that filled her with a little alarm – because it seemed to imply that she was as shallow as Morgan himself.

"So will you do the leaflets for Elsie?" she persisted, since it seemed to be the only thing they had to say to one another now.

"I dare say," he said coolly.

"That's not good enough. If you could get them done by next Wednesday, Elsie can start distributing them."

"No chance. Wednesday week or nothing. So how many?"

By the time they walked back down the hill, separately instead of giggling and snuggling together as usual, he had agreed to the price and number required. Immy held her head high as she went home to report to Elsie.

And a lone figure lifted his head out of the long grass, staring at his sister's stiffly retreating back, disappointed not to have seen anything more interesting to feed his vivid adolescent imagination.

Time didn't stand still just because the fabric of the Caldwells' lives were changing. If anything, it raced by at an ever-increasing and frightening speed. The shop remained open, the stock was being sold at highly discounted prices because Quentin would rather serve his faithful customers himself than sell on anything to the imperious Prestons.

Aunt Rose and Uncle Bertie decided to remain with them for a week, while Aunt Rose gave her expert advice on how to adapt the house to accommodate paying guests while retaining some family privacy.

By then, Teddy had become fully indoctrinated with the idea that he was going to live at the seaside for a while, where the sea was always blue and the sands were always soft and warm for him and his new dog to romp on. Uncle Bertie would take him fishing every day, and life would be one long blissful holiday.

"It almost makes me wish I were going too," Elsie said, hearing Teddy going on and on about it. "I'm sure Mother thinks she's going as well, though, from the way she keeps smiling and nodding at him. She's going to have an awful shock when she finds him not clinging to her any more."

"I'm not so sure," Immy said. "Have you heard her mention Miss Lindsey this past week? I'm sure she's forgotten her existence already."

Elsie looked distressed. "I had the same feeling myself, Immy, and I can't bear it. It means that her mind's going much quicker than we thought." She hesitated. "I don't like to say this, but do you think Father should listen to what Doctor Wolfe says about sending her somewhere safe?"

"What can be safer than here, where we all love her?" Immy said fiercely. Then she sighed. "Oh, I know what you're saying, and we can't be her eyes and ears every minute of the day. She looks so pretty and normal when she walks about, as if she's a lady who's simply dreaming and taking the air. If she were to wander near the river, nobody would consider that she might be in danger."

"We must all watch her, then, and be sure she's never allowed to go out unsupervised."

Immy nodded slowly. "I know you're right, darling, but I feel so sad for her. She had the world at her feet, and now she's a virtual prisoner in her own home, isn't she?"

"But for her own safety," Elsie stressed. "And you must admit, we're the ones who are suffering on her account. *She* doesn't seem to suffer at all, and she's perfectly happy in her own world, restricted though it might be.

"I know, and we must all thank God for that."

Immy also thanked God that she had never confided anything about Morgan to Elsie and Daisy, especially not Daisy.

Morgan had come into the shop to show Elsie a dummy of her leaflet, and she had approved it at once. He had said he would deliver the finished articles when he could. It was so vague that it told Immy more clearly than words that their Wednesday-afternoon liaisons were well and truly over.

"He seems quite nice," Elsie remarked after he had gone. "Where did you meet him, Immy?"

"It was when the delivery boy failed to come with our newspaper and Father's trade magazine a few months ago, and I went to the offices myself to collect them," she explained.

"He's Welsh, isn't he?"

Immy suddenly realised her sister was showing a special interest in Morgan Raine, and that it must be curbed at once. And it had nothing to do with jealousy, she told herself fiercely.

"Yes, but don't let that lilting accent distract you. He already has a young lady, anyway."

And before Elsie could ask her how she knew that, she turned to smile at a new customer who had entered the shop.

"Good afternoon, sir," she said. "What can I do for you?"

He was tall and darkly good looking, and about the same age as Morgan, she guessed, which made him in his early twenties. But that was where the similarity ended, because this young man had a brooding look about him that reminded her sharply of Heathcliff in *Wuthering Heights*.

How absurd that was, to reach such an instant conclusion . . . but when he spoke, she realised she had been more intuitive than she knew.

"I'm not too sure about that, lass, but you can direct me to the proprietor of this establishment, if you would be so kind. You can give him my card, if you will, and tell him that Robert Preston's come to see him."

Immy's face flooded with colour, and she heard Elsie gasp beside her. Thankfully, Daisy was at home with Frances today, or she would no doubt have been toadying up to this film-starry character, no matter who he was.

"If it's my father you've come to see, I'm not so sure that he'll want to see you," she heard herself say freezingly. It was certainly no way to speak to a customer, let alone this man, but since Preston's were buying the entire building up, lock, stock and barrel, no matter what was said, she didn't bother to heed her words.

The man's eyes widened. They were very dark, flecked with hazel . . . and she had been reading too many romantic stories, Immy raged.

"So you're one of the daughters, are you? I heard they were a bonny bunch of lasses. And is this another one?" he enquired in his flat nasal tones, nodding towards Elsie.

The damned, insufferable gall of the man! Immy had hated anyone to do with Preston's sight unseen, and the actual presence of this one didn't do anything to change that view.

And then he smiled, and held out his hand, and before she could stop herself, her natural courtesy made her extend her own hand without thinking.

His fingers curled around hers, firm and strong, and she almost snatched her hand away from his. She just managed to resist rubbing her fingers on her skirt.

He knew, of course. She could see it by the way his eyes were amused now. His accent might be raw and rough to their southern ears, but she had no doubt that he was an educated man. His clothes were impeccable, and those finger nails were clean and buffed without being effeminate in any way.

This was no Yorkshire tyke straight off the moors, *à la* Heathcliff . . .

"Is your father available, Miss Caldwell?" he continued in that cool, assured voice.

"I don't know . . . I'll see," Immy stammered, and fled to the back room, thankful there had been no regular customers in the shop at that moment to witness her lack of composure.

What on earth was wrong with her? It wasn't as though he attracted her in the very least. If anything, he reminded her too much of Morgan, with his dark good looks and his smooth and easy manner.

"Is there a fire?" her father said mildly, as she went storming through to him.

"Only in my heart," she said savagely, and then winced, knowing that such histrionics were more worthy of Daisy than her normally self-sufficient self! It seemed a long time since she had felt that way, however, she admitted, and from the way her heart kept leaping about in her chest for all kinds of reasons lately, it was a wonder she didn't suffer a heart attack.

Her father was even laughing gently now, and it was good to hear the sound, even if she had been the butt of his amusement.

"My goodness, something's definitely rattled you, hasn't it, my love? What's happened?"

Immy handed over the business card in silence, waiting for the explosion as he digested the gilt words printed on it. It was a vulgar card, she tried to tell herself derisively, knowing that it wasn't. It was perfectly tasteful.

"Ah," said her father without surprise. "Please ask Mr Preston to come through, Immy, and perhaps you would make us a pot of tea."

"Did you know he was coming?" she demanded, unable to grasp the fact that her father seemed so willing to sit down with the enemy and drink tea.

Or was she being totally naive? There was no point in being antagonistic, she supposed, when the young man in the shop was presumably a son or nephew, and not the almighty owner of Preston's Emporium.

"Darling, we might as well be sociable," Quentin said. "What's done is done, and there's no changing it."

"But what does he *want*?"

"I don't know until he tells me, and unless you're going to keep him waiting all afternoon, I suggest you do as I ask."

She went back to the shop, where Elsie was trying to keep up a stilted conversation with the stranger.

"Will you come through, please?" she said stiffly. "My father is expecting you – apparently."

"Thank you," he said civilly, making her ashamed of her churlishness, and resentful because she felt that way.

She shot a warning glance at Elsie as she followed Robert Preston into the back room and then disappeared to make a pot of tea and take it to him and her father. She poured out the two cups silently, offering milk and sugar, her hands shaking just a little as she felt the man's eyes watching her movements.

"What was *that* all about?" Elsie said at once, when Immy rejoined her. "Did you know he was coming?"

"Of course not! Father did, though. It's all so mean. Why didn't he tell us? I feel as if he doesn't trust us any more."

"He trusts you to do the books, and that's trust enough, isn't it? You're so clever with figures, Immy; I wonder why you couldn't see that things weren't going so well?"

"Well, I didn't. Don't you trust me either?"

"Don't be a goose, of course I do."

"As for the books, it was little more than stock inventories mostly. The accountant did the real work."

"Or lack of it," Elsie pointed out.

"We'll probably never know the truth of it, and I'm not sure I want to know any more," Immy told her. "From now on, I'm going to take each day as it comes, and give up worrying."

If Elsie believed that, she would believe anything. But thankfully there was a small rush of bargain-hungry customers to keep them busy for the next hour, and when their father emerged with their visitor, he was smiling.

Robert Preston shook his hand, and nodded to the girls.

"You'll join us for dinner next week at the Grand, then, Mr Caldwell? And if your daughters would care to be our guests too, I know my father would be delighted."

Immy held her breath as he left the shop without waiting for an answer. She couldn't help the feeling that in accepting this dinner invitation, her father had well and truly sold out. But worse was to come.

"Well, I'm not sitting down to dinner with them," she said indignantly, even though she had never been inside the Grand Hotel in her life before and had always wondered how it would feel to be entertained amid such splendour.

"You will, and you will be perfectly well behaved, Imogen," Quentin said. "You too, Elsie, though I think Daisy might be too much of a risk in polite company."

"But why should we go?" Immy said, even though they knew it was a command they couldn't ignore.

"Because I have just been offered the position of under-manager in the new shop, and I couldn't afford to refuse, since it will make all the difference to our futures."

"Well, I think that stinks!" Immy burst out. "How could you even consider it, Father? After being your own boss, and now to bend over backwards to the likes of those people—"

"I considered it, my dear, because if the worst comes to the worst, which seems most likely, and we have to put your mother in a residential home, I simply won't be able to pay for it unless I have a good job."

His face twisted as he spoke. The thought of sending his beloved Frances away was almost too much to bear, but he had known for a long time that it had to come. She needed professional people to look after her, and however much they loved her, the family simply couldn't give her all that she needed.

"Does this mean we won't be taking in lodgers, then?" Elsie said, since Immy seemed deprived of speech for once.

"Perhaps. I don't know. Obviously I would prefer not," Quentin told her, deciding to be blunt.

"Just as long as you don't expect us to work for Preston's," Immy said. "Because I won't."

"That's a pity. Robert Preston said his father was particularly keen to offer us all jobs if we were interested. They're not unaware of how our circumstances will be changed, Immy. Give them credit for that."

"For trying to make us all dependent on them? For humiliating us even more! It's not enough that they've taken our shop away; now they want to gloat over us by having us work for them as if we're paupers!"

"*Immy*," Elsie said uneasily as her sister's voice rose.

"No, let her have her say, Elsie," her father said. "We're not paupers, Immy, and I hope we never will be. But I've done some very foolish things. It's my fault that we're in the state we are, which is why I'm doing my damnedest to put things right. I had hoped that my family would feel the same. Even Baz, for all his knockabout ways, has found himself some useful work instead of bemoaning his fate."

It was so rare for him to chastise her in this way, especially setting Baz up on a pedestal in comparison, that she almost wept.

"I can't imagine you doing anything foolish," she said, trying to prove her loyalty.

"Well, if you're fishing to find out what it is, you'll wait for hell to freeze, my dear," he replied, making her feel more rejected than before, because she hadn't meant that at all.

He strode off to the back room again, and she stared at Elsie miserably.

"I can't seem to please him, can I?"

Elsie gave a half-smile. "Join the rest of us, darling. You've always been his pet; it comes as a bit of a shock to find him so pithy, doesn't it?"

"I'm not his favourite, if that's what you mean!"

"Oh yes you are, and you always have been."

Immy felt embarrassed by her sister's frank words. She didn't set out to be a favourite – nobody did – and she certainly didn't want the rest of her family to be put out because of it.

"Elsie, I don't know what to say."

"Oh, for pity's sake, it doesn't matter! I wish I'd never said anything at all. It doesn't make any difference to the way we feel about you, anyway."

It wasn't the time or place to be getting emotional about family values and loyalties, but for the life of her Immy couldn't get the conversation out of her mind as she served customers with their bargain goods and rang up their payments. It was ironic, she thought, that they were so exceptionally busy now. If the goods had still been at their regular price, they would have been laughing.

"So are you prepared to go to this dinner at the Grand?" she asked her sister during a welcome lull.

"Of course. Daddy expects it, doesn't he? We have to show a united front, Immy. I thought you'd have seen that."

There it was again – that little bit of censure she wasn't used to. Or perhaps she was just being extra sensitive to nuances in a voice now, even if the words were artless enough.

"I'm going to see Helen again as soon as I can," she said, in an effort to sound normal. "Sometimes I think we've become too insular, Elsie. We're like Siamese quins."

"Don't you mean twins?"

"I was thinking of the five of us actually, though as you can hardly count Teddy, it should probably be quadruplets – no, *triplets*, since Baz is hardly there. And Daisy can be a bit offish at times—"

"There you are, then," Elsie said, laughing. "It's twins – just you and me, kid," she added out of the side of her mouth in the best Western movie style. "But I know what you mean."

"Do you?" Immy said, knowing it was Morgan who had led her to this way of thinking.

"Yes. We go out with each other, eat, sleep and care for each other. As well as being family, we work together and we confide in one another, which is what best friends do. But that's not such a bad thing, is it?"

"No," said Immy, knowing there were plenty of things she didn't confide to anyone except Helen. "But there's a big world out there, and whether we like it or not, we're part of it. Preston's have proved that we're not the only ones who matter, and even our cosy little world can be shattered when we least expect it." She shivered. "I'm talking nonsense, aren't I?"

Elsie put her arm around her. "Of course you're not. You're thinking of all these war rumours too, aren't you?"

She hadn't been, but any reply was curtailed as the door of the shop suddenly opened and a couple entered to look around. The woman was young, the man with her probably her father, and he was wearing dark battle dress that looked brand new. On the shoulder was a strip of insignia proclaiming him as an air-raid warden.

The woman saw Immy staring at it and laughed, hugging the man's arm affectionately.

"I told him it was daft to be wearing it in the daytime, but it's just like my old dad to brag about it. They all love their uniforms, don't they, Miss Caldwell?"

Immy nodded, taking care not to look at Elsie's told-you-so face.

Five

The following week the girls dressed with care and shaking hands for the dinner at the Grand Hotel, still with the feeling that the invitation had been almost a royal command. After changing her mind half a dozen times Immy finally decided to wear her best pale green frock, which complemented her brown eyes and glorious red hair, and Elsie chose her favourite cream ensemble.

Daisy was openly envious that they were going to such a posh place, and complained bitterly that she never went anywhere. Baz, on the other hand, couldn't have cared less.

"I suppose it's a sensible thing to do," Aunt Rose said dubiously. "Better the enemy you know, and all that."

"They're not our enemies," Quentin said evenly. "I'm told they're meeting all the shop owners in the row socially, and since I have decided to take them up on their offer of a job in their clothing department, the least I can do is be civil to them."

"*Et tu, Brute,*" Rose murmured beneath her breath, still *in situ* despite her earlier decision to go home a few days ago. Frances's slight cold had made her choose to stay and play nursemaid instead.

Quentin gave a heavy sigh. "Please keep out of it, Rose. I have to do what's best for my family. You're already getting your way over Teddy, and I'll hear no more about it."

Immy saw her aunt tighten her lips until they resembled a thin pink line and just managed to resist a giggle at the effort she was making. The brother and sister were old sparring partners, and she could just imagine Rose's joy on the day she met Bertie Painter and realised that he more than lived up to the sibling rivalry she and her brother had always revelled in. There was more than one way of showing love, and those two were certainly proof of that.

Finally they were ready to leave Vicarage Street. The girls sat tensely behind Quentin in the big old Rover that was to take them to the Grand Hotel.

Immy considered herself more worldly wise than her sister, if only because of her secret romance with Morgan Raine, and if her own mouth was dry, she couldn't imagine what Elsie's must be like. The hotel was grand in every way, and they were all awed by its magnificence as they entered the foyer at the appointed time.

Immy presumed that the man who came forward to greet them was the ogre, Owen Preston. Behind him were two younger men, one of whom was the fellow they had met the previous week.

"My dear sir," Owen Preston said, in the same flat tones as his son had used. He pumped Quentin's hand enthusiastically. "We meet at last – and not before time, after all the paperwork nonsense that's gone on between our two parties, as they call us these days. And these two bonnie lasses must be your daughters, of whom I've heard such good reports, though now that I see them, I realise none of it quite does them justice. You're a very fortunate man."

Such glib compliments were probably the hallmark of the canny businessman, thought Immy cynically, and shouldn't be taken seriously.

"This is Imogen and this is Elsie; they're my two eldest," her father was saying, at which they murmured back politely.

"Aye, and a prettier pair a man couldn't wish to see. Now, you've already met my son, Robert. He'll not be staying in Bristol, but seems to think I need a bit of watching over when I travel," he added with a bucolic laugh that probably meant Robert was quite correct. "T'other fine specimen is my nephew Joseph – Joe – who'll be taking over as manager of the new establishment. But you'll not want to talk about that now, and we don't need to stand on ceremony. This is a social occasion, and we'll have a drink to wet our whistles and get to know one another."

Once he was in full flow, they realised they hardly needed to talk at all and to their surprise they found themselves more relaxed in his larger-than-life company than any of them had expected. As the evening progressed the two older men developed an easy rapport between them, but that was more than could be said about the younger generation. Foolish or not, Immy still smarted at the thought that these people were taking away all her father's dreams and ambitions – even if he was able to so successfully abandon them, by the looks of things.

She couldn't stop thinking that Robert Preston thought himself superior to them, and at first Joe didn't say very much at all. He wasn't what she would call management material, Immy found herself thinking, but presumably he was more comfortable dealing with staff and customers than with social guests he didn't know.

It gradually dawned on her that Elsie was coming out of her shell more than usual, as if to compensate for Joe's lack of social skills. Two of a kind, maybe, she reflected. And it was herself, normally the more confident of the sisters, who found herself tongue-tied and annoyed because of it.

"Have I done something to offend you, Miss Caldwell?" she heard Robert Preston say at one point. It was surprisingly easy to have a few words of private conversation under cover of his father's frequent raucous laughter.

"No, of course not. I hardly know you," she replied.

"I'm sorry I'm not able to stay in Bristol more than a few more days, then, for I'd very much like to put that right. But we all have to be in York by the end of the week. My sister's getting wed."

"Oh," she said, not knowing what other comment to make. She didn't know whether to be more surprised that these giants of industry had a normal family life involving a sister's wedding, or by the fact that if she'd heard him correctly, he'd just implied that he'd like to know her better. Well, if he had, he had better forget it, because she would as soon snub him as look at him!

At that moment he smiled at her with that Heathcliff smile again, and spoke softly.

"Don't hate us, Miss Caldwell."

"I don't," she muttered.

She wasn't attracted to him either – at least, only in the mildest way. And after Morgan, she had no intention of being attracted to any other young man for a long while yet. Maybe never, she thought dramatically.

She turned away from him as she heard her sister's laughter, and to her astonishment she saw her sister gazing up into the eyes of Joe Preston. To any astute onlooker, there was more than a tingling attraction going on there.

Immy felt shocked. Not because she'd thought that Elsie couldn't attract a young man, but because she had never shown a great deal of interest in them before. And to be interested in one of *these*, of all people . . .

"Well, well," she heard Robert say, and as she met his amused eyes she knew he had seen it too. "Worse than selling your soul to the devil in your opinion, I dare say."

She ignored him, seething. He clearly knew very well what her feelings were at that moment, and she wished they weren't sometimes so obvious to other people.

"It's what makes every young man fall for you," Helen had once observed. "It's the mixture of that smouldering look in your eyes and that cool, cool voice. Oh, and then there's that delicious laugh! I wish I had it!"

"You're mad," Immy had told her, her helpless laughter having prompted Helen's final remark. "And I do not have every young man falling for me!"

She remembered the silly conversation now, thinking that, of the two of them, it was Elsie who had Joe Preston looking admiringly at her and "hanging on to her every word", as the coy storytellers in the women's magazines had it. For a crazy moment she wanted to put her arms around Elsie and protect her, and beg her not to be hurt. Like a mother hen, she thought . . .

"I'm afraid we must go," her father said regretfully, a while later, "but it's been a very enjoyable evening, Preston."

"We'll do it again when I come down next time," the other man responded, slapping Quentin on the back. "And the name's Owen. There's no need to be formal now we've got to know each other. And no hard feelings, I hope."

"Not any more," Quentin reassured him. "But I'm still curious as to why you decided to move some of your business down here in the current climate."

"All this war talk, you mean?" Preston said with a shrug. "Insurance is the word, Quentin lad. That'll take care of anything should it come to the worst."

"I don't know of any insurance company who'll pay out for an act of God or an act of war," Quentin said doubtfully.

"I do. It means I pay enormous premiums, but in return I've got a cast-iron clause included in the policy to pay out for war damage to any of my properties. It's called forward planning,"

Preston added, touching his finger to his nose. "Preston's were looking to expand, so why not come south, and why wait until the moon turns to cheese? I'm also a patriot, Quentin, and I prefer to keep my business in this country rather than selling my goods to those bastards on the Continent, begging your pardon, lasses."

Robert spoke with some irony. "Make no mistake, Mr Caldwell, my father will have us all in uniform the minute the prime minister makes an announcement."

"There's nowt wrong with that, lad. We saw enough of them conchie buggers in the last campaign. If I was still young enough, I'd be off like a shot the next time it happens, and so should any red-blooded Englishman."

"And Welsh and Scots and Irish, presumably," Immy murmured, realising that Preston senior had had more than enough to drink over dinner, and would benefit by sleeping it off as soon as he reached his hotel room.

"Oh aye, them too," he slurred. "Well then, Caldwell, if you must go" – he got to his feet, swaying gently – "we'll say goodnight to you all and hope to see you again soon."

"What a hoot, wishing us goodnight as if we were all the best of friends," Immy said, the minute they were back in the car again, and feeling unaccountably put out for no particular reason. "Hoping to see us again soon, indeed! Hoping to take over our shop, that's all, which he's already done anyway!"

"I thought he was nice," Elsie said. "He's not doing it to us personally, Immy. It's not a vindictive thing."

"It's calculating," she snorted. "All that stuff about insisting on a clause in an insurance policy to pay out if their property was damaged in an act of war. As if he's as rich as royalty or something! It's obscene. It's as good as wishing for bombs to fall – and who could possibly afford the insurance payments for such an eventuality?"

"Somebody who has become very wealthy by his own efforts, and isn't a fool with his money," her father said. "Now that I've met the man, I've got every respect for him. Your prejudice is far too obvious, Immy."

She didn't answer. She hadn't actually disliked Owen Preston, but she had felt uncomfortable at the whole command performance. Now she began to feel as if she was the only one who hadn't fully enjoyed this evening, and found it a trial to sit through everyone else's mutual admiration.

"The young men were agreeable, too," her father went on. "Elsie certainly seemed to be enjoying Joe's conversation."

"I was." Elsie hesitated as if she would say more, and then changed her mind. But Imogen was feeling more belligerent than usual and wouldn't let her stop.

"Go on. What else were you going to say?"

"Nothing, really. Well, I was thinking about my working at home. Of course I know it's the right thing to do for now, and I expect to do my share of looking after Mother. But one day perhaps, when – well, one day – perhaps I could work in Preston's repairs department. Joe said he was sure there would be an opening for me if I wanted it."

Immy was crisp. "This 'one day' that you're talking about. Is that when something happens to Mother? Because even if we do send her away, there'll still be the guest house to run – *if* we ever start it – and I don't intend to be the sole skivvy!"

"Will the pair of you stop it?" Quentin suddenly thundered. "We've had a pleasant social evening, and I want to hear no more talk of your mother being sent away or my girls being skivvies. Now be quiet until we get home."

Immy bit her lip, appalled at the way she had let her tongue run on. The last thing she had meant to do was to upset her father when he had been in such a rare mellow mood. Nor Elsie, who was sitting hunched up in the back seat of the car now, as far away from her sister as possible. How quickly things could turn sour, Immy thought miserably, well aware that she was mostly to blame.

And all because she had suddenly become more unsure of herself than ever before. She had always been the confident one, the one the others looked up to, the oldest daughter, with a secret lover . . . Now it was all going wrong and she didn't know who she was any more.

She must have made a small sound in her throat, because she felt Elsie's hand reach out for hers and give it a small squeeze. She could just make out her sister's pale face, lit by the glow of the street lamps and the headlights of the other vehicles, and she squeezed back, knowing they were friends again.

That was the best thing about families, she thought fervently.

They always had each other. There was no such thing as having to make an elaborate apology. You just *knew*.

When they got home Quentin opened the letter he had been handed as they left the hotel. He studied it for a long time before he spoke.

"Well, I'm blessed. My instincts were right, then. He's not such an unfeeling fellow."

"What is it, Father?" Immy asked him, knowing the letter had come from Owen Preston.

"It's a formal letter to all employees of the row of shops shortly to be converted into a new Preston's store. Read it if you wish, since it concerns all of us."

Immy read it aloud for the benefit of Elsie and of Daisy, who had begged to be allowed to stay up long enough to hear about the dinner.

"To all my loyal staff. By the time you read this you will have met me informally and we'll know something about each other. Some of you have already been offered posts in the new establishment. This to formally offer jobs to each of you. I shall need a considerable number of staff, and you all deserve the first offers. We shall not be opening until the middle of November because of the necessary conversions, but hopefully it will be in good time for the Christmas trade . . . An eye to business as ever," Immy muttered.

"Go on, Immy. Or is that all?" Elsie said.

She shook her head, reading to the end of the page.

"I realise that the interim time may be difficult for all who take up my offer of employment, so I propose to pay each of you a modest retainer wage from the day your usual business closes. For your added information, the store will have various departments, including general clothing, books, toys, babies and childrens' apparel, and a mechanical and tools section. If any of this interests you, please respond in writing before your closure date. I trust this will show my fairness to all. Cordially, Owen Preston."

"Well! What do you think of that!" Elsie said. "And a modest retainer wage. I wonder what that means."

"It could be anything," Immy said.

"But a fair man, wouldn't you say, Immy?" her father insisted, and she couldn't argue with that.

Daisy spoke slowly. "It sounds different from what I expected. Working in the children's or toy department sounds like fun."

"Well, I won't be doing it," Immy said aggressively, resisting the urge to call them all turncoats. "We were always a small family business, and I don't want to be part of a big concern that will swallow us up."

"I suspect there may be plenty more of them in the future, darling, and you can't fight progress," Quentin said.

"No, but you don't have to like it."

Frances was well enough by the weekend for Quentin to insist tactfully that Rose and Bertie should go home and take Teddy with them. They had all had enough of each other's company by then, and they knew that if Teddy didn't go soon he would start rebelling at the idea. As it was, he couldn't wait to go to the Unwanted Dogs' Home and buy the pooch Bertie had promised him.

"We'll all be back for Immy's birthday tea, of course," Rose promised. "So you'll hardly notice we've gone before we're back with you again."

"Us – and George," Teddy said importantly.

"Who's George?" Immy said.

"It's what he's going to call his dog," Daisy sniggered. "Who ever heard of a dog called *George*?"

"It's his name," Teddy howled. "And I won't let you hold him, so there."

"Thank heavens for that." Daisy grinned. "Dogs are nasty, smelly things, like most animals."

"You won't want to meet our farming friends when you come to visit us, then, Daisy," Aunt Rose said smartly. "Their daughter's about your age and she has a couple of horses. I thought you once said you wanted to ride."

"I did once, and anyway, horses are different. They don't make doggy and piggy smells all over the place—"

"No, they just make horsy smells," Bertie teased her. "So I take it you'll be quite happy to meet Lucy, then?"

"I dare say," Daisy said with a shrug. "If I ever come down your way, that is."

"That girl needs a good shaking, Quentin," Rose told her

brother after Daisy had sauntered outside. "She's becoming a proper little madam."

"Takes one to know one," Quentin said beneath his breath, with a sly wink at Immy, just near enough to overhear him.

She smiled back mischievously, thankful they were on good terms again. Her father seemed more cheerful than he had been in a long time. And if that was down to his – and Elsie's – decision to work for Preston's, then so be it. It was their choice.

As yet, she didn't know what she was going to do, except stay at home and look after Frances. Though not permanently, she amended quickly. The days of an elder daughter being obliged to be a companion to her mother were long gone.

Was it selfish to think that way? She didn't think so. Especially as Dr Wolfe had spoken very seriously to Quentin about getting Frances into a residential home quite soon. And after that . . . ?

Immy couldn't think that far ahead. In any case, first they had to see Teddy and the relatives on their way, and it was more of a tearful goodbye than expected.

Teddy had been a little pain in the neck for a long time, but when the moment of parting came they all realised how much they were going to miss him. The girls cuddled and kissed him, and smelled the lingering infant smell of him. He wasn't such a big shot yet, and right now, at just five, he looked young and vulnerable.

Even Quentin, who had never spent much time with his youngest son, looked uneasy, until Rose reminded him that hundreds of children as young as Teddy had been sent away from their London homes for their own safety, and would be living with strangers, so they should all look on the bright side.

Milking it for all he was worth, Teddy clung to them all and wailed for his mother, who seemed totally unaware of what was going on. Smilingly she told him to be a good boy and be sure to eat his crusts so his teeth wouldn't fall out.

Bertie finally broke up the uncomfortable goodbyes before they became too much to bear.

"Come on, old chap, or George will be wondering what's happened to us," he said firmly. "We don't want somebody else to take him home, do we?"

*   *   *

The house was very quiet after they had gone, and Immy couldn't settle to anything. Quentin had disappeared into his study; Daisy had flounced off somewhere; Elsie had offered to read to Frances; and Baz was out as usual.

Without warning, she pictured the Preston family still revelling in the joyous aftermath of a family wedding. She wondered if it would ever happen to any of them.

She had been so sure it would, and that she would be the one to marry first. It was the right order of things. But now she wasn't so sure. Now, with all the changes in their lives, and losing Morgan, she felt as cast adrift as an old ferry-boat without a rudder.

She grimaced at her own thought. What a state to be in, thinking herself stuck on the shelf at nineteen years old! It was far too gloomy around here today. There was only one place to go to cheer herself up.

Helen greeted her with open arms.

"Thank goodness. The parents have gone to Gloucester to see my grandmother and I'm bored, bored, bored!"

"I get the idea," Immy grinned. "And I need cheering up. Teddy's been banished to the country, and I have a horrible feeling I'm going to miss the little pest after all."

"Oh dear. So tell me what happened about MR," Helen said, with little interest in small boys. "Did you patch things up satisfactorily, or do I sense a hint of despair?"

"Sometimes I think you and Daisy would make a fine double act, Helen. You're both so dramatic!"

"That's dodging the issue, darling. Now then, what happened with the Welsh boyo? Tell me before I burst."

"It's finished," Immy said abruptly. "It *was* him I saw with another girl, and he didn't deny it. We argued, and I'm off men for good."

Helen was silent for a minute, and then she shrugged. "Of course you're not. There are plenty more fish in the sea, and you're not likely to be without a beau for long, Immy."

"Aren't I? When do I ever meet anybody? I don't go to charity functions like you do, where all the huntin', shootin' and fishin' set go—"

"You can always come with me, darling, you know that."

"Thanks, but I didn't really mean that. I'm stuck in the shop, and soon I'll be stuck at home. What am I going to *do* with my life, Helen?" She was as pathetic as any drama queen now, she thought, but she couldn't seem to help it.

"What do you want to do?"

"I don't know. Travel. Write books. Paint pictures. All the impossible things I'd be no good at!"

"How do you know if you don't try?"

"I think the furthest I'm likely to travel is down to Weston to see Aunt Rose and Uncle Bertie, or ride around Bristol as a bus conductress. How does that sound?"

"Bloody awful, if you're asking me seriously what I think," Helen said coolly.

"Thanks. I knew I could count on you to give me an honest answer," Immy said with a grin. Helen's plummy voice always made the occasional swear word sound unspeakably elegant.

"No, really, though," Helen went on, clearly seeing this as her crusade of the day. "What are you good at? Accountancy, in a small way. So apply for a job as an assistant to an accountant. You can type, so why not a secretary's job? Don't underestimate yourself, Immy. In my opinion, you're the sort who can do just about anything you put your mind to!"

"My father's going to work for Preston's," Immy said abruptly. "And Elsie's toying with the idea, though she won't commit herself fully yet. Don't you think it's a betrayal?"

"It's common sense. Is that the bee in your bonnet?"

"Perhaps. They took us out to dinner with them at the Grand the other night—"

"My God, Immy, and you're complaining!"

"And I swear that any of those Preston men could twist anyone around their little finger."

"Except you," Helen said shrewdly. "So how many of these super-gents were there?"

By the time Immy had explained about the garrulous Owen and the way Joe was so attentive towards Elsie, and got around to mentioning Robert, Helen's eyes were knowing.

"Aha! So do I take it the gorgeous Robert didn't come up to expectations on the flattery front?"

"I didn't say he was gorgeous."

"You didn't say he wasn't."

"Actually, Helen, since we've been talking I've had an idea." Immy changed the subject, ignoring the thought that she could be remotely attracted to Robert Preston. "Wild horses wouldn't make me work in that new store, and Mother will need someone around, so even if the others all turn traitor, I'll probably be the one to stay home . . ."

"Don't make yourself out to be a martyr, darling. It doesn't suit you," Helen said drily.

"I know," Immy said, more cheerfully. "But you're right. I can type and I'm quick and neat at it. So if Elsie can consider working at home, why not me? I could take out an advertisement offering my skills as a typist. What do you think?"

"I think you're brilliant, and I'm not going to make you more swollen-headed by telling you more than once. So what sort of things are you going to type for people?"

"Whatever they want. Letters, stories, wills," Immy said vaguely. "Lord, I don't know. I've only just started to think about it. I'll be a sort of jobbing typist."

"A roaming secretary," Helen suggested.

"Who stays put," Immy added, at which they both fell about laughing. "It's an idea, though, isn't it?"

"It's a wonderful idea. Where will you place your advert? In the local newspaper?"

"Ah. Perhaps. I haven't got that far yet. I may just put a card in a newsagent's window to start with."

Helen shook her head. "That won't do. You only get housewives looking for second-hand prams or women offering their services as dailies. You need to attract a different kind of people. And you'll need business cards."

Immy knew Helen didn't mean to be snobbish. She just lived in a different world, where people moved in a different way.

"My father could help. He has plenty of contacts. You could work for him if he didn't have old Miss Phipps, who'll be his adoring secretary until she's too old to crawl up the path to his chambers." But she said it without malice, and Immy shook her head at once.

"Thanks, Helen, but I'd be far too nervous to work in a solicitor's office. My skills are fairly limited – but if your father can offer me any small typing jobs that are beneath Miss Phipps's dignity, I wouldn't object."

"I'll ask him," Helen promised. "But at least you're looking more cheerful now, so let's decide what to do for the rest of the day, and forget about boring work." Since she never had to do any, it wasn't difficult for Helen to do.

They linked arms as they left the spacious house and strolled across the Downs, where the grass was sweet with summer, and the graceful span of Brunel's suspension bridge joined the two sides of the dizzying Avon Gorge, with the winding ribbon of river far below.

It was a favourite place for the more fashionable folk of the town to go walking, to see and be seen. And if the elegant and honey-blonde Miss Helen Church attracted admiring attention, it was met in equal measure by her companion with the blazing red hair and doe-brown eyes.

"So now tell me more about Robert Preston," Helen demanded, never one to let go.

The past few weeks had been taken up with so much anxiety and nervous tension within the family that Quentin Caldwell had hardly had the time to read the newspapers properly. Usually, he scoured every inch of them, national as well as local.

He wasn't what some modernists called a political animal, but as a businessman he felt it his duty to know what was going on in the world. Folk liked to do more than pass the time of day when they came into his shop. It had always been something of a social occasion, time for a chat with an intelligent man and the opportunity to put the world to rights.

Now it was nearing the middle of September and closure day was looming, but just because it wasn't going to be his shop any more, he saw no reason for things to be any different. Now that he had cause to think more positively about the future, at least on his family's account, he settled Frances in a deck-chair in the garden and took a rare hour to sit beside her indulging in his favourite pastime.

It wasn't happy reading, however. It never was these days, and it was no use burying their heads in the sand. War was coming – maybe not this year or the next, but it was inevitable, and only a fool could deny it. And only a madman or a fanatic would think he could overrun neighbouring countries and not have the rest of the world come to their defence.

"What did you say, my dear?" he heard Frances murmur as he swore silently.

"Nothing, darling. Go back to sleep."

"Is it night?" she said in bewilderment. "And where is my nightgown? Quentin, am I in bed with all my clothes on?"

As her voice rose in panic, he kissed her quickly, his eyes clouded with pain.

"You're in the garden, my love, and I'm here with you. Try to rest now."

He ached to see her concur as obediently as a child, when she had once been so vibrant and dynamic. It was all gone now, and she was dependent on him – on them all.

He remained as silent as he could as he scanned the article that had caught his attention. The government was urging the construction of Anderson shelters now, in advance of the air raids that could be expected in the event of an attack. They were pompous words, written by pompous reporters, uncaring of the fear they put in ordinary people's hearts. And the next reports were even worse.

Some factories were already being turned over to the production of thousands of gas masks which would protect the face and lungs. It was intimated that every person would soon be given one of these hellish masks and instructed how to use it.

For a moment Quentin imagined his beloved Frances being forced to put the rubbery, alien thing over her face, and knew she would simply choke. And Teddy too . . . and all of them. He wasn't a man given to panic, but right then he wished he had the means to remove every one of them to some far-off place where they would be out of harm's way.

But if you believed the direst pundits, there was going to be no such place left in the world.

He read on, all his former calm slipping away. He thought Frances was asleep until he heard her soft, carefree humming, as sweet as a nightingale, and his throat constricted.

Six

O wen Preston was nothing if not efficient. Another circular
arrived to inform all ex-shop managers that, as a further
gesture of goodwill to those who were joining his staff,
he would install a telephone in every home, so they could
keep in touch when necessary. And a week before Imogen's
birthday on September twenty-third, the Caldwells were the
proud possessors of their own black bakelite instrument.

It was a grand gesture that impressed everyone, though to
someone like Helen Church, who had never known what it
was like not to have a telephone in the house, it was less of
a wonder than it was to the family in Vicarage Street.

"You know what this means, don't you?" Quentin had said
delightedly. "It means we can be in touch with other folk as
well, including my sister for news of Teddy. Bertie can get an
instant message to us through his Lodge."

"So his funny old Antelopes will have their uses at last,"
Imogen said with a grin at the thought of solemn and portly
Uncle Bertie wearing the regulation Antelope horns for his
meetings. "It's a good job their Lodge is in Weston and
not somewhere out in the woods, isn't it?" She herself was
thinking more along the lines of being able to telephone
Helen whenever she liked, once she had got the hang of the
new-fangled thing.

Quentin chuckled back as images of his community-minded
brother-in-law flitted through his head.

"It gives us some status too, my love. We're not the cast-offs
we might have been. It proves that Preston's take care of their
people, and that's not something to be taken lightly. No, maybe
their take-over wasn't such a bad thing after all."

His eldest son scowled, out of sorts because Enoch Bray's
ferry-boat had been slightly damaged and was in for repairs.

Now he had little to do but twiddle his thumbs all day. He hadn't even been taken on officially on a proper wage-paying basis yet, because Enoch was a stickler for getting the boy's parental approval before he agreed to it. And so far, Quentin hadn't given it.

"You've changed your tune, haven't you, Father?" Baz grumbled. "I thought Preston's was a dirty word around here. I thought we all hated their guts."

Quentin looked at him in annoyance. Big though he was for his age, his son was not beyond receiving a cuff about the ears if necessary, even though physical violence was not something Quentin entirely approved of.

"You just mind your tongue, young man, and remember who you're talking to. I'm not one of your riff-raff friends, and I won't have their gutter talk brought home here." It was hardly gutter talk – in reality it was little more than bravado – but Quentin didn't see why he should have his bubble burst by the likes of this squib.

Immy put in her pennyworth, supporting her father. "I don't know why you want to spend so much time there, anyway, coming home stinking with your boots caked in mud half the time, and looking as if you've been pulled through a hedge."

Baz rounded on her, his eyes gleaming with a kind of malicious triumph. "Oh yes? I suppose you'd rather spend your time rolling about in the long grass up on the hill then."

The small silence that followed seemed full of accusation and betrayal, and Immy felt her face go crimson.

"What's all this, Imogen?" Quentin said at once. "Do you know what the boy's talking about?"

"I can only think he's been spying on me and Helen," she invented furiously. "We often go up there where nobody can overhear us when we want to talk about private things, but now we know differently, don't we? We didn't know we'd been *followed* and *spied* on, and it's just the kind of thing this little sneak would do."

She babbled on, emphasising the words scornfully, and taking the initiative for all she was worth. Staring Baz out, her brown eyes bored into his, daring him to betray her completely.

At last she saw his gaze flicker, and he shrugged and spoke sullenly.

"It's all dull girl stuff anyway. It's not half as exciting as listening to the foreign sailors and the old seamen. They talk about faraway places and *men's* things. That's why I want to work with old Enoch on his ferry, and not have to listen to stupid girls all the time. There's enough of that at home. I wish somebody would realise it's what I really want to do and not scoff at me all the time."

He stared back at his sister penetratingly, so that she could read every little blackmailing thought going through his devious mind.

You persuade Father to let me work on the river, and I won't say anything about you lying in the long grass with a boy and letting him kiss you, was his message. What else might he have seen? Immy wondered in sick horror.

Well, she supposed that if he'd seen her the last time she met Morgan, at least he would know there was no likelihood of any of it happening again. Despite her resolve she couldn't help feeling a huge pang of loss for something that had been lovely and was gone for ever. And with it, a deep fury that this litle wretch had seen and overheard it all.

"You know, he's probably got a point, Daddy," she said, turning to him as if the thought had just occurred to her. "Apart from yourself, we're a household of females, and he hasn't even got Teddy to tease any more, poor little love. You followed your ambition to open the shop, and I suppose it's only natural for Baz to have an ambition too. For what it's worth, he has my vote to do what he wants."

"I wasn't aware that I was asking for votes," Quentin said coldly.

"Oh, why can't we let him go and work on his old ferry-boat and give us some peace?" Daisy said. "He never stops grumbling about the shop, and it gives me a headache."

Immy hid a smile at the dramatic declaration. Meanwhile, Elsie decided not to bother adding her voice to the debate at all, sure that Baz would get his way in the end. Boys always did, in her opinion.

After a few minutes, Quentin spoke reluctantly. "Well, you can give it a try – and we'll see how long it lasts when it comes to winter, when nobody wants to cross the river in the bad weather."

Baz gave a whoop of joy.

"You mean it? You'll have to give me written permission, mind, because Enoch won't accept me otherwise."

"Well, at least the man's got some integrity," was all Quentin would say, knowing when he was beaten.

As soon as she could get him alone, Imogen grabbed her brother by his shirt collar, and none too gently.

"Now you just listen to me, you little sneak. We're even now, and I don't want to hear another whisper about this business *anywhere*, in or out of this house. Do we understand one another?"

He didn't pretend to misunderstand, and nodded quickly, aware of how incensed she was. The waterfront louts had jeered at him that temper went with red hair. Well, he had that too, and prided himself on using his fists when they were needed. But his sister was older and just as fiery – and surprisingly strong, he thought, as her grip on him tightened.

"I wouldn't really have told anyone, not in normal circumstances," he defended himself, choking and spluttering.

She let him go, pushing him away from her in disgust, and knowing very well that he would have done, given half a chance.

"The little blighter," Helen said indignantly, when Immy reported the incident to her.

They were drinking tea in a cafe in the town. Immy had contacted Helen by telephone, but only to arrange the meeting – this was something that had to be relayed face to face, without any interested operator listening in. Immy was still getting used to using the instrument. As yet she had no idea how private any telephone conversation was, and she wasn't taking any chances.

"You did well to cover your tracks so quickly, though," Helen went on. "And your father believed you, of course. He'd never believe less of his angel."

"I'm anything but an angel," Immy exclaimed. As Helen's eyes widened, she went on hurriedly. "It's not what you're thinking, and I've told you so before. But that doesn't mean I didn't think about it sometimes."

"Crikey," Helen said. Her own senses had been completely untouched by romance so far. They were intended to stay that way until a certain knight on a white charger came along: she much preferred reading about King Arthur's exploits to the miseries of Jane Eyre.

"I've never heard you talk like that about MR before, Immy," she went on.

"Well, I'm not going to talk about him now, so forget I said anything. The last time I saw him was when he delivered Elsie's leaflets and asked for a larger fee than we expected. It was out of spite, I suspect, because he's not used to being turned down by a girl."

"That makes you pretty special, then, doesn't it?"

A smile replaced Immy's look of annoyance.

"I suppose it does," she said cheerfully. "Anyway, do you want to join my family for my birthday tea? We've decided to have a picnic on the Downs, since Dr Wolfe says he sees no reason why Mother can't be there. She loves the fresh air, and Aunt Rose and Uncle Bertie will be bringing Teddy for the day. James could come too, if he's around."

"Oh, you don't know, do you?" Helen said excitedly. "He's enlisted in the Royal Engineers."

"Already? But there's not a war on."

"Not yet, but you know what everybody's saying, especially now Mr Chamberlain's meeting that horrible little Hitler in Munich for talks over Czechoslovakia. All the papers are full of it. Don't you ever read them?"

"Not if I can help it. Well, yes, of course I do sometimes," she amended, at Helen's raised eyebrows. "Father insists that we should keep abreast of national affairs, but I try to avoid all that stuff as much as possible."

"Immy, you shouldn't."

With a solicitor for a father, and a mother into Good Works, Helen could be just as intense when she chose, and clearly had decided to take a more serious interest in the state of the nation now that James was one of His Majesty's soldiers.

"I promise I'll try to catch up," Immy promised. "So will James be around for my birthday?"

"He might. I'll try to telephone him tonight. He's with his training regiment in Winchester, and Lord knows how soon they'll let him out."

"You make it sound like prison," Immy said with a laugh.

"It is, as far as I'm concerned. I bet he looks a whizz in his uniform, though." Helen giggled, her sombre mood gone. "He always played toy soldiers when he was little, marching around with a toy gun and making me be the enemy."

"Good Lord!" Immy said, laughing as the pictures filled her mind. "I suppose you fancy yourself in uniform as well – and you might have to wear one if it comes to conflict. We all might, like women did in the last war – or we may even end up having to dig fields to grow turnips. What a thought!"

They looked at one another as the idea began to sink in that this might not be play-acting at all, but very real.

"I'm simply not going to think about it, except to say that if it *does* happen, we must always stick together, Immy. We'll both be nurses, or both grow the damn vegetables, or drive cars for officers—"

Imogen hooted. "Oh yes! That's all right for you, but I can't drive a car."

"You'd better learn, then," Helen advised her. "But whatever happens, we'll stick together, right?"

"Through thick and thin," Immy said solemnly, and they shook hands over the table, before she burst into nervous giggles again. "Now stop it."

"All right," Helen agreed. "Tell me what I can buy you for your birthday instead."

Immy couldn't decide. There were only two things on her mind as she bicycled home again in the heat of the day. One was that she had begun to think it might be a very good idea if she learned to drive a car, and that she would do her best to persuade her father to teach her.

The other, gloomier thought was that Morgan wouldn't be giving her the small gift he'd promised. She shouldn't care . . . but it was hard to accept the blow to her pride caused by his discarding her so easily. Even if she had known she would never fully trust him again, he hadn't put up much of a fight to keep her as his girl.

He hadn't wanted her as much as she thought, and if she

had any sense, she'd keep reminding herself that she didn't want him.

In the end, the birthday picnic was delayed for a week because Teddy caught a bad cold, and Rose wouldn't bring him to Bristol until he was better.

So the day of celebration coincided with the jubilant newspaper and wireless reports at the end of September that Mr Chamberlain had pulled off a massive success in Munich, and returned home to cheering crowds at Heston airport, with the news that there was to be no war. The Munich Pact had been signed, and an almost palpable sigh of relief seemed to envelop the whole country.

"Isn't it wonderful news?" Immy asked a handsome and newly uniformed James Church when her friends joined the family on the Downs in the middle of that sunny afternoon. "You needn't have bothered to enlist, James!"

"I wouldn't say that," he told her. "It's what I always intended to do, and besides, this is only the beginning."

"How can you be such a pessimist? I don't believe you, anyway. Don't you dare put a damper on my party, James!"

He laughed at her pouting face, and stroked his finger down her cheek. "I wouldn't dream of upsetting the prettiest young lady in all Bristol!"

Immy's face went pink. He didn't pay compliments lightly, and as she caught sight of Helen's grinning face she remembered her teasing words, "You can always marry James." But she had never thought of him in that way before, and she didn't think of him that way now. He was an old friend, no more . . .

"Oh, pooh," she answered him lightly. "Stop teasing me, and come and have some lemonade and sandwiches before Baz and Daisy scoff them all."

He laughed again and put his arm carelessly around her waist as they joined the others, the way old friends did.

"Now then, Imogen, what have you and this young man been plotting with your heads together?" her Aunt Rose asked.

"Well, James is plotting how to win a non-existent war, and I'm plotting how much of my delicious birthday cake I can decently eat without ending up looking like a barrel." Immy giggled, serenely confident that she had the neatest figure of all of them and never put on an ounce, no matter what she ate.

"I want some cake. Me, me!" Teddy bellowed, tidier than of old after Aunt Rose's fussing over him. The rampant George, the new Yorkshire terrier pup that he had adamantly refused to leave behind in Weston, got so excited at Teddy's shouting that he had to be restrained from trampling over the entire feast.

Quentin took charge, insisting that the pup be tied to a convenient tree before they all ended up having mashed cake and sandwiches for tea. But it was all so light-hearted on that blue and golden day, an afternoon of Indian summer, that nobody really got upset.

Immy felt a sudden crazy and irrational need to hold this whole scene in her memory and fix it there for evermore. She wished she had her box Brownie to do the job for her, but she hadn't remembered it. What a shame.

All her family and her closest friends together . . . her darling mother enjoying the sunshine . . . and not a war cloud anywhere in the sky. It deserved to be photographed for posterity as a permanent reminder of this glorious day.

There were other groups out on the Downs as well, and it was as if the newly buoyant mood of the country and the fair weather had combined to bring everyone out of doors. There were older couples, and a number of other families with young children and babies in prams.

Away to the right of them, too near to the edge of the steep cliffs overlooking the gorge in Aunt Rose's opinion, a child of about Teddy's age was having a small tantrum, and his nurse was vainly trying to quieten him and stop him screaming and upsetting other people. It was the only jarring note in an otherwise beautiful day, but few people took any real notice. The Caldwell party were all laughing and teasing Teddy that he'd never get George to do tricks until he was out of the puppy stage.

Teddy wouldn't give up, and by now George was yapping excitedly, rolling on to his back to be tickled. Everybody was taking turns obliging when Elsie suddenly spoke loudly.

"What's Mother doing? Where's she going? Daddy – oh, Daddy, stop her!"

They stopped tickling the dog, and everyone began crying

out at once as they turned and saw Frances, her graceful arms outstretched, her feet skimming over the grass as nimbly as they had ever done in her dancing days.

They heard the joy in her voice as her arms reached out as if to embrace the screaming child, who had torn away from his nurse now and was staring at the vision in the floaty summer frock coming towards him.

"My baby. My sweet baby. Come to Mama, Teddy," Frances was crooning sweetly. "Mama will kiss and make it all better."

"Dear God in heaven," Quentin croaked as he rushed to cover the ground between him and his wife. Everyone else was at his heels, except for Rose, who held Teddy close, burying his head against her bosom as if to stave off the inevitable.

"Frances, come back," Quentin shouted hoarsely. "It's not Teddy. Teddy's here with us. Keep away from the edge, for God's sake."

As she heard his voice, she turned around in bewilderment, and the other child let out the breath he had been holding in a blood-curdling scream, as if he thought this madwoman was about to take him away.

The child's nurse began to shout at Frances, and it clearly unnerved her. They saw her teeter for a few seconds, her feet twisted and somehow tangled in one another, and then the terrified screams were hers as she plunged over the steep cliffs of the Avon Gorge and disappeared from view.

From then on one of the best days of Immy's life became the worst. The ambulance men told them that Frances had never had a chance, and by the time they had recovered her torn and bleeding body and taken it reverently away for examination and pronouncement, they had all realised that the next place for her would be the hospital chapel of rest.

Quentin was inconsolable. Crowds had gathered on the Downs, and there were many more on the river bank and the roadside far below. Some of them would be clearly thinking it was just another suicide, for which these cliffs and the suspension bridge were favourite venues.

The hell of it had been that the family hadn't been able to get to Frances quickly. There was no path down the cliffs, and the cars took an age to reach the valley far below. By then someone had already sent for an ambulance, and someone else had covered Frances's body with a blanket for decency's sake. All the family could do was cling together and weep, knowing the only consolation was that she must have died instantly.

Immy had wanted to scream at people not to cover her mother's lovely face with the blanket and to let her breathe . . . even though she knew how heartbreakingly foolish it was. Like their father, Elsie seemed numb with shock now, while Daisy stood shaking, her eyes terrified and distraught.

Rose and Bertie had swiftly cleared up all the picnic things, and taken Teddy and George back to Vicarage Street before the child could see what had happened. They would explain the facts more gently later. Baz had gone with them, unable to face up to what had happened.

James Church kept his arms around Immy and his sister, as if to shield both of them. None of it helped. Nothing could change the fact that on this day of all days, fate had so cruelly taken Frances away from them, and in so ghastly and horrible a way.

"It's so dreadful for it to happen so publicly," Helen whispered, not knowing what else to say.

"It's dreadful for it to happen at all," Immy retorted through shivering lips. She gave a strange, strangled laugh. "But you know what I keep telling myself? I think that in a weird way Mother would have loved the drama of it all. She had an audience, and that's what she lived for."

"Oh Immy, that's an awful thing to say."

"No, it's not," Immy said, flinching at her friend's censure. "She'll have had her last moment of glory, because this will surely be splashed all over the local newspaper. Now everyone will remember her as she was, and probably ask my father to provide details of her earlier years in the theatre. And if they *don't* think about reminding everyone how talented she was, I shall damn well insist that they do!"

"Good for you, Imogen."

She recognised the voice immediately. A voice that was marginally less arrogant than usual, showing suitable respect for a tragedy.

She spun around, her heart thumping, knowing it would

be Morgan, as curious as anyone else in the Gorge valley that day, whether they had actually witnessed the accident or simply heard the scream of the ambulance. They were all ghouls, thought Immy savagely, knowing it was human nature all the same.

Morgan wasn't alone. The girl she had seen before was there with him. They had obviously been out for an afternoon stroll, but now she had a notebook and pencil in her hand.

"I'm very sorry, Imogen," Morgan said roughly. "This is a terrible thing to happen, and we've only just discovered who the lady was. But if you want to let us know exactly what happened, I can promise you the true facts will get into the paper as soon as possible, instead of any garbled reports. Catherine's a trainee interviewer," he finished lamely, as Immy's eyes burned into him.

Since she seemed to have temporarily lost the power of speech, James assessed the situation and took charge at once.

"I think that would be a sensible thing to do, and far better than any wild suppositions. But as you can see, Miss Caldwell's in no state to give a statement. If you permit me, I can tell you exactly what happened."

"And you are?" the girl called Catherine asked, as James drew her and Morgan to one side, well away from eavesdroppers.

"A close friend of the family," he said.

There had to be an inquest, and the verdict was the expected one of Accidental Death, but long before that the local newspaper had given endless column inches to the once glamorous stage artiste, Frances Caldwell.

It resulted in the funeral becoming an even more harrowing occasion then expected, since it seemed that half of Bristol had turned out to witness it as if it was some kind of spectator event. "It only needs the sandwiches and deck-chairs," Rose said sourly.

Quentin was both moved and appalled at the crowds intruding on their personal grief, but Immy still had the macabre feeling that her mother would have loved it all, that she was somewhere Up There watching, and approving.

Because of the sudden interest in what most people living

outside the area would have seen as merely passing news of a one-time star, the newspaper's coverage seemed to go on for several weeks. As other interviewers requested details about Frances's life and career, Imogen became the spokesperson, knowing that she was feeding that interest with an almost frantic desire not to lose her mother, and that in this small way, she was keeping her with them, still in their midst.

Since her father couldn't face it, she had been the one to search for her mother's memoirs and loan the newspaper the old programmes and posters that were reproduced in full. Theatre managers and stage hands were interviewed, as well as prop designers and a retired dresser who had known Frances at the beginning of her career. All gave their version of the beautiful and talented dancer who had been out of the public eye for so long.

Eventually the family began to feel she hadn't belonged to them at all, but to the world.

"This has gone on long enough, and it has to stop," Quentin finally said harshly, when Immy asked if she could borrow his favourite photograph of her mother – the one that never left his bedside. "I want no more of it, Imogen. Your mother was the one who revelled in the publicity, not me, and now she's had her fill. Let her rest in peace, for God's sake, and stop tormenting me."

She stared at him dumbly, seeing the gaunt lines on his face that had never been there before. Too late she realised that all this attention was killing him. She ran to him and hugged him, feeling his silent sobs against her body.

"God knows I miss her and I'll love her until the day I die, my darling," Quentin finally muttered, "but I had years of sharing her with the world, and now I just want to be selfish and keep my memories of her to myself."

"I understand, Daddy," Immy whispered. "It seems that you and I have been pulling in opposite directions, when we should be pulling together. I know now we have to accept what can't be changed, don't we?"

The others seemed better at doing that than she was, although she couldn't see into their minds and supposed that it might be their method of coping. Everyone had their own way of dealing with grief. She knew that. But she was the eldest, and her memories of her mother were sharper and longer. She couldn't really settle to anything. Like her father, without the shop to occupy herself, she seemed to be in a kind of limbo.

Condolence cards and letters kept coming, even from the Preston family, who had somehow got to hear of the tragedy. Immy didn't hate them any more, but the cards served to remind them all of a part of their lives that was gone for ever.

After the funeral Baz had immediately gone to work on the river, as if he couldn't bear to be inside the house any more than he had to. Elsie shut herself in her room for much of the time, and Daisy declared fervently that she no longer wanted to go on the stage.

In fact, she begged to be allowed to go back with Rose and Bertie, if they would have her, so that she could help to look after Teddy, at least for a while. And if she was too much of a bother she'd quite willing to go and work in a village store, or something, she added vaguely.

"Are you sure about this, my love?" Rose asked her carefully, since it was such an odd request. "I think you should take your time over this. You always wanted to follow in your mother's footsteps, didn't you?"

"Not any more. Nobody could," Daisy said simply. She took a deep breath, suddenly more self-controlled at sixteen than any of them realised. "I'm perfectly sure I don't want to do that any more. Mother loved all the fuss, but I don't think she'd like the way it's been happening lately. I think if those interview people found out her favourite food and drink, they'd plaster that all over the newspapers too. It's invading her privacy, and ours, and I know Daddy hates it."

"Then of course you must come to us, my love," Rose said, hearing the note of desperation creeping into her niece's voice now. "It will be good for Teddy too, poor little lamb. He doesn't understand, and he keeps crying and asking for his mother. It's upsetting your father, though I don't know if we should be taking Teddy away just yet."

"I'm sure we should. I know Teddy can't help it, but he just reminds him all the time," Daisy said, wiser than her years. "Please let's go soon, Aunt Rose."

"The girl's right, my dear," Bertie said. "The sooner we all get back to some sort of normality, the better. And young Lucy will be more than pleased to show Daisy how to ride a horse, I'm sure. Daisy'll be competing in the local gymkhana before you know it."

"I doubt that!" Daisy said, with the glimmer of a smile. "But I do know one thing. It will be good to get George out of the house and back to the country. He's chewed up nearly everyone's slippers by now!"

The house was very quiet after the departure of Rose and Bertie, along with Teddy, Daisy and George. Imogen could hear the scratchy sound of the gramophone coming from Elsie's room, and when she knocked on her door and went inside, she found Elsie lying motionless on her bed, arms locked behind her head and staring at the ceiling.

"This was one of Mother's favourite tunes, do you remember?" she asked Immy without turning her head. "Sometimes I think I can still hear her humming it."

"Stop it, Elsie. It does no good."

"What? To remember Mother? Should we pretend she never existed, then? You're a fine one to talk, letting those awful newspaper interviewers have what they want all the time," Elsie said, brimming with anger. She sat up, hugging her knees to her chest. "I think you were enjoying the limelight, if you must know."

"That's a dreadful thing to say, and you know it's not true," Immy said, shocked.

"Do I?" She wilted. "Oh, I'm sorry. I don't know what I'm saying, and I'm just feeling lost and miserable."

"I know, Elsie. We all are. But you're not alone. We're still the Caldwell clan, aren't we?"

"Even if we're a bit depleted," Elsie said sadly.

Immy said nothing for a few minutes, and then said something that had been on her mind for a while.

"Shall I tell you what I think?"

"Go on. I know you will, anyway," Elsie said, turning off the gramophone as the music ended, to Immy's relief.

"I think you should forget your idea of working at home and take that job at Preston's new shop. I don't know whether Father will still want to take in paying guests now, and I daren't ask him yet. But you need to get out of the house and meet people, Elsie – and you haven't done anything with those leaflets yet, have you?"

"Hardly. It's been the last thing on my mind," Elsie muttered. "I haven't really thought about it."

"Think about it now. If Father's working for Preston's, it will boost his spirits to know you're there too."

"And what about you?"

"I'll probably stay home for a while and take in typing," Immy said, as if she had always known it would come to that.

"Well, that's a turnaround, isn't it?" Elsie exclaimed indignantly, not sure whether or not she liked the thought of her sister using her own idea. "And will you hire the dashing Morgan Raine to print your leaflets too?"

Immy shook her head decisively. "I definitely will not. That's the last thing I'll do. And don't even ask why, Elsie."

Seven

Personal tragedies always overshadow world events. It took a long while for the Caldwells to recover from the trauma of Frances's death, and even longer for the unwelcome ballyhoo surrounding it to die down. It was as if Bristol had suddenly remembered its once famous artiste, and was doing its guilty best to keep the interest alive. But enough was enough.

As October slid into November Baz's fifteenth birthday came and went without fuss. Baz wasn't one for fuss, anyway. All he wanted was to notch up another year on his mental calendar and calculate when he could decently ask to leave home. Enoch Bray had said he could move into his cottage with him and his missis, if he was so minded, but as yet he hadn't dare mention it to his father.

There was plenty more to think about as the newspapers screamed out the news. The early euphoria over Neville Chamberlain's "peace in our time" declaration became a mockery as Hitler marched into Czechoslovakia.

Britain wasn't involved, but everyone said it was only a matter of time, egged on by the gloom-spreaders giving dire predictions of *when* the war would actually begin, rather than *if*. Some of the more daring newspaper cartoonists were already depicting various factions placing bets on the date.

The old salts at the waterfront openly bragged about their part in the last one, firing Baz with enthusiasm to be in on something. He didn't know what, except that it had to be something to do with water.

Bristol was a traditional seafaring city. It was full of daredevil stories of the sea and of the old press-gangs who had forced men into service. There were hair-raising tales of those who escaped their clutches, disappearing into the many twisting tunnels under the old pubs such as the famed Landogger Trow, and accounts of heroes such as John Cabot and Isambard Kingdom Brunel and his great ships. Adventure on the high seas was in every true Bristolian's blood. Or so Baz told himself.

"Why would we have to get involved in a war, anyway?" Elsie asked one of her workmates in the spanking new Preston's Emporium, which had opened to a fanfare of publicity, or vulgar razzmatazz, according to some. "I'm not sure it's our business to interfere with what Hitler does."

"It is if he thinks he can gobble up the whole of Europe," the older woman from gents' neckties and cravats said.

"But we're not Europe. We're England!"

"Tell that to those who fought in the last one. Ask your father what he thinks! He was in it, I suppose." She gave Elsie an arched look. "Or was he a conchie?"

"He certainly was not!" Elsie said. "He fought in France like everyone else."

"And came back. Mine didn't."

"Oh Doris, I'm sorry," Elsie stammered, red-faced.

The woman shrugged. "'S'all right. I hardly knew him. I was only a kid when me mum got the telegram. But I still remember wondering what was going to happen to us, me mum with six kids an' all, and another on the way."

"And what did happen to you all?" Elsie said, humbled.

"Nothin' much. We had a lot of uncles who helped out."

"You were lucky to be part of a large family, then." She stopped, realising that Doris was laughing at her.

"Blimey, girl, you're a bit wet behind the ears, ain't you? I'd have thought, coming from a theatrical family, you'd have known what was what."

"A theatrical family?" The pain rushed in as she got Doris's meaning. "If you mean my mother, she was the only one involved with the theatre. The rest of us were just, well, normal. My father saw to that."

"He didn't mind, then – her mixing with all them flashy folk, I mean, and knowing what went on in some quarters."

"What exactly do you mean by that?" Elsie said, her heart starting to thump.

"Hey, kid, I don't mean nothing," Doris said, seeing how upset Elsie was becoming. "I'm sure your mother was whiter than white, and nobody ever heard a word against her as far as I know, but by all accounts some of them Hollywood film stars carry on a bit, don't they?"

"I dare say they do, but my mother was never like that." Elsie was stiff with anger now. "She always came home after a performance except when she was on tour, and then my father or my aunt went with her, so just you keep your nasty insinuations to yourself."

"Well, I'm sorry!" Doris snapped, ruffled. "Blimey, touchy ain't the word for it with some of you young 'uns."

She flounced off, but it put Elsie out of sorts for the rest of the day. She was scratchy with Doris and everybody else with whom she came in contact, with the result that Joe Preston, newly appointed manager of the store, asked her to come into his office at the end of the day.

She remained standing by the door of the office while he sat at his desk, pencil in hand, his good-looking face thoughtful as he looked at her rigidly held figure.

"You sent for me, sir," she said tightly, sure that she was about to get the sack.

"Come in and shut the door, Elsie, for goodness' sake. I'm not going to eat you."

She felt her mouth curve into the smallest of smiles at his words, and edged nearer to his desk.

"So what's this fuss all about? I can't have my staff going around looking as if somebody's just died—"

The minute the light-hearted words had left his lips, Joe knew what he'd said. As Elsie's face crumpled, he came around the desk in horror, hesitating a moment before pulling her to him, and wrapping his arms around her. His voice was hoarse with embarrassment and concern.

"My God, lass, I didn't mean to be so bloody insensitive – and now I'm making it worse by blaspheming, aren't I? My tongue sometimes runs away with me. By now you'll have realised 'tis a Preston failing, but I was just trying to cheer you up, that's all."

"You've got a funny way of doing it, reminding me that my mother's just died," she choked.

Her voice was muffled, since her face was pressed so close to his chest, and as always she felt a huge sense of shock and disbelief at having to say the words at all.

Aware of their closeness, Joe released her gently, but he still held her hands, as if afraid she would take flight at any minute. He didn't want her to. With a fierce sense of shock he realised how deliciously warm and soft she had felt in his arms, and he wanted her back there.

He looked into her velvety brown eyes, shining with the tears she was too proud to shed, her cheeks flushed with pain and embarrassment and however many other emotions he and that wretched Doris had inadvertently stirred up in her.

Elsie felt his gaze on her. As she returned it, she felt an answering echo of something that she didn't understand, but which both frightened and moved her.

She almost leapt away from him, rubbing her hands down the side of her work overall in the smart Preston colours of blue and mauve stripes, suddenly as nervous as a kitten.

"Are you going to fire me?" she said in a small voice. "If so, I wish you'd tell me and get it over with."

"Good God, why on earth would I do that?"

He had returned to his side of the desk, and told her abruptly to sit down. She did so quickly – if she hadn't, she was sure she might have fallen down. They all thought they were coping well enough after Frances's death, but sometimes it just hit you all over again . . .

"I haven't exactly been a model Preston's employee today, have I, sir?" she asked.

They all knew by now that it was the yardstick by which Preston's worked. Posters were pinned up in each of their stores to announce the model employee of the month. Most of the new Bristol employees had thought it pretentious and a bit of a laugh at first, until one of them got the accolade and preened for the whole month because of it. Elsie knew she was hardly going to qualify for that on today's performance!

Joe smiled gently, admiring the way she tilted her chin and stared him out, challenging him to agree with her.

"I have to admit that you have not," he said. "But since I also believe you were provoked into it, and having heard Doris's reckless words myself, we'll say no more about it."

She found herself sitting back in relief. She *liked* working here. Imogen had been right in saying she should get out of the house and see something of the real world – even if it was from behind a shop counter in the middle of town. And her old clients knew her and asked for her, bringing in their garments for her neat repairs, and the occasional order for a new hat.

"Shall we shake hands on it?" Joe Preston said.

As their hands touched, he blurted out, as gauche as any schoolboy: "I shall be going back to York for a week at Christmas for our usual family gathering, but the shop will only be closed for the two days' holiday, of course. When I come back, would you come to the cinema with me one evening?"

"Is it proper for a manager to ask a shop-girl out?" Elsie said, too flummoxed to say anything else.

"I don't see why not, but if you want me to ask your father's permission—"

"That won't be necessary. I *am* eighteen, and I'm sure he respects you, Mr Preston."

"Does that mean yes?"

She hesitated, flushed to her ears. "I believe it does."

"Marvellous. And Elsie, if you don't stop calling me 'sir' or 'Mr Preston', and start calling me Joe, at least socially, I shall withdraw the invitation at once."

She started to laugh at his teasing, because despite the greyness of the November afternoon, the day began to feel sunnier than any day had done for a very long time.

"Joe Preston has asked you out?" Immy said, when Elsie reported the news that evening. "What does Father say about it?"

"I haven't told him yet."

"And what will your workmates think about you hobnobbing with the boss? I'm not sure it's a good idea, Elsie."

"I wasn't asking what you *think*. I'm just telling you what I'm going to do. You're not my governess, Imogen, and I'm not a child any more. Just because you've never had a young man interested in you doesn't mean that I'm going to stay a spinster all my life. The days when a younger sister had to wait for her elders to get married before she did are long gone, in case you hadn't noticed."

As she paused for breath, the temptation for Immy to inform her sister all about Morgan Raine came and went. It wasn't worth it. *He* wasn't worth it. Immy had seen him out with several other girls since the days of Catherine, so presumably that particular fancy had come and gone too.

"You're thinking of marrying Joe Preston, then?" she asked instead, sarcastically.

Elsie blushed. "Of course not. I'm only going to the pictures with him. And since it's not to be until after Christmas, because we'll be *far* too busy in the shop until then, I can take my time before telling Daddy. I thought you'd be happy for me."

"I am, darling. I just think you should be careful, that's all."

"I'm not going to do anything I shouldn't, if that's what you mean. I do know about things, Immy!"

"Of course I don't think that," Immy said, knowing her sister was as green as grass when it came to men, and having an enormous advantage over her in that respect – if advantage it was. "I just think that if Joe Preston *was* thinking of marriage – eventually – that would be all right, I suppose. But if he wasn't, and if it all went wrong – well, it would be very difficult for you both, wouldn't it? Working in the same place, I mean. And for Father too."

"Oh, you're just being beastly, and spoiling everything!"

"I'm only thinking about you, sweetheart," Immy said in distress. She hesitated, and then spoke more softly, saying what was in her heart at that moment. "If Mother were here, Elsie, and still capable of understanding and caring for her girls, I know she'd be saying the very same thing to you."

Elsie bit her shaking lip, and slowly nodded.

"Perhaps I should go and ask Father's advice, then."

"That's a very good idea," Immy said, relieved that she wasn't to be the one to destroy her sister's dreams.

But to her surprise, Quentin didn't object, saying that Joe Preston was a decent, upright man, and that since everybody liked a bit of innocent romance, it wasn't such a bad thing for it to happen in these troubled times.

"It's only the pictures, Daddy," Elsie told him with a nervous giggle. "It's hardly a romance!"

But in her heart she knew it could be. And when Joe left for York a few days before Christmas – and her father was elevated to temporary manager because of his experience in the haberdashery and clothing trade – Elsie realised how much she missed him.

It was then that she started dreaming about him, and waking up with certain hot and shivery feelings she had never felt before. She began feeling not at all sure it was all going to be so innocent, either.

But first they had to bolster one another up for the first Christmas without Frances. Preston's was closed for the two days' holiday, and the frantic buying of gifts and wrapping paper was over. A decorated Christmas tree stood in the front foyer of the shop, but for the Caldwell family there was no heart for trimming the house or the usual festivities.

"You should get right away," Helen Church advised her friend Immy when she said how much she was dreading it all. Immy had described how the family had always played charades on Christmas night, and how her mother had loved it so much, laughing and clapping, even when she could no longer take part.

"Oh yes?" Immy said. "And where would we go? We don't have a seaside cottage in Devon like you. We're not—"

"If you dare to say you're not in the same class, I shall hit you, darling," Helen said fiercely. "In any case, we're not using the cottage at Christmas, so . . ."

"Thank you, but no thank you," Immy said. "It's very generous of you, but I know Father would never hear of it. It's only for two days, anyway."

Even they seemed to stretch endlessly ahead. The family were still lost after Frances's death, and so far they had done nothing about the guest-house idea. Privately, each of them thought it would never happen. In the meantime, Immy had advertised her secretarial skills and got a few responses, and done some typing for Helen's father, but that too seemed pathetically like grubbing for work. It wasn't her style. She knew she would have to get a real job, if only to hold her head up high.

The Christmas problem was decided, however, when Bertie telephoned to say Christmas was taking place at their house that year, and Rose wouldn't take any excuses. They were to drive down to Weston-super-Mare on Christmas Eve to be all together, which was how families should be. His and Rose's personal – and early – gift to each other had been the installation of a brand-new telephone, he added, which he was using now, instead of having to rely on the Antelope instrument.

"Your aunt's a good soul," Quentin said, when he put down the receiver, resisting a smile at the image the words conjured up. "And when she gets in one of her planning and organising moods, there's no arguing with her."

He was pleasantly surprised at having been made manager for the next week. It gave him back some much-needed status, although everybody said it had been on the cards all the time, and there was little resentment from anyone.

"Did Joe give you anything?" Immy whispered to Elsie when they were all bundling into the old Rover car, with Baz grumbling all the while at having to leave the city.

"Of course not!" Elsie said in astonishment, surprised that Immy could even ask such a thing. "We're not *courting*, Immy. Not yet, anyway, and maybe not at all. He's been far too busy to say anything much to me lately, and I sometimes think he may regret asking me out, or even have forgotten it."

If he had the hurt would be too great to bear, but she wasn't telling Immy that. She regretted ever having had any foolish romantic dreams about him at all, almost sure now that he had only asked her out on impulse, and was far too grand to go along with it.

But she wasn't going to think about him at all for the next couple of days. They all had to be as bright as possible for their father's sake. Their parents' first meeting had been at Christmas time, and it had always been an extra special, magical time for them all. His two elder daughters were determined not to let him slip into despair.

Once Christmas was over, and there was a new year to think about, surely they could start to think about living again. They just had to get over this hurdle . . .

Rose and Bertie lived in a rambling old Victorian house on a hill with a glorious view of the sweeping sandy bay of Weston-super-Mare. The house had originally been built for a large family with many servants, but since Rose and Bertie had none of either, they had filled it with assorted cats and dogs over the years. As Rose grew older, however, her increasingly finicky nose had begun to object to the various aromas the animals left behind.

Now, in the "beastie department", as Rose called it, there was only George, Teddy's exuberant pup. But Teddy filled a large gap in their lives, and there was also Daisy, though she spent most of her time whizzing down the hill on her bicycle to the Luckwell farm or helping out at the village store.

The first time Daisy had met the Luckwells, she had thought them a very odd crowd. With the superiority of living in the city, she thought the parents caricatures of farming folk, large and jolly, with red-apple cheeks like the pictures in a child's story book. Ben, the son, was in his twenties, the spit of his father and already nearly as rotund.

Lucy was the real surprise. Daisy had fully expected them to have nothing in common at all, except that they were both girls, and she was impatient with Aunt Rose for even insisting she and Teddy went with her to the farm that first weekend.

"Do I have to go?" she had asked sullenly. "I know we won't like each other. She'll think I talk posh and she'll probably have hayseeds in her hair."

Rose snapped, "That's being snobbish and I won't have it. Lucy's promised to show you how to ride, so behave yourself."

"I *can* ride," Daisy sulked.

"A *horse*, my love, not a bicycle," Uncle Bertie guffawed. "Anyway, when your aunt's made up her mind to something, you might as well get used to it and enjoy it."

Daisy decided she definitely wasn't going to enjoy it.

Lucy Luckwell, with a name that would have done justice to a music-hall star, to Daisy's thinking, was the opposite of her family in shape and style. She was thin and wiry, with long brown hair like a horse's mane, a ready smile and a pale complexion due to an illness that had apparently kept her confined to bed for the previous summer months. She was the same age as Daisy, which was supposed to make them instant soulmates, according to Aunt Rose. And to Daisy's agreeable surprise, she wasn't far short of the mark.

"Do you want to see Star?" she asked Daisy as soon as they arrived at the farm. Teddy had been taken off by Ben and the menfolk to feed the chickens and take a look at the pigs while the women drank tea and gossiped.

"Stars?" Daisy echoed.

Lucy burst out laughing. "Not *stars*, you goose. You can see them any night of the week. *Star*, my horse. Come on, I'll show you how to make friends with him."

She chattered on until they reached the stable, where there were several horses. Daisy eyed them apprehensively, her bravado deserting her at once. The horses were smaller than the dray horses who pulled the beer wagons about the city, but they were still much bigger up close than she expected.

"I'm not sure about this, Lucy," she said.

"Star won't hurt you. He's as soft as Weston mud. Stroke his nose, go on."

Daisy reached out a tentative hand to touch him, then drew it back as the horse whinnied gently.

"Don't worry, it's just because he doesn't know you yet," Lucy said confidently. "Blow gently up his nose."

Daisy staggered back as Lucy pulled her forward. "Are you potty or something? I'm not blowing up any horse's nose!"

"I don't mean like a force-nine gale! It's just to let him know you want to be friendly, and he's not going to do it back to you! Look, I'll show you."

She stroked Star's nose and then blew very gently into his nostril, as soft as a feather, and he nuzzled against her hand in response.

"You see?" Lucy said. "Now you."

Daisy moved gingerly forward, thankful none of her family could see this charade. Star responded to her by whinnying again and pressing his nose against her cheek.

"You see?" Lucy said in delight. "He likes you. Now you can do the same to Baby, and you can ride her if you like. She's a mare and a bit smaller."

By the end of the afternoon Daisy had formed two new unexpected friendships – one with Lucy, and the other with the piebald mare called Baby. She had also managed to climb on to Baby's back without sliding straight off again and by clutching grimly to her neck as well as the reins, she had stayed on for a gentle canter around the field.

"We'll have you entering the local gymkhana next year," Lucy said, confirming what Aunt Rose had surmised. "That is, if you're interested, and still around. You're only here on a kind of holiday, aren't you?"

Daisy looked at her dumbly. The afternoon had been so exhilarating, and she had been able to forget . . .

"I'm here because I couldn't bear to stay in Bristol after my mother was killed," she said brutally, wanting to wipe the smile off this nice girl's face, just as if it was all her fault. Nobody had the right to be smling and happy when other people's hearts were breaking.

"I heard about that," Lucy said sympathetically. "It must have been awful. I know how I felt when my nan died last year. Nothing's ever quite the same again, is it? But everything has to die sometime. Animals and crops; it's all the same as far as nature's concerned."

She gave a brief swallow and carried on. "That's what my Gramps told me when I couldn't stop crying. He said my tears were probably doing a powerful lot of good in watering the flowers on Nan's grave, so to just keep on crying until I'd done enough and she'd be satisfied."

"Crikey," was all Daisy could say after this tirade. "Don't you miss her, though?"

"'Course I do. I loved her lots, but I can't have her back, can I? Only in my heart – and now you'll think I'm a real loony. That's something Gramps said too, though."

"I think your Gramps sounds lovely," Daisy said, all her city toughness slipping away at this girl's simple logic. Country folk weren't all hayseeds after all.

"So do I. You can share him, if you like. If you want to be friends, that is."

"I do," Daisy said, as solemn as a vow. "And I'm probably going to be staying with my Aunt Rose for quite a while."

In the new year, Quentin Caldwell was officially appointed under-manager of Preston's Bristol Emporium, with a rise in salary and a sense of relief on his part that he wasn't going under after all. For a time his debts had assumed gigantic proportions in his mind, but now they were being paid off at a sensible rate, and he was beginning to see light at the end of the tunnel.

Frances's needs had been far more of a drain on his resources than he'd ever revealed to anyone, but he hadn't begrudged a penny of it, and if he could have had her back, he would have sold his soul to the devil. But he couldn't ever have her back; instead, they all had to make the best of their lives.

Now his daughter Elsie was officially courting Joe Preston, albeit in a discreet fashion to avoid shop gossip, and a nicer fellow he couldn't imagine for a future son-in-law. He gave a wry smile at the thought. If anyone had told him a few months ago that he'd welcome the prospect of having a Preston in the family, he'd have felt like punching him. But time and circumstances changed everything.

His smile faded. Time and circumstances were changing even more than the domestic doings of the Caldwells were. The government was sending out signals a mile high that war was coming. Before Christmas plans had been unveiled for a National Register of reserved occupations in time of war, and by February it had been announced that free air-raid shelters were going to be distributed to thousands of homes where the annual income was less than £250 per annum.

Quentin read the current newspaper report out loud to his daughters. "Priority will be be given to London and other potential targets around the country. And Bristol will be one of them," he added grimly.

"Do you really think so, Daddy?" Elsie asked in alarm.

"I'm certain of it, my love. We'll probably have to build our own shelter to the specifications laid out. It has to be partly underground to be effective, so Baz will have to help dig out the plot for it in the back garden."

"He'll love that," Imogen grinned.

"I won't. I hate the thought of being underground in any way," Elsie said, shivering.

Immy changed the conversation at once, knowing she was thinking of their mother.

"Did you know Baz has been thinking about asking you if he can live with Enoch Bray and his wife, Father?"

She waited for the expected explosion, but it didn't come. Quentin's mood changes could be swift, and it troubled Immy more than she had let on to anyone but Helen. She couldn't decide if he was truly mellowing of late, or if he just didn't care what was happening to his family any more.

Teddy and Daisy seemed very settled in Weston now, and it looked as if everyone was happy to keep it that way. Teddy was going to start at an nearby infant school at Easter, and if that didn't make him a permanent fixture in Aunt Rose's house, Immy didn't know what would.

"If the boy wants to live with the waterfront rats, so be it," Quentin said coolly in answer to Immy's query.

"Oh Daddy, that's not fair!" Elsie said. "Joe and I went across on the ferry last week, and old Enoch is as nice as pie. Doris says Mrs Bray's cottage is as neat as a new sixpence, and Enoch has to take off his boots and mind his manners before he even steps inside. I don't think Baz will come to any harm there."

"Well, that's all right then, isn't it? My family all seem to do exactly what they want, anyway, so I wonder anyone bothers to ask me anything at all."

He left them to themselves in the sitting-room, taking his newspaper with him and closing the door behind him with a bang that made them both flinch.

"He's lonely," Imogen stated. "Don't take his mood changes personally, Elsie."

"I don't. But I don't think he's lonely, Immy. He still has us, and his new position at the shop, and the customers and staff all like him. Why should he feel alone?"

The minute she'd said it she called herself a thoughtless idiot. Of course she knew why. The trouble was, when you were inwardly glowing with your own happiness, you didn't always stop to think how others might be faring.

"I'm sorry, Immy. I didn't think. It's because of Mother, of course. Do you think he'll ever get over her?"

"No. And in a perfectly selfish and shameful way, I don't want him to, either. Not if he ever thought of getting someone to take her place."

Elsie stared at her, surprised at the fierceness in her sister's voice, and shocked at having to confront a thought that had never occurred to her before.

"Get married again, you mean? Oh, Daddy would never do that, would he?"

"People do," Immy said roughly.

"Well, I wouldn't live here any more if he did. I couldn't bear it."

"You wouldn't have to," Immy said. "You'd have Joe."

Eight

The vague plans to turn the house in Vicarage Street into a paying-guest establishment had been resolved by the beginning of the year. No longer content to stay at home and feel insular and isolated, Imogen had accepted the offer of a job as a receptionist within a housing agency and been given free advice about the guest-house idea.

The outcome was that Quentin had agreed to hire a builder to turn the top floor of the house into a self-contained flat with its own kitchen, bathroom and entrance. By the middle of March two middle-aged widows had taken up residence there.

While he was about it, the builder had offered to include the garden air-raid shelter at a job-lot price, which was both a comfort and an uneasy reminder of why it might be needed.

The outlay had been considerable, but the agent assured Quentin it was as good as an investment, and the widows now provided a reasonable income without making the Caldwells feel that their privacy was invaded. Cook had been persuaded to stay on – after throwing a fit at the thought of being head chef and bottle-washer for a crowd of strangers, as she called it – and a daily help was hired to "do for" the tenants.

Imogen liked the new arrangement. Like her father, she and Elsie were out all day, and it made her feel that they were now a proper business family.

It wasn't the family business of old, but she felt they had gradually made a successful move from despair into something positive.

But if things seemed more buoyant on the home front in the early months of 1939, they were less so generally. It hadn't helped the general anxiety when a group of volunteer ARP personnel had invited people to come to the hall near Vicarage Street and bring along their gas masks for a demonstration on the fitting and wearing of those items for varying periods of time. This move, intended to gee up any lethargy on the public's behalf, made the advent of war seem all too real — although most people were beginning to see it coming.

Many people turned up at the hall out of curiosity, to laugh and joke with their neighbours at the alien beings they represented in the hideous masks. And more than one section of the public declared they would never wear the beastly things; they would rather die from the inhalation of mustard gas, or whatever else the Germans sprayed them with.

"Some of them haven't got a clue!" Quentin Caldwell snapped. "The young 'uns weren't around for the last lot, and the old 'uns seem to have forgotten what it was like. Perhaps they think it's better to live in ignorance than to remember."

"It's better than not living at all," Immy murmured, knowing why her father was extra tetchy.

The anniversary of her parents' wedding was in March, and it would be a good thing when the day had come and gone. Each anniversary that came along had its significance, and there was some truth in the saying that it took a year before the mind could accept what it knew to be true.

There was always the nostalgia and pain of looking back to what was happening this time last year . . . or the year before that . . . or any of the years that made up the tapestry of their lives together.

The end of March was also the time of one of the local gymkhanas in and around Weston. The Caldwells planned to spend the weekend at Rose and Bertie's for the event, since both Lucy Luckwell and Daisy were taking part. Daisy had taken to riding a horse the way she took to everything else, with great enthusiasm and determination to be the best.

The only one of the family who refused to go was Baz, now firmly settled in the Brays' cottage and totally bored by anything that had four legs.

"I'm surprised you and Elsie could be spared from your shop duties, Quentin," Rose said, after she had greeted them, George had run rings around them, yapping excitedly at their heels and trying to lick everyone at once, and they had all exclaimed at how big Teddy was getting now.

"That's what comes of being under-manager," her brother

said smugly. "There are certain advantages to be had, and a Saturday off occasionally is one of them."

"It doesn't hurt that the manager's besotted with the under-manager's daughter either, I dare say," Rose murmured.

"I wouldn't say he's besotted with me," Elsie said with a nervous giggle, knowing very well that he was, because he had told her so. Not in those exact words, of course; his had been far more romantic.

Joe was definitely a romantic, she thought, her heart swelling with love. In her moonstruck state she wished her elder sister could find a young man too.

Apart from the housing estate agent, who was forty if he was a day, she never even mentioned anyone. Oh, except James Church now and then – but he was serving somewhere with his regiment, and Immy hadn't seen him in months.

But she mustn't think of Joe to the exclusion of all else, Elsie reminded herself. This was to be Daisy's big day. They had left Bristol early to be in Weston before midday, so that they would all be able to cheer her and Lucy on at the gymkhana that was being held at the Luckwells' farm.

Before arriving at Rose and Bertie's house on the hill, they had driven along the seafront to get a welcome breath of sea air and watch the diminishing tide go out, leaving the town sand-locked – and "mud-locked", as Rose called it. Bertie always added importantly and predictably that it happened because the Bristol Channel had one of the highest rise and falls of tide in the world, so at least the sand got well laundered every day. And the heaps of seaweed that were washed up really *didn't* smell too bad . . .

Daisy came into the house with the speed of a whirlwind, having been let off her afternoon stint at the village store for this special occasion. She hugged and kissed everyone, and the excitement on her face made her extraordinarily beautiful. She was so much like Frances that Imogen drew in her breath and hoped it wouldn't upset her father to see it.

Immy was also struck by how much her sister had filled out and altered in the few months she had been here. The sea and country air was patently doing both her and Teddy a power of good.

"Lucy expects to win some rosettes, and I suppose I just

might get one," Daisy told them with a laugh. "But you just wait until you see me on Baby. Even Ben Luckwell says I'm a natural. He doesn't normally bother with girls, but he comes to watch us jump the practice hurdles sometimes."

"He's got two sisters to be proud of now, that's why," Bertie told her.

Daisy laughed again. "I doubt he thinks about it like that! You know Ben; if he's proud of anything it's fattening up his old pigs and getting the best price for them at Yatton market."

Immy listened to her in amazement. It was so unlike the starry-eyed Daisy of old, who had always wanted to follow in her mother's dancing footsteps. Here she was, sounding more like a farmer's daughter herself.

Quentin clearly saw it too. "You're happy down here in the sticks then, are you, my love? Not yearning to come home again and keep your old dad company in his old age, now that everyone's deserted me?"

"You're not old!" Daisy protested. But as if some sixth sense made her realise what was behind the question, she danced across the room and hugged him. "And you'll always be my Daddy, no matter what."

"This isn't the sticks, either," Rose told him smartly. "And Daisy's free to go home whenever she wants to. She knows that. We're only borrowing her, Quentin."

It was quiet for a moment; then, before the atmosphere became more tense and emotional than any of them wanted, Bertie spoke again.

"We're getting another one soon. Maybe even two," he said. "You know what your sister's like, Quentin. Always a glutton for punishment, as they say."

"Another what?"

"Child. Evacuee. Applied to the Town Council, she did, and said we've got plenty of room, so if they want to send us another one – or two – they could," he said, hardly able to disguise his pride. "We haven't heard anything yet, though."

"Good Lord, Aunt Rose, aren't you brave!" Immy exclaimed. She turned to her brother. "Auntie might get another one like you, Teddy," she teased him.

"I hope we do. It'll be company for him, and Bertie

can take them both fishing and keep them out of my hair when I'm trying to do my baking." But Rose was smiling as she said it.

Because there were so many of them they drove in two cars to the Luckwell farm. It was a fine spring day, with no sign of the British rain that could make such an event a wash-out.

Daisy left them to explore the stalls selling home-made preserves and cakes made by the ladies of the WI, cartons of young plants, saplings wrapped in balls of soil, and more bric-a-brac than ever found its way to the local scrapyard.

The next time any of them saw her, she was with Lucy, both of them elegant in jodhpurs, white shirts and riding hats. The Caldwells hardly recognised the young lady their youngest girl had become.

"Did you buy her all this kit?" Quentin asked his sister.

Rose shrugged. "You have to indulge me if I spoil them sometimes, Quentin. What else do I have to spend my money on if not my brother's children?"

It was one of the rare times she alluded to the sadness of not having any of her own, and she turned away, not inviting further comment.

The centre of the field had been roped off and set up with hurdles and jumps, and during the warm afternoon the competitors took their turns in the various events to the accompaniment of loudspeaker announcements and generous applause for the winners of each trial.

Teddy quickly became bored with it all, and when Ben Luckwell offered to take him – and any other children who wanted – to see the animals being fed, nobody complained.

By the time he left the field, now grandly called the arena, there was a trail of small bodies following him.

"He's a love with the young 'uns," Mrs Luckwell said comfortably, beaming at them. "He might be fourpence short of a bob, and he allus has been in his big old clumsy way, but he'd make somebody a lovely wife," she added. She shrieked with laughter at her own joke, as she went around smiling and welcoming everyone visiting the farm that day.

"If you dare say there's a catch for me, I shall thump you," Immy murmured beneath her breath to Elsie as they watched his lumbering frame disappear.

"I wouldn't dare," Elsie grinned back. "Not when you've got the delectable James Church hovering in the background. Oh, and I forgot to tell you the worst news. Robert Preston's coming down here for all of May, and Joe has to go back to the York store. Joe says his uncle's always been keen for his managers to do that kind of exchange, and even though they're family, they have to do it too. He says it keeps them on their toes – but I don't see why Joe has to go away so soon. I shall miss him like fury."

She went on prattling and grumbling, but Immy hardly listened to the rest of it. She was remembering the dinner at the Grand Hotel, and Robert Preston saying he wished he was staying in Bristol because he'd like to get to know her better. She recalled her instinctive reaction – that she was glad he was going away, because he was too dangerously attractive.

She hadn't put the feeling into words or even coherent thought at the time, but the idea was indubitably in her head now – together with the quickening of her hearbeat, and the image of his face, which was suddenly so vivid in her mind that he might have been standing in front of her.

"Immy, are you all right? I swear you haven't been listening to a word I've been saying!"

She blinked as her sister's face came into view.

"Of course I'm all right," she said crossly. "I just hear so much about Joe's virtues that my mind sometimes drifts."

"Well, I'm sorry!"

She was contrite at once. "Oh Lord, I didn't mean to be rude. I know he's a lovely man, and I'm truly happy for you, Elsie. I wasn't really concentrating because I wanted to be sure we didn't miss Daisy's event," she invented wildly.

She was angry with herself for allowing her heart to give even a single lurch at the thought of seeing Robert Preston again. After the disastrous affair with Morgan, she had vowed to beware of smooth talkers, especially rugged young men with a brooding Heathcliff appearance, who looked as if they'd be more at home tramping the moors than managing a shop.

Now she was doing it again, she thought in annoyance. She was letting him into her thoughts and her mind, when she had every intention of keeping him out.

"Here they are, then," Elsie was saying, as the tinny voice

on the loudspeaker announced the hurdle race for the sixteen to eighteen-year-olds.

Immy forced herself to concentrate. It was what they were here for, to encourage Daisy in the faint hope of her getting a rosette, and to cheer Lucy on in the certainty that she would.

"Thank goodness we left George at home," Rose remarked, seeing that several noisy dogs had to be restrained by their owners every time an announcement was made. "Just imagine what he'd be like."

"I'd rather not," Immy said. "I don't want to imagine what he's doing to your house either, Aunt Rose."

"Oh, I think he's got over the wild puppy stage of tearing everything to bits now."

"You hope," Elsie added as an aside.

But there was no more time to speculate on what George might or might not be doing. The riders were coming into the arena.

"She looks so grown up," Quentin said, as if he had only just noticed the air of confidence with which his youngest daughter sat astride Baby.

"So she should. She's nearly seventeen," Rose said.

"She's still a child—"

"She's the same age Frances was when you met her," Rose pointed out, as if determined to keep her sister-in-law's name alive, since he seemed just as determined not to mention her at all. "And only a year younger than her mother was when you married her, Quentin."

"That was wartime," he said abruptly. "And a very long time ago."

"If you two don't stop talking and glaring at one another, we shall miss the start," Imogen said, admonishing her elders. Sometimes they needed it – those two could bicker as volubly as siblings of any age.

The starter's pistol went off, and the race began. The spirit of the afternoon was light-hearted and the competitors raced around the arena to the accompaniment of cheers and screams from their supporters.

As expected, Lucy was easily the best rider in her category and she finished with a flourish, knowing she would take the blue rosette.

Daisy came a creditable fourth. It meant she took nothing, but she was triumphant at having finished the course at all and proved to her family that she could do something other than serve in a shop or make hats or type at a fair rate of knots. When you had two clever older sisters, you had to prove yourself at something.

At that moment one of the excitable dogs who had caused problems for his owner suddenly broke free of his lead and went tearing towards the horses in the small winners' enclosure, circling their legs and barking madly.

Thinking he was going to injure Star, Lucy shouted at the dog and automatically kicked out at him, forgetting that her feet were still in the stirrups. As she leaned over Star's flank, he seemed to stumble, and she lost her balance and cried out as she fell sideways to the ground. Her foot was still caught and Star stamped the ground nervously, dragging her forward as she screamed at him to stay still.

It all happened so quickly that only those near to her were really aware of what was happening, and the main crowd of spectators saw little of the incident.

Daisy had a clear view, however, and immediately saw the potential danger. If Star really got spooked by the dog, who was still barking frantically and being pulled away by his red-faced owner, Daisy knew the horse could drag Lucy along the ground or even trample her. She wasn't about to let that happen.

In the general confusion, she ran forward and pulled at Star's reins, talking soothingly to him and gentling him for all she was worth. His eyes were rolling, and she caught hold of his nose, stroking him and breathing softly into him, while Lucy tried to extricate herself from the stirrup and struggled to get away from those agitated hooves.

"I'll take the nag, girl," she heard Ben Luckwell say, appearing as if from nowhere. "You'd best let somebody see to our Lucy now."

Daisy blinked, realising that the small group of people nearby were applauding her and praising her skill with the horse. She was less concerned with that than with taking in what Ben had said, however. Lucy wasn't really hurt, was she?

Her friend was still sitting on the ground, holding her ankle and groaning, and Daisy sank down beside her as the call went out for the St John ambulance people to come to the winners' enclosure at once. One look at the ankle and Daisy knew it was sprained. It was swelling inside Lucy's boot, and Daisy knew it would already be turning a lovely mixture of purple and red.

"I feel sick," Lucy said.

"Take deep breaths and don't close your eyes," Daisy instructed at once. "Keep looking ahead."

"God, it hurts," Lucy muttered. "I have to get my boot off," she added, tugging at the laces.

"No, don't do that. You've got to keep it on until you get it seen to properly."

"You seem to know a blooming lot about it," Lucy said, the stinging pain making her aggressive.

"It happened to my mother during a performance. I was watching in the wings, and I can only have been about eight years old, but I can still remember the doctor's instructions."

"The young lady's quite right – but you can leave it to us now, my dear," said a male voice.

The St John ambulance men had arrived at last with their bag of tricks, and were kneeling down beside them both. By now Lucy's mother had reassured herself that it was only a slight accident and was busily announcing to everyone that her daughter was perfectly all right, and that the next event would continue after a short interval.

Whatever else happened, the show must go on. Daisy knew that. Her mother would have approved. As other hands tended to Lucy and a stretcher carried her into the farmhouse, she followed on behind, feeling suddenly nauseous herself.

"You'd better sit down, love," she heard the second ambulance man say. "It takes folk that way after the event sometimes. But you did well to keep your head. Got the makings of a proper little nurse, I'd say."

He turned away from her as her colour began to come back, and concentrated on Lucy. "Now then, let's see to this poor ankle and get it strapped up before the doctor comes to take a look. There'll be no more riding for you for a while, my duck."

"Never mind; I'll come and cheer her up," Daisy forced

herself to say. Lucy gave a squeal of pain as they examined the ankle. "I think I'm off riding for a bit, anyway."

It had only ever been a pleasant pastime, and now she had other things to think about. She had always had a butterfly mind, but not in the way her family used to tease her about. She had flitted from one airy-fairy idea to the next because she hadn't ever been able to make up her mind what she really wanted to do. But now she knew. She was going to be a nurse.

"It's just another fad," Imogen said in the car on the way back to Bristol on Sunday afternoon. "We all know what Daisy's like. This week she wants to be a nurse. Next week it'll be something else."

"I'm not so sure it will," Elsie said. "She seemed pretty determined about it."

"She always does, but Aunt Rose will sort her out. She's going to take her along to her volunteer first aid class, and she's also got an old medical book for Daisy to read. Once she discovers all the nasty things a nurse has to do and the thousand and one ailments there are, I bet she'll start feeling squeamish and change her mind."

They were both laughing by the time she had finished speaking, but to Immy's surprise her father was not.

"I think you do the girl an injustice. Nursing's an honourable profession, and if Daisy does decide it's what she wants to do, I shall back her one hundred per cent. And I'll tell you something else. Your mother would be proud of her."

"Oh, Daddy, I know she would!" Immy agreed hurriedly, moved by his words. He rarely spoke of Frances these days. She was a taboo subject, since his memories of her were so bittersweet.

It was odd to think Daisy's new ambition might be the catalyst that would make him think differently. That, and Aunt Rose's mission to never let Frances be forgotten. Not that she *was*, or ever could be. But they should all take heart and speak of her as naturally as possible in future, the way Rose did.

"I was amazed that Daisy remembered the doctor's instructions when Mother had her bad sprain, though. Daisy was such a little thing at the time – do you remember, Father?" Immy went on bravely.

"Of course I remember," Quentin said after a moment's pause. "For a while we wondered if Frances would ever dance again – but *she* knew she would, no matter what the doctors said." The pride in his voice was almost tangible. "Nobody was going to take that away from her."

"Nobody can take her away from us, either," Elsie said softly, unerringly following Imogen's lead. "Not as long as we can still remember."

"I know, my dears. But now, if you two don't let me concentrate on my driving I shall probably have us all in the ditch!" Quentin went on crisply. The girls both knew he had turned a small corner, however, and that they had helped him do it. In the back seat of the car, they reached out and squeezed each other's hands for a moment, each blessing Daisy for being such an unlikely angel.

"Imogen," Quentin said a little while later, "if you still want me to give you a few driving lessons, you'd better take advantage of my generous mood. We'll start after the shop closes tomorrow evening, God help me!"

"Wonderful!" Immy said in delight. The idea had been abandoned for so long she had all but forgotten it and was sure he'd had no heart for it.

By the time they returned home to Vicarage Street it was still a mellow early evening, and after a wash and change of clothes, she bicycled up to Helen's house to report the weekend's happenings.

"You're joking," Helen stated in amazement, when she heard the news about Daisy. "She'll freeze the minute she sees a blob of blood on somebody's finger."

"Actually, I don't think she will." Immy came quickly to her sister's defence. "I think perhaps the idea has always been there, deep down. I've been thinking back to all sorts of occasions when she played the little nurse, even persuading Elsie to make her a nurse's outfit one Christmas so she could look after Teddy when he was born."

"Playing at being a nurse is a bit different from the real thing, darling," Helen said mildly. "But good luck to her if that's what she wants to do. She'll probably be in her element when we go to war, anyway. Imagine having all those vulnerable wounded soldiers depending on you." She gave an elaborate sigh, her eyes mischievous. "It's quite a thought, isn't it, Immy? I might even consider becoming a nurse myself."

"I thought you weren't interested in men."

"I never said I wasn't interested. I just haven't found the right one yet. But watch out for fireworks when I do!"

Immy was thoughtful. "Do you think you'll ever fall in love, hook, line and sinker, then? Enough to throw off all your inhibitions, I mean, and – well, *do* things?"

"Lord knows. Probably, if he's masterful enough." Helen laughed easily, since she had never been tested. "Why, would you? *Have* you? You said you hadn't done anything with MR—"

"I didn't say I hadn't done *anything*. Just not *it*. Of course not *it*!"

"What, then?" Helen said. "You've got to tell me now, Immy. As your best friend, I demand it."

"I don't even want to remember him. But if you *must* know, he touched me here. Pressed me tight, I mean."

She passed her hand over her breast, feeling an idiot as she did so. Fast girls might be complacent about such things, but she wasn't fast and never had been. Despite having a glamorous mother who some might think of as bohemian, Frances had always taught her daughters to be virtuous and modest, the way good girls should be.

Just sometimes, however, Immy had wondered what it might be like to be less inhibited. Morgan Raine had certainly proved that she had a sensuous nature lurking beneath her air of Caldwell respectability.

She wished Helen hadn't stirred it all up again. She didn't want him any more, nor think of him any more, but she couldn't deny the passionate feelings he had awoken in her.

"What was it like, then? Him pressing your bosom, I mean?" Helen persisted. "I only ask in the name of research, Immy."

"Well, it's not much different from when you wash yourself in the bath. You have to touch them then, don't you?" Immy said crossly, knowing it was totally, erotically different to have a man's hand caressing them. But there were some things you just couldn't share, even with your best friend.

"I refuse to talk about MR any more," she said. "The other thing I came to tell you was that Father's decided to teach me to drive at last."

"Hooray. So if we do have to join up we'll be able to put our names down as drivers for the officers. You meet a much better class of person that way," she added, only half serious.

Immy burst out laughing. "Oh Helen, you really are the most terrible snob!"

"I know, darling," she said cheerfully. "Isn't it a ghastly hoot?"

They took the car well out of the city before Quentin was prepared to change places with Immy and let her anywhere near the steering wheel. By then, she had learned where all the gears and instruments were, and managed not to grip the wheel so tightly that her knuckles turned white.

It wasn't as easy as it looked, Immy admitted, and it didn't help her nerves to have her father shouting whenever the wheels approached the grass verge instead of steering a straight line down the middle of the road.

Both tempers quickly became frayed, and they had soon each had enough of it. Quentin drove them home with more speed than judgement.

"You'll have to find some other person willing to put his nerves to the test, Imogen," he told her shortly. "It's not all your fault, mind. I just don't have the patience to be a driving instructor."

"I was pretty useless all the same, wasn't I?" she said.

"Not useless. Just inexperienced, which is to be expected. Let's leave it a few weeks and perhaps we'll try again."

And perhaps they wouldn't. She was thankful Elsie had gone out to meet Joe by the time they got back so that she wouldn't have to see her crimson face. And by the time her sister came home for supper, gloomy with the news that Joe would be leaving for York the following Friday, Immy could laugh about her first efforts at controlling a car.

She did want to learn, though, since it seemed a useful skill to acquire. There must be someone who could teach her without the two of them getting hot under the collar and screaming at one another.

Helen had owned her own small car for two years, given to her courtesy of her well-heeled father as a very special eighteenth birthday present, but Helen certainly wouldn't do as she would be far too soft as an instructor. It needed a stranger with no other interest than advising her how to keep her wheels securely on the road and assuring her she was in no danger of killing them both.

At the beginning of May, Quentin came home from the shop to say that Robert Preston seemed as capital a fellow as his cousin Joe. He had already settled in well, charming most of the shop-girls into the bargain, and Quentin thought he might ask him home for tea one Sunday afternoon.

"Do you think mixing business with pleasure is a good idea, Father?" Immy queried at once.

"Why not? Your sister doesn't object to my suggestion, so why should you? I'm sure Cook can manage to bake an extra cake or two and cut a few extra ham sandwiches. We're not inviting the king and queen, my dear."

"But he's the manager. Your boss."

"He's also a decent young man far from home, whose family sent a wreath and a genuine letter of sympathy when your mother died. The least we can do is show similar thoughtfulness, or has your generosity of spirit entirely deserted you?"

Imogen flushed to her ears. "Of course it hasn't. I was only thinking it might be a bit awkward for you and Elsie, that's all."

"Well, it won't. Besides, he particularly asked after you, and I told him you badly wanted to learn to drive a car. We decided he should teach you."

"*Father*! You didn't, did you?"

"Why on earth not? Of course I did. You can discuss it with him when you see him. Now then, I want to listen to the wireless, so go and do something else while I try and tune in to the station before the wretched battery runs out."

Imogen went off, fuming. It was bad enough that they would have to sit and be polite to Robert Preston all through a Sunday afternoon, but the thought of having to sit beside him in the close, cosy proximity of the car while he taught her to drive . . . his hands reaching out to correct her steering, and perhaps touching hers, by accident or design . . .

She knew she was letting herself become totally irrational over the whole thing, but by the time she sought out her sister, she was in a foul mood.

"You can't imagine what Father's done now, Elsie," she said furiously.

Her sister didn't look up from the hat she had brought home from work so that she could finish off the delicate stitching on its frivolous little veil.

"You're talking about Robert, I dare say," she murmured, biting off the fine thread between her teeth and inspecting her work with a critical eye, knowing the hat would make its appearance at Ascot in the summer.

"Yes. *Robert*. As well as inviting him here for tea, father's wangled it so that I have to take driving lessons with him. How *could* he have asked him? He can't possibly want to do it, and I'll be just mortified."

"Actually, it was Robert's idea. I heard him offering his services when Daddy mentioned it."

Nine

The telephone rang that evening.

They still hadn't got used to the sound of it, and invariably jumped when it happened. It was usually Aunt Rose with the weekly gossip about Teddy's doings, or how well Daisy was doing at her first aid class with her bandaging and her soothing bedside manner for the mock casualties.

There was always a faint note of surprise in her voice, which sent Imogen and Elsie off into peals of laughter when they had finished talking. Daisy with a bedside manner would be something to see – but it was the actress in her, of course, Elsie would say solemnly, which would start them off again.

"Hello," Imogen said into the telephone mouthpiece, already smiling at the expectation of chatter from her aunt.

"Am I speaking to Miss Imogen Caldwell?" she heard a deep voice say. A voice that was unmistakably northern, the flat tones even richer and more resonant over the line than they had been on the one occasion she had been face to face with their owner.

"You are," she said, unable to say more for the moment, and hoping that the wild beat of her heart wasn't as evident to him as it was to her. And why was it beating so rapidly in any case? she asked herself furiously. He was nothing to her.

"This is Robert Preston."

"I know who you are."

And for the life of her she couldn't think of anything else to say in the small pause that followed. What *did* you say at such moments?

What do you want? It was hardly polite to ask so bluntly.

Thank you for calling? That sounded like goodbye, and was also inane, since he hadn't said anything yet.

Thank you for offering to teach me to drive, but no thank

114

you? No, because he hadn't offered it personally yet, and anyway, she knew how ungracious it would sound.

She heard a short throaty laugh at the other end.

"My, my, we are touchy, aren't we, Miss Caldwell? Have I caught you at a bad moment?"

She stared at the phone, thinking him outrageous for speaking so familiarly when she didn't even know him. Didn't *want* to know him, if the truth were told.

"Is it my father you want to speak to?" she asked in her most frigid tone.

"It's you I want," he said, and her heart gave an enormous leap in her chest, because the words were far too soft and emotive and seductive, and they scared her.

"What can I do for you?" she said, refusing to let him think she understood him all too well, and realising too late that she was leaving herself wide open with her artless words.

"It's what I can do for you, Imogen," he said.

Before she wondered whether she dared slam down the phone, since the sitting-room door was open and the others had probably heard every word she said, he spoke more crisply.

"I understand you want to learn to drive a car, and you probably know I told your father I'd be happy to teach you. But naturally it has to be your decision. The lady always has the last word."

Was there a hidden meaning in that remark? Did he mean that if he planned on seduction she could refuse and there would be no hard feelings between them?

What in heaven's name was happening to her, if she could even think such a thing? Her palms were damp as she held on to the telephone, and she was furious with herself for letting him affect her so.

"I'll think about it," she said in a strangled voice.

"Good. We'll talk about it again when I come to tea. I shall look forward to it."

She hung up before she could say any more and rejoined her father and sister in the sitting-room, hoping her cheeks weren't as fiery as they felt. Not that they would notice. Each of them was too wrapped up in their own little world to wonder what was happening to *her* . . . Now she was in danger of becoming paranoid, she told herself.

"That was Robert Preston," she announced, knowing they would ask. "Just wanting to know if I'd like him to teach me to drive, and I said I'd think about it."

"What's to think about?" her father said. "It'll be easier on my nerves, anyway," he added with a chuckle, before going back to his newspaper.

Elsie was engrossed in her letter from Joe, who had promised to write with devoted regularity.

"I think Robert's quite nice," she murmured without looking up. "All the lady customers think so, anyway."

I suppose you'd think it nice if we ended up having a double wedding, sister dear, Immy found herself thinking, with a shock of annoyance at her own wayward thoughts. She had no intention of falling into that trap.

Knowing more about the ways of the opposite sex than her sister, she had decided very early on that Robert Preston was one of those charismatic men who appealed to ladies of all ages – and traded on it. And she wasn't going to be one of his conquests, thank you very much.

"What have you got against him?" Helen said curiously.

"Nothing, I suppose. I just don't trust him."

"But you're going to let him give you driving lessons? Out in the country with a strange man?" she teased her.

"I can handle that," Immy said crossly. "And I'll *have* to agree, since my father's so keen on the idea. It's all too embarrassing!"

Helen looked thoughtful. "I think I'll pay a visit to the shop and take a look at this paragon. Elsie seems to think a lot of him, doesn't she?"

"Elsie's moping over Joe's absence, and since he and Robert virtually grew up together, I think she spends half her time pumping Robert for information about Joe's childhood. She's always coming home with some new revelation about cut knees and getting lost on the moors and stuff like that."

"Crikey, she really is besotted, isn't she?"

"That's not the word for it," Immy said drily.

"I wonder if we'll ever be that much in love with anyone. I can't see it for myself, or not for ages, anyway," Helen said, complacent in her self-sufficiency. "I'm not sure I want to be that dependent on another person's feelings, anyway. Being in love's a responsibility, isn't it?"

Immy laughed. "When did you take up philosophy – or should it be psychiatry? Are you going to start analysing me?"

"I wouldn't dare. You're far too complex for me to want to delve into your secrets, darling. Apart from the ones I know, of course."

But Helen didn't know all of them, Immy thought, as she cycled home. Helen didn't know how bitterly betrayed she had felt over Morgan, and she didn't know the depth of the turbulent feelings Robert Preston could arouse in her.

"You will be polite to Robert, won't you?" Elsie asked her on the Sunday he was due to come for tea.

"Why wouldn't I be?"

"Well, I know you're put out because Daddy and he seem to have cooked up the driving lessons between them, but if it's what you want, I don't see any point in getting all fussed about it. Robert's only going to be here for four weeks, so you might as well make the most of it."

Her voice implied that the sooner these four weeks were over the better, because then Joe would be back. Immy didn't miss the yearning in her voice, and didn't have it in her heart to make any teasing comment about it.

"Oh well, I'm sure a couple of lessons is all I need. I do know the basics now, and then I'll be able to go wherever I like, providing Father will lend me the car. I'll be as independent as Helen."

The thought of it was starting to open up a whole new world to her. It was merely the usefulness of being able to drive that had prompted her originally, coupled with Helen's airy remark that they could both apply to be drivers for officers if war came. Her face broke into a smile as she remembered the unwittingly snobbish remark. Helen could always make her smile.

Robert Preston had clearly set out to be at his most charming when he came to the house, bearing a huge bunch of tea-roses and stephanotis that took up several vases. As the girls arranged them Immy whispered to her sister that Robert could hardly have got a more ostentatious bunch of flowers to impress them if he'd robbed a graveyard.

"Stop it; he'll hear you." Elsie grinned. "It was a lovely thought – and he's very dapper, isn't he? I know you're determined to dislike him, but if I didn't have Joe I could almost fancy him myself. You know Helen came into the shop this week, don't you? Her eyes were like saucers when she met him, and he certainly took his time showing her around the store. *More* than enough time, I'd say."

"Really?" Immy feigned as little interest as possible. She was curious and a little put out that Helen hadn't phoned her to report, though.

"So when shall we have the first lesson, Imogen? How about this evening?" Robert asked her after tea, when he had chatted with her father and quizzed Baz – at home for his regular Sunday afternoon – on his activities.

Immy's heart jolted. "So soon?"

Baz sniggered. "She'll need time to think about it, Robert. She'll be too scared of making a fool of herself."

"Of course she's not," Robert said, ignoring Immy's glare at her brother, though he was looking directly at her with his gypsy eyes. "I assure you there's no need, and I'm a very gentle teacher."

"I'm sure you are," Immy muttered.

Quentin seemed quite unaware of any undercurrents. "Take advantage of the offer, Imogen. It's what you want, isn't it?"

"And we only have a few weeks," Robert added, his gaze still unwavering, and causing that uncomfortable little leap of her heart again.

"All right. Let's get it over with," she muttered.

Her father and brother both hooted.

"Good God, girl, anyone would think you were going to the devil, instead of having a driving lesson," Quentin laughed.

"Perhaps she is," Baz sniggered again, his eyes bright and knowing.

Once she was ready for the lesson, telling herself her nerves weren't really intensified at all, Immy went into the garden to catch Baz before he returned to the Brays' cottage. Glancing around, she saw Robert still talking to her father inside the house, and she grabbed Baz's arm firmly.

"Listen to me, you little sneak. You just keep your hints to yourself, do you hear? Or I shall have to put in a few words to Father that you're getting into bad company. He's still capable of hauling you back home and changing his mind about all this ferry-boat nonsense."

He scowled at her. "All right, you don't have to make a meal of it. I was only having a bit of fun, anyway. Nobody noticed anything."

"*I* noticed, and it wan't funny, Baz. It's never funny to make someone else feel uncomfortable. You seem to have forgotten how Mother always instilled that in us."

It was the first time they had discussed Frances since her death. He was such a toughie now, and so self-contained . . . but to her astonishment she saw his face suddenly twist in a look of pain, and his throat worked a little before he replied.

"It won't happen again, I promise."

"Well, that's good," she said. "The family's important, Baz. We may have separated a bit recently, but we must always stick together when it comes to basic things, family things. Mother used to say that too, before—"

"Yes, all right," he said, and from his edgy voice she knew she was going a touch too far now.

He wouldn't remember her mother's little sayings the way she did, but he would be remembering her sweet voice now, and it didn't hurt to remind him now and then that he wasn't as tough as he liked to think. She gave his shoulder a more gentle squeeze and saw him blink rapidly.

"I have to go now. I'll see you next week, sis."

He hadn't called her that for a long time, and she stared after him as he strolled jauntily down the hill towards the waterfront. He was big for his age, but he was still her little brother, and she felt unaccountably tender towards him.

"Ready?" Robert Preston's voice said behind her.

"Not really, but I suppose it's now or never," she said staunchly.

He laughed. His teeth were even and pearly white. For a totally illogical moment Imogen remembered Daisy telling her solemnly that you could tell a lot from a horse's teeth.

Did that apply to humans as well? If so, Robert Preston must be very even-tempered and very pure at heart . . . but she instinctively doubted both of those assessments.

"It's only a driving lesson, Immy," he said softly.

He had already cranked the engine with the starting handle, and now he opened the car door for her to get into the driving seat. She gave him a freezing look.

"I'm only Immy to my friends," she said, knowing she was being petulant, and feeling unable to help it. He simply brought out the worst in her – and this behaviour meant that her recent words to Baz had been nothing more than the pot calling the kettle the darkest shade of black.

He started to close the car door again, and she looked at him, startled.

"I refuse to teach anyone to drive while they're in a bad mood and a possible danger to others. I know fate has thrown your family and mine together, and we may not be friends. But if we can't at least be civil to one another, then we'd better forget it right now."

His eyes challenged her, and out of the corner of hers she could see her father and Elsie at the sitting-room window. She swallowed her pride with a huge effort.

"I'm sorry. I'm nervous, that's all. Of course we're friends – sort of."

He smiled again, and opened the door wide. It was a bit like offering her entrance into the lion's den, Immy thought stupidly. But she slid inside the car without another word, and he closed the door before moving around to the passenger seat, enclosing them both inside. He turned to face her.

"Well then, Imogen, shall we begin? You know the procedure, I believe?"

An hour or so later Elsie was keen to hear how she had got on. By now Quentin had taken Robert off to his gentlemen's club in the city for a "well-deserved" drink or two, in his chuckling opinion.

"I managed surprisingly well," Immy said reluctantly. "He's a good teacher, I'll say that for him. I'm having another lesson on Wednesday evening, and next Sunday as well, since Father has apparently asked him for Sunday tea every week until he goes back to York."

"What did I tell you? All the Preston men are charmers, aren't they?" Elsie said happily, thinking of the only one who interested her.

"I daresay they have their charms."

"Oh Immy, you're so stubborn. Can't you ever admit you're wrong about people?"

"What do you mean?" Immy objected in genuine astonishment.

Elsie shrugged. "It's the way you are, darling. You may not realise it, but you've got some pretty rigid ideas, and nothing on earth will change them. You should take a leaf out of Daisy's book."

"What, and flit from one idea to the next as often as changing my stockings?"

"She's growing up, Immy, and she's pretty set on this nursing idea. She telephoned us while you were out, full of excitement, to say she's got an interview at the local hospital tomorrow afternoon to be taken on as a nursing auxiliary."

"Good Lord," Immy said, everything else forgotten. "I wonder how long that will last."

She caught Elsie's look, and grinned.

"All right. I'm doing it again, aren't I? I wish her luck, anyway. She's cheerful and pretty, so she'll certainly brighten up the wards if nothing else."

Daisy intended to do far more than that. Nursing was her vocation, she declared to her friend Lucy, advising her on gentle exercise as she tentatively put her foot to the ground to test out her sprained ankle, which had been slow to heal.

"You're a blooming doctor now, then?" Lucy said, tetchy with the boredom of inactivity, and missing her rides on Star.

"Of course not, but I probably could be," Daisy said airily. "You have to start somewhere, don't you? And once I'm taken on as an auxiliary, I'll be all ready to be sent to war when the call comes."

Lucy groaned. Having little imagination herself, she sometimes found it difficult to follow Daisy's mercurial train of thought. She herself didn't care for all the war-mongering stories gathering tempo now, either. Her life was geared to slower and steadier country ways.

"You won't catch me going to war. Me and Ben will help Dad on the farm. He says now that the government's offering farmers two pounds an acre to plough up the fields and plant more seeds for food production, we'll be laughing, anyway. Besides, war's not going to happen."

"Of course it is," Daisy said, impressed by this bit of knowledge. "Why do you think they've started conscription? Uncle Bertie says it can't be more than months away now. Oh, and did I tell you we've got two more? That's another reason why I'll be glad to start my new job."

"Two more what?"

"Infants. Evacuees. Arrived from Kent with a school supervisor, all snotty-nosed and too scared to talk, poor little squirts. Aunt Rose is in her element, and they'll be playmates for Teddy. And if *that* doesn't make it sound like there's going to be a war, I don't know what does."

"What, sending two snotty-nosed kids to live at your Aunt Rose's house to be spoiled with cake and kindness?"

"*No*. Getting them all out of London and the south-east counties ready for when the German bombs fall. Honestly, Lucy, don't you know what's going on?"

"Of course I do. Dad reads the papers and listens to the wireless all the blessed time and bores us silly with it, but I don't pay much attention to it, and I didn't think you did either."

"I didn't, but now I do," Daisy said solemnly. "You can't stay blinkered for ever, can you?" She started to giggle, her sombre mood gone as quickly as it came. "Did you hear what I said just then? Blinkered! As if we were Star and Baby."

Immy's next three driving lessons went smoothly. She was pleasantly surprised at how patient Robert Preston could be, and how calmly she responded to his instructions after her outbursts with her father. Robert was aware of his position in the city regarding his father's business, of course, but he made no attempt to be other than polite and friendly.

If deep down that attitude mildly piqued her, Immy told herself she was being ridiculous. She didn't want his attention. She just wanted to be able to drive competently.

She reported her success to Helen, expecting her friend to be hugely approving and supportive, since she had put the idea of driving lessons into her head in the first place.

"Lucky you," was all Helen said.

"Lucky? That's an odd word to use, isn't it?"

Helen's face was a deeper colour than usual.

"I mean good for you, of course, darling."

"No, you don't. That's not what you meant, nor what you said. You said lucky me. Why lucky me?"

"You're starting to sound like a parrot, Immy."

"And you're evading the question."

"Good Lord, is this the Inquisition or something?"

Immy stared at her. They had always been able to say anything to one another, or so she thought. But there was a secretive look about Helen today, and she was definitely edgy. Immy had a sudden rush of intuition.

"Elsie says you've been to Preston's, so I know you've met him."

"Why shouldn't I? It's a shop, isn't it? People go there to buy things. I didn't think Robert Preston was your exclusive property, anyway."

"He's not! I never heard anything so daft. It's not as if I'm going *out* with him. It's only driving lessons, for heaven's sake."

She stopped, suddenly seeing all there was to see.

"You've fallen for him, haven't you? I thought you didn't believe in all that love at first sight stuff!"

"It wasn't at first sight," Helen muttered.

This took a moment longer to sink in. "Have you been *seeing* him, then? Has he asked you out?"

Helen glared at her. "You're not so pretty when you're jealous, darling. Your eyes have gone a positive shade of green. Yes, he's asked me out, and I've gone. We went to the pictures one night, if you must know, and we're going out again on Saturday night."

"I see!" Immy said, shocked.

But as Helen said, Robert Preston wasn't her exclusive property. He wasn't her property at all, nor ever likely to be. Now that the initial Heathcliff attraction had faded, she wasn't sure she even liked him all that much.

What annoyed her most was that Helen should have kept

all this to herself, when they had always told one another everything – almost.

"I think it's time I went home," she said stiffly, standing up to go.

Helen capitulated at once, jumping up from her garden chair and squeezing her arm.

"Oh Immy, I would have told you, honestly. It just took me by surprise, that's all, and it – well, it scares me, I suppose. I've never felt like this before. I don't quite know what to do with the feeling."

"How very unlike you! I thought the so-sophisticated Miss Church could cope with anything."

"So did I. But I've never been in love before, and I'm not at all sure if I'm in love now. How the heck do you tell? Come on, brainbox, tell me that if you can!"

She looked so comical and bemused that Immy felt her lips twitching, and because it sounded so ridiculous they found themselves laughing helplessly together, arms around one another, practically holding one another up.

Helen's mother came into the garden, as ever the gracious hostess, a tray of lemonade and bourbons in her hands, and smiled at them indulgently.

"Now then, you two girls, what wicked little schemes are you planning today?" she enquired, serenely sure there could be no undesirable secrets between her dutiful, sweet-faced daughter and her lovely friend.

At which the two of them became convulsed all over again.

Ten

Robert Preston had no intention of seducing the Caldwell girl. It had only ever been a passing thought, since she was the most alluring of the bunch. But he liked them more pliant, and Imogen Caldwell was far too strong-willed for him to take on. In any case, he was far too aware of his position to get caught up in that little trap. Desirable as she was to any red-blooded man with heat in his loins – and he was certainly that – she was a canny lass who would read him like a book. And she was still the daughter of a small-time shopkeeper.

His cousin Joe was more liberal-minded than he was in that respect, and if he wanted to dally with the other one, it was his affair. Robert himself had ambitions of a higher order, however. He had the smouldering looks and his father's go-getting personality, and he had proved on plenty of occasions that he could get any girl he wanted. And right now, he wanted Helen Church.

He felt a tingling in his nether regions just thinking about her, but he hadn't made his real move yet. He was sure she was a virgin, and therefore he had to go slowly if he didn't want to frighten her off.

Her classy, non-Bristol accent and her well-heeled connections were the main attraction, of course. Robert's father was a self-made man with a bluff and gritty Yorkshire exterior, and a girl with a bit of class had always appealed to Robert. Not least because he revelled in the triumphant idea that his wild gypsy looks could always tame them.

There was one insurmountable problem regarding Helen Church, though. He had to be back in York at the end of May, and there simply wasn't the time available to woo her as slowly as he knew was wise.

But the more he thought about her, the more he ached to

have her. So if he was to make a conquest, the only way was to overwhelm her with charm and seduction and a profusion of small, acceptable gifts. And now it was time for the kill.

He took her for a drive in the country on Saturday evening, and eventually parked his car in a secluded copse well away from the city. He turned to Helen and handed her a small gift-wrapped box.

She accepted it with a squeal of delight. She wasn't unused to receiving expensive presents from her parents, and occasionally her brother James could surprise her with something unusual and exotic, but Robert's selection of gifts had been very sweet so far. A china dog for her bedroom; a hair-tidy; a box of Turkish Delight; a discreet bottle of lavender-water; nothing to which her parents could object.

But before today she had never in her life received anything from a young man – other than her brother, who didn't count – that came in a jeweller's box.

It had to mean something. It had to mean he was falling as headlong in love with her as she as with him. She was dizzy with the thought, and she opened the box and took out the glittering crystal pendant with shaking hands.

"Oh, Robert, it's beautiful," she breathed.

"So are you," he said, his voice thickening. He caught her hands in his, and the trail of gold chain draped over them both, enclosing the crystal. It was symbolic, Helen thought dreamily, as besotted with love as Elsie Caldwell.

"I wonder if you know just how beautiful you are, Helen, and just how much you tantalise a man."

"Tantalise you?" she protested with a shivery laugh. "I don't mean to do any such thing!"

"But you do. You make me want to do things I've never done with anyone before," he said, so convincingly that she could do nothing but believe him as his dark eyes bored intensely into hers.

She ached with love for him, and it had happened so suddenly, so amazingly and spectacularly suddenly, that she couldn't think straight. Couldn't sleep without dreaming of him. Couldn't eat.

He took the slender chain out of her hands and she leaned

126

forward as he fastened it around her throat. It lay shimmering against her pale skin, and he bent and kissed it.

Her heart pounded as she wondered fleetingly what her mother's reaction to such a gift from a young man would be. It was terribly personal. Too personal, by her mother's strict reckoning.

But it was becoming difficult to concentrate on anything other than Robert's hands, warm on her body, caressing her breasts and sending exquisite shooting sensations right through her. All her senses were alive to his touch and the wickedness of it all . . . the shameful, delicious, decadent wickedness . . .

He was unfastening the buttons on her afternoon frock so gently and skilfully that she hardly noticed it, nor realised that his lips were moving downwards over her skin. She was simply drowning in the new sensation . . . Suddenly she was frightened as she felt his hand slide inside the bodice of her frock. His fingers squeezed her nipple, and she heard his breathing quicken.

"No. Don't. Robert, please," she appealed.

"*Please* is what I want to hear. A bit of begging is as good as sweet music. Be nice to me, lass," he whispered.

"I didn't mean that. Please don't do it, Robert."

But he wasn't listening to her. It was now or never, and the ache in his loins was too great to be denied. He tugged her breast out of its confining bodice and his mouth fastened over her nipple, his tongue caressing and tasting, and whipping up more of these strange sensations in her that she didn't understand and knew she didn't want.

They were too powerful. Uncontrollable. And she had never lost control of her own emotions before. The feeling of alarm far outweighed the dizzying sense of pleasure his touch had evoked. She was also sick with furious embarrassment, knowing now that he had expected this as a reward for his gift. Any thoughts of love vanished as quickly as they had come, and in her mind he was an animal slavering over her.

She jerked away from him, scarlet with shame at the sight of her own breast exposed to the daylight, with the slickness of his tongue still on it.

She covered herself quickly, and spoke through shuddering

lips. "Take me home, please. And give this to someone who will be glad to pay in kind for your generosity."

She wrenched the pendant from her throat, uncaring that the clasp of the chain broke. It was as tawdry as she felt.

"There's a name for girls like you," Robert snarled, sparks of anger lighting his eyes. "You're worse than a street tart. At least they ply their trade honestly and don't tease a man to death."

"I never tried to tease you," Helen almost sobbed. "I thought you liked me. I thought you *loved* me."

He heard the catch in her throat and sensed the romantic idealism of a girl not yet schooled in lust. His attitude gentled again until he was as seductive as a panther stalking its prey.

"Well, my lovely girl, isn't that exactly what I want to do if you'll let me?"

He wasn't giving up just yet, not while she had soft tears brimming in her eyes, and her lips trembled so enticingly. He let his hand rest on her knee over her silky skirt, stroking her upper leg with imperceptible movements, and pressed his cheek to hers as he felt her relax again.

"Love means trusting another person, lass," he whispered, his mouth on hers now. "You can trust me not to hurt you."

She didn't understand what he meant until she felt the heat of his hand beneath her skirt and the harder pressure of it. Felt it sliding quickly upwards and inwards as his breath hoarsened again, and she could smell the lust in him.

Helen was gripped by fear, but she couldn't let this happen. *Wouldn't* let it happen. With an instinct stronger than fear she clamped her knees together and rammed her fist into his face with all her strength.

"You little vixen," Robert yelled. He let go of her at once as he reeled back in the car to clutch at his nose. His elegant nose, that had a streak of blood coming from it now . . .

"If you don't take me home this minute, I shall get out of this car and start running," Helen screamed, even though she had no idea where they were. "I shall shriek rape to anyone within hearing distance, and we'll see what all your fancy clothes and your daddy's reputation does for you then!"

"And who do you think will believe you?" But his sneer

was fast becoming a bluster, and all his fight and libido was shrivelling as he saw the cold fury in her eyes.

Bloody *class* did this, he found himself thinking furiously, the breeding that was denied to his sort. She would never be persuaded into the hay. She had iron control when it was needed, and she had it now. The bitch had dragged it up from somewhere.

"Who would believe you?" he snapped again, when she had stared him out, unnerving him even more.

"Anyone who sees this," Helen snapped back, and calmly ripped the bodice of her best Sunday frock as if it was tissue paper. He supposed it was of no consequence to a girl whose father could always buy her more. "Now drive me home. Providing I get home with no one seeing me, I'll forget this ever happened. Except that I always confide everything to my best friend."

He stared at her in shocked disbelief, his face a picture of impotent rage. "You surely don't mean Imogen Caldwell?"

"The very same," Helen said grimly, knowing she had the upper hand now, and aware that several other cars were in the vicinity on this lovely evening. If she chose to shout for help, there was nothing else Robert Preston could do to her now, without others being aware of it.

They drove back to her house at speed, and in total silence. Helen thanked her stars that her parents were away for the night, and wouldn't witness her humiliation. Nor would she be obliged to explain her disgraceful appearance to them.

She slammed the car door in a final gesture of defiance, and heard Robert curse before he drove off in a temper.

Only then, when she was safely indoors and alone, did her knees buckle, and she leaned against her own front door with tears streaming down her face.

"What a fool. What a mad, bloody fool I was to be so taken in by looks and smooth talking," she finally whispered savagely into the empty house. She never swore in anger, and hated him still more for reducing her to it.

She went to the ornate bathroom her father had had installed and stripped off every bit of clothing while she filled the bath with hot water. Then she scrubbed every inch of her body and soaked herself for half an hour, until the water ran cool and her skin was wrinkled and alabaster white, but bore no more traces of Robert Preston's touch.

Finally, with no more tears left to weep, she put on an everyday frock and systematically destroyed every single thing he had bought her. Only then did she feel moderately cleansed. And only then did she realise that she couldn't bear to be alone any longer.

There was only one person she needed. Only one other person who would understand. She called her on the telephone, praying she would be the one to answer.

"Immy, I need to see you right away," she croaked.

The shock in her voice transmitted itself at once.

"Where? Do you want me to come to you, Helen?"

"No. Somewhere out of doors. I'll drive to the park near you and meet you there in ten minutes. I have to talk to you. I feel" – she gulped – "so dirty."

"I'll be right there," Immy said. "Whatever it is, we can sort it out, Helen."

A sixth sense told her exactly what she was going to hear. She left Vicarage Street and walked quickly to the grassy park, which was busy with parents and children on a balmy evening, telling herself not to condemn. Not to be an I-told-you-so friend. Telling herself she could be wrong, and probably was.

One look at Helen's feverish face told her she was not. She took her friend's hand tightly in her own, and they sat on a park bench near the pond in the shade of one of the graceful weeping willows. It seemed ominously appropriate.

"Was it Robert?" she asked quietly.

Helen was brittle with hurt, and lashed out at once.

"How did you know? Did he try it with you too? Why didn't you warn me? You *should* have warned me, Immy."

"I didn't know, and he didn't try it with me – and I'm only guessing, darling. Tell me what happened."

Apart from any physical hurt, it wasn't hard for Immy to see what the experience had done to her friend. The old confident Helen had temporarily gone, and in her place was a terrified girl who had seen something far uglier than she had known before. Helen would have thought it all a delicious game, and now she knew it was not. You didn't play with fire and not expect to get burnt. The trouble was, Helen did.

"Helen, he didn't . . ." Immy's voice sharpened. "You know it's a criminal offence for a man to force himself on you, and your father would take him all the way—"

"My father's not to hear a word of this," Helen stuttered. "Nobody but you, Immy. Promise me. *Please.*"

"Of course I promise, if you're sure you weren't hurt."

"He didn't rape me. I know that's what you're thinking, and you'll probably think I'm making far too much of it all. But I was so *scared*, Immy. I can't tell you how scared I was, and if that's what love is, I want no more of it."

She shuddered a breath. "Not that it was love on his part, nor mine. I was just infatuated. A stupid, pathetic girl who got her head turned. But not any more. I hate him now."

Immy knew she had to tread carefully. There was a time for an intimate discussion about the difference between love and lust, and it wasn't now.

"What exactly did he do, Helen? Just between us. It *is* why you called me, isn't it? To unburden yourself?"

"Yes," Helen muttered, drawing another deep breath. "Oh, it all seems so silly now. But it was so sordid at the time."

She described it quickly, her face as hot as fire as she did so. Immy slid an arm around her friend's shoulders, feeling the tension in her whole body.

"I know you won't believe me right now, but love . . . it's not as awful as it seems, Helen. At least, it won't be when you find the right man. You have to know that. He was only after one thing, but they're not all the same."

"What about your MR? You thought he was the right one, didn't you? How does anybody know?"

Helen's eyes burned with aggression, prepared to argue with anyone, and although Immy tried to placate her she still wasn't calm by the time the air grew chilly and the park had become more or less deserted except for themselves.

She came to a decision. "Helen, I'm going to take you home and make us some hot cocoa, and then I'm going to call my father and tell him I'm staying the night with you because your parents are away. Is that all right?"

Helen's voice was husky with relief. She wilted against her

friend. "It's more than all right. You're the best pal, Immy, and I'm an idiot to be making such a fuss."

"No, you're not. You've had a shock, but I bet we'll be laughing about it tomorrow."

She doubted it, and her head pounded with the irrational thought that the responsibility for this all harked back to the Caldwells.

If her father and Elsie hadn't gone to work for the Prestons and invited Robert home, and if *she* hadn't talked about him more than she realised, Helen would never have been agog to see this wonder man – and then entered into a kind of unspoken rivalry with Immy. They both knew about that one, even though neither of them ever voiced it.

"I'm not sure I can even drive home. My hands are shaking too much," Helen said abruptly when they reached the road where her small car was parked.

"You don't have to. I'm a driver now, remember? If you'll trust me with your car, of course."

"You're the only one I do trust," Helen said, and they both knew she wasn't just talking about the car.

It wasn't familiar, but a car was just a car, Immy told herself, and by the time they reached Helen's house, with a few jerks and false starts and under-the-breath curses, she knew there would be no more driving lessons with Robert Preston.

It would be her father or Helen. Or nothing. But that was for later. They had to get through this night, and tomorrow there were other things to sort out. Helen wasn't the only one who was a crusader when the need arose, she thought grimly.

Helen's parents were due home during Sunday morning, and if she wasn't exactly laughing by the time Imogen left, the first shock had faded, and she was viewing things more calmly.

Immy knew which hotel Robert was staying at, and she had no qualms about marching into the foyer and asking the receptionist to let him know she wished to see him.

"Whom shall I say is calling, madam?" the man said, his eyebrows marginally raised at the sight of a young lady with hair like fire and eyes like fury entering the hotel unaccompanied in the middle of a Sunday morning.

"Miss Imogen Caldwell," she said coolly. "And it's a matter of urgency, if you please."

She wasn't intimidated by the air of superiority all these people assumed. They worked for a salary, the same as she did. She waited unblinkingly while he contacted Robert's room on an internal telephone.

"Mr Preston will be down shortly, Miss Caldwell. If you would care to wait in the lounge."

"I'll wait in the garden," she told him, having already assessed the tables and chairs under shady umbrellas for guests' use. She suspected that what she had to say would be less likely to be overheard outside than inside.

She had to wait a good ten minutes before he appeared, which did nothing to cool her temper. She stared at him without speaking, resisting any reaction or comment as she saw the darkening bruise around his nose and beneath his eye. Helen had done a good job.

"I had a fall," he said abruptly.

"No, you didn't. You were punched by a young lady resisting your unwanted advances," she said deliberately.

"Keep your voice down, for God's sake," he hissed.

Seeing the hunted way he glanced around, Imogen sat back, knowing she was going to make the most of this, and intending to make him cringe until he wished himself back in Yorkshire.

"It was my intention to do so, and also the reason I suggested meeting in the garden. But now I'm not so sure I want to keep quiet about the kind of man you are. The kind who is outwardly a pillar of society, who charms all the elderly ladies who come into his store, but who sees fit to lure naïve young girls into the country and then tries to seduce them."

"My God, who are you, the Virgin Mary? It wasn't like that, anyway," Robert blustered. "And she's not naïve. She knows what it's all about."

"Helen Church is the sweetest girl I know, and she certainly does *not* know what it's all about, as you so crudely put it. By the way, did you know her father's an eminent solicitor in this city?"

It was sweet to see him blanch. He had an outdoor, rugged

complexion, but it went an unattractive sickly yellow at that moment.

"She's not telling him, is she? My God, Imogen, you've got to stop her. My reputation is at stake!"

"Your reputation is that of a river-rat – it stinks," Immy told him coldly. "And we haven't decided whether or not to tell her father yet."

"*We*? You don't know what actually happened, do you?" He tried to bluff it out now. "You weren't there. All this fuss over a few kisses! It's only a stupid girl's word, and none of your damn business, anyway."

"You bastard!" Immy said in a low vibrant voice. "You despicable *bastard*."

Her violent reaction shocked him. She shocked herself, but she was too incensed on Helen's behalf to care.

"I *do* know what happened, because when she got home Helen called me in a terrible state and I spent all night at her house, listening to her and comforting her."

"Over a few kisses?" he sneered.

"Over what would be construed in a court of law as attempted rape."

She had him now. She could see it by the way his knuckles whitened, his fingernails biting so hard into his palms they would surely draw blood eventually. She could see it by the way the pulse in his throat throbbed as if it would burst, and by the way the veins in his forehead stood out like purple ropes. He was scared stiff, and she was *glad*.

She stood up, smoothing down the skirt of her frock with hands that trembled slightly. Now that it was almost done, she felt faint, but she wasn't going to let him see it.

"One more thing. I want no more driving lessons from you, and you will not come to tea with us again. You will make whatever excuse you like to my father, but if you set one foot inside my house again, I shall have no alternative but to tell my father everything."

"I can hardly avoid seeing him at the shop!"

"The shop is a different matter – and, thank God, you'll be leaving it soon. If there are any more arrangements about exchanging managers, please ensure that you don't come back to Bristol again. I won't have you violating my mother's house with your presence. We're a decent family, and we don't take kindly to scum. Have I made myself clear?"

"Perfectly," he snarled. "And I was right. You are the bloody Virgin Mary. So do you want to shake on it?"

He oozed sarcasm, adding blasphemy to everything else. He held out his hand to her, and she took a pace backwards.

"I wouldn't touch you if you were the last man on earth," she said vehemently.

No one glancing out of an upper window of the hotel could have resisted a comment about Imogen Caldwell's hair, its sheen caught in the glow of morning sunlight that turned it to a blaze of fire.

The chambermaid sighed enviously to her older companion as they stripped the sheets and pillowcases off the bed, ready for laundering.

"Wish I had hair like that, don't you, Lizzie? My boy likes red hair. Says it goes with a hot nature, if you get my meaning," she added with a giggle.

"I don't know nothing about that, but I reckon the bloke with the funny way of talking's a bit of all right. You know who she is, don't you?"

"Never seen her before."

"Yes you have, ninny. She's one of them Caldwell girls. Family fell on hard times 'til they started working in that new emporium. Bit of a come-down for the father, of course. The mother fell off the cliffs last year. *You* know. But did she fall or was she pushed?" Lizzie commented sagely.

As Dolly looked blank, she went on irritably. "I been watching them two down there and all, and I reckon there's a lot of summat going on."

"Is there? I only noticed her hair."

"That's because you're too dozy to notice anything that's not spelled out for you. Well, you'd best start noticing this bedding before you get a rollicking from the housekeeper for idling, and stop getting cow-eyed over the nobs."

Dolly would forget all about the little scene within minutes, Lizzie thought, but *she* wouldn't. Not when she had a tasty titbit of news to tell her sister, who cleaned at the newspaper offices, about how one of them haughty Caldwell girls had spent half the morning in the company of a guest at the hotel.

Sunday morning, too, when you might have expected a family like hers to be at church. Not the toff, though. Working at the hotel as long as she had, Lizzie had seen all sorts, and knew a thing or two about men.

This one had wicked eyes and a flat way of talking in that come-hither voice of his, and he called her "lass", which made her feel quite young again. She had smelled the stuff in his bathroom – which was a bit poncy for a man, in Lizzie's opinion – and had looked through his dressing-table drawers. She'd seen the saucy magazines he read, which had made her eyebrows rise a little.

But he wasn't above sharing a joke and having a bit of a laugh, slapping her backside playfully when she did his room and tossing her a few coins for her trouble.

She had a fair idea about that nasty bruise around his eye this morning, too. She'd seen a few of them in her time. Maybe that was also down to the Caldwell girl. Lizzie wasn't above elaborating a bit when it came to telling a good tale about the goings-on in the hotel business, and getting an extra half-pint of stout for her trouble.

With her imagination, she sometimes reckoned she could have been writing some of them penny dreadfuls, she thought cheerfully. *And* writing them better!

Eleven

It was late in the evening when Quentin Caldwell came back to the sitting-room where his two daughters had just closed the books they were reading and decided it really was time they were in bed.

"What an extraordinary thing," he said to them. "I can't quite make head nor tail of it, but I've just had Owen Preston calling me all the way from Yorkshire on the telephone to say I'll be temporarily in charge of the shop as of tomorrow."

"*You*?" Elsie said in astonishment. "But why?"

"I do have managerial experience, Elsie," he said drily.

"I didn't mean that, Daddy. But what about Robert? He won't like it at all, and it's going to put his nose right out of joint, isn't it?"

Imogen kept her face as immobile as she could, thinking that Helen had already done that, and that although Robert's nose was the least of his worries, it too would take some explaining to his father, if what she suspected was happening.

The next minute she knew her intuition was right.

"It seems that Robert is required in York, and has to be back there right away. I've no idea of the reason, and it wasn't my place to ask. Owen seemed brusque enough as it was."

He smiled archly at his second daughter. "Aren't you going to ask the next question?"

"I don't know. Am I?" Elsie's face suddenly flooded with colour, and Immy saw how radiantly beautiful she was when thoughts of her young man filled her mind.

"Oh, *does* this mean Joe will be coming back sooner than expected?" she asked, clasping her hands excitedly.

"It does. I'm in full charge only for a short time. Joe will be back at the end of the week, so you'll probably see him on Sunday. He and I will have plenty to discuss."

137

Immy cleared her throat. "Father, I wonder if this would be a good time to ask you a special favour, since you're in such a good mood."

"Well, you can always ask, and I can always say no," he added, teasing her.

But he was indulgent, with the way things were going. Robert was a good fellow, but lately he had become a bit too pompous and sure of himself. Power didn't suit everyone and, like his daughter, Quentin much preferred Joe.

"I hope you'll say yes! It's about the car."

"What about the car? The last time I saw it I believe it was all in one piece."

Immy mentally gritted her teeth at having to say the next bit, but knew there was no other way.

"Robert says I've done very well, and he thinks I should do some solo driving now to get proper experience, so I was wondering if I could borrow it on Sunday. I'll be very careful with it, and go out in the country where there won't be any traffic. What do you think?"

Quentin didn't say anything for a minute, but Immy desperately hoped he would agree. She might even ask Helen to accompany her, to take her out of herself . . . but that would defeat the object. She needed that feeling of total independence.

"I don't see why not, but if that's to be the way of things, you'd better start saving up to buy one of your own, miss. And don't pick up any strangers," her father said with a smile, sure that she wouldn't.

"Oh, Immy would never do that," Elsie said, in a rosy glow at the thought of Joe coming back. "She's far too sensible. No stranger would dare to take advantage of *her*!"

"Good Lord, what a dreary image you have of me!" Immy said, not at all pleased at the thought that she was being compared to a dragon lady. "You make me sound as middle aged as the Marys upstairs."

Among themselves, they had taken to referring to the quiet widows in the apartment upstairs as "the Marys", after discovering they both shared the same first name. It brought a smile to Immy's face, and Elsie laughed.

"No one could ever accuse you of being middle aged, Immy,

nor dreary. All I meant was that you're far too intelligent to be taken in by people, and it's something to be admired."

Immy couldn't argue with that, though it had taken her a while to see through Robert Preston, she admitted. But now that he was in the past, she could forget him.

Lizzie Reed's sister Meg worked as a cleaner in the newspaper office, and was keen to pass on the bit of gossip she had heard about the handsome Yorkshire bloke who had been in charge of Preston's Emporium for such a short time.

"Ever so good looking he was, according to our Lizzie," her sister said with a sigh.

"Your Lizzie would think anything in trousers was good looking," her fellow cleaner grinned.

"That's true, but she always says it pays to be nice to people in her line of work, and before the bloke left the hotel he gave her a good tip for her trouble."

"Oh, yes; and what kind of trouble was that, then?" the other woman sniggered.

"I think it included keeping her mouth shut about certain goings-on," Meg said, lowering her voice. "But between you and me, it had a bit to do with that Caldwell girl. You know the one I mean. The snooty one. Don't work at the shop no more, but went up in the world with her office typing, so they say."

"You mean the one with the funny name? Imogen or summat?"

Meg nodded. "That's her. She ain't so snooty that she can't chase after a man, though. Lizzie says she seen 'er with him at the hotel early on Sunday morning, so tell me that ain't saucy if you like! They was having a right old barney in the garden, and Lizzie reckons he was giving her the brush-off and she was pleading with him to stay."

"Blimey. You wouldn't catch me pleadin' with a bloke."

"Nor me," Meg said. "Unless he was as loaded as that one. I might be tempted then."

They laughed bawdily together as they got on with their floor cleaning. At that moment a junior reporter took a batch of papers into the print room.

"I've just heard a spicy bit of gossip that might interest you," he said to the smooth-talking Welshman working there, hoping it might boost his status.

"I doubt that," said Morgan Raine, with undisguised loathing for the little sneak. He'd probably make a good reporter someday, though, he acknowledged, since his nasty little ear was always to the ground for anything sleazy.

"Didn't you do some advertising leaflets for one of those Caldwell girls, whose father used to have his own shop before he went down in the world?" Davy Batt went on, hiding his resentment at the way Morgan always looked down on him.

He'd caught Morgan's attention now. He was presumably referring to the second daughter, but Morgan instantly recalled the times he'd had with Imogen. He remembered her with a lustful yearning, and more than once he had wished he'd never done the dirty on her. She had been a sparky little thing; his new girl was nowhere near as responsive in certain quarters.

"This had better be good. You're running down a family who've had a rotten share of bad luck recently," he snapped as the idiot fidgeted from one foot to the other.

"The one I'm talking about is the other one. The oldest one. Some call her the snooty one."

Morgan's heart jolted.

"Imogen Caldwell? What about her, you loon?" he said sharply, forgetting he wasn't supposed to know her.

Davy Batt knew he wouldn't get anywhere unless he came out with it. He spoke more boldly.

"She was with one of them Yorkshire fellows in some posh hotel early on Sunday morning. Don't that make for a juicy bit of gossip?"

One second Morgan couldn't believe what he was hearing. The next, he had caught the boy by the throat and was twisting his flesh in his hands.

"You lying little bastard," he hissed.

"I ain't lying!" he choked. "Ask them cleaning women if you don't believe me. It's them spreading the gossip."

"And you're adding to it, you toe-rag," Morgan grated, letting him go so fast that he staggered back. "Get out of here before I throw you out."

Davy dashed for the door, turning to yell back at Morgan when he was out of arm's length.

"Bloody Welsh turd. Go back to the bloody land of your fathers – if you know which one is yours."

"What in God's name's going on here?" Morgan heard his boss say above the rattle of the machinery. By then, however, he was out looking for the cleaning women. He found them leaving after their morning session with their mops and buckets.

"Which of you is spreading wicked lies about Imogen Caldwell?" he demanded.

"'Tain't lies, Welshy," Meg said at once. "My sister seen 'em canoodling in the hotel where the gent was staying. I'd say she'd been staying there too, if you get my meaning."

Her sly wink incensed Morgan so much that he had a job to keep his hands off her, except that she smelled of carbolic and bleach and stale clothes.

"Miss Caldwell has a respectable home and family, and if you repeat any more of this I'll have you up for slander – and your sister too," he ranted.

"Here, I didn't mean nothing by it," Meg said, scared by the look in his eyes. "It was just summat my sister said."

"Well, tell your sister to mind what she says in future, because it can have serious repercussions."

He doubted that she knew the meaning of the word, but his tone was enough to scare her still more. Her companion nudged her and said they'd better be off or they'd miss their bus.

"I won't say no more about it, then," Meg said at last, "and I'll tell Lizzie she was prob'ly wrong. Will that do?"

"It'll have to," Morgan said.

He turned away, but not soon enough to miss hearing Meg tell the other one that she knew Lizzie wasn't damn well wrong, and that one with the fancy name was prob'ly no better than she ought to be.

Which was a damn silly phrase if he ever heard one, Morgan fumed, still not too sure why he was so het up over Imogen's reputation. She was nothing to him any more – though she could have been, if only he hadn't been so careless in walking out with another girl on that Sunday afternoon last year.

Well, it was a long time ago now, and the dust had settled by now. But the need to see her again came over him with an urgency that took him by surprise.

* * *

141

"You'll never guess who came into the shop today," Elsie told her sister after work the following evening.

"I don't know. Surprise me," Immy said with a smile.

"That young man who did the leaflets for me – and that was a waste of money, because I never did work at home."

"What did he want?" Immy broke in, realising from the faraway look in Elsie's eyes that she was going to start musing that if she had worked at home, she would never have had the opportunity to see Joe every single day.

"What did who want? Oh, that man. He was asking after you, and I must say, Immy, he sounded rather keen. You said he was only an acquaintance, but he made it sound as if you were more than that. Have you been keeping things from me all this time?" she teased, clearly not really believing it.

"Certainly not," Immy said crossly. "He is – *was* – only an acquaintance, and I haven't seen him in months. I can't think why he would have asked after me."

She ignored her erratic heart beats, thinking guiltily that Morgan Raine had been far, far more than a mere acquaintance. More than a friend, or a sweetheart. He had been the love of her life, as she had been his . . . or so she had thought, until he had shattered those illusions.

"Anyway, when he asked what you were doing these days—"

"Elsie, you didn't tell him, did you?"

"I didn't think it was a secret. He could have walked into your office any day of the week and seen you there. People visit a housing agent's office all the time. And why are you getting so cross with me?"

Immy tried to calm down. It wasn't Elsie's fault that she was so sweetly and innocently involved with Joe, and had no idea of the dark forces raging inside her sister's head right now. And not just in her head, either.

"I'm not cross with you," she said. "It was just the surprise of hearing you mention him again, that's all."

"Well, if that's your reaction to an old acquaintance turning up, I dread to think what an old boyfriend might do."

Elsie started to laugh, and then saw the momentarily unguarded expression on Immy's face.

"My heavens, that's it, isn't it? You knew him far better than you let on. And you never told me!"

Since that last fact seemed to be the sum total of her indignation, Immy managed to laugh it off.

"That's because there was absolutely nothing to tell. I knew him for a few weeks, and we hit it off rather well before we went our separate ways. And now I'm going to bed!"

She needed to be alone, to try to slow down her hammering heart, and to forget all the memories Elsie had so unwittingly brought to life.

But as she undressed quickly and slid between the cool sheets, she couldn't rid her thoughts of that one phrase, "We hit it off rather well."

She closed her eyes in the soft darkness of her bedroom and remembered all too vividly how wonderful it had been before all her girlish dreams had been destroyed.

She had loved him with all the passion of first love, trusting in his words, in his deep, lilting Welsh voice, in his sensuous touch that could arouse her in a way she had never known before. She shivered, curling into a ball in her cotton nightgown, hugging her body tight, and remembering just how magical it had been.

She had awoken to his kisses and his love like a flower opening in the sun, wanting him, welcoming him, ripe and ready to take the next step, no matter how she had tried to deny it to herself, and to Helen . . . and it had all been so loving and so different from the crude way Robert Preston had tried to force himself on her friend.

Her thoughts shifted again. She remembered that awful night when Helen had called for her help, and her eyes flew open now, staring up into the darkness.

Morgan had never been like that, but she was older and wiser now, and who knew whether a gentle seduction was any the less a violation than the crudest kind? How could you tell?

She moved restlessly in her bed, turning to watch the patterns of moonlight dappling the curtains of her room as the breeze scurried through the trees outside. Wondering if she would ever have taken that final step if Morgan had asked her, and knowing in her heart that she would.

Love would have made her accept that it was the natural

thing to do. Love, and the persuasion of a lover skilled in the ways of seduction. And even the thought that she would have given in so gladly made her wicked. Wanton. As bad as any waterfront street-woman. And she was thankful that she had never been put to the test after all.

She looked up from the letter she was typing the following afternoon with her usual professional smile, expecting to see a client. Then her heart jumped into her throat.

"Hello, cariad," said Morgan softly, using the Welsh word for "darling" that had always sent delicious shivery feelings shooting through her. This time, however, she refused to let them in.

"What do you want?" she stammered, angry with herself for behaving in this way, for being reduced to a schoolgirl again, just because he had the same dark brooding look he had always had. Even the sight of his smiling mouth could remind her of his kisses, and how she had always wanted more . . .

She struggled to remember where she was, and who she was, and that he had betrayed her.

"We need to talk, Immy," he said quietly.

"We don't have anything to say to one another."

"It's important. But not here. Perhaps on Sunday."

"I shan't be here on Sunday. I have to go somewhere."

It gave her a childish satisfaction to say it, to not be readily available whenever he chose to drop by. And then she went and ruined it all.

"I could manage tomorrow afternoon if it's *really* important, though I can't imagine that you have anything to say that will interest me."

"Trust me, Immy, it's something you'll want to hear. Where, then?"

Up on the hill, in our favourite hollow? She could almost hear the words leaving his lips, and knew she couldn't bear to hear them. It would be too emotional, and she wasn't sure she was ready to have her heart opened again.

And to trust him . . . ? She had done that once before, and look where it had got her.

"I'll meet you for a few minutes in the park, near the lake," she said quickly. "I can be there about three o'clock. If that's no good, I'm sorry—"

"It's perfect. And Immy, you look wonderful. I'd forgotten just how lovely you are."

"Tomorrow, then," she said quickly, not wanting this. "But I shan't be able to stay long."

She was still staring into space when her employer came out to the reception area from his own office. He was forty, sandy-haired, pudding-faced and kindly, and very partial to having such a "vibrant" young lady fronting his establishment. He used the word as often as he could, hoping that the ungrammatical but transatlantic sound of it proved that he was up to the minute and not as fuddy-duddy as his appearance might suggest. *Did* suggest, he thought mournfully.

"Are you all right, Imogen?" he said, suddenly struck by her stillness. He was used to hearing the clatter of the typewriter keys whenever he came to speak to her.

"I think so. Yes, of course I am." She realised what she was saying, and where she was. "Sorry, Mr Harris. I was dreaming. I'll get back to work right away."

He put a fatherly hand on her shoulder, even though he had begun to feel anything but fatherly towards her. But he would never have said anything about his feelings. In any case, they were not the feelings of a typical Romeo. He had always known he was lacking in the passion department, and it had relieved rather than concerned him. Caring and devotion were something else, however.

He had devoted his life to his mother until her death, and he would have devoted it to any woman who cared for him in a calm and platonic way with few other obligations. But most women wouldn't want that, especially not this one. He knew well enough that Imogen Caldwell was not for him. Not this lovely, vivacious young woman who could surely have any young man she wanted – and who, curiously enough, had never mentioned one.

Most gossipy young women couldn't resist talking about their sweethearts to anyone who would listen, but in his eyes that was another thing that set her apart from the rest. She was unique. She was his Imogen, his shining star, his humble slave

– even though he was her employer and paid her wages – and he was content just to see her every day.

"Shall I put the kettle on?" he heard her say.

He blinked and turned away, as if afraid she might be able to see into his soul.

"Please do, my dear. I feel the need for sustenance."

Immy always thought him a bit eccentric with his frequently pompous way of talking, but she always felt safe with him. He was like a father figure or a favourite uncle.

In the tiny cupboard that passed for a kitchen area, she filled the kettle with cold water and lit the gas ring with a match, then put two cups and saucers on the tin tray he had brought back from a long-ago holiday in Cornwall with his mother. They were adorned with pictures of tin mines and pixies, the ruins of Tintagel Castle, and strange words in the Cornish language all around the rim.

Immy deliberately dissected her employer's character all the while she prepared the tea and biscuits, simply to keep her mind off the man whose image was really claiming her thoughts. She veered off Morgan, and concentrated on Kenneth Harris.

Sometimes she couldn't make him out. She knew he had never been married. Nor was he particularly attractive, though she supposed he was the kind of man some women might want to mother. Now nobody would ever say that about Morgan . . .

She sighed, giving up the attempt to keep him out of her mind. She didn't want to think of him, but she had arranged to meet him and she wouldn't go back on that. Whatever he had to say, she would tell him firmly that this was the last time. She wouldn't risk her heart being broken for a second time. It was why she had suggested they meet openly in the park. Let him say what he had to say and that would be the end of it.

"I hope you know what you're doing, darling," Helen said, when she reported the news to her that evening.

They were sitting in the Churches' fragrant garden as usual. It was a tribute to Helen's mother's green fingers. Right now it was a profusion of heavenly scented roses, tobacco plants and the delicate perfume of honeysuckle, and was alive with the contented hum of summer bees.

On such an evening, how could anyone ever imagine that war was on the horizon, or that the tranquillity of England could ever be decimated again, the way it had been twenty-five years before?

The thought flitted in and out of Immy's head as she tried to concentrate on what Helen was saying.

"Whatever he wants, I'm going to make it perfectly clear that I don't want to see him again."

"So why did you say you'd see him at all?"

"I don't know. It sounded important, that's all. Or perhaps I want to prove once and for all that I can meet him socially, and that he means nothing to me any more."

"Is that the truth?"

"I want it to be," Immy said honestly. "I know I can never feel the same way about him again. I could never trust him, Helen, and without trust, it wouldn't work. You have to be able to trust a man. You know what I mean, don't you?"

"You don't have to ask me that," Helen said. "It will be a long time before I trust anyone again."

"But you will in time. We both will. Anyway, let's forget Robert Preston – and MR, too. How's James? Have you heard from him recently? It seems ages since I saw him."

"He's transferred to the Tank Corps. God knows why, but I think it's some mannish thing. Riding around in that powerful metal machine makes him feel like Hercules, I suppose."

"Well, I'm impressed," Immy said, awed. "I'm thinking of driving my father's car to Weston on Sunday to pay a surprise visit to the folks, but I couldn't handle one of those monstrosities."

"I just hope James can," Helen said drily.

When Imogen arrived at the park the following afternoon, Morgan was already there. She saw him before he saw her, and deliberately made her face impassive as he jumped up with a ready smile from the bench where he was sitting. He made to shake her hand and she touched his briefly, then drew away as she sat down.

"I told you I couldn't stay long. What is it you have to say?" she enquired coolly.

"Immy, don't be like this," he said softly.

"Is that it? If this was all a ploy to get me here—" She half rose, and his face sobered at once.

"It's not. But I thought you should know what people are saying about you."

She stared at him, not understanding. All around them, people were laughing and enjoying themselves on a Saturday afternoon in the park. Small boys were sailing wooden boats on the lake, and pretending they were Drake or pirates. A man was flying a brightly coloured kite, his children cheering as its long tail snaked up into the sky. The rippling blue of the lake glittered like diamonds in the afternoon sun, and everything was perfectly normal, except for the chill that had suddenly filled Imogen's heart.

"Saying about me? What do you mean? Why on earth should anyone have anything to say about me?"

"You were seen, Immy. And gossiped about. I hope I've stopped it, but I thought you ought to know."

"Are you going to explain, Morgan, or am I supposed to guess what rubbish you're talking about?"

"I hope it's rubbish, cariad. I thought I knew you well enough to believe that."

"Tell me this minute, or I'm leaving," she snapped. She suspected that this was his way of getting around her again – and somehow, here in the daylight, now that she was used to the fact that he was still in the world, she was absolutely sure that she no longer wanted him. It was almost a shock, but a perfectly wonderful one.

"You visited the hotel where that chap Preston was staying," Morgan said flatly. "You were seen in the garden with him early one morning."

Imogen stared at him. He wasn't making sense. *Seen* with him early one morning? What was that meant to imply?

When she realised, her face flooded with colour, and she felt faint with a far more unpleasant kind of shock.

"You can't believe what you're saying," she whispered.

"I didn't say I believed it. I think I know you better than that, Immy. I'm just telling you what was overheard. If you should go there again, you'd better take great care."

"I won't be going there again. He's gone – and anyway, it

wasn't at all like you're trying to imply. If you must know, we were having a furious row."

"I don't need to know the details. I'm just saying you should be careful in future. Dirt sticks."

She swallowed. He was making something sordid out of something that had been so innocent, so well meant on behalf of a friend . . . but if he was doing so, then so must those who had passed the rumour on.

"How did you hear about it?" she said huskily.

"A chambermaid who works there has a sister who cleans at the office. They were discussing it and one of the juniors heard them and came to me, thinking I'd like to hear a juicy bit of gossip. His words, not mine, but when I realised who he was talking about, I squashed it at once. I don't think you'll have any more trouble."

"Well, thank you for that."

He caught hold of her hand and squeezed it, and she let it lie there for a moment. His voice softened.

"Did you think I wouldn't defend you, Immy? You know I think too much of you for that. I always have."

She pulled her hand away from his and stood up. "Morgan we can never mend what's irretrievably broken. I'm grateful for what you did, but let's just leave it there."

"Do you really mean that?"

"Believe me, I mean it. Goodbye, Morgan."

She walked away with her head held high. She felt humiliated at the thought of being the subject of gossip, but she wouldn't let him see it. She was the cool and collected Miss Imogen Caldwell – and she had no intention of crawling away as if she had something to hide.

It was galling to think she couldn't go and tell Helen what the meeting with Morgan had been all about, but if she did that, Helen would know she had gone to confront Robert, and that the ensuing gossip was all her fault.

Immy knew she couldn't let that happen. Helen had been too traumatised by the whole thing to risk shattering her world all over again. As it was, she was putting the events in perspective with her usual resilience, but if the reason for Immy visiting the hotel ever came to light, she would be devastated.

Instead, Immy called her on the telephone as soon as she

got home, rather than see her face to face. She told her crisply it was as they had thought. "MR's fling with that other girl is over and he wanted me to go back to him again. I told him what I thought of him, though."

"And that was all the mystery?" Helen said, clearly disappointed that there was to be no great drama unfolding.

"That was it. They don't always get their own way, Helen, and I relished telling him so."

"Nobody ever got their own way with you, darling," Helen said with a laugh. "Enjoy your day out tomorrow."

"I will," Immy said, but her hands were shaking slightly as she replaced the receiver, and she wasn't quite as confident as she sounded.

What if the gossip hadn't been stopped? What if it got to her father's ears? Or what if Morgan decided to do a little moral – or immoral – blackmailing on his own account in order to win her back? She wouldn't put that past him.

And who was becoming a cynic now? Immy asked herself crossly. She turned in relief as her brother Baz came breezing into the house on an unexpected Saturday afternoon visit home.

Twelve

An hour after she had left home late the next morning, having had a sandwich and cold drink to keep her going, Immy began to doubt that the solo driving trip was such a good idea after all.

Inside her cotton gloves, her hands were clammy. She knew she was gripping the steering-wheel far too tightly, but she couldn't seem to judge the distance between the car and the grass verge as well as when Robert had been guiding her.

Thinking of him set her teeth on edge. She was determined to do this all by herself. She had set herself a goal, and she didn't intend to be beaten. She prayed that other cars on the road would give her a wide berth, though the occasional horse and cart made her hold her breath in case the horse should rear up or take fright, sensing a novice driver. Didn't animals have an instinct about somebody nearby expiring with nerves, or was that all a myth . . . ?

"For pity's sake, get hold of yourself, girl," she muttered to herself as she negotiated the winding lanes and narrow roads that seemed endlessly longer than they had the times her father had been driving.

At last the sign on the road told her she was nearing her destination. She could swear the smell of salt was in the air now, and with a wave of nostalgia she remembered when her parents used to take the older Caldwell children on regular visits to their aunt and uncle. Frances had always promised a penny to the first one to spot the sea.

How long ago and how dear it all seemed now. And how *sad*, knowing that such days could never come again. She drew a deep breath, knowing she was in danger of becoming maudlin, and it wouldn't do.

Aunt Rose would think there was something wrong with

her, and Uncle Bertie would get all gruff and embarrassed. So she straightened her shoulders and got on with it, telling herself that the dampness in her eyes was simply due to a bit of dust from the road, and nothing more.

She finally stopped the car outside Aunt Rose's house with a huge sense of relief, choosing to forget for the moment that she had to drive it all the way back again. Instead, she allowed herself a surge of triumph, because she had actually done it. She was here, unscathed – and, once she had got her breath back, quite ready to brag about her achievement.

She stepped out of the car, her legs shaking only fractionally, and paused for a moment as she heard the sound of laughter coming from the garden.

Childish shrieks were coupled with the deeper, older laughter of adults, and just for a moment she let herself imagine it was themselves a dozen years ago, before Teddy was born . . . Immy and Elsie and Daisy and the infant Baz, playing their favourite games with their delightful mother and father in the garden at home.

Selfishly, Immy longed for those days to return with a fierceness that almost overwhelmed her, until the vision cleared, and she knew how foolish she was being.

She didn't know *what* was wrong with her today, she thought crossly, but, needing to blame someone, she put the blame squarely and unfairly on to Morgan Raine.

She pushed open the gate, hearing the familiar squeak of the hinges. Uncle Bertie always said cheerfully that he left it deliberately to warn them of strangers in the camp. Today there was so much noise it seemed that no one else noticed it.

Bertie was on his hands and knees on the grass, playing trains with three small boys and a yapping dog. Aunt Rose was sitting on a deck-chair knitting, after her usual gargantuan exertions with the Sunday dinner.

It was such a homely, cameo scene that Immy wanted to cherish it for ever – until one of the little boys turned to stare at her in disbelief, and the mood was broken.

"It's our Immy," Teddy yelled, hurling himself at her, almost pulling her down. "Our Immy's come to see me!"

Rose stood up at once, her knitting falling to the ground as she moved swiftly towards her niece.

"My dear girl, what's wrong?" she said at once. "Where's your father?"

"Nothing's wrong! Why should there be? Oh, I know I should have called you to say I was coming, but I wanted to give you a surprise. I drove here by myself!"

"You *what*?" Bertie was beside her now, enveloping her in his usual bear hug. "You mean your father allowed you to drive his pride and joy? I didn't even know you knew how."

"Well, I do. Aren't you a little bit proud of me?"

"I've always been proud of you, my love. I'm afraid you've got here too late for Sunday dinner, though."

"Oh, we can always rustle up something," Aunt Rose said easily. "We'll leave you to your own devices while Immy and I go into the kitchen, dear. Daisy's gone out with that friend of hers, Immy, but they'll both be back in time for tea."

Once inside the house she looked at Immy quizzically.

"Now then, my love, what's *really* wrong? I'm sure there's no illness in the family, or I'd have heard, so it must be something else. And I'd say it's something to do with the heart rather than the head. Am I right?"

"It's nothing, really."

"Whenever someone says 'it's nothing, really', you can be sure it's *something* really. So out with it before you burst, and be sure it will go no further than these four walls."

"I shouldn't really say anything. It's not my secret to tell," Immy said at last.

"Then you'd better not tell me," Rose said firmly. "Unless you're involved, of course. Are you, Imogen?"

"Yes. I feel responsible, and I can't rid myself of the guilt, even though I know how ridiculous it is. I mean, how was I to know she would take such a fancy to him, and that he would turn out to be such a – such a—"

"A rat?" Rose supplied.

When Immy nodded, she went on thoughtfully.

"You know, darling, no one could ever take your mother's place, and it would be stupid and heartless to try. But if she were here, and if she saw you in such distress, I know she would want you to confide in her. Won't you let me try to be a substitute, just this once?"

It hadn't occurred to Immy until that moment how important this was to her aunt. Rose would have loved a daughter, and the Caldwell girls were the nearest she had ever got to having one of her own.

So she found herself pouring out all the trauma Helen had gone through with Robert Preston, and telling her aunt how she had helped Helen through the night, and then gone storming off to Robert's hotel to have it out with him.

"You should have seen him, Aunt Rose," Immy said, finally allowing her mouth to stretch into a tremulous smile now that the worst of the telling was over. "Helen had really packed a punch, as they say in the pictures. He had a lovely bruise on his face. The next thing we heard was that he had been recalled to York, which made Elsie very happy, of course, because it meant that Joe came back to Bristol yesterday."

"And?" Rose said patiently.

"Well, that's it. It's a relief to get it off my chest – but it's our secret now, isn't it?"

"Of course, but why don't you tell me the rest of it?"

"Are you psychic or something? How do you know there's something else?"

"I know when one of my girls is troubled, and you haven't told me everything, have you? That's Helen's story, but what's yours, my love?"

Immy looked down at her hands for a moment. Then she unclasped them and gazed out of the window.

"I had a young man once," she said slowly.

If she thought her aunt would be shocked by all that she had to say, she was mistaken. In the telling, Immy was able to put Morgan Raine ever further into the past, and her aunt made it clear that she doubted that the gossips would make anything more of her little expedition to the hotel to confront Robert.

"They'll have forgotten it by now, because something more interesting will have occurred. It's the nature of the hotel business and the people who work there," Rose said sagely.

"But you don't really think I committed a *faux pas*, do you?" Immy said anxiously.

"Of course I don't, not for a minute. Now then, do you want something to eat, or not?"

Immy gave her a beatific smile, the first one in ages, it seemed to her. "I certainly do. I'm suddenly ravenous."

By the time Daisy and her pale friend Lucy came back from the farm, Immy had made friends with the evacuee children, and promised that when she came again she'd go to the beach with them all.

"We've had a wonderful time today," Daisy announced, when she had got over her astonishment at seeing Immy there.

Immy was equally astonished at seeing how grown up her sister seemed since the last time she had seen her. Daisy had grown apart from the rest of her family, she thought, but that was the way of things and there was no changing it.

"What have you been doing?" Rose asked indulgently.

"Riding, of course, and watching the airmen."

"*Daisy!*"

"Oh, it's all right, Aunt Rose. Part of Lucy's farm backs on to the airfield, and some of the recruits were doing their marching routines or whatever it is they call it. Ben knows a couple of the new ones, and he says they're going to start doing hurdling exercises on the promenade on Saturdays. They have to get fit for when they start flying practice. We're going to watch. Doesn't it sound like fun?"

"I'm not so sure about you watching these young men—"

"Oh, everyone will be there, not just us! We'll take the boys if you like."

Daisy caught Immy's glance, and read it correctly. *Any excuse*, it said – but by now the boys were leaping about excitedly, and they all knew there would be no stopping them.

"So how's the work going, Daisy? Father said I was to ask you especially," Immy said, when she could make her voice heard above the din. "You haven't killed anybody yet, I hope?"

It was a testimony to the passing of time that they could say such things light-heartedly now, without feeling guilt on behalf of their mother, Immy thought. It wasn't that they had forgotten her, or ever could, but you couldn't wear sackcloth and ashes for ever.

"I like it a lot," Daisy said, more soberly, adding cheekily, "I hope war won't come for a while yet, though, so that I'll be old enough to join up and be a proper nurse when it does."

"That's an awful thing to say! I hope it won't come at all," Immy said, thinking instantly of James Church and his tank, and the unpleasant possibility of young men she knew being wounded – or worse. She shied away from the thought.

"There's no chance of that hope, my love," Uncle Bertie told her. "It's a question of when, not if."

"But how can you be so sure?"

"How can you not, when all the signs are there? When all the newspapers and wireless reports are so full of gloom, and the government is giving us hints a mile high?"

He nodded towards the evacuees squabbling noisily with Teddy over who was going to be the engine driver now.

"And we wouldn't have these little inkspots with us if it wasn't for the threat of war, so at least we can be thankful for something, if not much else lately."

It was an odd way of looking at things, Immy thought as she took her leave of them all several hours later, and started on the drive back to Bristol. It was an odd way for Rose and Bertie to finally have their house filled with children's laughter, the way they had always wanted it.

All because of a beloved sister-in-law's death, and the threat of a war. If this was God's will, He had a funny way of determining things for people.

She gave up philosophising, and concentrated on the road, realising that she was a deal more confident behind the wheel now than when she had started out.

It was partly because she had done it once and knew she could do it again. And everyone knew that the road home was never as long as the road that took you away from it.

But it was also partly because of the catharsis of unburdening herself to Aunt Rose and hearing her logical reponse to it all. Uncle Bertie always said that nothing was so bad that it couldn't be fixed, and for once, she believed it.

Her father greeted her with relief when she arrived home, commenting that he was glad his car was still in one piece, and so was she.

"I'm not sure which of those comes first in your mind," she

said with a smile, "but I'll take it that you meant it kindly, Father."

"Of course I did."

"So where is everybody? Where's Elsie? I'm dying to tell her how well I did."

"She's out for a walk with Joe, so you'll just have to tell me how everybody is – unless you want to bore the Marys with your driving tales. They'd like to hear it, actually," he added. "I mentioned where you'd gone when I saw them going to church, and they think you're a very modern young lady."

"Do they?" Immy said with a grin. Not half as modern as she had once thought herself in certain areas. "Oh, I don't think I'll go up to them. I'm pretty tired tonight."

"Oh, well. But did you know Mary Yard was a munitions worker in the Great War? She was interested when I said one of the Bristol factories is stepping up production of aeroplane parts. Old ladies are never just old ladies, Immy. They would appreciate a chat with a bright young girl like you."

She sighed. "All right, then, if you think I should. I dare say I'm too wound up to sleep yet, anyway."

She hadn't had much to do with the Marys; why should she? They were just the upstairs tenants. Elsie had spent some time with them, though, and they weren't really old; they just seemed it. But half an hour wouldn't hurt . . .

A couple of hours later, after several cups of tea, she was still mesmerised by the tales the two of them had to tell. Their neat sitting-room was full of old-fashioned knick-knacks and potted plants, and she had looked through a dozen photograph albums. They were stuffed with sepia photos of young men in unfamiliar uniforms, newspaper cuttings about daring deeds and formal occasions, and more sombre ones too.

"This was my Harry," Mary Yard said in matter-of-fact tones, pointing to a handsome young man in a captain's uniform. "He was killed in the last push of the war, so we were never able to celebrate victory together. Mary's husband went even earlier."

"During Passchendaele." Mary Baxter nodded. Her sad eyes took on a faraway look. "Ever so handsome, he was. We'd only been married a month before he went. We wanted babies so badly, but we never got the chance to have them. We even named our boy. Raymond would have been twenty-three or four now."

"And just right for signing up for this next lot," Mary Yard, the more cynical of the pair, said.

"You think it's inevitable, then?" Immy said quickly.

"No doubt, my dear. Let's just hope there aren't as many widows left this time as there were in our day. Nor so many young lives wasted. Where are all those beautiful young men now? Just white crosses in a graveyard – and those are the lucky ones, leaving something behind to grieve over."

The other Mary chipped in. "Oh yes. There were thousands who didn't get any grave at all. Just blown away to dust as if they were nothing. It makes you wonder what it's all about, doesn't it? Is that what you're born for? To grow up and fall in love and then get cut down in your prime? Sometimes it's hard to equate all that with a loving God."

"But you still go to church every Sunday," Immy reminded her, guiltily knowing that she only went on occasion.

"Of course," Mary Yard said in surprise, as if there could be any doubt. "If you don't believe in something, what have you got left?"

"Anyway, dear," Mary Baxter went on, "my advice is that if you've got a young man and you love him, then you should marry him and make the most of him. I told your sister the same thing. Enjoy every day, because it will never come again."

"My goodness, all this is getting too solemn for me," Immy said. She spoke gently, however; she could see that these two sweet-faced ladies meant every word they said, and no doubt Elsie would have taken them very seriously.

Mary Yard laughed. "Oh, you young things only think about your careers these days. But we did it right, didn't we, Mary? We were both quite a bit older than you when we married, and we cherish every day we had with our sweethearts."

And now all they have is memories, Immy thought as she went back to her own room. Neither of the ladies had remarried, though presumably they could have done.

As she undressed for bed, Immy couldn't get the conversation out of her mind. It had really touched her soul, she realised. In an unlikely fashion, it was if she had suddenly received a deep understanding of something very fundamental.

She had recognised that what those two faded ladies had known was real love. *Real* love, not shabby fumbling on a hillside or in a motor car. Not the kind you saw portrayed at the pictures, all glossy and fake. Real love. The kind that neither she nor Helen yet knew. The kind of love Elsie had with Joe.

Daisy Caldwell knew she had found her vocation at last. In the hospital some of the patients and proper nurses had begun calling her "Daisy-Daisy" after the silly song.

She didn't mind. She was the youngest auxiliary on the wards, and the patients said it made them feel better just looking at her, because she was bright and cheerful and pretty. She hadn't been asked to do anything *too* nasty yet, she admitted, but if she had to, she was sure she could cope. She wanted to be a nurse, and a good one.

She was trying really hard to persuade Lucy to join her. So far she had resisted, but Daisy knew she had a stronger personality than her friend and hoped to bring her round to the idea in time.

"You shouldn't try to coerce her, my love," Aunt Rose told her. "It takes a certain kind of person to be a nurse, and if Lucy doesn't have the stomach for it, it would be wrong to force her into it."

"I bet nobody said that in the Great War when you were all keen to do your bit, Aunt Rose," Daisy said slyly. "Didn't you help with the ambulance service?"

"Yes, but you and I are the same kind of people, Daisy. Strong-willed and willing to get on with things, no matter what we're asked to do. Whereas I'm not so sure about Lucy. She doesn't have a lot of stamina, and I've noticed she has that worrying cough all the time."

"She tends the horses when they're not well, and you have to be a bit tough on a farm. She's not as soft as she looks," Daisy defended her. She was more pleased at being compared with her forthright aunt than she let on, however.

"Oh, well," Rose said, laughing. "Perhaps she should be a vet instead of a doctor, then."

Daisy shuddered. "I've seen the vet at the farm, and I know I couldn't do some of the things he has to do."

"Then we won't think about them, and we certainly won't

talk about them," Rose said briskly, remembering the unpleasantness of George's recent worming problem.

"Agreed," Daisy said, perking up. "I'll see you later then, Aunt Rose. I promised to meet Lucy at the beach."

"Are you taking any of the boys with you?" Rose called out, but her niece had already gone, flying out of the house like the wind, her hair glowing in the sunlight, an absolute picture of health and glorious young womanhood, Rose thought fondly. And since such sentiments didn't often come to her practical mind, she yelled at the boys to stop making that racket this minute, or she'd box all their heads together.

But she was smiling as she said it, and she knew they didn't really believe her. Bertie had told them more than once that her bark was worse than her bite, and that she loved them all in her peculiar way. And so she did.

Whether the house rang with the sound of children's laughter, or squabbling, tears or tantrums, she was fulfilled in a way she never had been before. She was more than content, and she refused to look ahead to a time when it would all have to change. As they all knew it must.

Daisy caught sight of Lucy sitting forlornly on the sea wall overlooking the wide sweep of sand that made up Weston Bay. The sea was its usual distant glimmer on the horizon, with the hazy view of Wales across the Channel, and unless you were fated to catch sight of the tide, or studied the posted details of the times it appeared, you sometimes marvelled that it ever came in twice a day to wash the sand clean at all. The fact that boats were beached haphazardly and mournfully on the mud at the Knightstone end of the bay were the only reminders that any craft ever rode majestically on a full tide.

"Why are you looking so glum?" Daisy demanded, the minute she joined her friend. "You look really pasty today, Lucy. Honestly, you could brighten yourself up a bit. You look as if you've lost a sixpence and found a penny."

"You'd be miserable if you felt like I did."

"How *do* you feel, then? You're not ill, are you? Shall I practise my nursing skills and save you?"

She was laughing, teasing her friend as she so often did, but to her horror she saw Lucy's eyes well up.

"My mother made me go to the doctor about my cough, and I have to see a special man for a second opinion."

"A second opinion about what?"

Her heart beat faster as she saw Lucy's lips tremble. With her new-found knowledge – even though it amounted to little more than snippets gleaned from the nurses at the hospital and from Aunt Rose's medical books – Daisy knew darned well that a second opinion meant something serious was suspected.

"You'd better not touch me or come too close," Lucy said abruptly. "Not until we know for sure. They say it's catching. I'm not sure if horses can catch it, though."

"Lucy, for goodness' sake, tell me what's wrong! You're scaring me now."

"It might be TB. Consumption. Whatever they call it. Don't know yet."

Her voice was jerky with fear. And to her shame, Daisy felt herself edge slightly away from her. But she knew enough to know that Lucy was right. TB – consumption – whatever name you put on it – was highly infectious. It took forever to cure, and the only treatment was rest and sunlight and cold air and taking life easy in a sanitorium for months at least.

There would be no nursing career, no horse riding, nothing but rest and boredom for a sixteen-year-old.

"Lucy, I don't know what to say. I'm knocked sideways."

"What is there to say? Anyway, we don't know for sure yet. Might be nothing. But let's keep well apart for now, right?"

Her eyes were steadier now, huge in her pale face, daring Daisy to mock her this time, to pooh-pooh the thought that anything could be really wrong with her. Wanting Daisy to give her the dignity she deserved.

"Right," Daisy said. "Just until we know for sure."

"Ben brought me here in the truck today," she went on. "I didn't feel up to riding my bike. He had to see somebody in town, and he'll be collecting me in a while. I'm sorry, Daisy. I didn't want to come out at all really, but I couldn't tell you on the phone, either. It wouldn't have seemed right."

"No. It wouldn't."

All of a sudden there seemed to be a great distance yawning

between them. Not so much physically, despite the self-imposed few feet between them, but the distance that illness made. It separated people.

Daisy knew that from her own mother. She knew it from the hospital visitors who came to see their nearest and dearest and couldn't think of anything to say except the most trivial and trite words. Illness prevented people opening their hearts, at a time when they most needed to.

There was a small, embarrassed silence, and they both turned with relief as Ben tooted at them. Lucy stood up and brushed down her skirt.

"I'd better go. I'll ring you as soon as I hear any news. Or you can ring me. You can't catch anything over the phone – at least, I don't think so," she added, scared and uncertain of what might be happening to her, and the effect it would have on every single thing in her life from now on.

"Of course I'll phone you," Daisy said roughly. "And I'll find out everything I can about you-know-what, just in case. But I'm sure it'll turn out to be nothing, and we'll be laughing about it very soon."

And without a second thought, she pulled Lucy to her and hugged her close. No damned disease was going to make her turn her back on her best friend, she thought fiercely.

She sat on the sea wall for a long while after Ben and Lucy had gone, still shocked by what she had heard. She was in no state to go back to Aunt Rose's yet. She just sat, breathing in the salty air, absorbing the carefree sounds of high summer like a sponge, and registering none of it. Not the visitors, nor the donkey rides, the beach games, the ice-cream vendors, the swooping, screaming gulls or the flurries of sand that blurred the eyes. And it wasn't only the sand that stung so painfully.

Eventually, she began to walk aimlessly along the beach, needing to clear her head and try to make sense of it all. Lucy had always seemed so active, if a little on the puny side compared to her robust family with their traditional farmers' rosy cheeks. That delicacy of skin had been something to envy, though, not to think of as ominous.

"Somebody seems to be lost in dreamland," she heard a voice say teasingly. She realised she had been walking with her head down, and had almost barged into someone.

Someone large and lean, with laughing brown eyes and a wide smile. Someone wearing a checked, open-necked shirt and casual trousers who stood squarely in front of her now.

"Excuse me. I'm sorry," she mumbled, but as she went to move sideways, so did he. He blocked her path, and she glared at him irritably. She wasn't in the mood to exchange pleasantries, even with a young man who would certainly have caught her attention at any other time.

"Where's the fire?" he asked.

"*Excuse* me?" she said again, more haughtily this time.

"Haven't I seen you somewhere before?"

Daisy sighed. She had been to the pictures often enough to know that this was a line that actors employed. She didn't think this one was an actor, of course – he didn't have that starry, unreachable look. He just had a nice face.

"I doubt it. Will you let me pass, please?"

"I know where it was. You and that other girl have been watching us through the perimeter fence a couple of times. It's a devil when you can't remember something, isn't it? I'm Callum, by the way. Cal to my friends."

Daisy automatically took the hand he was holding out to her. As she did so, she got the most extraordinary feeling. She would have liked to report to Lucy that it was love at first sight, and that a tingling sensation ran right through her entire body, the way the love stories told you it would.

What she actually felt was a sense of horror that she was touching this young man with the hand that had recently touched Lucy's. If she had caught something from her friend, she was probably passing it on to him.

She shook off the feeling blindly, but she couldn't stop trembling, and her knees threatened to buckle beneath her.

"Here, are you all right? You look as if you're going to pass out. I don't usually have such an effect on people," she heard Callum – Cal – say in concern. "Sit down on the sand for a minute. I can call someone if you like. There's always ambulance people around somewhere."

"I don't need anybody. I'm all right," Daisy muttered, but she did as she was told and sat down abruptly on the warm sand. He sat beside her, rubbing her hands between his, as if she was chilled and needed her blood warmed.

"What are you, a bloody doctor or something?" she snapped, immediately appalled at saying such a thing. "Letting yourself down," she could almost hear Aunt Rose say.

Cal smiled. "Hardly. Just an RAF erk."

"A what?"

"The lowest of the low, in RAF parlance. Just starting my training at Locking Camp."

It all became clear now. He probably hadn't been stringing her a line at all. He must have seen her and Lucy looking over the fence and watching the RAF boys going through their paces. It was easier for them to place two girls than for the girls to recognise any of the large group of young men.

"I'm sorry I was so rude just now," she said humbly. "I'd just heard a bit of worrying news, and I was trying to get used to it."

"That's all right. About you being rude, I mean. Not about the worrying news. Bad luck. Want to tell me about it? It sometimes helps."

"Certainly not. It's private."

What was she doing here, sitting on the sands with a young man when they hadn't been properly introduced, and he didn't even know her name? She groaned inside at the primness of her own thoughts, but her head was still in a total muddle. Some nurse she would be, if Lucy's news threw her into such panic . . . but nurses dealt mostly with strangers, not best friends, and that made a difference.

"How about an ice-cream, then? Or a donkey ride? Or we could always paddle in the mud. Weston's famous for it, I understand."

God, he was persistent! She started to smile, despite herself, and he looked relieved.

"That's better. What's your name, by the way?"

"Daisy," she said, without thinking, before she could start to wonder why the dickens she should tell him.

"So, Daisy, give me your answer, do," he said. "I think an ice-cream's favourite, isn't it?"

"Don't you ever take no for an answer?"

"No," he said, and they both started to laugh as if he had said something excruciatingly funny.

"All right. Just an ice-cream, then."

After all, she thought, watching him go off to one of the vendors, sitting on the sands eating an ice-cream with a nice young man would make no difference at all to the outcome of things. Not to Lucy's problem, or the prospect of a war, or whether she would make a good nurse.

It didn't mean she didn't concern herself with any of those things, but just for now, while she could, she was putting it all to the back of her mind.

Thirteen

D aisy wasn't going to tell anybody about Cal. Normally she would have confided in Lucy, but she didn't think that was wise until they knew what was happening. She certainly couldn't tell Aunt Rose, who would be scandalised to think she had virtually allowed herself to be "picked up", as they said.

Then again, she might not, Daisy mused, since Aunt Rose was more progressive in her thinking than many women her age. But she couldn't take the risk. Not when something as delicately fragile as a blossoming relationship with a young man was concerned. If it *was* a relationship.

She shivered at the very thought of the word. It sounded almost too decadent. And it wasn't really blossoming, either, she thought with brutal honesty. It was more like – well, more like *budding*. He'd only bought her an ice-cream, and he hadn't said anything about seeing her again. Only in the most casual way.

"We're going to be doing exercises on the promenade at the weekends," he'd said. "Hurdling and so on."

"I know. My friend told me."

"Maybe you'll be watching that too, then," he'd said with a grin. "I'll try not to make a fool of myself, tripping over my big feet."

"And I'll try not to laugh if I see you doing it."

And that had been that. It was hardly big-time passion, Daisy thought gloomily, her head stuffed full of Hollywood romances. He probably thought she was too young for it, anyway. He had joined up, so he was obviously older than her, probably eighteen or nineteen or more. He'd think she was still a child.

It was one more depressing thing to think about at the end of a depressing day, by which time she had studied her aunt's medical books to find out all she could about the disease that used to be called consumption, and was now known as TB. She supposed it was a mite less intimidating than its proper name of tuberculosis, but people still died of it.

She couldn't bear to think of Lucy dying. You never thought of young people dying. Dying was for older people, not for girls. Nor for boys who dressed up in uniforms and thought themselves men and went off to war – and that hadn't really occurred to her before, either.

Did she *really* want to be a nurse? The answer came with surprising ferocity. Yes, she damned well did. She might never be a Marie Curie or a Doctor-Foster-went-to-Gloucester, thank you very much, she thought childishly, but she wanted to care for people.

Her mother had enchanted and uplifted her audiences with her dancing, and it had taken time for Daisy to realise that she didn't want to do the same thing, and why.

There could only ever be one Frances Caldwell, and in Daisy's eyes no one could ever follow her. And whether or not it was egotistical, Daisy knew she couldn't bear to be a second-rate anything. Instead she would be a first-rate nurse. It was decided.

"They're really getting serious about evacuating folk out of the cities now, especially London," Bertie remarked a few weeks later, his head deep in his morning paper as usual. "From the sound of it, they'll be practically empty soon, and the countryside's population will have swelled by millions."

"It's just as well we got our little charmers while the going was good then, isn't it?" Rose said smartly. "We did well for ourselves, didn't we?"

She beamed fondly at Ronnie and Norman, busy scooping up their breakfast cereal as fast as they could in competition with Teddy. She knew she should scold them, but it did no harm, and there were worse things in life to contend with. Having heard the shocking news about poor little Lucy Luckwell being sent off to some sanitorium, a bit of leeway at breakfast seemed nothing to get het up about. Rose was just thankful that Daisy was taking it fairly well, even offering to exercise Lucy's horse for her, and writing to Lucy every week, since she wasn't allowed visitors outside the family for a while.

Daisy had made a point of finding out a lot more about

Lucy's illness. She knew about the regular temperature and sputum checks, the vast quantities of milk and eggs Lucy had to swallow, and the need for rest. She responded by sending her books and magazines to read, and writing her lots of letters.

Daisy was really showing what she was made of, Rose thought approvingly. Her mother would have been proud.

"I saw Cal again on Saturday afternoon," Daisy wrote in one of her letters to Lucy, unable to keep it to herself any longer.

> It's a shame you didn't meet him. Though perhaps I shouldn't be too sorry about that! He might have fancied you more than me. Not that I know if he fancies me or not.
>
> I wonder how you can tell. He waves to me if I see him over your fence when I'm taking Star out for exercise, but he can't make it so obvious when he's hurdling on the promenade. Too many people around. But that's the trouble. I never see him alone. But do I want to?
>
> It's a bit scary in a way, and I don't really know what I feel about him. My heart beats faster as soon as I see him, in a kind of sick way. I know that sounds odd, but I can't think of any other way to say it. I probably couldn't say it out loud at all, but it's much easier writing it all down and knowing you wouldn't tell anybody.
>
> I do miss you, Lucy, but at least I can write masses and masses to you and know that my secret's safe with you. That's a laugh, too, isn't it? It's not exactly much of a secret. Not exactly the *grand passion*, as they say. Oh well.

She ended with lots of kisses, knowing guiltily that until Lucy was better, they were safer on paper than on lips.

She didn't say how frustrating it all was, either, because that was a word that was somehow a little suspect, a little *risqué*. But it was how she felt. Frustrated. Even thinking it made her feel a little peculiar, the way it felt when you wanted something you couldn't have. Except she wasn't quite sure what it was she wanted.

* * *

Elsie Caldwell knew exactly what it was she wanted. There was nothing so heavenly as basking in the knowledge that you were in love, and that your beloved was every bit as much in love with you. It was the most magical feeling on earth, and made you feel expansive towards the whole world, wanting everyone to share in the euphoria it brought.

She didn't think her sister Imogen had felt it yet, and Daisy was too young. Immy's friend Helen was too bright and breezy and cynical to fall for a man, but she – Elsie Caldwell – was so in love she sometimes thought she would die from it. Except that of course she wouldn't.

Not unless Joe died with her and they could continue loving one another far above the clouds on some blissful, ethereal plane . . .

"I wish I could see inside your mind and see just what it is you're thinking about," Joe said lazily, as they lay on the grass in the park that Sunday afternoon. "Your eyes are half closed, and your mouth has gone all dreamy and relaxed in a half smile. It's also extremely kissable. If we weren't in a public place, I would do something about it right now."

Elsie opened her eyes at once, twisting her head to gaze up at him. The smile widened.

"I was just thinking how lucky we are. So many things had to happen to bring you here, Joe, to bring you into my life. When I think about how happiness depends on such a thread, and how different it might have been, it makes me shudder."

His hand closed over hers, warm and strong.

"Well, don't even think about it. Nor about the past. The future's what matters, yours and mine, and the fact that we'll always be together from now on."

"Will we?" she said, her heart giving a leap of pure joy. "You're sure of that, are you?"

"As sure as any of us can be, sweetheart."

He didn't want to spoil this lovely day by any talk of war, even though the moment it came – or possibly sooner – he would do the same as every other patriotic man did for his country. Only cowards or conscientious objectors would remain behind while the rest of them enlisted.

Elsie wasn't stupid, however, and as she sat up to look down at him, a grey cloud hovered over the edge of the sun, gilding it with a rare golden beauty only an artist could capture. For a moment the air went a shade cooler, and she shivered.

"I know what it is you're not saying, Joe, and I thank you for it. But we all read the newspapers and listen to the wireless – we can't help it at home, as my father has it on night and day – and we have to be realistic, don't we?"

"I'm afraid we do, darling," he said gently, his fingers lightly caressing her bare arm with feather-light strokes that curled her toes and thrilled her senses.

If he knew . . . if he only knew, thought Elsie achingly, how she longed for him to make love to her. Wicked though it was for a well-brought-up girl to think that way, – and dangerous too, in view of the possible consequences – she ached for him so much. She dreamed of it too, with no idea if those dreams were anything like reality.

She had never told him, or anyone. Once she had thought of telling Immy, when she fancied there might have been a spark of something between her and that Welsh fellow. But Immy had got all closed up lately, and spent all her spare time with Helen Church – or in talking to the Marys, surprisingly enough – rather than staying at home. And anyway, Elsie didn't want to share her dreams with anyone but Joe.

"If you have to join up" – she said it deliberately, facing the fear – "what will you do?"

"Army. Infantry, same as my father."

The fact that he said it so quickly, and so definitely, with unmistakable pride, told her far more than his actual words. She would never lose him to another woman, but she was going to lose him all the same, and to something far more lethal.

He sensed her mood at once, and pulled her down beside him, uncaring that other people might be glancing their way. Let them, Joe thought savagely. If all the world was supposed to love a lover, let them see true love.

"I want to ask you something, Elsie. War is coming – we both know that it must," he said. "I want to know before I have to leave you that you belong to me."

Elsie's heart throbbed wildly. She had so wanted to hear those words, wanted him to make love to her so badly . . . but when the moment came, could she do this? Could she really forsake all the principles she had ever learned, and could he really expect it of her?

Her mouth was dry as she tried to speak. She loved him so much, but she wasn't sure how she was going to answer him.

Joe's fingers stilled her lips.

"I'm not asking for an immediate answer, but I want you to marry me, Elsie," he said softly. "If I have to go away to war, I want to go knowing that we belong as man and wife."

"Oh, Joe," she croaked, ashamed of her doubts.

"We may not have known one another long, and I don't know what your father will think of this haste, but there could never be anyone else for me. If you feel the same, then I think we should get engaged right away."

He took his fingers away from her lips, and she stopped caring if the world was watching. She caught him to her, and pressed her cheek to his.

"Of course I'll marry you, Joe," she breathed. "I want nothing more than to be your wife."

He kissed her then, in full view of a small family taking a boat-ride on the lake. And nobody minded. It was summer, the dark shadow had already bypassed the sun, and war clouds hadn't yet filled the sky.

"I'll ask your father formally tonight," he promised. "And then I shall buy you the biggest diamond I can find."

"Or three smaller ones," she said. "I always liked the idea of three diamonds. It sounds silly, but it always makes me think of a family. Mother, father and baby. Or am I being too forward?" she said, going pink.

"You're delightful," Joe said, loving her.

They were totally taken aback by Quentin's reaction. Elsie had been so sure of her father's liking for Joe that she had begged to be allowed to come with him when he made the formal request for her hand.

How *very* formal that sounded, she thought, when he was asking for so much more than her hand. For all of her, body and soul, for the rest of their lives . . .

"Have you forgotten so soon, girl?" Quentin said angrily, looking past Joe to his daughter.

"Forgotten what?" she stammered, as red-faced as if she had been caught out in some childhood misdemeanour.

But she wasn't a child. She was a woman, and a man loved her and wanted to marry her. Her father had no right to diminish her like this. Enraged, she rushed on before Joe could say any more.

"You must have expected this, Daddy, and I don't understand you. I thought you'd be pleased. I thought you'd want me to be happy."

In the next instant she saw the anguish in his eyes, and she knew. She thought about how often he went quiet in the middle of an ordinary evening, going to his room and closing the door, from behind which would emanate the faint sounds of his gramophone playing one of Frances's favourite songs.

It was his way of keeping her alive, and keeping her close to him. She knew how difficult it was for him to express his grief, and how deeply that grief went.

Joe stood in silent embarrassment as she ran to her father and put her arms around him, whispering close to his cheek.

"Oh, Daddy, I'm sorry. It's because of Mother, isn't it?"

He almost shook her off, his voice harsh with pain.

"She's not been gone nine months yet, and you expect me to think of wedding celebrations already? Have you *no* respect for her memory? Besides, you're far too young. You don't know what you want out of life yet."

"Yes I do, Daddy. I want Joe. I'm lucky enough to have found a good man who loves me, and we want to be married. You and Mother set us a wonderful example, and we want to find the happiness that you had. Is that so terrible?"

This lovely day was turning out to be terrible, she thought. Somehow it was all going wrong, and she couldn't think what else to say – until Joe took up the cause.

"Mr Caldwell – Quentin – correct me if I'm speaking out of turn, but Elsie once said her aunt told her that you and your wife were married when she was about Elsie's age."

Quentin glowered angrily, but Joe went on relentlessly.

"It was wartime, and you desperately wanted to be together, and to feel that you belonged together. I believe Elsie's Aunt Rose said that the two of you thought it made you invincible,

172

despite all the horror that war brings. Knowing you belonged in the eyes of God and the law was a kind of talisman for you. It's exactly the same for Elsie and me."

Elsie held her breath, wondering if he had stepped too far over the line. Her father wouldn't like to be reminded of what some might consider to be sentimental weakness, nor that Aunt Rose had been talking out of turn and revealing heart-breakingly private and personal truths.

She found herself clinging to Joe's hand, her eyes pleading with her father to understand, to remember what it had been like for him and her mother.

His tormented look finally slackened, and he spoke in more measured tones.

"I suppose I'm being selfish, very blind, and very foolish. As for a future son-in-law, I couldn't wish for a better man for my daughter than you, Joe. In normal circumstances I would insist that you have a long engagement to get to know one another properly. But these are not normal times, any more than they were in 1914."

As he paused, his voice faltering, Joe spoke firmly.

"Then does this mean we have your blessing, sir? I love Elsie with all my heart, and I'll never let her down."

"If I thought that, I'd do the Germans' work for you," Quentin said with grim humour.

"*So*, Daddy?" Elsie said, unable to bear any more of this hedging. *Men* . . . why didn't they just get on with it? It only needed one word . . .

"Patience, girl," her father answered with a small smile, then held out his hand to Joe. "Yes. You have my blessing."

Elsie gave a cry of pure delight and threw herself into his arms, and the three of them stood close together for a moment, arms entwined, one unit.

"It was awful for a while. I thought Daddy was going to have a blue fit!" Elsie told Immy excitedly, a long while later. She couldn't sleep, and didn't intend to let anyone who would listen sleep either.

She sat on the foot of her sister's bed in her cotton night-gown, hugging her knees tight. With her excitedly glowing face scrubbed clean for bedtime, she looked about ten years old, Immy thought.

"I really thought Daddy was going to refuse. My heart was in my boots, until Joe reminded him of what Aunt Rose told us. He and Mother did marry young, and it *was* because of the war, so he didn't have a leg to stand on after that."

She sobered for a minute. "I did feel anxious for him, though, Immy. He looked quite stricken. But it couldn't have been that much of a shock for him, could it? He must have known how Joe and I feel about one another."

"Perhaps he realised he's about to lose you too, Elsie."

"What do you mean? I'm not going anywhere!"

"When you and Joe are married, you'll want a home of your own, won't you?"

"Well, of course, eventually. But I'm resigned to the fact that he'll be joining the army. He'll be away for most of the time until things get settled between Chamberlain and Hitler. So I shall carry on living here, and when Joe comes home on leave, we'll just share my room."

Her face flooded with colour at the thought, and her heart raced.

"That's what I mean, darling," Immy said softly. "Once you're married, you won't be Daddy's little girl any longer. He'll be losing you, even though you'll still be living here. Because you'll be living with Joe."

"It's a bit scary, isn't it? All *that*, I mean. You know, the intimate things. Even undressing . . . oh, I do love him madly, Immy, but I have no idea what to do, and Mother's not here to tell me."

"You could always ask Aunt Rose. She'd probably draw diagrams for you," Imogen said, starting to grin.

"I certainly could not!" Elsie hesitated. "You don't know any more than I do about it, I suppose?"

"Afraid not. Well, not *afraid*. But in answer to your unspoken question, no, I haven't experienced any of *that*."

After an awkward little pause, Elsie said: "I know what I'll do. I'll ask the Marys. They're both so nice, and I know they won't think I'm odd or forward or wicked or anything. I just want to get it *right*, you see. When the time comes, I don't want Joe to be sorry he married me."

Immy scrambled down the bed and gave her a hug.

"I think Joe will be very glad he married you, darling. He's a very lucky man."

Elsie shook her head, her eyes full of dreams.

"You're wrong, Immy. I'm the lucky one. I'm the luckiest girl on earth. And I'm going to bed now, or he'll be telling me off for being late at the shop tomorrow morning."

She laughed delightedly, blowing her sister a kiss as she left Immy's bedroom, knowing that even if she was late, it would simply be an excuse to go to Joe's office for a secret kiss before she started work for the day. She was sure of herself, and of him, and the future they were going to share, with the special kind of confidence that comes from being in love.

Immy envied that feeling. She thought she had known it once, but it had faded so quickly, she decided it hadn't really been love at all. At least, not the kind of love that would last a lifetime. It had been infatuation, and the thrill of being desired.

She moved restlessly in her bed, wishing she could find someone to love. No matter what happened in the months to come, Elsie would always have Joe coming home to her.

Unless the unthinkable happened, of course. A chill ran through her then, because people died in wartime. The Marys had both been as madly in love with their husbands as Elsie was with Joe, and they had both ended up as young widows.

Was it worth all the suffering afterwards? She asked herself the question seriously, and knew that it was. The Marys had told her that. They wouldn't have missed a moment with their husbands – and anyway, you couldn't foretell the future. You had to grasp happiness where it came, and good luck to Elsie and Joe. It was funny, though. She had always been so sure she would be the first to marry . . .

"So when's the big day to be?" Aunt Rose said over the telephone when Elsie had bubbled out the news the following evening. "I shall need a new hat, of course. You must design one for me, Elsie – if you've got the time, that is."

"I'll have plenty of time. We don't intend to rush into it immediately, Aunt Rose. We're going to buy an engagement ring next weekend, though, and Joe's taking me up to Yorkshire to meet his family. I know his uncle and cousin, of course, but

I have to meet his parents. I've already spoken to them on the phone when Joe told them the news, and they sounded really nice – when I could understand them!"

"Are they foreign or something?"

"No, of course not, but they do talk differently. Joe went to college and is educated, but they're country folk. Oh Lord, I hope that doesn't sound patronising. I don't mean it to!"

"I'm sure you don't, and I'm sure they'll love you, Elsie. So when's the big day?" she asked again.

"We haven't decided yet. Fairly soon, I think, but we haven't set the date yet."

"Elsie dear, if you need some advice of an intimate nature, you know you can come to me, don't you?" Rose offered delicately. "I think you know what I mean."

"It's all right, Aunt Rose, really. I have a book," Elsie explained, glad her aunt couldn't see her fiery cheeks. She hadn't intended the conversation to take this turn.

"Oh well, if you have a *book*, I suppose that's all right. I didn't know they printed such details nowadays, except in medical books, and I'm not sure I approve of it."

"Mrs Yard – Mary from upstairs – gave it to me earlier and explained a few things. It's all very proper. She was a nurse during the last war, and thought it might be useful."

"I see. Well, that's all right then."

Before her aunt became too ruffled at being usurped in her duty by one of the Marys, Elsie quickly changed the direction of the conversation.

It had been far less embarrassing talking to the Marys. They had been so frank, assuring her that the act of making love for the first time was not something to be afraid of. Nor should the details be kept secret and furtive, in their opinion. They were something every bride had a right to know.

"And it really won't hurt too much?" Elsie had asked apprehensively.

"If you love and trust one another, and your young man is gentle and takes his time, it will be no more than a momentary sting, my dear, and maybe not even that," Mary Yard had told her.

And yes, there *were* diagrams in the book the Marys had given her. It still seemed an awesome thing to happen, this transformation in a man's body that was the means of making love . . . of making babies. Elsie, who had never touched her own private parts, except when she was bathing, wondered how she would ever get over the embarrassment at having someone else touching her there . . . seeing her . . .

"It's the most natural thing in the world," Mary Baxter had said gently, seeing her eyes darken with fright. "If it wasn't for the act of love, none of us would be here, my dear. *You* wouldn't be here. Without the act of love between a man and a woman the world would have ended before it even began. You read your Bible, don't you?"

"Oh yes," said Elsie hastily, knowing she hadn't read it properly in quite a while. "And Mother always used to read the stories to us when we were small."

She had choked a little then, remembering Frances's sweet, melodious voice relating the stories of Adam and Eve, and Moses, and of Jesus dying for them all. Magical stories that were fact and fable all rolled into one.

The other Mary added her own common-sense finale.

"As long as there's love and trust between you both, it will be as wonderful as you want it to be."

"I know we have that. And you don't think I'm too forward for asking you both such things?" she said anxiously.

"You're a very sensible girl," they assured her.

Fourteen

Sunday was the day that Baz made his duty visit home, and on the same day Joe arrived for a leisurely afternoon in the garden with his new fiancée, her sister and father. It was a gorgeously warm day, and even the Marys from upstairs had descended into the garden at Quentin's invitation.

Cook had made a fresh batch of lemonade and biscuits for the weekend, and Immy was in the act of fetching them from the kitchen – and wondering, idly and impossibly, if her father was taking more than a friendly interest in Mary Yard – when the front door bell rang.

She ran to answer it, throwing open the door, prepared to berate Baz for not coming to the back entrance as he always did.

"Have you lost your sense of direction since leaving home, you goose?" she said gaily, the words out of her mouth before she realised it wasn't her brother standing there at all, but two strangers.

At least, the dumpy little woman with the straggly grey hair and troubled eyes was a stranger. The other was a man she had seen before. He was weather-beaten, and obviously felt awkward at dressing up for Sunday. His collar was almost choking him and his hands were gnarled with half the knuckles split. The ferryman.

"It's Mr Bray, isn't it?" Immy said quickly, a sense of foreboding almost knocking her sideways. "Enoch Bray."

"That's right, Miss," he said, almost humbly. "And this is my old lady, Sarah Bray."

The woman nodded, as if too afraid to smile. The small, cramped house at the waterfront where Baz lived with these two was really little more than a hovel, so presumably the tall house in Vicarage Street was somewhat intimidating.

It was all relative, ofcourse, but the thoughts kept spinning around Immy's brain as if they were in a whirlpool. And everybody knew how awhirlpool could suck you down . . .

"What's happened? It's Baz, isn't it? Is he ill?"

Or worse . . .

"Oh, no, miss, he's not ill," Sarah Bray said at once, her old head nodding and bobbing as if to deny the words she said. How odd, thought Immy. It should be shaking fit to burst, to reassure her, and it was doing the exact opposite.

She gathered her stupid senses together, wondering why on earth she was analysing their behaviour at such a time. But she didn't have to wonder. She knew exactly why. It was to put off the moment . . .

"I'm forgetting my manners. Please come inside and tell me why you're here," she said. "It's far too hot to be standing on the doorstep."

Especially in those stuffy clothes. Indeed, there were beads of perspiration as big as mothballs on their foreheads. Immy was thankful they hadn't wanted to shake her hand, feeling the clamminess on her palms as if they had actually done so.

"Come on, Sarah," Enoch urged, as the woman hung back. "Miss Caldwell won't eat you, and it has to be done."

For pity's sake! Immy almost screamed as she ushered the two of them inside.

"Now, tell me what it is you've come to say," she ordered, as she closed the front door.

Her heart thudded uncomfortably. She didn't even offer them a seat. First things first. *Important* things first.

From the back garden she could hear the faint sounds of chatter and laughter, and her heart as well as her head told her it was a scene that was about to be shattered.

"He left this letter for us, and another one that we was to bring to your father, miss. We didn't know nothing until we got up this morning and found he'd gone. It was a terrible shock, and Sarah's still not over it. She were very fond of the boy, see, and allus treated him like her own."

The indignation in his voice was too much for Immy. Baz *wasn't* their own. He belonged to the Caldwells, and she couldn't forget that she had been the one to urge her father to let him go. It had been the price for Baz's silence over her half-baked love affair with Morgan.

She snatched the letter out of Enoch Bray's hand. His letter. She needed to see that first. Her father had to be the one to open his.

She recognised Baz's scrawling handwriting and careless spelling. He'd never been much of a scholar . . . as if any of that mattered now! She was furious at her own pathetic attention to detail.

"Dear Enoch and Sarah," Baz had written.

> By the time you get this, I'll be gone. I've bin taken on as cabin boy on a trawler, leaving early Sunday morning. I just want to thank you for all you did for me. Please give the other letter to my father and ask him not to think to badly of me. You've both been good freinds to me. Yours faithfully, Baz Caldwell.

Immy looked up at the sound of Sarah Bray's snivelling.

"That's not going to do any good, is it?" she snapped. "I'm sorry, but you have no idea what this is going to do to my father. How *could* you have let him do this?"

"You can't blame us, miss!" Enoch railed back as Sarah snivelled louder. "The boy had a mind of his own, and sure as God made apples he was never meant to be a shopkeeper."

"So you thought you could do better for him by filling his head with tales of adventure at sea? For what? So he could go to sea on a stinking trawler ship!"

"What the devil's going on in here?"

They all heard Quentin's voice at the same time, and Immy spun around to see her father filling the rear doorway. Against the bright sunlight outside he looked large and menacing, and Mrs Bray gasped and clung to her husband.

Immy's stomach was knotted now, and she could have bitten out her tongue for her viciousness. It wasn't Sarah's fault.

"Come into the sitting-room, please, where we can all discuss this more sensibly," she said quickly, taking charge before her father could get another word in.

"Would someone tell me what's going on?" Quentin thundered as he followed them, not at all pleased at having his Sunday afternoon disrupted. "Who are these people, Imogen? And where's Baz?"

"I don't want to sit like comp'ny, beggin' your pardon," Sarah mumbled. "I want to go home."

"So you will, my duck," Enoch told her roughly. "Just as soon as we do what we came here for."

"And that is?" Quentin snapped.

"Father, I think you should hear what Mr Bray has got to say. There's a letter for you from Baz."

"A *letter*? What's all this? Has the boy got literary aspirations now?" Quentin was full of sarcasm.

He took the letter silently and ripped it open, and then his face darkened. He didn't say anything for a few moments, which was worse than if he'd exploded with rage. Then he turned on the unfortunate Brays.

"Did you know about this? Have you been hatching up this scheme with my boy all this time?"

"I have not, sir!" Enoch shouted back. "'Tis as much of a shock to me and my old lady as 'tis to you, and she's fair shook up about it. She loved that boy."

"And so did I," Quentin rasped.

Sarah Bray spoke up hoarsely. "The sea was his life, Mr Caldwell, sir, and everybody knew that. There was never no holding him, not when his heart was so set on it."

She stumbled over the words awkwardly, unused to voicing her feelings. But the statement was eloquent enough.

"We have to accept that, Father," Immy said quietly. "This had to come someday."

"But not yet. He's only a boy. Only fifteen. He's still a child." He drew a deep breath, aware that he was in danger of showing how raw his feelings were to these two. And it wasn't done. Even now, in the midst of his heartbreak at what he saw as losing another of his children, he remembered his dignity.

"This has been a shock, Mr Bray," he said harshly. "But I've always been a fair man, and I know my son was doing a job he favoured. He's done wrong to leave like this, but I cast no blame at your door."

"Thank you, sir," Enoch said in obvious relief. "Then we'll be off. 'Tis a pity, though. He were a good 'un, and I'll have to be looking round for another ferry-lad now."

Immy ushered them out quickly before her father could

throw a fit at such crass insensitivity. From his set face, she knew his sarcastic tone hid his true feelings.

"Oh well, that puts it all into perspective, doesn't it? I've lost a son and he's lost a ferry-lad."

"You haven't lost Baz," she said, putting her arms around him. "You'll never lose any of us."

"No? Think about it, Imogen. Daisy and Teddy are settled in Weston with your aunt and uncle. Elsie – well, she may still live here for a time, but she'll be closer to Joe than any of us now, and rightly so, of course. And now Baz."

"And then there was one," Immy said, echoing his thoughts. "You've still got me, Daddy."

"Thank God for that," he said, his arms tense around her.

Her eyes were blurred and troubled, however. Because what did that make her? The last one at home. The spinster daughter, dutifully staying at home to care for a widowed father, the last relic of a time long past . . .

She shook off the feeling, knowing it was unworthy. Besides, her father wasn't old. He wasn't yet fifty, and although she was quite sure he wouldn't entertain the idea just now – and neither would any of his children – the day might come when he would even consider marrying again.

"Do you think you're up to telling the others what's happened yet, Father?" she said, before her thoughts travelled too far along that uneasy road.

"I suppose it has to be done. I still can't condone the boy's actions for going off like that, but—"

"But would you have agreed if he'd come to you and suggested it?" she said shrewdly. "It's not exactly running away. You must admit that he's shown a lot of backbone."

"I do admit it," Quentin said. "Perhaps I've got too stuffy in my old age to remember what a spirit of adventure is like. We had it in abundance in the last war, and folk have become spineless since then."

"Whatever you are, Daddy, you're not old!"

Immy refused to even think about war making men out of boys.

Later, when the telling was done, and the outrage had been dealt with, it became obvious that the Marys didn't think Quentin was old, either. But then, they were all of a similar age. They had gone through a war, not together, but with similar experiences. And they had all known bereavement.

While Elsie was indignant over the sneaky way Baz had done this, and Joe was pointing out that it could be worse because Baz was alive and happy, doing something he had always wanted to do, the Marys were sympathising with Quentin, and putting the smile back on his face.

There was something to be said for the companionship of like-minded people, Immy thought. She resolved to invite them downstairs more often. It wasn't that they had shut them away or that the Marys had chosen voluntary isolation, like forgotten pictures in the attic . . . but they just hadn't socialised much.

Until now.

And if they ever had to share the intimacy of the air-raid shelter that stood like a sentinel at the bottom of the garden and was now tastefully covered with earth and plants, all discreetly held in place with chicken wire, then perhaps they should all get better acquainted.

Daisy was also thinking about new acquaintances. The news that her sister Elsie had just got engaged had filled her romantic heart with all sorts of thoughts. She had told Lucy about it in her last letter. Lucy was now allowed to write back, and they exchanged the kind of secrets in letters that you couldn't seem to say face to face, even with your dearest friend.

Daisy, of course, had now discovered enough about life to know a bit more than most girls her age. Some of her new friends at the hospital had told her plenty, and it was a nurse's duty to know everything, she told Lucy loftily.

"I wonder if they've done it," she wrote.

> I can't imagine our Elsie getting all hot and bothered, somehow, but Joe's nice enough to persuade her. What do you think? If they're going to get married quite soon, do you think she'd go to hell if they did it beforehand?

"You're a wicked person to even think of such a thing, Daisy Caldwell," Lucy wrote back.

> But if it was me, and he was as nice as you say, I might. Only *might*, mind you.

183

I've never met anyone like that, and I'm not likely to while I'm stuck in here. By the way, they say I'm progressing nicely, whatever that means. I miss you. Why aren't you telling me more about this Cal person? Would he get you all hot and bothered, do you think?

Daisy laughed at that. Their letters were of the grasshopper variety, jumping from one topic to another in random fashion, as cosy as if they were sitting beside one another. It was just as well, though, that nobody saw the letters but themselves.

She reflected on Cal a bit more. Would he get her hot and bothered? Did he do that already? He certainly made her heart go pit-a-pat whenever she saw him, but she didn't feel the storming surge of passion that some of the older nurses told her about, teasing her and calling her Miss Greenery.

Thinking about *that* made her heart beat faster. Passion was another of those lovely words you never used, but which apparently was important when you were in love.

Daisy sighed. Obviously she wasn't in love yet. Or if she was, it was only growing very slowly. Perhaps it would help if she could meet Cal alone, but so far it hadn't happened. It was such a long-distance affair that it wasn't an affair at all.

"There's someone asking for you, Daisy-Daisy," one of the older nurses said on Friday afternoon, at the end of her working day. "I think you've been holding out on us!"

"Asking for me?" Her thoughts went at once to her family. Something had happened to her father. Or Baz had been hauled back to Bristol. Or Immy had had an accident . . . or Elsie . . . or *Teddy* . . .

"Come on, you dark horse," the nurse teased her. "I know what a young man's after when he's got a certain light in his eyes. *And* looking all slick and Brylcreemed, too."

Daisy's face flooded with colour. Cal. It had to be Cal. But coming here, to the hospital where she worked, especially to see her! To ask for her! If her heart wasn't thudding fast enough to start up a steam engine now, she didn't know what would.

"Bye, Winnie," she said in a stifled voice, racing out of the hospital with the nurse's laughter following her.

He was there. Standing by the stone wall alongside the pavement and looking somehow brash and sheepish at the same time. She stopped racing when she saw him, and tried to behave like a young lady should.

"I guessed it was you," she said inanely.

"Did you? I didn't know whether you might have thought it was someone else."

"No; why should I?" She wondered frantically where the easy rapport between them had gone. They'd had no trouble conversing on the beach when he'd bought her an ice-cream that first day, so why did it seem as if they were oceans apart, even though there was only a couple of feet between them?

"I thought you might have some other caller."

It was such a quaintly old-fashioned way of putting it that an intuition worthy of someone older than herself flashed through Daisy. He was just as nervous as she was. Boys got nervous, too. Even boys who usually dressed in men's uniforms and played at being soldiers or pilots. She could see it from the small twitch at the side of his mouth. And he was here without the prop of that uniform or the regulation sports outfit and the support of his fellow erks . . .

"I don't have any callers at all," she said, smiling sweetly. "Anyway, I'm not sure my aunt and uncle would want me to have one, unless we had been properly introduced. Or unless I asked a certain person home with me for them to look over."

"And would you ever feel like asking a certain person home for them to look over?" he said, his face relaxing into a half-nervous smile.

Daisy felt her heart sing. She had flirted harmlessly with customers at her father's shop, but it hadn't meant a thing. Her sisters had called her a silly girl and indulged her for it. But this was different.

This was teasing in a far more delightful way, a kind of hedging around one another because they both wanted to see one another again. It was obvious, or why would Cal have come here especially?

"Well, I might," she said. "What do you think?"

"I think you should. I definitely think you should get your aunt and uncle's approval, otherwise how could a certain person ever ask a certain young lady to go to the pictures with him one evening?"

Fifteen

Teddy loved talking on the telephone. He loved it when Aunt Rose handed it over to him, and he could talk to his sister Immy just as if she was in the room. He especially loved it when she promised to come and see him sometime soon, and said that she might take him out in their Daddy's car.

"You and the other little boys," Immy said generously, praying than none of them would feel ill. "And Daisy, of course, if she wants to come."

"Our Daisy won't come. She'll be out with her boy," Teddy said importantly.

Imogen stared at the wall above the telephone for a few seconds, thinking it really was time they changed the cabbage-rose wallpaper that was fading in the sunlight. Pausing before she answered, so that she could organise her thoughts properly before she asked.

"What boy, Teddy?"

She heard her small brother snigger. "The one who's going to fly an aeroplane. He's called Cal, and he came here with our Daisy the other day, and Aunt Rose gave him some tea, and said they could go to the pictures together."

"Oh, *did* she?"

Imogen couldn't decide whether she was more annoyed that she didn't know anything about this, or astonished that Daisy was actually walking out with a boy. At her age. A whole three years younger than Immy herself!

"Teddy, let me talk to Aunt Rose again, please," she said imperiously.

"But I want to tell you about George and the hedgehog," he howled at once.

"I don't want to hear about George and the hedgehog. I want to speak to Aunt Rose."

186

"I don't like you any more," he said, sulking.

"I'll hear all about it another time, poppet. I promise. Now, will you *please* let me speak to Aunt Rose!"

She was trying hard to hold on to her patience when she heard her aunt's laughing voice on the phone.

"He's a card, isn't he, Immy?"

"Oh yes. Now then, Aunt Rose, what's all this about Daisy seeing a boy?" Immy asked, forestalling a long discussion of Teddy's antics. "Do we know him?"

"My goodness, dear, you do sound like a headmistress! He's a very nice young man serving as a cadet with the Royal Air Force at Locking Camp, and of course we know him."

She was liberal with the truth, and saw no reason to reveal that Daisy had met him first – she had got the full facts out of her niece now. But she also prided herself on being a shrewd judge of character, and she would certainly vouch for Air Cadet Callum Monks.

"And you've agreed to them going to the pictures?"

She bit her lip at her aunt's continuing hoot, beginning to realise that she did indeed sound like a headmistress, or a disapproving spinster aunt. It wasn't a comparison that charmed her.

"Immy dear, don't take on so. Daisy is a very well-adjusted young girl, and I promise you neither your uncle nor I have any qualms about the propriety of the invitation. Cal will bring her home afterwards and stay for some supper before going back to camp. It's all perfectly proper."

As the voice became a little sharper, Immy realised she was in danger of offending her aunt and questioning her ability to look after Daisy at all.

"I'm sorry, Aunt Rose. I never doubted you for a minute. It was just a bit of a surprise to hear Teddy blurt it out like that. I've been feeling a little over-protective since Baz went off," she invented wildly, "and wondering if I've been looking after the younger ones in the way Mother would have expected."

She closed her eyes, knowing guiltily that she had been thinking of no such thing, and glad there was no one else in the house to hear such a glib and shameful reply.

"I understand, my love, but you needn't worry on that score. Your mother would be proud of all of you," Rose said more gently. "And you're welcome to come here any time to talk to

Daisy about it – though I suggest you don't make it too obvious. She's always been high-spirited, but she's growing up now, and wouldn't take too kindly to it."

"Perhaps it would be a good idea if we all came down one weekend," Immy said at once. "It's ages since Father's been to Weston, and he and Mother always did love the seaside."

"You can come here whenever you like, darling. Our door is always open, you know that."

It was silly to let the news that Daisy was walking out with a young man affect her, or make her feel so restless, Immy thought as she replaced the receiver. And she knew that for all Aunt Rose's seemingly relaxed attitude, she would keep a very keen eye on Daisy and this Callum Monks who was going to fly aeroplanes.

She heard the sound of creaking floorboards above, and knew the Marys would be having afternoon tea, their ritual at four o'clock every afternoon. She knew she would be welcome to join them if she knocked at their door – and a few minutes later, without even knowing why, she found herself doing just that.

"Well, isn't this nice!" Mary Yard said, beaming. "We were just talking about your sister, Imogen dear, and wondering what we could buy her as a gift."

Immy looked blank, until she realised they were talking about Elsie and a wedding present.

"It's very sweet of you to think of buying her anything at all. I'm sure she won't expect it."

"Then it will be all the nicer for being unexpected, won't it? Now then, what little problem is creasing that lovely brow of yours?"

Mary Baxter poured them each a cup of tea, and the older women sat expectantly on either side of the fireplace – a bit like matching bookends, Immy thought irreverently.

"What makes you think I've got a problem of any size?" she asked, taking a sip of tea far too quickly, and wincing as it scalded her mouth.

Mary Yard laughed. "Oh, come now. When a pretty young lady prefers to spend her time with two old codgers like us on a lovely summer's afternoon, there has to be something afoot!"

"You're not old codgers!" Immy protested, pinking.

But it was true. They were always smartly dressed, their hair always immaculate, their fingernails buffed and neat. It was a shame neither of them had thought to marry again, but it said something for the depth of their feelings for their first loves.

Immy moved her thoughts quickly away from the unwelcome idea that downstairs was a widower who could do worse. She did *not* want to think of that.

"So what do you have on your mind, Imogen?" Mary Baxter prompted again.

"Have you ever been to Weston-super-Mare?" she said, not really knowing where the question came from.

"Once, a long time ago. We went on the train, didn't we, Mary?" she asked her friend. "It was such a happy day out, and we'd never seen such lovely golden sand."

The other woman nodded, her eyes unblinking.

"Is everyone well there, Imogen?"

"Oh yes, they're fine, evacuees and all. My sister Daisy's actually met a young man, and my aunt's agreed to let them go to the pictures together."

Oh God, she *did* sound like a headmistress or a disapproving spinster aunt now.

"Ah," said Mary Yard. "And you think you're being left behind, is that it?"

For a moment Immy was angry at the assumption, and then she had to admit that it was exactly how she felt.

As if such things mattered when the country was in such turmoil over the imminence of war, with an inept government seemingly powerless to stop it. Those matters should be the most important things in a patriot's life.

But they weren't. The two things were completely unrelated, and at this moment, politics were of no importance to a person who didn't know what life had in store for her any more. Whose life had once been so ordered and so settled, with a darling mother and a stalwart father, and a loving family all around her . . . and childhood not so far behind . . .

To her horror she found the cup shaking in her hands. The next minute it had been taken from her and she was being held in Mary Baxter's arms.

"Tell us what's really wrong, Imogen. We don't like to see you like this. It's so unlike you. You're usually so bright and cheerful. You are happy about Elsie's engagement, aren't you, dear?"

Immy gulped back the tears, feeling very foolish.

"Of course I am. I'm very fond of Joe, and I know they'll be happy – providing Mr Hitler lets them be," she added, crossing her fingers as she spoke the name, the way everyone did.

"And from what we've heard of your aunt, she'll keep a weather eye on Daisy," Mary Yard put in. "But my guess is that you feel a bit put out because they've both found a new interest, and you haven't. Isn't that it?"

"Perhaps it is," Immy said reluctantly, knowing darned well that it was. "Perhaps I'm just plain jealous – and that's silly, and a bit shameful, isn't it?"

"Of course not. It's perfectly natural. But what about that friend you were telling us about – she doesn't have a beau, does she? And goodness me, the two of you are still very young. What age are you both – nineteen?"

"Twenty. And no, Helen doesn't have a young man. But it doesn't concern her too much." Not after Robert Preston. . . .

"There you are, then. You take a leaf out of her book and make the most of your youth. Enjoy being carefree young girls together. There's plenty of time for falling in love."

"My parents were married very young, and so were both of you, weren't you?" Immy pointed out.

Immediately she wished she hadn't, as a shadow fell over both their faces. She felt she had been far too intrusive. But Mary Yard's quiet words suggested no offence had been taken.

"That was out of necessity, dear. We all had to snatch at happiness while we could in those days, because we never knew how long it would last."

In the sudden silence, the only sound was the ticking of the grandfather clock in the corner of the room, beating with monotonous regularity. All three of them were thinking the same thing. Time was rushing them towards the inevitable again, when no one knew how long happiness was going to last.

"I think I'll pay Helen a visit. I haven't seen her in a while, and she'll be tickled pink at Daisy's new pash," Immy said quickly. "I doubt it will last, anyway. They never do."

Much as she had felt that the Marys' apartment was a small refuge a short while ago, now she wanted to get out of there, feeling oddly stifled by the rich perfume of the potted plants and the onerous ticking of that darned clock. Ticking time away. Ticking life away . . .

She got out her bicycle and pedalled like fury towards the part of town where Helen lived. Earlier that afternoon, it had been lovely and sunny, but predictably for English weather, long before she reached the Church house the rain had pelted down.

She felt a straggly mess by the time she pressed their front door bell, but was prepared to put on a clownish grin, knowing Helen would see the funny side of her appearance. Shaking the drops from her hair, she pushed the bell again.

The door flew open and an irritated voice told her it only needed pushing once, not fifty times. And then the voice stopped, and its owner gaped at Immy.

"Good God, Imogen, you do look a sketch!"

"James!" she stammered. "What are you doing here?"

He started to laugh. "I live here, remember? For heaven's sake, come inside – but do try not to drip all over the Persian carpet, or my mother will have a blue fit."

"I thought you were away driving tanks or whatever it is you do," she said, feeling ridiculously disorientated and out of breath from battling against the elements. "And where's Helen?"

He caught her arm and pulled her inside. She felt incapable of moving, even though the rain was beginning to drive into the hallway. And she was indeed dripping. The rain clung in rivulets to her skin and her hair hung in rats' tails on her shoulders. Water ran off the hem of her frock, and her shoes were sodden. How could this all have happened in so short a time? She wondered, bemused.

"Are you all right? You look pretty seedy to me." His voice came swimmingly towards her.

She blinked. "I'm perfectly all right," she said crossly. She had no intention of swooning like some Victorian heroine when faced with a young man she had known all her life, even if he looked quite unlike himself now.

That was a thought that had no place in her head either. She asked quickly for a towel to rid herself of some of the drips.

"And where *is* Helen?" she asked again, as if it was of paramount importance.

"Helen and the parents are out, so you'll just have to make do with me. You'd better come up to the bathroom and dry yourself off properly, and then I'll make us some tea."

Her instinct was to ask him if he knew how, since she presumed the servants did it for him. Then she realised how ungracious that would be, when he was being so kind and understanding. But it also occurred to her that she was alone in the house with a very handsome young man, and her father certainly wouldn't approve, even knowing of James's integrity.

"Look, perhaps I'd better go," she said.

"Rot. You're in no state to be cycling home again, and just look at the way the rain's coming down now."

His eyes challenged her. "What's the matter, old thing? Don't you trust me? I assure you my intentions are honourable. Disgustingly and boringly so, if you must know. I'm not in the habit of seducing my sister's little friends."

Immy's face went scarlet. If he only knew how that bruised and wounded her. Not that she *wanted* him to seduce her, nor had she ever thought of him in that way, but to know that he only thought of her as his sister's "little friend" was the worst possible humiliation.

"You don't think of me as a scarlet woman, then?" she found herself saying through chattering teeth as he led her upstairs to the bathroom and offered her a selection of large fluffy towels. She was trying to be provocative but knew she had failed miserably. It was hard to flirt when you knew your hair was dripping and your frock was clinging to you everywhere it touched.

He laughed. "Good God, no. More as an old chum."

"Good. Then get out of here and let me try to repair the rain damage," she told him crisply. She could still hear him laughing as she shut the bathroom door and shot the bolt.

She sat on the edge of the bath, feeling all kinds of a fool for saying what she had. It was all thanks to Helen for saying James would marry her like a shot and that they could be sisters.

She jumped a few minutes later when she heard him tap on the bathroom door, and her heart pounded like a drum.

"In case you think you still look too disreputable for polite company, I suggest you put on the bathrobe behind the door and then go along to Helen's room to borrow one of her frocks. I'm sure she won't mind – and the tea will be brewed in ten minutes."

"Thank you," Immy croaked.

Thank God he couldn't read her mind. Thank God he hadn't realised that for one wild moment she had thought he might be going to make some seductive suggestion. And thank God he would never know that for an even smaller moment, she had toyed with the idea of what it would be like . . .

Ten minutes later, scrubbed and tidied, and wearing one of Helen's day frocks, she presented herself in the Church dining-room. She sipped the welcome cup of tea he had made – brewed to perfection, she told him airily.

Her hair was still damp, and as she gave an unavoidable sneeze, he offered to rub it dry for her.

"It's not necessary," she said hastily.

"Sit, and behave," he ordered, just as her mother used to when she was a child. Just as Teddy had begun ordering the boisterous George about, she thought, with the glimmer of laughter in her eyes.

But she sat and behaved, and James stood behind her and rubbed her long hair dry with a towel, raking it gently with his fingers until the natural waves returned, and sending unexpected waves of pleasure rushing through her.

She couldn't be sure, but as he lifted the weight of her hair off the nape of her neck, she thought she felt the touch of something far warmer than his fingers on her skin. But he couldn't have kissed her – could he?

Not an old chum like her. She must have been mistaken.

"Right, that will do. I'll fetch you a comb so you can make yourself look respectable again," he said abruptly. "The folks will be back soon, and they won't want to see you looking as if you've been pulled through a hedge."

"Thank you, James. You're a pal," Immy said sincerely. "You'll make some girl a great husband one of these days."

"I might, when she's ready to be asked," he said.

"You've met her, then?" she asked.

"I didn't say that."

"You didn't answer the question either," she pointed out, her spirits revived.

"That's because some questions are best left unanswered," he said enigmatically.

He left her to ponder on that and brought her back a comb,

but she only gave her hair token attention, knowing it would fall naturally into place anyway. She was far more interested in what he was saying – and what he *wasn't* saying.

"*So*? Have you met Miss Right?" she persisted.

He laughed. "Have you and Helen ever thought of starting one of those matrimonial agencies?"

"Certainly not. I think it's an awful idea."

But she was becoming more exhilarated by the minute now. It was always fun talking to one of the Churches. Few things got them down – disregarding the unfortunate affair with Robert Preston, of course. But James didn't know about that, and Helen seemed to have recovered fully.

"I hear your sister's become engaged," he said casually. "Nice fellow, is he?"

"Very nice. And you're avoiding the issue."

"My dear sweet Miss Caldwell, you must allow a gentleman some privacy regarding matters of the heart," he said teasingly.

She laughed with him, and caught her breath as she saw just what a very personable young man he really was. She had never considered it before. She idly considered it now . . . and then common sense rushed back, reminding her that if this was a reaction to her sisters' new attachments, it was in very poor taste.

"I think I'd better go," she said in some confusion. "The rain's stopped, and if you'll explain to Helen what's happened, I'll bundle my frock into a paper bag and bring hers back tomorrow. She'll be here then, I suppose?"

"She will, but I won't. I was only home on a forty-eight hour pass, and it's up tonight."

"Oh Lord, James, I haven't even asked you anything about your tank. What is it like?"

"Big, hot, noisy, smelly – and exciting," he answered.

"Well, at least that got some reaction!"

"I'll be able to tell you more when I've been in action in my Bertha," he said.

"Bertha? Does everyone have names for them?" she said, starting to laugh.

"God knows, but I do. It makes her more human, and we'll all be needing a bit of humanity when we take our killing machines into battle."

He was suddenly serious, and she didn't want him to be.

He was one of the frivolous Church siblings, whose family had money and position, and could always make her laugh. Fair-haired, handsome and a dear friend . . . and as if his words had given her a glimpse of some nameless horror, she had a wild urge to cling to him and wish him God speed.

She didn't, of course. Instead, she leaned towards him lightly, and pecked him on the cheek, the way old chums did.

"Well, I wish you happy times with your old tank, James, and I'll dream of sweeter things."

"And so will I," she thought she heard him say softly as she whirled out of the door.

She phoned Helen later that evening, with many apologies for borrowing her frock.

"Don't worry, old thing," Helen said, laughing. "James entertained us royally, describing the state you were in. I'm sorry I missed it. We had to go to a meeting of one of Mother's fund-raising committees, and Father came along to add weight. Anyway, you're invited to tea tomorrow, so you can tell me all the gossip then. We'll be in the doldrums, since James will have gone back to his regiment, so you can cheer us up."

"I'm not sure about that, but I'll do my best," Immy said, realising other people had worse troubles than she did. Well, hardly worse, but different, she amended.

Talk of war was getting really serious now, and young men of a certain age were becoming resigned to the fact that either that they were going to be conscripted, or would have to volunteer anyway. Patriotism was running high, and was likely to increase.

Immy was glad Baz was too young to even think about it, but she knew Elsie lived on a knife edge of anxiety, wondering if Joe would think it his duty to volunteer before waiting to be called up. Many of his peers did. It was a *man* thing, Daisy would have said dramatically.

It was Daisy that she wanted to talk to Helen about, but by the next afternoon the unworthy thoughts of jealousy had vanished, and she could laugh at herself.

"I felt like driving straight down there an... the young madam out," she told her, relaxing in... und – well, a little

"Honestly, Immy, you are sta...

elderly, darling!"

"Elderly?"

195

Helen wouldn't be deterred. "You know what Daisy's like. She's always flirted. It doesn't mean anything. And I'm quite sure your aunt has vetted the boy very carefully."

Immy was still smarting over the word "elderly" to take too much notice of her friend's reassurance.

"I'm not being *elderly*. I'm just concerned for my sister, and I think you of all people should know the dangers of flirting, Helen."

"That's really hitting below the belt, darling!"

"That's just what I mean – *darling*."

For a moment the tension between them was palpable, and then Helen's mouth broke into a grin, and she reached across and squeezed Immy's hand.

"I'm an idiot, aren't I? I dare say if I'd been the oldest in the family and had younger sisters instead of an older brother who's always looked after me, I'd be concerned too. But you really shouldn't take on the role of mother and saint all rolled into one, Immy. You should let go of them and remember that you have a life to live too."

Immy stared unseeingly down the length of the lovely garden, so heavily perfumed now that it almost stunned the senses, and wondered.

"I'm certainly no saint. Nor would I want to be."

"You're not their mother either – and I make no apology for reminding you of your darling Frances. I'll tell you what. Let's put a wager on who finds a young man first – and gets the first kiss."

Immy began to laugh. "Oh, yes? It's easy for you, going to all those functions with your parents and meeting eligible bachelors. What chance do I have, stuck in the office with the portly Kenneth Harris?"

"Well, you could always consider him, of course."

"What: old, fat and forty? I'd have to be desperate," Immy retorned with a giggle. She felt much revived by Helen's company.

"We'll treat. Oh, and a trip to the cinema as first prize. Winner's on relentlessly. the way, James doesn't count," Helen went

"What's that supp a leap for no reason at an mean?" Immy said, her heart giving

"In the wager. You can't count falling for James as a possibility, because it would be all too easy."

"Would it?"

"Of course. You know he's always had a thing for you, don't you? A pash. A crush. Whatever you like to call it. Only being James, of course, he'll never show it. He'll just pine in secret. But I know. Sisters always do."

She was laughing, but Immy suddenly felt upset. She didn't want to think of James pining away with a secret "pash" on her. It sounded so shallow. If it had to be anything at all, it had to be the real thing.

She wasn't sure that she wanted that either, though. He was like a brother to her, and it was incestuous to think of falling in love with your brother. It wasn't right.

"I think that's nonsense," she said crossly. "Anyway, nobody could look less like pining away than James. He's got the physique of an ox."

"You've noticed, then," Helen said archly.

There was something about her tone that made Immy suspicious. "I've noticed your little scheme! You're trying to put me off the most obvious in order to win your own wager! So who's your victim? There *is* someone, isn't there?"

"Maybe. Probably not. Well, Mother's organising a dance at the end of August to raise money for servicemen's comforts. We've been discussing it this weekend, and one of the men on the committee is rather nice, that's all."

She paused. "The trouble is, they all seem nice at first, don't they, Immy?"

Her voice faltered, and Immy knew she was remembering Robert Preston.

"They're not all the same, darling. I told you that before, didn't I?"

"You just remember that about Daisy's young man, then, and trust her to behave. She comes from good stock, anyway."

"Like a filly – and just as flighty," Immy said, and they began laughing again.

Sixteen

As July merged into August, Quentin received a second letter by post from his son. It outlined Baz's guilt and sorrow at upsetting his family by his departure, but assured them that he was well and thought of them all constantly.

Quentin had had to accept many things in his life – not least the traumatic death of his beloved wife, and the loss of the business he had so proudly built up. He had weathered it all with stoicism, and he wasn't going to let his son's misdeamour affect that resolve. He knew the only way to save face was to accept the fact that Baz had probably fulfilled his destiny, so he had decided to praise the boy's ingenuity and sense of adventure instead.

"I'm sure he's having a high old time by now, and good luck to him," he told his cronies at his club. "It takes a man's courage to recognise his destiny and do what the boy did. And naturally I blame myself for being short-sighted enough to ever think he could be a shopkeeper. No, Baz was always a seaman in the making."

The more he said the words, the more he made himself believe them. Whether or not his listeners believed them was another matter.

The Marys certainly did, or were canny enough to say so for the sake of his dignity.

"Another slice of seed cake, Mr Caldwell?" Mary Yard said, when he joined her at four o'clock on Saturday afternoon, alone for once since Mary Baxter was out visiting.

"I belie me Quentin will, Mary. And I'd be honoured if you would call and it seems youngsters don't stand on ceremony these days, likely we'll need for us to do so. Especially as it's more than the days to come." re the confines of the air-raid shelter in

"It looks very much that way, and I agree that there'll be little point in standing on formality then," Mary said quietly. "We remember the last time, don't we?"

"We do indeed," Quentin said grimly. "And none of us ever thought it would come again. What a cruel farce it was to call it the war to end all wars. That statement was the biggest invention in history! . . . I beg your pardon for getting so heated, Mary."

She put her hand over his. There was a pleasing scent of lavender about her, Quentin thought approvingly.

"There's no need to apologise. Evil men will always want what they can't have, and that includes trampling over other countries, no matter how many lives they take in the process."

"How perceptive you are," he said, patting her hand with his other one. "It's relaxing to talk to you, Mary."

Then, as if realising how close they were, he drew back at once, and saw her blush a delicate pink. She turned away and busied herself with pouring more tea.

At this rate, he'd be awash with it, he thought, but felt no inclination to go back downstairs yet. Everyone was out, and he was almost surprised to discover how much he enjoyed this easy and uncomplicated companionship. It was good to have a woman to talk to, other than his daughters.

"It's because we're of an age," Mary said gently, echoing his thoughts. "We don't share personal memories, but we do share memories of that other war, and it's natural to dread what will happen in the next one. We know what to expect."

"But do we? I don't think we have any idea of what's to come. I think this will be a very different war."

He hadn't meant to alarm her, but he saw her hands shake, and she spoke in a more impassioned way.

"However different it is, it comes down to the same in terms of human suffering. Mothers will lose their sons, and wives and sweethearts will lose their menfolk. Nothing can be more terrible than that. Women are always the losers in the end, no matter how great the victory."

Her trembling had become greater now, and she bowed her head so he wouldn't see the tears that were normally locked up inside, and weren't for public viewing.

"Mary, my dear, I didn't mean to upset you," Quentin said, embarrassed and appalled. He squeezed her hand again.

She said nothing for a moment, then raised her flushed face to his.

"You didn't, and I'm a foolish old woman to take on so."

"Whatever you are, you're not old," Quentin said, with a feeble attempt at gallantry. "I respect you for still having such feelings after all this time."

"Why wouldn't I? Once you love somebody, it's for life. You never lose those feelings, do you?"

"Of course not," he said, removing his hand and wondering if he had intruded too far upon a private grief.

His own feelings for Frances were as deep as ever, though he had long since admitted to himself that it had been years since she had been a proper wife to him. But her illness had claimed her faculties, and he had never blamed her for it, nor asked for anything different. He had been content to care for her as lovingly as he could – but a man was still a man for all that. There had been times when he had yearned to take her in his arms and feel her respond to his passion as she had done in the heady, early days of their marriage.

When he realised where his thoughts were going, he stood up awkwardly. He had been ensconced in this cosy atmosphere for too long, and far from comforting him, it had suddenly begun to stifle him.

"Time I made a move and watered the garden," he said.

"High time," Mary said steadily, and he knew very well she had followed his wayward thoughts just as clearly as if he had said them out loud.

The invitation came in the morning post, although Helen could just as easily have handed it to Immy herself. She opened it curiously, taking out the gilt-edged card inside and gaping at the printed words before reading Helen's scribbled note.

> Before you say no, Immy, think about our wager! You can look over You-know-who, and also see if anyone takes your fancy. Do say yes. It will be such a lark!

"What have you got there?" Elsie asked her sister, who had been silent for some moments.

"It's an invitation to one of Mrs Church's fund-raising dances for servicemen's comforts on August the twenty-sixth. I don't think I shall go. I'd be right out of my element."

"Of course you must go! It's a chance to see how the other half lives, if nothing else."

"Exactly. All those chinless wonders and bright young debs. I'd have nothing in common with them, and I'd stick out like a sore thumb."

"Immy, for goodness' sake! You're becoming far too insular lately. You hardly ever go anywhere, and you certainly don't have Baz's adventurous spirit. I'd really like to see you spread your wings a bit more, and this might be just the opportunity."

"This sounds far too much like the happily engaged sister dying to play the matchmaker."

Elsie laughed. "Well, hardly, since I haven't been invited to this posh do. Where is it, anyway?"

"It's in Bath, at a large hotel. Knowing Helen, she'll probably suggest that we all stay overnight."

Elsie's smile widened. "All the more reason for taking a chance then, you ninny. Who knows who you may bump into along a dark hotel corridor?"

Over his eggs and bacon, Quentin had been half listening to the banter for the last five minutes. Following Elsie's teasing words, he closed his morning newspaper with all its grim news, feeling that he must say his piece.

"I think that's enough of that, Elsie. But there is another little matter, of course. There's the fact that Imogen hasn't asked what I might think about her accepting the invitation to a dance, *and* possibly staying in an hotel overnight." He paused as Immy drew in her breath.

"*Do* you object, Father?" she said, knowing that if he did, it would definitely turn the tables on her hesitancy about accepting the invitation. Contrary to the last, as Aunt Rose would say . . .

"I was about to say that I don't think it's such a bad idea to have one or two frivolous evenings while you can, darling. Mrs Church is an admirable fund-raiser, so it's all in a good cause, and who knows when such times may come again?"

"Oh, Daddy, don't say that," Elsie said quickly, knowing what he was implying.

"It's no use burying our heads in the sand, my love. The news is dire. The ARP wardens are already insisting that we prepare our black-out curtains, and they'll be around to inspect them soon. We can't hide from it any longer."

At her crestfallen face, he added with a small attempt at humour: "Cheer up, Elsie. Think of the silver lining as far as Preston's is concerned. We're already doing a roaring trade in selling black-out material. If it's good for business it puts money in Joe's pocket, doesn't it?"

"I'd rather know that Joe was safe at home than gloating over profits for the shop, and planning on going to war," Elsie burst out, and rushed from the dining-room before anyone could say anything else.

Immy made to go after her, but her father stopped her.

"No. Leave her, Imogen. She needs to deal with things in her own way, the same as we all do. And what I think you should do, my love, is to accept your friend's invitation, and have a thoroughly good time."

"And should I stay at the hotel overnight, if Helen suggests it?"

"Absolutely," her father said.

Why she should think it so daring, Immy couldn't think. It made her cross to be unable to stop prevaricating. Where was her backbone, her strength of character?

She called Helen on the telephone before she could change her mind and told her she would love to come.

"Wonderful!" Helen said in delight. "And since we'll have danced the night away, we're going to stay at the hotel until Sunday. Mother's already booked our rooms, so you can share with me. Our treat, of course – and it'll be such fun, Immy. You're not going to argue about that, are you?"

"Good Lord, no. Whatever made you think I would!"

She put down the receiver. Now that it was done, she started immediately panicking about what she was going to wear. She had nothing suitable at all. She didn't go to fund-raising dances organised by the elite.

"I've done it," she told her father as he came out of the dining-room. "Helen's ecstatic."

"Good. So should you be. And before you say anything else, I've had an idea. You may not be comfortable with it, but I want you to hear me out."

*　　　*　　　*

On Sunday, Immy made her long-promised visit to see the family – and especially to see Daisy. During the journey she kept going over that last emotional chat with her father. She would never have dreamed of asking him for what he'd offered in a million years, nor would she have expected him to suggest it.

Once she had recovered from the usual exuberant greetings from Teddy and the boys, admired George's new antics and learned of his tentative friendship with the hedgehog in the garden, she managed to get her aunt alone. Daisy was out for the afternoon, but she was expected back about four o'clock, and bringing Cal for tea. So the inspection must wait.

"You can't imagine what my father's done," she said to Rose bluntly.

"Well, since I can't imagine it, you'll have to tell me, won't you? I'm sure it can't be anything too dreadful, though. Quentin was always a cautious man."

"It's not dreadful at all. It's – it's really rather wonderful," Immy confided, suddenly choked.

"My dear girl, this isn't at all like you!" Rose said in astonishment. "You'd better tell me at once."

As her aunt patted her back, Immy gulped, feeling more like a five-year-old than a responsible young woman of twenty.

"I'm going to a dance in Bath and staying at a hotel overnight with Helen and her parents. It will be a very posh affair, and Father said I should wear something really beautiful. Then he opened the closet where Mother kept her dance dresses, and said I could choose whichever one I liked."

"My heavens! I thought he'd have got rid of them all."

Immy shook her head. "He couldn't bear to do that. They look just as beautiful as I remember them."

"But surely . . ." Rose spoke carefully, not wanting to offend her niece, and sensing how fragile she was now. "Aren't they a little dated, darling? Your mother hadn't danced for years before she became ill."

"That's the strangest thing, Aunt Rose. Stage costumes aren't the same as ordinary wear. They simply don't date in the same way. And you know the kind of thing Mother wore. All those lovely, gossamer dresses that we all adored."

Her voice trailed away, her mind's eye seeing her mother's

sensual dancing, seeing Frances as she once was, slender and lovely and vibrant and alive . . .

"And have you chosen one of them to wear at this posh dance?" Rose's brisk voice penetrated her thoughts.

"Yes," Immy said. "Luckily, I'm the same size as Mother was before she got so thin. It's palest blue chiffon with silver threads running through it, and there are silver shoes to go with it."

"I remember." Rose nodded, blinking. "Has your father seen you in it, though? It might be too much for him."

"Actually, I think it released something inside him to see me try on the dress. I'd never want him, or any of us, to forget Mother, but he's kept all her things locked away, like a shrine to her memory. He hasn't really wanted to let any of us in, and I think it's been a good thing to bring those memories out into the open."

"And there speaks the wise child," Rose said.

Immy pulled a face. "Oh, I'm not wise. But I'm thrilled to have Mother's dress. Helen always wears such lovely clothes, and I didn't want to look like the poor relation."

Rose declined to say that whatever she wore, Imogen would always turn heads. Her striking colouring and mobile, expressive face would always do that. She was turning into a real beauty, even if she couldn't see it herself. Of course, all the Caldwell girls had inherited their mother's legendary beauty, Rose thought loyally.

The door opened, and Daisy came breezing into the room, bringing a welcome change from the charged atmosphere of the last few minutes. Behind her came a tall young man with an open face who was introduced as Callum Monks – Cal to his friends, he insisted with a smile.

"And you're stationed here at Locking, I understand?" Immy asked him.

"For the time being. Lord knows where we'll be sent when we've finished our training," he said, with all the pride of a young lion. "But as long as it's somewhere where I can get in plenty of flying hours, I'll be happy."

"There's not much doubt of that, my boy," Uncle Bertie said, coming indoors exhausted after romping in the garden with three small boys and a dog. "Once operations begin you'll go to wherever the powers that be decide to send you."

"Operations, indeed," Rose scoffed, as usual bringing the talk down to size. "Men's talk again!"

"At least it's better than Daisy's descriptions of hospital life, Mrs Painter," Cal said with a laugh. "Military operations are an honourable affair, but some of the things that go on inside a hospital are beyond talking about."

"Then we'll not talk about them today, thank you, Cal," Rose said, seeing that three small sets of ears had pricked up at the interesting thought of hearing anything gruesome.

She had begun to be far more careful of late, knowing how they got their small heads together to pick over any snippet of gossip. As bad as three little washerwomen, she thought, with real affection for them all.

Immy could see how well Cal was liked by the family here, and Daisy was clearly smitten. He passed, Immy decided.

"How's that friend of yours, Daisy?" she remembered to ask. "The girl from the farm. Is she any better?"

"It takes time, but her letters are much more cheerful now," Daisy said. "So what are you all doing lately? Have you heard from Baz again? And what of Elsie's wedding plans?"

To Immy, it was odd how detached she seemed from them all. How she was one step removed from her real family, and so firmly established in this one. Odd, and a little sad.

"Baz is fine. Elsie's still dithering, and I'm going to a dance with Helen and her parents soon," she said abruptly.

"Lovely," Daisy said carelessly, her enquiries done.

Later, Rose took her eldest niece aside.

"Don't take too much notice of Daisy's apparent lack of interest, Immy dear. She doesn't mean anything by it."

"I know. We've all moved on, though, haven't we? Ever since Mother – well, that changed everything, didn't it?"

It had torn the family apart in a way none of them had imagined, but it seemed too churlish to say as much to Aunt Rose, who had welcomed two of Frances's five children into her home out of love, with no thought of duty.

"You still have her memory, and nothing can change that, Imogen. And she'd be so proud to think you were going to wear her lovely dress at your dance."

She turned the conversation neatly, and all the way back to Bristol in the car – she now considered herself a competent driver

— Immy thought what a diplomat Rose could be when she wanted to be. No wonder they all loved her.

By now she knew there was one more thing she had to do before she finally decided to wear her mother's dress. She needed to get Helen's opinion of it, knowing she would get an honest one. If Helen thought the dress was unsuitable, then she would have to think again — at the risk of breaking her father's heart.

"Helen, can you come here one evening?" Immy telephoned her as soon as she reached home again. "I need to show you my dance dress and see what you think."

"Oh, spiffing! I can be with you around seven o'clock tomorrow if you like. I'll bring along one or two of mine, and you can help me choose what I'm going to wear. We can have a trying-on session. It'll be fun."

Everything was fun to Helen, Immy thought, still smiling as she put down the phone. And of course Helen would have a selection to choose from . . . well, so had she, she admitted. Her father had offered her the choice of her mother's dresses. But she still thought the blue and silver was the one.

The following evening in Immy's bedroom, Helen gasped. Her eyes widened even more as Immy paraded in it.

"It's absolutely gorgeous, darling. It must have cost a fortune. But when did you get it made, for heaven's sake? You always say you don't go to many social occasions, but I'm beginning to doubt it. You are a dark horse, Immy!"

Immy burst out laughing, glowing at Helen's reaction, and ready to tease her a little longer.

"You don't think it looks a little dated, then?"

"It's right up to the minute and you know it. Come on now, where did you get it? I need the name of the designer."

"It's not new, though I think it was only worn a few times. It was my mother's. One of her stage dresses."

Helen sat back on the bed.

"Good Lord," she said at last. "I hardly know what to say. It's really beautiful, Immy, and I shall be as jealous as old Harry. You'll be the belle of the ball."

"Stop it, for heaven's sake. You're embarrassing me. I'm just so thankful my father offered me the choice of them."

"You mean there are more?" Helen almost squeaked.

"Lots."

"Then you have to get out more, Immy, if only to wear them. I shall take you in hand and see that you do."

Immy laughed. "Don't be silly. Elsie's going to be allowed to choose a special dress too, for when she and Joe go on their honeymoon. Mother had such lovely things."

"Well, if they're all like this he'll love her in it."

"So show me what you're going to wear," Immy said, suddenly remembering Elsie's tearful comment that it wasn't fair that even a honeymoon might have to be arranged according to the arrogant demands of Adolf Hitler.

"I think it will be the pink brocade," Helen announced. "Or perhaps the green. I'll try them both and you can tell me what you think."

Whichever one it was, they both knew it wasn't going to be a patch on the lovely fluid blue and silver gown that had once graced the stage and held the audience enthralled as it undulated to Frances Caldwell's exquisite dancing.

"We may bring the wedding forward," Elsie told her sister. "I don't know what Daddy will think, though I've got his written permission in advance. But Joe doesn't want to wait until October to enlist, and he wants us to be married before then."

"Elsie, you can't arrange it too near to the anniversary of Mother's death. I thought you had enough sense to wait until after that, at least. It would be far too emotional."

"I know all that! But life has to go on, doesn't it?"

Immy glowered at her. "How can you be so selfish and so thoughtless? Life ended for Daddy eleven months ago."

"No, it didn't, Immy, and if you only had eyes to see, you'd know he's already found some consolation."

Immy scoffed. "The Marys, you mean? Just because he spends a little time with them doesn't mean he's feeling amorous about them."

"Not them. Her. Mary Yard," Elsie stated, her voice clipped and resentful.

"I think you're imagining things. But would it be so very awful – after a decent few years, of course – if Father did think of marrying again?"

"I don't even want to think about it."

"Neither do I – but you obviously *have* been thinking about it, or you wouldn't have mentioned it," Immy pointed out. "What brought it up, anyway?"

"Joe and I were discussing how small a wedding we could have. But if we were to invite one or two friends, Daddy said maybe we could include the Marys."

"And that's it?"

"It was the way he said it, especially Mary Yard's name. I have a bad feeling about it, Immy."

Immy put her arm around her sister. "Well, you shouldn't have. I can't say I've thought about it seriously, but if Daddy wants to find a little happiness again, we shouldn't begrudge him the chance. And I can't think of anyone nicer than one of the Marys."

Though it would be different having her as a *stepmother*, of course . . . In unspoken agreement they changed the subject.

"Anyway," Immy said determinedly, "about your wedding. Whenever it is, you know Aunt Rose will insist on that new hat, don't you? And Daisy will expect to be a bridesmaid."

Elsie groaned. "It all gets a bit much, actually! I've been reading about all the fuss and planning that's involved in Mother's old etiquette book, and we really don't want to spend time on all that. We'd much rather keep it private, just the two of us. I wish I had the nerve to do what Baz did. Run away and leave a note, telling everyone we've tied the knot and we're staying in some little hotel, out of reach of everyone, blissfully happy just to be together and on our honeymoon. It's a far more romantic idea."

"You're not serious, I hope?"

"Of course not. Would I dare?"

She went off, laughing and blushing red, and Immy stared after her for a good few minutes.

Yes, sister dear, she thought, in answer to the airy question. *I do believe you would.*

Reading the morning newspaper over breakfast had become a necessary ritual for Quentin and his children, in addition to listening intently to the daily wireless bulletins.

"Though it's little more than a masochistic exercise these

days," he told anyone who would listen, since all that the rags and the dour radio presenters' reports contained was bad news. This mid-August day was no exception.

"Good God. We're all going to have to carry identity cards now," Quentin exploded angrily, glowering at the newsprint. "What damned impertinence! We'll each be given a personal number, just as if we're pigs being sent to market. They may as well stamp it on our foreheads and be done with it."

"It's for security reasons, I suppose," Imogen said, knowing that with every new regulation imposed on them, the certainty of war came ever closer.

Quentin snorted. "Do they think there's any doubt about who's British and who isn't? You only have to look at us and listen to us."

His daughters tried not to smile at his indignation, knowing he was perfectly serious.

"I don't know about listening to us, Father. Not all of us talk the same. Joe's accent is very different from ours, for a start," Elsie pointed out.

"I'll grant you that, but we can understand it – just. It's not foreign – or Welsh."

Immy flinched. The mere mention of anything Welsh could instantly remind her of Morgan Raine.

"Welsh isn't foreign!" she said.

"I don't mean the boyos who work at Welsh Back market," Quentin went on. "But the national Welsh language might just as well be foreign for all anybody could understand it."

Little did he know that he had a daughter who had once been charmed by the lilting sound of it, and by the soft and seductive way Morgan had called her cariad and caressed her breasts, making her toes curl and her blood sing . . .

"What are you two mooning about now?" her father asked irritably. "Don't you have jobs to go to?"

"He's getting more upset as it gets closer to September," Elsie remarked to her sister as they went upstairs for their outdoor shoes. "I'm really sorry for you, Immy."

"Sorry for me? Why?" Startled, and still thinking about Morgan, she wondered for a ghastly moment if Elsie had heard any rumours about her liaison with the Welshman.

"Well, Mother dying a week after your birthday. You'll

always remember it, won't you? But at least you can be thankful we didn't have the picnic on the day itself."

"And that's why you think Father's getting upset?"

"Of course. Well, and all this war talk doesn't help, naturally."

Immy's heartbeat slowed to normal again.

"Sometimes I think the talk's gone on so long that that's all it will ever be. Just talk."

"Tell that to Joe," Elsie said. "He doesn't think it's only talk for a minute. Nor do any of the girls at the shop. Some of them are talking about leaving Preston's and working in a munitions factory making aeroplane parts. Joe says Bristol won't be a safe place any more, what with the docks and the aircraft industry here. He says—"

"Good Lord, Elsie, don't you have a single thought of your own? I'm sick of hearing what Joe says!"

"Well, pardon me. But at least he talks sense and doesn't go around with his head in the clouds thinking it's all a mirage. Helen's mother obviously thinks it's serious, with her fund-raising schemes for servicemen. *And* her brother."

"All right, I'm sorry. The fact that I don't want to talk about it doesn't mean I don't think about it."

"There's no point in *not* talking about it, is there? It's not going to go away, Immy."

"Well, it's not here yet, and now I'm going to work," Immy said rudely, needing to get away from this newly serious-minded sister, who seemed to be showing far more political sense than she herself was.

She got out her bicycle and pedalled to her office in the city centre in a fury, noting as if for the first time just how many young men there were in uniform about the city now; how many older men were wearing the dark battledress of the ARP warden; how a general air of gloom and anxious activity seemed to have settled over what had been, until now, a mellow and lovely summer.

Kenneth Harris looked up and smiled as she entered the reception area of the office. His expression changed when he saw her flushed face and noted her prickly countenance.

"Good morning, Imogen," he said with the heartiness of bolstering her up. "You're looking a mite less cheerful than usual this morning. Nothing wrong, I hope."

He was as sweet as ever, as round as a butterball, and full of concern for her. He fussed over his clients' welfare, and he worried about her like a mother hen. But right now the attention was too much.

She burst into tears and rushed through to the back room where the tea-making things were stored. She thrust the kettle under the cold tap with shaking hands, just to busy herself.

Blindly, she felt him take the kettle from her, then put his hands firmly on her shoulders.

"My dear girl, what have I said?"

"Nothing, Mr Harris. It's not you. It's me. It's the news. It's *everything*."

"My goodness," he said in bewilderment, not really understanding such passion at nine o'clock on a Monday morning. "The last thing I heard, you were practically floating on air because you were going to a dance with that nice friend of yours. Has it all fallen through?"

She gave a tremulous smile. She knew he loved hearing about her family, and took a vicarious interest in all their doings. He led such a small, narrow life compared with hers.

In fact, she thought shamefacedly, it was far narrower than hers. She had a family who loved her; he had no one and lived in a small cottage with only a cat for company. She was lucky compared to him.

"No, it hasn't fallen through. I'm just having a few bad moments. It's because the anniversary of my mother's death is coming nearer. Sometimes the awfulness of that day comes over me again."

"Of course it does. I still remember when my own dear mother died. You never really get over it, especially if you were as close as fleas on a dog's back . . . That's better," he went on, as she gave a watery smile at his tasteless simile. "Now then, you go and dry your eyes, and I'll make us some tea."

"It's really me who should be doing it," she mumbled.

"Nonsense, dear. I've been making tea for years."

Seventeen

"God Almighty, so the prodigal's returned," Quentin said, opening the door to the virtual stranger standing there.

The thought was in his head before any other, because even in that first startled instant he could see how his son had broadened and matured in these few short weeks. He had gone away a boy, and come home a man.

His natural anger surged up at the memory of Baz's leaving note. A son was still a son for all that, and answerable to his father.

"I suppose you expect me to welcome you back, do you?"

"I hope so, Father," Baz said, refusing to be intimidated in the way he had once been, though his heart banged uncomfortably in his chest in a less than manly way. He held on to the fact that as far as physical endurance went, he'd had more perilous encounters in those few weeks than his father had ever had. And come out of it triumphant. Wanting more. Eager for more.

He looked at his father unsmilingly, making no attempt to step inside the house until he was invited, still defensive.

"I'm sorry for the way I left, Father, but it's all I ever wanted, even if the sea gets a bit rough at times."

At such an understatement, a muscle at the corner of his mouth twitched, and without warning his lips went with it. He was suddenly vulnerable, wanting approval, wanting his father to say everything was all right and not to condemn him. They both knew it.

"You'd best come inside and tell me about it, then," Quentin said gruffly. He held the door wide, and the next minute his son was clasped in his arms.

Just as quickly they broke apart in hot embarrassment, but

not before Quentin had felt the thickness in his throat, and Baz had dashed away the shine of tears.

Then Imogen came rushing out of the sitting-room and hugged him tight, and the moment was gone.

"You little wretch, have you any idea what you've put us all through?" she burst out. She was too full of gladness to see him safe to be cross for long, however. "You shouldn't have done it, Baz, but I must say you look well."

"I am well," he said, wriggling away from her. "Why wouldn't I be, when they call me the ship's mascot now?"

"Good God, they must be desperate if they put their faith in a ferry-lad for a mascot. Father Neptune must be squirming in his watery grave," Quentin said with heavy humour, his sarcasm tempered by a stronger feeling that all was right in his domestic world, if not outside his front door.

Immy laughed. "He's not such a boy now, is he? I swear you've grown two inches already, Baz."

He grinned with pleasure, discovering to his surprise that it was good to go away and come home again. It made them look at one another differently. Respect one another differently. Yes, it felt good.

"Where's Elsie?" he said next.

"Out with Joe, as usual," Immy told him.

"Are they married yet?"

"Hey now, boy," Quentin said, "you've only been away a few weeks, not an eternity. There's time enough for Elsie to be thinking about marriage."

"What about you, Immy?" He looked at her with mischief in his eyes, telling her that he knew far too much about her and Morgan for comfort. "Don't tell me you're letting our Elsie leave you behind."

"That's enough of that talk," his father said, reminding him that he was still an adolescent. "Besides, not every young woman wants to be married, especially in such troubled times."

"I do eventually, Father," Immy said indignantly, in case he should think otherwise. But she wouldn't spoil Baz's homecoming by getting upset because he had unintentionally made her feel the spinster sister.

Baz didn't stay very long. He was glad to have made his

peace, but he was eager to see Enoch Bray and get his head down there for a night or two until the crew were off on the next trip. But he promised to visit them all again soon.

"Make sure that you do. This is always your home, Baz," his father reminded him.

Elsie was annoyed that she'd missed her brother, but she and Joe had had far more important things to discuss. Private things that concerned no one else but themselves – for the time being, anyway.

She was tempted to confide in Immy, but some secrets weren't for sharing with a third person, however much you loved them. There'd be time enough for that later. In any case, Immy was getting too het up about this dance in Bath and staying in hotel for a night.

What a narrow world they all inhabited! As if it was the end of the world to be sleeping in a strange bed for one night. Her darling Joe would be going away to heaven knew where soon, sleeping in tents or camps wherever the army sent him. She didn't care to question him too closely.

Elsie shivered, not understanding the madness of men. For months now, if not longer, there had been talk of war. If it was so imminent and so inevitable, why didn't they just get on with it, instead of planning their strategies and marshalling their troops and building up supplies of evil weapons as if they were pushing toy soldiers around a make-believe battleground or playing with men like marionettes on a string? Why not just begin?

The sooner it began, the sooner it would end, and all this nonsense of putting up black-out curtains at the windows of their houses so that no chink of light would show through to warn an unseen enemy would be over. All the evacuee children separated from their mothers could go back where they belonged, and people wouldn't have to carry those nasty little cardboard boxes containing gas masks around with them all the time. There would be no need for her father's despised identity cards to be issued.

She had said all this to Joe in an impassioned voice, proud of using the kind of logic that was usually attributed to Imogen. And alone in his room at his digs, where the landlady turned a blind eye since they were a betrothed couple, he had kissed her lips and her eyes with tenderness, and spoken to her gently.

"Darling Elsie, don't you know that the government is desperate to do everything in its power to ward off the evil day for as long as possible, and is doing its best to keep the peace negotiations with Hitler alive?"

"But it won't work, will it?" she said, angry at his patronising attitude. "Hitler's riding roughshod over everything in his way. He won't rest until he conquers the world."

"That's why he has to be stopped, one way or another. We'll go down fighting before we see him conquer Britain, but only when the last hope of peace has gone. But I'm glad you're taking it seriously."

"Please don't treat me like a child, Joe! Of course I'm taking it seriously. I just want to get it over with, so we can all get back to normal. Do you think I'm eager for you to go to war? Do you think I want to send you away to be killed?"

Her eyes brimmed with unshed tears as the horror of it engulfed her, and with a smothered oath he folded her in his arms and held her very tight.

"I don't plan on being killed when I'll have you to come home to. I'm planning for our future, Elsie, for my wife and my children, and if this monster has to be stopped before that's possible, then so be it."

"I'm sorry. You make me ashamed," she whispered.

"Don't be. Just remember we have a future to share. Meanwhile, let's make the most of the present."

He put the words into action very satisfactorily, and for a blissful hour they forgot everything about wars and partings, and cherished the time they had together.

As the day of the fund-raising dance in Bath grew nearer, Imogen did her best to forget all talk of war as well, though it was almost an impossibility now. Talk of it was on everybody's lips, and the entire city seemed to vibrate with anxiety and fear. Children were being sent out of Bristol to the country on extended visits to relatives, and everyone knew it was in expectation of the announcement.

By now Quentin was constantly tuning in the wireless for news reports, and cursing under his breath whenever the battery ran out without warning, and someone had to rush along to the motoring garage to get it recharged.

Immy shared her sister's feelings. Why didn't they just get on with it so that everyone knew what they were doing? All this indecision was setting everyone's nerves on edge.

Even Kenneth Harris, normally so cheerful and almost childishly boisterous, was saying gloomily at the end of a quiet day that he didn't suppose many folk would want to be buying or renting houses until they knew what was what.

"People will always need somewhere to live, Mr Harris," Immy pointed out. "People will still get married and need a home of their own. Others will have more children and need larger homes, or they'll move to Bristol from other towns for the industrial work. I'm sure we needn't worry too much."

For once, he looked at her as if she didn't know what she was talking about, and without his usual tolerance.

"That's very short-sighted of you, if I might say so, Imogen. Who do you think will want to move to a city that's likely to be a prime target for German air raids?"

"Well, Preston's Emporium did, for a start."

She defended them, which was ironic in the extreme, since Preston's plan to open in Bristol was the start of a chain reaction resulting in her father losing his business.

It hadn't really turned out so badly, she admitted. Baz had got his way. Daisy had forgotten her one-time dream of going on the stage and seemed remarkably set on a nursing career. Teddy adored his life with Aunt Rose and Uncle Bertie. Elsie had found happiness with Joe.

And she *liked* secretarial work, she found herself thinking, almost in surprise. Perhaps she hadn't been destined to be a shopkeeper. She would probably never have learned to drive a car, either, if things had stayed the same. Things had a habit of turning out for the best – usually.

"I'm thinking of closing down," Kenneth Harris said gently, gauging her reaction as he did so.

"What did you say?" she gasped, wondering if she could possibly have heard him properly.

"Think about it, Imogen. We've done hardly any business lately. You know that as well as I do. Look how quiet we've been this past week. It's only been the two of us catching up on the administrative work. It's no way to run a business, and much as I love your company, my dear, I'm not sure I can really afford you if things continue this way."

Her heart was beating so fast she felt sick.

"But I don't want to leave," she stammered. "I don't want you to close down. What will you do?" She just managed not to say, "What will *I* do?"

"What everyone else is doing. Decamp to the country. I have a married brother in Cornwall who runs a market garden. He's been asking me to go in with him for ages, and I think I shall probably do so."

"I see. It's all cut and dried, then?" She tried not to feel that he was throwing her to the wolves without a second thought.

The next moment she knew how wrong she was. He caught both her hands in his, his face as red as fire.

"Not quite. Why don't you come with me, Imogen?"

"What do you mean?" she said, her heart thudding even faster now. At this rate she'd expire soon — and then her future would be settled without any problem, she thought.

She suppressed a hysterical desire to laugh, since she realised he was being deadly serious. Excruciatingly so.

"I know I'm not the most demonstrative of men, nor the most handsome. I've never considered marriage before, but you and I have always been comfortable together, haven't we?"

She felt as if she was being strangled as his clammy hands tightened over hers. She struggled to free herself.

"Mr Harris, forgive me if I'm misunderstanding you," she croaked, knowing darned well that she was not. "I do hope you're not proposing to me. If you are, then I'm afraid it's out of the question."

He stepped back a pace, his face as crumpled as an old newspaper now. He spoke with clumsy embarrassment.

"Of course it is. I can't think what possessed me to make such a suggestion, and I beg you to forget it ever happened."

"I will — but I won't forget the honour you do me, Mr Harris, and I don't mean to hurt your feelings."

"You haven't. No, indeed." He was almost fervent now. "As I said, I have never considered myself a marrying man before, and it was a moment of madness on my part. No, far better to go on as we are for the time being."

"But how long will that be?" Immy said.

"One more week," he said decisively. "I plan to close at the end of next week and move to Cornwall."

Whether or not this decision was so final because of her rejection, Immy didn't know. In those startled seconds she was alternately thankful she wouldn't have the embarassment of working with him for much longer in the circumstances – and appalled that she was so soon going to be unemployed.

But to wed a man whose one reason for wanting her to marry him was that they had always been *comfortable* together? It wasn't the way she wanted to think about marriage. Her parents' relationship had been a loving and joyful one, until Frances's cruel illness had changed everything. She was sure it had been completely fulfilled, and right until the end, the love had been there. Even Aunt Rose and Uncle Bertie, for all their frequent spats, couldn't hide their love for each other. That was the way they expressed it.

Elsie and Joe too . . . she didn't need an interpreter to give her the reason for Elsie's glowing cheeks whenever she came home from seeing Joe. That was what love was like, and what it should be like. That passion, and that feeling that you couldn't exist without the other person, that you were only half alive when they weren't there. It certainly wasn't enough to be merely *comfortable* with one another.

"I think it's time I went home, don't you?" she said abruptly, suddenly feeling sad for a man who had obviously never known the meaning of passion, and didn't seem likely to do so. But she wasn't sorry enough to marry him.

"Another day tomorrow, then," he said, as he always did. "See you in the morning?"

He looked at her desperately, as if afraid she was going to tell him he could rot in Hades. Either that, or he was scared that she was about to spill his ridiculous proposal to the entire world.

"Of course. There's going to be a lot to tidy up in a week, isn't there? At least that will keep us busy."

She was rewarded by seeing a huge flicker of relief on his face. And no, she thought, cycling home, he had never been the marrying kind, and she doubted that he ever would be.

* * *

"You are joking, aren't you?" Helen said with a hoot of laughter. They were driving to Bath in Helen's car, since her parents had gone ahead earlier. "He didn't actually expect you to marry him?"

"You promised not to say a word about this, Helen," Immy said crossly. "I was shocked at first, but then I felt quite sorry for him."

"But what did he actually *say*? Did he go down on one knee and profess his undying love?" Helen giggled, in her element now, trying to imagine Kenneth Harris's struggle to get down on the floor at all.

"Of course not. Hardly! He said we'd always been comfortable together."

"Good God. Well, if that's a not a passion killer, I don't know what is," Helen said scornfully. "You deserve far more than that, darling."

"I know. I *want* more than that. I'd never settle for less, either. If anything, his sad proposal has made me realise it, Helen. I'll never settle for second best."

"Good for you. I suppose that's why those Marys of yours have never married again. Once you've tasted champagne, why settle for beer? Mind you, they've been a long time without, haven't they? Maybe they've forgotten how."

Immy didn't follow her meaning for a moment, and then she laughed. "You've got a saucy mind, Helen Church!"

"No, I haven't, just a normal one. It has to be more than twenty years since they were widowed."

"They probably never even think about it any more."

"Why not? Do you suppose all the urges stop when you reach forty – or even fifty?"

"I don't know!"

"Well, neither do I," Helen admitted, "but it seems a great waste of married life if they do."

"Can we please get off this subject?" Immy said, her thoughts reverting to her father, who was not yet fifty, and spent considerable time with the Marys nowadays. She certainly didn't want to think of him having urges. But she grinned to herself. It was impossible, of course.

"What now?" Helen said.

"Nothing."

"Oh well, I suppose you'll tell me when you're ready. How are the great lovers, by the way? Elsie and Joe?"

"Blooming, of course, as you would expect."

"I wonder if they've done it yet," Helen said thoughtfully.

"*Helen!*"

Helen laughed, since the response was exactly what she had expected. Considering Immy had had a pretty torrid affair with that Welsh fellow, by all accounts, she was extraordinarily reticent about her sister's romance. Still, she couldn't fault Immy's loyalty.

"By the way, did I tell you James will be at the dance tonight?" she said casually. "He got home late last night on a measly thirty-six hour pass. He'll be joining us at the hotel later, so at least we'll have one partner to share."

"How lovely," was all Immy said.

What she was remembering was the way his hands had gently raked through her tangled hair, and the sweet way he had dried it for her. She was remembering that moment when she was sure she had felt the warmth of his lips on the nape of her neck, and his words in response to her own.

"I'll be dreaming of sweeter things," she had said.

"And so will I," he had replied softly.

She shivered as the car rattled over the bumps in the road. They were nearing the glorious city of Bath with its elegant buildings and beautiful abbey. What an insult it had been for a man of forty years old to half-heartedly propose marriage to her because they had always been comfortable together!

She would feel quite differently about a proposal from a man of her own age. A virile, dynamic young man with heroic ideals and film-star looks. Even though she had known him as a friend for so long, she experienced a sudden yearning in her soul to feel those same hands in her hair once more, to feel the touch of his lips on her neck – and in other places – just to reassure her that she was a desirable young woman and could stir a man's senses. And she was very much aware that it was a dangerous game to play.

"Here we are, Immy," Helen said, breaking into her turbulent thoughts.

She realised they had drawn up outside a very large and impressive hotel with flags flying over the portals. A uniformed doorman appeared at once to open the car doors and give them a smart salute. Immy had never been in such a splendid place before, and she felt momentarily overawed.

"Imagine them in their flannel underwear, darling," Helen whispered. "That will always bring them down to size."

She turned to the porters coming out of the hotel foyer now and gave them a dazzling smile.

"The bags are in the boot for Miss Church and Miss Caldwell's room," she told them.

Immy was impressed by such cool confidence, but then, Helen was well used to this. Well, if she didn't want to look as if she had hayseeds in her teeth, she decided she had better appear used to it too.

The room was what Kenneth Harris would call very well appointed. It was deeply carpeted, with twin beds covered in deep red brocaded eiderdowns and solid oak furniture that had been lovingly polished. There was even an adjacent bathroom.

"Gosh," was all Immy could say, when she had inspected everything minutely.

"Put your eyes back in their sockets, darling, and pretend you're used to it," Helen advised, reminding her of her own conclusion. "That's the way to get by. You don't think my family lives in such grand surroundings every day, do you? In fact, you know we don't! But if you want to be treated like rich folk, you have to act like them. That's the secret. Let's unpack quickly and then go downstairs and hobnob with anyone we can find who looks interesting."

The bags had arrived in the room before they had, and they quickly hung their evening gowns in the wardrobe and despatched everything else to the dressing-table drawers.

"Ready for the fray?" Helen said.

"Quite ready," said Immy.

She wasn't really, but without warning one of her mother's sayings came into her head.

"Hold your head up high and let them see you think you're worth a king's ransom, my darling. If you think it, so will everyone else."

It echoed Helen's reasoning. Immy gave a wistful little smile, murmured a silent thank you to Frances, and lifted her head and swept out of the room behind Helen as if she had been born to high society.

Helen's parents greeted them both warmly, thankful that their daughter had got there safely.

"More safely than if I'd been driving, Mrs Church," Immy said smilingly.

"Nonsense, Imogen. You're becoming quite an expert, going all the way to Weston-super-Mare to visit your relatives."

"Mother still doesn't think it quite ladylike to drive a motor car, though," Helen said teasingly.

"It just wasn't done much in my day, dear – save when we were required to drive ambulances and suchlike in the war, of course, but those were exceptional circumstances."

"And very likely to come again," Helen said, as her mother drifted off to greet more aquaintances.

"She's really in her element, isn't she?" Immy said, seeing the ease with which she greeted all comers.

"Oh, Mother's a whiz at organising. If she had her way she'd organise Hitler too. She'd have no truck with all this shilly-shallying."

"Let's forget it for now," Immy said swiftly. "We're here to enjoy ourselves, remember?"

"Of course. Laugh and be merry, for tomorrow we—"

"Tomorrow we'll probably all have aching heads and even worse feet," Immy forestalled her. "Do they serve afternoon tea here, Helen? I'm parched after holding on to my hat and my nerves with worry about your driving."

They went into the tea lounge with linked arms, still teasing one another. Watching them, Helen's mother thought what a superb example of graceful young womanhood they were. Helen with her blonde curls framing her pretty face and her typically English blue eyes, and her beautiful friend with delicate features and that glorious red hair falling in natural waves to her shoulders.

She turned with a sigh as someone claimed her, and at once became her efficient self again, with no time to waste on nostalgic reminiscences of a time when she too had been young, and brimming with health and vitality of a different kind.

They were to have an early dinner in the hotel dining-room,

and then dress for the dance which officially began at eight o'clock.

"There's no point in getting there on time, though," Helen said, with prior knowledge of such events. "People drift in at least half an hour late, and we don't want to stick out like sore thumbs, or even worse, look like wallflowers. We don't want to seem too eager to catch a man, either."

"I presume you mean to dance with?" Immy said, with a smile in her voice.

"Oh, of course! What else could I mean?"

"And what's the name of this committee man you were so interested in?" Immy continued archly.

"Paul. Paul Stevens."

Helen said it too quickly for it not to have been on her mind, and she blushed.

"Oh, all right, I admit I'm keen to see him again. I only met him once, but he was quite charming."

"And he's probably got a wife and ten children at home."

Helen's face was a picture of dismay. "Good Lord, do you know, that never occurred to me. But you may be right. Not that he'd have *ten*. He's hardly old enough for that. He must be nearer thirty than twenty, though."

"Oh, *old*," Immy said, hearing the almost imperceptible loss of interest in Helen's voice. She knew her friend too well. Until she was really, properly, madly in love, she was quite happy to flirt harmlessly. And just as ready to flit from one possible to the next.

It made her sound shallow and fast, when in reality, Immy knew she was not. The traumatic experience with Robert Preston had told her that. Helen was just waiting for the right man, that was all. The same as Immy was.

When they had fastened each other's evening gowns, brushed their hair to a sheen, applied as much face make-up as was decent and doused themselves in their favourite scent, they turned and assessed each other, and then looked at their dual reflections in the long mirror.

"Wow!" they said simultaneously, and then laughed at their own vanity.

"We're so modest, aren't we?" Immy giggled. "But I do think we look rather spiffing, Helen, don't you?"

"I think we shall make quite an entrance," Helen agreed. "Shall we do just that?"

Immy still had to make an effort to hide her nervousness. She had never been to a function like this, and when they reached the ballroom, festooned with balloons and Union flags, the glitter of it all nearly took her breath away.

The orchestra was playing a waltz tune, and a dozen couples had already taken to the floor while others chatted amicably as they greeted old friends.

"You see? Hardly anyone's here yet, except Mother's committee and a few others," Helen whispered. "And him."

"Who?" But she already knew who it would be. She could tell by the coolness in Helen's voice that the male half of the couple her eyes were following must be Paul Stevens. She also guessed that the rather prim-looking lady holding his arm was almost certainly his wife. So much for romance.

"Oh well," she began.

"Oh well," Helen agreed, cutting her off. "Never mind, there are plenty more fish in the sea, as they say. And Mother always insists that people *mingle* at these affairs, so that's what we shall do. Lovely word, isn't it?"

Immy admired her poise. Helen would never get entangled with a married man, or one who was promised to someone else. No more would she herself. She couldn't imagine anything worse than having to share a lover. She had discovered that awful feeling for herself when she had seen Morgan Raine with his arm around another girl.

She brushed off the memory. It was over. In the past. She was here to enjoy herself, and to forget all of that.

Many more people were coming into the ballroom now. It was a thrill just to see the dazzling jewels the ladies were wearing, and how rich and important they looked. Mrs Church would surely do well with her fund-raising for servicemen's comforts tonight, Immy found herself thinking.

Eventually it began to be almost too crowded for comfort. There was a roll on the drums and the MC took his place on the platform, clearing his throat.

"Ladies and gentlemen, I've no intention of holding up your enjoyment for more than a few moments," he said, to the accompaniment of a few polite cheers, "but there are one or two formalities I can't ignore.

"The first is to thank Mrs Church, our indefatigable hostess, and her committee, for arranging this gathering tonight." He waited for further cheers to die down. "The second is to remind you why we're here. As well as to enjoy ourselves, we want to raise as much money as possible for our gallant servicemen, so when the raffle tickets come around, please dig deeply into your pockets to stand a chance of winning one of the valuable prizes to be awarded at the end of the evening.

"And I've one last request. Whatever tomorrow may bring, we've pledged not to make a single mention of war this evening. We're here to have fun, and that's what we want you all to do, in the best possible way we know."

He was almost deafened by the roars of approval. The drum rolls continued until he had left the stage and the orchestra began playing again. From then on, everyone took to the dance floor, and did exactly as they had been told.

Immy and Helen had no lack of partners. At one point Immy lost sight of her friend. She was taking a short breather after the exuberant whirling of her most recent, perspiring escort. Right now she was more than happy to watch the more energetic dancers jigging frantically to the Gay Gordons for a few moments while she caught her breath.

When it ended, the lights dimmed and the dance floor cleared before the slower strains of a dreamy waltz tune coaxed the romantics back again.

"May I have this dance?" she heard a deep, masculine voice say right behind her.

A voice she knew, and one that made her heart leap. She turned around quickly.

"You look simply stunning, and you take my breath away," James said quietly, the moment before she went into his arms.

Eighteen

Imogen couldn't have pinpointed the exact moment she realised she was falling in love with James Church. She couldn't even decide if it was love that she was feeling.

It could just have been the effects of the magical evening, which had seemed headier and more vibrant than usual, perhaps because of everyone's determination to follow the MC's instructions and give no thought to an impending war.

Whatever it was, Immy felt happier than she had at any time since breaking up with Morgan. James became her sole escort for the evening, and when she asked him laughingly if he wasn't expected to ask some other young ladies to dance, he shook his head decisively.

"Why should I, when I'm already dancing with the girl of my dreams?" he whispered seductively in her ear, his arm tightening around her waist for yet another slow waltz.

"I just thought your mother might think you had a duty to do so," she murmured, too much on fire to question whether his words were just a tease.

"Not at all. I'm not one of Mother's committee sheep. I don't conform, Immy. I never have. I thought you knew that. I could never follow in my father's footsteps and be a lawyer."

"Is that why you joined the tank regiment? Is there some special kind of excitement in that?"

He looked down into her face, his voice definitely teasing now. "You have to pay a penalty for that remark."

"What do you mean?" she said, her heartbeat quickening.

"Our glorious MC declared that there was to be no hint of war tonight, and you've just broken the rule by mentioning my regiment," he said solemnly.

"I have not!" Immy protested. "I think you're stretching the rule a little, James!"

He shook his head. "I insist that you take the punishment."

"Oh dear. Should I start quaking in my shoes?"

"You may well do so! Such penalties cannot be paid in public. We have to go outside on the terrace to spare your blushes."

He took her hand and began weaving his way through the dancers, so that she had no choice but to follow him. It was all delicious nonsense, but the ballroom *was* becoming unbearably hot and stuffy now, and a breath of fresh air on the wide terrace adjoining it would be very welcome.

He led her across the marbled floor, and they leaned over the edge of a secluded corner of the terrace, breathing in the scented air from the gardens below. By now the shadows had deepened and the night was a soft indigo, peppered with stars and lit by the crescent of the new moon. It was a night made for romance, for secret whisperings and vowed intentions.

Far below them the winding river Avon meandered through the city, glittering in the moonlight and reminding Immy for one heartbreaking moment of the way it had looked on that fateful day when her mother had spiralled to her death from Clifton Downs. But she blinked the image away, not wanting to spoil these perfect moments with such anguished thoughts. Frances would never have wanted that.

James was now turning her to face him, his hands gentle on her slender shoulders. She could feel the heat of his fingers softly caressing the skin at the nape of her neck, making her shiver – but not with cold. Never with cold, when there was fire raging inside her. And she was instantly certain she had not imagined that other time. None of it.

He still said nothing, but her nerve ends were tingling with sweet anticipation now. Her mouth opened in a tremulous smile as she looked up into his face.

"Well, James?" she said.

And though she could hardly bear to play the waiting game any longer, her words were slow and long drawn out, as if something inside her wanted to hold on to this moment for ever. She was sure that whatever had been between them all the time she had known him was about to be changed for ever.

"Well, my lovely Imogen," he said softly. "Are you ready to pay your penalty?"

"I believe so," she whispered, knowing what it would be. His arms went around her, and she melted against him, raising her face for his kiss.

The first kiss between them had all the passion of lovers. It was a kiss that was deep and possessive, parting her lips so that she could taste the freshness of his mouth and feel the sharpness of his teeth against her tongue. A kiss that stirred her soul as she wound her arms about his neck and held him close, so close that she could feel every sinewy part of him and revelled in it. A kiss that reminded her that she knew what it was to feel unrestrained passion, and to have a man wanting her. And there was no doubt in her mind now that James wanted her.

They broke away after a few minutes in order to breathe. They remained close, still locked in one another's arms, their mouths still no more than a breath apart, their hearts pounding in a mutual dance of desire.

"For the first time, I regret having to rejoin my regiment so soon," he said huskily. "And now I've broken the rule. You'll have to extract a penalty from me, my love."

"If I must," Imogen said, feeling a delicious sense of fun at his banter. For of course he knew what he was saying and doing, just as she did. The kissing went on . . . and on . . . and needed no more encouragement of rule-breaking to make them fully aware of the significance of this night.

"Where on earth did you get to? I lost sight of you hours ago," Helen complained, when at last she came to bed in the early hours of the morning, having danced until her feet throbbed.

By then, Immy was lying in bed, gazing up at the ceiling and realising how much truth there was in the old saying that love was blind. It had to be, if you could know a person for so long, and yet not really know him at all. Until now . . .

"Immy? Why haven't you put the light on?" Helen asked, switching on a bedside lamp and making Immy flinch. "Or were you asleep? Oh God, I'm so thoughtless."

"I wasn't asleep. I was thinking. Dreaming."

"You must have had a good time, then. So did I. I met the most marvellous man, and Paul Stevens can go and—"

She suddenly realised that Immy wasn't listening to her

ramblings. She sat down on her own bed in her petticoat, her lovely evening gown tossed carelessly on the floor, and stared at her friend.

"Who was it, Immy? You must tell! I've never seen you look so moonstruck before – well, not since MR."

"Don't even mention him. He's in the past."

"*And*?" Helen almost squeaked. "Who's going to be the future? The last time I caught sight of you, you were dancing with James and grinning up at him like a Cheshire cat."

"Was I?"

Immy felt her mouth curve at the memory of James smiling down at her, of her heart doing somersaults, and of the dawning emotions between them. Although if Helen was to be believed, James had harboured feelings for her for quite a while. And she was quite ready to believe it.

"*Immy*!" Helen breathed. "Am I reading the signs right? You and James – at last? So I was right all along in saying you would make the perfect couple!"

Immy gave a small laugh. "Hold your horses! We only had a few dances, that was all. And a breather on the terrace. And the rest is none of your business," she added teasingly.

But her flushed face and luminous eyes said far more than words, and for once, Helen took the hint and left her to her private dreams.

"Tell me tomorrow," she said, turning away from such blatant happiness. She finished undressing and turned out the lamp before climbing into bed and falling asleep instantly.

It was more than Imogen could do. She was still hearing the sound of James's rich voice in her head, feeling his arms around her waist, his hands gentle on her shoulders and elsewhere, his mouth on hers as the silly excuses for paying penalties faded out of existence.

Because they had known one another for so long, and had already discussed every topic beneath the sun, there was no need for the conventional explorations between tentative new lovers as they talked long into the night.

"Will you write to me?" he asked.

"As often as you want me to."

"All the time. And I promise to write back. I'll need to know that you're thinking of me, and missing me."

"You won't need my letters for that, James. Just keep the certainty in your heart."

It seemed the most natural thing in the world, on a night that was charged with tension, to be speaking so frankly. A beautiful summer's night, yet they all felt the threat hanging over them like a dark shadow. And with it the fear that the peace and tranquillity that was prevalent in their corner of England was so soon to be shattered.

"When I can't actually hear your voice your letters will mean a great deal to me," James said, interspersing each word with a kiss. "So promise me you'll write."

"Of course I promise."

He hesitated. "I won't ask for more right now, Imogen, but I'd like to think of you as my young lady. My special girl. What do you say?"

"I say that I can think of nothing I want more than to be your special girl, James," she said softly, her reply as solemn as a vow.

As she remembered those words her eyes were damp. He might not have asked for more, and maybe it was not the best of times to be looking ahead to personal happiness. But if you didn't look ahead and plan for the future, you might as well admit defeat.

And even though the words hadn't been said, Imogen sensed that there was already a very special unspoken promise between them. She finally drifted into sleep, content.

"So are you and James going steady now?" Helen demanded the next morning.

Imogen awoke with an enormous headache stabbing her behind the eyes and the sinking feeling that the previous night might all have been a dream. Had James Church really said those seductive things to her, kissed her so passionately, and made her promise to write to him as often as possible?

"I shouldn't think so," she said crossly. "One swallow doesn't make a summer, does it?"

"What the dickens do birds have to do with it? I hope you're not going to go all coy on me, Immy. You know I'm dying to hear everything."

"There's nothing to tell. James and I danced a lot, we had

some laughs, and we both probably drank a litle too much champagne. That's all."

"And I suppose you've no intention of telling me any more," Helen stated.

"Absolutely right. So don't ask."

"You're a selfish pig sometimes, Immy, but I still love you," Helen said cheerfully. "Anyway, if you won't tell me what went on, I won't tell you about Adam."

Immy sat up in bed, her red hair tumbling about her shoulders as she heard the dreamy note in her friend's voice.

"Adam?"

She knew Helen well enough to know she wouldn't be able to keep it to herself for long.

"He's Paul Stevens's brother – you know, the committee man I told you about. You were right about Paul, by the way. He's married with children – but Adam isn't. He's in the navy and he's adorable. So it seems we were both lucky last night."

She was blatantly fishing again, but Immy simply laughed and leaped out of bed, suddenly infected by Helen's enthusiasm. Remaining in this room a moment longer, when she could be downstairs in the dining-room having breakfast with James, seemed like a total waste of time.

The thought of sharing breakfast with him in a hotel also sounded delightfully decadent and intimate, even if it would be in the company of James's family.

"I'm first in the bathroom," she called out gaily. Helen was still yawning lazily.

"Goodness, you working folk depress me," she grumbled.

By then, Immy was picking up the envelope that had been pushed under the bedroom door. It was addressed to her, and she didn't recognise the handwriting. She opened it quickly. It was from James.

> Immy darling, this is the most awful luck, but my leave's up and I can't even see you this morning. We're almost certainly on the move, though God knows where. My guess is France, though I probably shouldn't say as much. I'll write as soon as I can. Meanwhile, keep the memory of our lovely evening in your heart as I will in mine. My love, James.

She was numb, staring at the letter and hardly taking in the words, just the fact that he was gone. They had been on the brink of something wonderful, and it had already been snatched away from them. She knew what "being on the move" meant – and now she also knew what it meant for one's blood to run cold, as they said in all the thriller novels. It was as if an icy wind was blowing through this luxurious room.

"Immy, what's up?" she heard Helen say. The next minute she felt the letter being taken from her hands.

"Oh, what rotten luck," James's sister said. "I said it was a measly leave, didn't I? Never mind—" She paused, seeing Immy's white face. "My God, you *do* mind, don't you? Did something happen between you two last night?"

"Not really. Just that I think we fell in love. Isn't that a crazy thing to do when a war is about to happen?"

She felt her throat closing up as all the implications of it washed over her, and she rushed to the bathroom, closed the door and leaned against it, her heart thudding.

Stories of the last war were still vivid in many people's minds, recounted over and over again. People like the Marys had lost young husbands. Mothers had lost sons. Children had lost fathers. The repercussions of war were endless.

She had envied her sisters recently for their romantic attachments. But she hadn't really thought it through properly. Because as soon as Adolf Hitler and Prime Minister Chamberlain decided there could be no avoidance of the inevitable, then all of them were going to be parted.

Elsie's Joe was about to enlist . . . Daisy's young man was already an air cadet and learning to fly . . . last night Helen had met someone called Adam who was in the navy and would be doing his bit . . . and she and James Church had fallen in love and promised to write to one another. And wherever he was sent, he was going to drive a tank, which everybody knew was a very dangerous thing to do.

The heady euphoria of last night had already faded. Daylight made you see things differently, and what Immy saw was that it was a terrible waste of emotion to fall in love at all, when some madman was threatening to wipe out all the young men who were patriotic enough to fight for their country.

Would you have him be a conscientious objector? the

treacherous little voice said inside her head. Of course she would not! She just wanted him safe, and here.

"Are you all right, Immy?" she heard Helen call out. "You aren't going to be all day in there, are you? I thought we'd take a walk around the city before we leave, unless you're anxious to get back to Bristol. I don't mind either way."

"I think I'd rather go home," Immy said in a choked voice. "If you're sure you don't mind."

It wasn't just that she couldn't bear to stay in a city that held such sweet memories for her. It was more a sense of urgency that made her want to be at home, inside the four familiar walls in the house where she had been born, surrounded by her family's love.

The sense of fear in her heart made her feel as vulnerable as a child, when just hours before she had never felt so much like a woman.

Aunt Rose was at pains to keep all news of impending war away from the three small boys in her care. Daisy didn't spend too much time reading the newspapers or listening to the wireless, preferring to maintain an ostrichlike approach to the whole thing. If she didn't see or hear too much about it, then it wasn't going to happen.

She still spent a little time at the Luckwell farm, exercising Lucy's horse and taking her own out for a trot. But she felt a little uncomfortable going there lately. Lucy's mother usually had such a red, blotchy face now. The recent news about Lucy wasn't good. Her state of health had suddenly deteriorated, she hardly ever wrote letters any more, and Daisy couldn't bear to hear the latest reports. She also felt guilty that her own robust looks must sharpen the difference between herself and Lucy.

For the first time in her life Daisy had to face the real possibility that a friend of her own age might die.

Working at the hospital made things seem worse. By now Daisy knew what happened to people when they died. She knew the gruesome things nurses had to put up with. The awful smell that came from a patient who was dying. The disgusting messes one had to clear up. And after death, plugging the orifices, as they called it, and the tasteful laying out, so that grieving loved ones could view the deceased as calmly as possible.

Many bereaved folk said how lovely and peaceful the deceased looked. To Daisy, they simply looked dead. Grey and dead. It was the one thing in her nursing work she hated, and the one thing she knew she had to accept if she didn't want to give it all up. And she had no intention of doing that. Even if her friend died – and every time she thought of the possibility, her heart gave a horrid little leap – in a strange kind of way she felt she owed it to Lucy to keep on nursing as a kind of perpetual piece of loyalty to her memory.

"I sound so bloody noble, don't I?" she said gloomily to Cal on the last weekend in August as they sat on the hot sands watching the tide go out. "I'm not, though. I'm scared of death, and yet I'm in the very profession where I'm likely to see it all the time. I hate the smell of blood and vomit, and if somebody starts to retch, I have to force myself not to do the same. Why did I ever think I could be a nurse?"

"Because you're good at it, that's why," Cal told her. "Because you have more compassion in your little finger than most people twice your age do. Don't belittle yourself, Daisy. We're going to need plenty like you pretty soon."

"You think I should volunteer to join a military nursing unit, then?" she said, following his thoughts. She shivered. "I don't think so! And besides, I'm probably not old enough."

Thank God, she thought.

"You may well be old enough before it ends," Cal told her. "Wars aren't fought and won in a day. The last one took four years, didn't it? You'll be twenty-one by then."

"Shut up, Cal. You're scaring me now. I don't want to think of a war lasting four years. Even Baz would be old enough to fight then. He'd be nineteen."

"Same as I am now."

They looked at one another. As if to remind them of Cal's passion for aviation, the steady drone of an aeroplane overhead made them both look up into the blue sky above the Bristol Channel, shielding their eyes against the bright sunlight.

"What's it like up there, feeling there's nothing between you and the ground but a piece of metal?" Daisy said suddenly.

"Marvellous," he said. "Providing the engine holds out and the wings don't fall off, of course. And as long as the pilot's had his eyes tested recently."

"Now you're making fun of me," Daisy said, grinning back, but feeling thankful that he was. You couldn't be gloomy all the time, especially when you were young and fancied yourself in love.

People were still bringing their children to the beach to make sandcastles with their buckets and spades, and paying for rides on the Weston donkeys. Their screams of laughter were the same as always, and such idyllic scenes made thoughts of war still seem a million miles away.

"Come on, I'll race you to the ice-cream kiosk. Last one there buys them," Cal said, dragging her to her feet.

She tore off behind him, laughing wildly as their feet kicked up the soft sand that impeded their progress. So glad that she had met him, and knowing that whatever happened, she was going to marry him one day. She had quite made up her mind to that.

Elsie and Joe had already planned their wedding day. It had been nothing more than a vague, romantic idea at first, not at all logical, and one to be dismissed at once. What would the family think? What would her father say? And the new hat that Aunt Rose intended to have made wouldn't be needed for the occasion. Daisy and Immy wouldn't be bridesmaids, and then there was Joe's family . . .

Elsie had put up all sorts of arguments as to why they shouldn't do this. Joe's nice, homely parents would be so upset, and his Uncle Owen would probably have a blue fit and disown him. Not that they would have spared the time to make the long journey, Joe had said – especially Robert, who seemed to have an aversion to coming south any more. It was too far, and his mother never travelled well. His father never travelled at all if he could help it.

"So what do you say, my love? Do we go ahead?" he asked. "You do realise that you'll be gaining a husband for a very short time."

"I know that," she murmured, knowing full well of his plans to enlist, and that he wouldn't put it off much longer. He had already informed his uncle of the fact, and Owen Preston had written to her father, telling him that in the event of his nephew going to war, Quentin was immediately to be made manager of the shop. It was the only thing that eased Elsie's mind about the whole thought of Joe being a soldier. His absence would mean a step up for Quentin, and put him back where he belonged, in charge of the shop.

She looked at Joe with clear brown eyes now.

"I'd rather have you as my husband for just a few days than not have you at all, Joe," she said softly. "And you'll always have me to come back to."

He caught her hand in his and touched her palm with his lips, enclosing the kiss inside it.

"That thought will be my talisman, my dearest. So we will make our plans."

The country awoke to the devastating news on Friday September first that the Nazi army had marched across the Polish border at dawn. Hitler's pact of non-aggression with Poland had been ignored, and in desperation Poland appealed to Britain and France for help. Both countries sent Germany ultimatums to withdraw that would expire in two days' time.

Entire communities began sending their children to the safety of the countryside in a panic. Evacuation had previously been an orderly affair, but what had been a comparative trickle before now became a flood, with roads and railways in danger of becoming clogged with the huge numbers of children and their teachers and helpers moving out of the cities with their assorted baggage, gas masks and labels. If many of the children thought of it as a great adventure, many more did not, and there was drama, tears and pandemonium at railway stations.

"We'll probably take another one," Rose declared on the phone to her brother. "We've plenty of room, and I've already put my name down at the Town Hall. The more the merrier, and the boys will enjoy having another friend to stay."

"You're mad," Quentin told her bluntly.

"Nonsense. I like having children around me. Besides—" She hesitated, not sure whether or not Daisy was in earshot. She decided that she wasn't. "You know that little Luckwell girl . . . It doesn't look too good for her, and her parents are going to be devastated if the worst happens."

"So you're surrounding yourself with children to soften the blow in case one of yours takes a bullet, are you?"

"Well, I wouldn't have put it quite so crudely! I prefer to say that this is my one chance of having the kind of family you and Frances had. Is that so wrong?"

After a moment, his voice was gruff.

"Not wrong at all, Rosie. Just take care of yourself, that's all. We can't afford to lose you."

"You don't get rid of a tough old bird like me that easily," she said briskly. "Now then, what's happened to Elsie lately? I thought she was going to make me a hat. Life goes on, Quentin, despite the worst that Hitler can do, and I still want to look my best for her wedding."

"She said something about coming to see you on the train on Saturday," he said with a frown. "I don't know if the news will alter her plans, though."

"She musn't let it. But why don't we all come and see you on Sunday? If she arrives here, we'll bring her back with us – and we'll also bring one of my large apple pies, since it will be a bit of an invasion. Ronnie and Norman have never seen Bristol – and families should be together at important times."

It was her one concession to the fact that Adolf Hitler was already dictating their lives.

Elsie was being decidedly secretive lately, Quentin thought with a frown as he rang off. He had said as much to the Marys over afternoon tea a couple of days ago.

"Now that your daughters are young women, you can't expect them to confide in you as they did when they were children, Quentin," Mary Yard said gently. "Especially Elsie, since she's engaged to be married. You must remember what it was like in your youth."

He smiled ruefully, his eyes full of memories.

"Oh yes. Frances and I shared plenty of secrets that were ours alone. Not improper ones, you understand, but private things that would seem like nonsense to anyone else."

"That's it exactly," Mary Baxter agreed. "And when it comes to children, you have to let them go, don't you?"

For two widowed ladies who had never had children of their own, they were extremely canny, he thought approvingly. It was why he enjoyed their company so much. The young ones were his pride and joy, but there were times when a man needed mature company.

And that was all it was. He admitted that there had been a few idle moments when he had wondered what it might be like to marry again, and he sensed that Mary Yard had considered it as well. She was the one with whom he felt most compatible.

But he wasn't ready for marriage. And in a strange way, he knew exactly when she too had mentally withdrawn from the idea. A kind of mutual agreement had emerged between them, never spoken about, but undoubtedly there. It was a relief, a comfort, and it meant they could continue to enjoy these friendly little tête-à-têtes without any embarrassment.

"Elsie's going down to Weston on Saturday, and I dare say she'll stay at Rose's and come back with them on Sunday morning," he commented.

"Good for her. Who knows how many more such outings we'll be able to take?" Mary Yard said. "Have you started getting the shelter ready for occupancy, by the way?"

Quentin grimaced. "The shop is a useful supply source for that. I've got candles and matches and flashlights – not that we'll be able to use them out of doors, of course. And some tinned food and a tin opener, and water bottles – oh, and blankets in case we're there for any length of time."

"Goodness me, you make it sound like a siege," Mary Baxter exclaimed. "We're not expecting to stay in there for ever, are we? It will be a little cramped, to say the least, and a bit earthy too. And tinned food, indeed! A camping stove and a kettle and tea would be more to the point, and some biscuits. It could be quite a little adventure really."

The three of them laughed, but the laughter didn't reach their eyes. All of them knew of old that it was going to be nothing like an adventure at all.

Nineteen

By Saturday the tension everywhere was almost tangible. The streets were strangely empty in many parts of the city. No one moved very far from their wireless sets, desperate to know if Neville Chamberlain's ultimatum to Hitler was going to be acknowledged and accepted.

Joe had decided that Preston's staff would prefer to be at home with their families, and since business was so slack the shop closed at lunchtime. He had had business of his own to attend to that morning, and had left the closure to Quentin.

Elsie's small suitcase was already at Joe's digs, and she hugged Immy tightly when her sister drove her to the railway station.

"Be happy, Elsie," Immy said.

"Goodness me, it's just Aunt Rose's, and I'll only be away for one night," Elsie said, her eyes bright. But everyone knew that one night could change a person for ever . . .

As soon as Immy had gone, Elsie waited impatiently for Joe to arrive. Bath was an elegant and beautiful city, he had told her, and Bath was where he had obtained the special licence that was going to make them man and wife later that afternoon.

Although Elsie had been tempted to confide in Immy, she would have bitten out her tongue first. But it was the most important secret she had ever kept from her sister.

Immy drove away, wondering if her deepest suspicions were true, and wishing her sister all the luck in the world if they were. She hadn't dared to ask. What she didn't know, she couldn't lie about.

She herself was frustrated that James Church still hadn't written to her. She knew it had only been a week, and that the needs of the army must come first, especially for someone training to be an officer, but it didn't help her feeling that perhaps it had all been a dream after all. Had James really implied that he loved her and wanted her? Or was she being a romantic fool?

Whatever it was, she felt an insurmountable need to be near his family and his home. She went straight to Helen's house, hoping they might have had news.

"No, old thing, he's gone incommunicado," Helen said. "Father says that's the army for you. We're not even at war yet, and already they're calling the tune . . . Sorry, darling," she added, seeing Immy's crestfallen face. "I didn't realise you were quite so smitten."

Immy tried to shrug it off with a laugh. *Smitten*? Was that the word for it? It seemed she had spent every waking moment since the fund-raising ball picturing James's face close to hers, breathing the same air, tasting his mouth, feeling the warmth of his arms around her.

Smitten? What a miserably ineffectual word that was for the strength of feeling she felt for James now! Stronger than anything she had ever felt for Morgan Raine. Deeper than she had ever imagined love could be. And yet she was also torn by the worry that she could be imagining the whole thing. Creating love out of need . . .

"Are you all right, Immy?" Helen's voice penetrated her thoughts. "Listen, I've had an idea. Well, it was Mother's, really. You know how good she is at these things."

"What things?"

"Organising and all that. The WVS is going to set up a sort of canteen at the railway station to provide drinks and cigarettes for soldiers coming home on leave or being sent home wounded. That sort of thing. They did it in the last war, apparently. Are you game to help, now that you're unemployed?"

Immy grimaced. "Thank you for reminding me! Your mother's obviously seeing war as a certainty. But if it is, I shall want to do something more useful than standing on a railway station dispensing tea!"

Helen looked at her steadily, her voice a shade cooler.

"Well, thank you for reminding *me* how useless I am! I'm sure I don't have your skills, but a bit of tea and sympathy goes a long way when you're facing the perils of war."

"Oh Helen, I'm sorry. I didn't mean to imply any such thing. Please don't let's quarrel. I'm so out of sorts today. Elsie's gone off somewhere, and although she hasn't confided in me I have a shrewd idea of what's happening."

"*Do* you?" Helen's scratchy mood changed at once. "Good Lord, Immy, you don't mean she and Joe have set up home together? Your father would never live down the scandal!"

"I don't mean that at all. Elsie would never do such a thing. But I do have my suspicions that they may be eloping."

"How utterly romantic!" Helen's eyes shone.

"How utterly irresponsible!" Immy snapped back. She immediately regretted it. Oh Lord, I didn't mean that, either. I rather agree with you, but I'm frantic about how Father's going to take it if I'm right. Baz ran off without a word, and if Elsie's done the same—"

"He's still got you, darling."

"The sensible one, you mean." When Helen didn't answer immediately, her voice became more passionate. "I don't want to be boring, Helen! Don't you think I'd like to kick up my heels too, and run away and get married and live happily ever after? But sometimes I wonder if it will ever happen for me."

"Goodness you do need cheering up. Let's go for a walk on the Downs. Unless you'd prefer somewhere else," she added, remembering Immy's mother.

"Not at all. A good dose of fresh air is what I need."

But a shiver of premonition crept into her mind at that moment. Who knew how much longer any of them would be able to enjoy England's green and pleasant land, once Hitler set his greedy sights on them?

There were only five people inside the small country church just outside Bath that afternoon. The elderly vicar who was officiating, the bespectacled verger and his wife who were acting as witnesses, and the bride and groom.

Joe wore the brand-new army uniform he had collected that morning, and Elsie was ethereal in one of her mother's more demure stage dresses in soft white silk that hugged her body in fluid folds. Her sheaf of white lilies symbolised her purity.

In Joe's eyes, she had never looked more beautiful. And

for Elsie, the sweet simplicity of the service and the empty little church seemed to emphasise even more the intimate relationship they were entering into.

She felt no more than a brief regret that there was no fanfare of rejoicing at their wedding. No family and friends to wish them well, or a feast to celebrate their nuptials. This was the true meaning of being joined by God, she thought, as the vicar intoned the solemn words. Committing their lives to one another . . . in sickness and in health . . . so long as they both should live.

She felt the coolness of the slim gold wedding band as Joe slid it on to her finger. He held it there while he said the words that bound them together for life.

"With this ring I thee wed. With my body I thee worship. And with all my worldly goods I thee endow."

His voice was thicker than usual as the vicar told him quietly that they were now man and wife, and that he might kiss his bride. He looked into Elsie's eyes for a long moment before taking her in his arms and holding her close.

In front of strangers it was the most chaste of kisses, a centuries-old ritual that each knew was a pledge of fidelity and love. It was a moment that would never come again, this first embrace as husband and wife.

Passion could wait, for they now had all the time in the world for belonging. No other thoughts of what might be happening in the wider world could dim the glory of this day.

Sunday morning in Rose's household was more hectic than usual. The small boys were taking an interminable time in getting ready to go to Bristol, squabbling over socks and sandals and generally making Rose wonder why she had ever thought having a family was such a desirable thing at all.

"If you three don't stop this, I'll box your ears for you," she bellowed finally, her nerves as frayed as everyone else's in the entire country. "Uncle Bertie's having enough trouble trying to persuade the car to behave, and heaven knows what's happened to Daisy."

"She's riding a horse at the farm and staying there all day," Teddy said, sulking. "She told you."

"Oh my, yes, so she did," Rose said, unusually flustered. "I'll forget my own head next. Now then, are we ready?"

"You said Elsie was coming to see me. Why didn't she come?" Teddy hollered next, determined to be difficult.

"Well, she must have had her reasons. We'll see her when we get you home. Come *along*, all of you."

She knew Bertie was uneasy about driving the old Morris motor with its growing habit of spluttering and stopping. It was always in doubt whether they would get to their destination or not.

"At this rate, we'll never get to Bristol before eleven o'clock," Rose snapped. "I so wanted us all to be together, and Quentin will be missing Baz as well as Daisy today."

"There's nothing we can do about it," Bertie told her. "If war's destined to happen, it will happen, whether or not we hear Chamberlain's words. Just hope this old blighter of a car gets us there before it finally gives up the ghost."

"Hope. Or pray," Rose muttered. "And since this is Sunday, that seems an appropriate comment to make."

She had never been a particularly religious woman, but right now, she was thinking that a few heartfelt prayers certainly wouldn't come amiss. And not just regarding the antics of their battered old car.

"It doesn't look as if your aunt and uncle are going to be here in time," Quentin said, as the hands of the clock moved inexorably round the dial towards eleven o'clock.

Immy looked at him nervously. What was he going to say when Elsie didn't arrive with them? It was more than a guess now, since she had looked in Elsie's room and discovered that her small suitcase had gone, together with her best clothes. She must have spirited them out of the house, and Immy was quite sure they weren't destined for Weston.

The final certainty had come when she discovered that Frances's filmy white dress that Elsie had coveted was also missing. Perfect for a wedding dress, her sister had said dreamily at the time. Lucky, lucky Elsie . . .

To Immy right now, the house seemed unbearably empty. Less than a year ago, it had been so full of life. Her darling mother had still been alive. Daisy and Teddy hadn't yet gone

243

to live with Aunt Rose. Baz hadn't left home, and Elsie and herself were the stalwarts, boosting up her father as his beloved business was being taken over.

Now, in the sitting-room that seemed far too big, there were only the two of them. Her father was tinkering with the wireless set, cursing beneath his breath as he tried to maintain a clear reception. It was as if the whole country was holding its collective breath. And Immy suddenly couldn't bear it.

"Shall I ask the Marys to come and join us, Father?" she said. "I'm sure they would appreciate the company."

"If you wish, my dear," he said abstractedly.

She fled upstairs and knocked on the Marys' door. It suddenly seemed important to be surrounded by people on today of all days – unless you were Elsie and Joe, of course. She gave a fleeting thought to how they might be spending this Sunday morning, and just as quickly blotted out the vicarious images. It was private.

It seemed that the Marys were just as thankful to join them downstairs, and at eleven o'clock they all sat silently around the wireless set as the premier's crackling words were emitted. Words that were to change their lives for ever.

The voice was as pedantic as ever, and as it went on, Immy found herself hating the deliberate, emotionless sound of it.

"This morning, the British Ambassador in Berlin handed the German government a final note stating that unless we heard from them by eleven o'clock that they were prepared at once to withdraw their troops from Poland a state of war would exist between us.

"I have to tell you now that no such undertaking has been received, and that consequently this country is at war with Germany. You can imagine what a bitter blow it is to me that all my long struggle to win peace has failed."

There was so much more. There were explanations and commitments and the outline of future plans, but Immy took in very little of it. Tomorrow, the speech would be in all the newspapers, and they could all devour it in its entirety.

For now, she was aware of the soft sound of Mary Baxter's tearful sniffling, and noticed the way her father had squeezed Mary Yard's hand for a moment, as memories of past conflicts were revived. These three had already been through another war, while she had not.

In a ridiculous way, it excluded her. She was momentarily the outsider, and it filled her heart with a huge emptiness. Then her father noticed her ashen face, and hugged her close.

"It's a bitter blow, but hardly unexpected, my love. We'll get through it together, the same as we've always done," he said in a rough voice.

As she nodded wordlessly, he went on more firmly.

"We've always pulled together, and we won't fail our country now. Whatever has to be done, will be done."

"Amen to that," Mary Yard murmured.

They stayed talking quietly for nearly an hour, listening to comments on the wireless from those who possessed more insight into what was about to happen. They tried to believe and accept that Mr Chamberlain had done the only thing possible in the circumstances. Finally, as a commotion began to be heard outside, Mary Yard glanced at her friend.

"I think your family has arrived at last, Quentin, so we'll leave you. Actually, we've been discussing whether or not to stay in the city, so now we must make up our minds."

Immy looked at her father sharply to see if this news might disturb him, but he merely nodded and let them go.

She turned thankfully as the three boisterous small boys burst into the room, with a red-faced Rose and Bertie close behind.

"What a morning!" Rose exclaimed. "I swear I thought we'd never get here. The car's almost expiring! But we know the bad news, my dears. The placards are already out, and there are people on the streets, some of them weeping openly."

She said this last quietly, not wanting to alarm the boys.

"I'm sorry Daisy's not with us," she went on, "but she wanted to be at the Luckwell farm with Lucy's parents."

"Where's Elsie?" Bertie said, finally getting a word in, and catching his breath after his battles with the temperamental car and three equally temperamental children.

"She's with you, isn't she?" Quentin said.

Rose stared. "No. When she didn't arrive yesterday we simply assumed she'd changed her mind about coming to Weston. It was all rather vague, anyway. Isn't she here?"

"She is not," Quentin said grimly. "I haven't seen her since yesterday, when Imogen took her to the railway station."

They all looked at Immy now, as accusingly as if she had committed a sin – when in reality she had done nothing at all, she thought indignantly.

She couldn't help thinking how ironic it was that domestic family problems could so quickly overshadow that of a nation's catastrophe. But perhaps it was better so, before imagination took them to places no one wanted to see.

"I don't know where Elsie is!" she said defensively. "I merely did as she asked and took her to the railway station."

"But if she wasn't going to Weston, then where was she going?" Quentin demanded. "You must have some idea, girl."

"I don't. I didn't."

Her mouth trembled, realising she was being treated like an accomplice now. It was all so unfair.

Her stomach felt as if it had turned to water, and all the romance of a suspected elopement was turning into something sordid.

"If the girl's really missing, shouldn't we inform the police, Quentin?" Bertie was saying. "There are some strange characters about these days."

"No," Immy said sharply. "I'm sure that's not necessary. Elsie would feel foolish if she was tracked down like a common criminal."

"She'll be a victim rather than a criminal if something's happened to her!" Rose snapped. "Was she alone or was she with someone? You must know her friends, Imogen. Think, girl."

Angry at the implied accusation that she was partly to blame, Immy took a deep breath. Now was the time; there was no more avoiding it. She spoke directly to Quentin.

"Father, this is only a guess, but I suspect that Elsie and Joe may have decided to get married without any fuss. Some of her best clothes are missing."

Rose exclaimed loudly. "The thoughtless hussy! How could she do this in such terrible times?"

"It could have something to do with wanting to feel she belonged to Joe before he went to war," Immy retorted, her eyes sparkling with fury now. "Maybe you've forgotten how it feels to be young and in love, Aunt Rose."

"Imogen, you will apologise to your aunt at once," Quentin roared. He had been silent with shock until this moment.

"No, the girl's right, Quentin," Rose said quickly. "But to go off without telling anyone *is* deceitful."

"And romantic and reckless," Immy went on relentlessly. "They were already engaged, and if they chose to bring the date forward to thwart Mr Hitler's plans, it's their lives, isn't it? *Daddy*?"

She pleaded with him not to hate Elsie for what she had done. They had always been such a close family unit, and even when they were apart, they were still strong. She willed him to remember that. She would defend Elsie to the death, just as she had supported Baz, and assured her father it would be good for Daisy and Teddy to go to Aunt Rose's.

She saw his mouth give the smallest twist.

"You were always a persuasive young baggage, Imogen. Well, what's done is done, even though I think the manner of it is unforgivable. I shall have strong words to say to Joe about it when they deign to contact us."

Since no one else could think of anything else to say on the matter, they reverted in some relief to more urgent thoughts of the future now that they were officially at war.

"I shall offer my services, of course," Immy said at once. "Now that Mr Harris has gone to Cornwall in partnership with his brother, I shall need to find some different work."

"There'll be no shortage of that," Rose said. "Women always come into their own when the menfolk have gone away to fight. I shall start a knitting circle for soldiers' comforts, and munition factories will want plenty of volunteers."

It wasn't really what Immy had in mind, but she didn't think now was the time to suggest that she and Helen might apply to be official drivers in one of the women's services. It was an idea that had been catching hold of her lately, and just as Elsie felt she would be mentally if not physically closer to Joe once they were married, Immy felt she would be a touch closer to James if she was in the same line of business. More or less.

She bit her lip, thinking how quickly life could change. Yesterday they hadn't been at war, and now they were. Yesterday she had been thinking vaguely that she might have to work in Preston's temporarily, and now she was thinking of leaving home herself and spreading her wings in a way she had never considered before. It was unnerving to think that war could be the catalyst for such changes.

The telephone rang. Quentin answered it, and eventually returned to the sitting-room with a flushed face.

"That was your sister," he said abruptly to Immy. "You were right. She and Joe were married by special licence yesterday and are staying in a hotel in Bath until Tuesday, when he has to report to his regiment. Joe enlisted several days ago, so the honeymoon will be very short-lived."

Immy had to ask. "Daddy, you did give them your blessing, didn't you?"

"How could I not? Despite her distress at having to confess to me, I couldn't miss the happiness in her voice. And she'll be back home with us on Tuesday evening."

But not in the same way as before, Immy thought. Not now that she's known Joe's love and become a part of him in the most intimate way a man and a woman can share themselves. She envied them that closeness so much.

The telephone didn't seem to stop ringing all day. Baz was as brash as ever, telling them that he had heard the news, and that he wished he was old enough to join up. Right now he was about to leave for the Cornish fishing grounds, but he promised to come and visit them as soon as his boat returned to Bristol.

Joe's distraught parents got through from Yorkshire after an interminable wait, to tell them Joe had managed to call them, and they hoped the Caldwells weren't too upset. Oh, and there was the war, they added, almost as an afterthought . . .

Daisy rang from the Luckwells to check that everyone was all right, and to say that Mrs Luckwell was taking the news badly, since she'd lost a brother in the last lot.

"That's how she put it," Daisy said to Immy. "Odd, isn't it? I think she's glad I'm here, though, so I'm staying for the rest of the day. And the best news is that Lucy's much better."

"I'm glad. You're a good pal, Daisy," Immy said softly.

"Oh, I know. A proper little saint, aren't I?" she answered breezily, covering her embarrassment. "Anyway, tell Aunt Rose that if I'm not back when they get home, she knows where I'll be. Love to you all, by the way."

"Oh, and Daisy—"

But she'd gone before Immy could tell her about Elsie and Joe. It didn't matter. Aunt Rose would do it far more eloquently face to face. She hung up the phone slowly.

Without warning, she was completely out of sorts again. In a kind of limbo. As deflated as if all the air had just been let out of her lungs.

She told herself severely it was hardly surprising. Her country had just gone to war, and nothing was ever going to be the same again.

But it was more than that. It was the feeling that everyone had something to do or say, someone to hold or to touch, when she had nothing and no one. The family was all around her, and yet she had never felt so alone.

She realised that the house was very quiet now, and there was only the occasional creak of floorboards from the Marys' rooms above. She hadn't even been aware of the moment when the grown-ups had gone into the garden to join the boys, though when she concentrated she could hear the sounds of the children's chatter, muted, as if they came from a long distance away. She could hear the deeper murmur of the adults' voices, more serious but determined not to let the trauma of this day affect three small lives.

In her head she could hear the echo of her mother, who had once filled this house with joy and laughter, and she blinked back the brief, stinging tears.

She felt as though the place was suddenly stifling her, and knew that if she stayed inside for much longer, she would go quietly mad. She had to get out.

"I'm going to see Helen," she called out to her father. "I won't be gone long, and I'll see you all before you leave, Aunt Rose."

"It's hardly polite to leave when we have guests, Imogen," Quentin began, but Rose put her hand on his arm, stilling his words.

"Let her go, Quentin. She needs to find her own peace."

"That's a bloody peculiar remark for anyone to make, if I may say so," he objected roughly, the words disguising his affection for her. "Considering we've just entered a war."

"I know," she said, her smile wavering and her eyes suddenly blurring with tears. "But then, I was always a peculiar woman, wasn't I, brother dear?"

Imogen kept her head down as she pedalled into the sudden blustery wind on her way to Helen's home.

She could have walked, but she didn't want to encounter people she knew, who would want to discuss this morning's announcement. She could have borrowed her father's car, but right now she wouldn't trust herself to drive sensibly. She rode hard, and she was out of breath long before she approached the lovely old house where the Church family lived.

There was a sudden noise from someone's garden, and a cluster of birds in a nearby tree flapped their wings and rose in a grey cloud into the sky. She wasn't a visionary, but in those few horrific seconds she had a weird sense of what the future might hold.

War clouds overhead, and the clear blue yonder being filled with the droning engines of enemy planes. Bombs being dropped. Buildings being torn apart as if they were as insubstantial as cardboard, reducing them to nothing but rubble and choking dust . . . and their occupants with them . . . destroying Bristol . . . bringing carnage and death to a once beautiful city . . .

She slewed her bicycle to a stop, shaking all over. If she hadn't, she knew she would have run into something. She was shocked by her own feelings of impotence and rage at that moment. Everyone had expected war for so long that some had almost become complacent. As if it was never really going to happen. It was all men's talk. All bravado.

Had she actually been one of them all this time? Never taking it as seriously as she should? Never thinking it would really affect her, or her family, even pooh-poohing Helen's talk of dispensing tea for soldiers on railway stations as something of a silly pastime for wealthy girls? How *could* she have been so blind? So shamefully self-centred . . .

"Imogen, by all that's wonderful! I was on my way to see you. Darling, you look so white. Are you ill?"

She felt someone take her bicycle away from her to prop it against a tree, not realising that she had been gripping the handlebars so tightly that she almost fell without their support.

But not quite. Because by then, that someone's arms were around her, and she was being pressed to his chest. The gruesome visions that had held her captive for those awful moments cleared, and she clutched James Church tightly as she gasped out his name.

"Oh James, I can't believe it's you. What are you doing here? I thought you were far away. You haven't written, and you promised—"

She was babbling incoherently, like a lovesick idiot, and she couldn't seem to stop.

"I know, and I'm sorry," he said, his voice vibrating against her cheek. "Field manoeuvres don't leave much time or opportunity for writing letters, I'm afraid."

"Not even one?" she said, brittle with unreasoning anger now, despite herself.

"Not even one. And I've only got a mouldy twelve-hour pass now before we get our orders for embarkation. But it doesn't mean I'm not thinking of you, Immy, darling. I think of you all the time. And you mustn't worry if you don't hear from me as often as you'd like."

She moved back from him a little, but he still held her close. She looked up into his handsome face and couldn't miss the determination there. He was like all the rest. He was St George and Sir Galahad all rolled into one. Eager to go, eager to fight, despite the fact he might be killed. And that was something she couldn't bear to think about.

"I don't want you to die, James," she said, hearing the tremor in her voice and despising herself for it.

"Well, I don't plan to, not if I have you to come home to," he said laughingly. The laughter faded a little, and he looked down at her less assuredly. "Do I, Immy?"

"You know you do," she whispered.

He bent his head to hers, and she felt the sweetest kiss on her lips, uncaring that they were in public, for there was no one around to see.

"Do you want to go and tell the folks?" he said softly.

She shook her head. "I don't want to tell anyone just yet. Let it be our secret, just for an hour or so. Except—" she went on, but hesitated, wondering if he would think her completely crazy if she said what was in her heart. Even as she felt her cheeks go hot, however, she knew she had to say it, and it was important that he understood.

"Could we take a walk over the Downs? I want to cherish the sense of freedom we still have."

"And you want to tell your mother's spirit that you've found your true love at last," he said, as if he could read every unspoken word.

She looked at him in real astonishment, and with a deep respect for such perception. "How did you know?"

"Call it intuition. Call it anything you like, but when two hearts are in tune, something far deeper than mere words flows between them."

She was more moved than she could say, never expecting a man to use such emotive words. But then, she had never known a man like James before. She had known him all her life, yet it was clearly going to take for ever to learn about him. It was a thought to fill her with joy, the first positive thought in her head on this momentous day.

"I do love you, James," she said daringly, forgetting all about the protocol of waiting for a man to say it first. It seemed such a silly convention now.

"And I love you. I always have and I always will. Even when we're far apart, and whatever the future holds, you must always remember that and take heart, my love. Promise me."

"I will," Imogen said. "Always."

Daisy's War

One

The small boys stared open-mouthed as Daisy pirouetted in front of them, as grandly as any film star at the local fleapit. The girl playing with the rag doll on the mat merely sniffed and refused to look at her. Daisy was going to ignore her anyway. Stuck up little madam that she was. *Vanessa*! Who ever heard of a name like that for a kid from the slums? No wonder she had airs and graces and thought herself better than anybody else.

'So what do you think, then?' Daisy asked her small brother and the two young evacuee boys. 'How would you fancy being looked after in your hospital bed by *Nurse* Daisy Caldwell?'

'You're not a proper nurse yet,' Norman, the older of the brothers, said, scowling. 'You're just a girl done up in a fancy uniform. Not like our dad. Our mum says he's got a proper uniform now . . .'

Vanessa hooted. 'Your dad ran off and left your mum years ago, stupid. The only uniform he's wearing now has prob'ly got arrows on it, like them jailbirds wear in my *Beano*.'

Daisy glared at her as the younger of the brothers howled, 'Our dad ain't in jail! He's flying one of them bombers and killing Jerries, that's what he's doing, Nessa Brown, and you're a pig—'

'Oh yeah? Tell that to the fairies, birdbrain. And don't call me *Nessa*! Anyway, I bet your dad's rotting in some 'orrible jail – and prob'ly dying of consumption by now,' she added for effect.

'Shut up, Vanessa,' Daisy whipped out at once. 'You don't know what you're talking about.'

'Yes I do, clever-dick nurse,' the girl said in a kind of triumph. 'Me old gran died of it, so there.'

All Daisy's pleasure in the brand new probationer's dress she was wearing disappeared at once. She tried to remember that this irritating girl had no idea that Daisy's own best friend was suffering from consumption – or TB, as those in the know called it, she thought, with a brief surge of superiority – and that the outlook was bad. Very bad, as it happened. After such a good start, Lucy's chances of survival were less than possible. They were nearer to nil.

It was all so unfair. Why did Lucy have to die? What had she ever done to deserve it? Everybody knew the Germans were rough-riding it over half of Europe and killing people now, ever since that pompous Mr Chamberlain had produced his 'Note' six months ago and plunged them into war with Germany.

'*Politicians*!' Aunt Rose always snorted – having no time for them as a breed – 'always meddling in people's lives and usually getting it wrong.'

But this was different. Lucy was different. She wasn't an anonymous face that Daisy didn't know. She wasn't one of the wounded soldiers who were starting to be sent to Weston General now, and cheerfully saying how much they liked to see Daisy's pretty face – even when some of them couldn't see at all through eyes that had been shot away or horrifically burned, and some of them had ghastly seeping wounds and not much chance of ever living a proper life again.

Daisy could cope with them – mostly – because it was her job, and she loved it. But Lucy was her best friend, stuck in a miserable sanatorium in deepest Wales, dying of TB at the age of seventeen; and there wasn't a damn thing anybody could do about it.

'Anyway, our dad's flying aeroplanes and killing Jerries, so that's all you know,' Norman was shouting furiously now, rounding on Vanessa as his brother began to snivel. 'Just like your boy, ain't he, Daisy?'

She snapped back at him without really meaning to, not wanting to think too much about the lack of communication from her young man right now.

'Maybe. I don't know. But I do know you'd better get this mess cleared up while I change out of my uniform. Then you can all help me get the tea started before Aunt Rose comes home from her knitting circle.'

Vanessa looked scornful again. 'Why would she want to sit around knitting socks for soldiers she don't even know? Why can't their mums do it for 'em?'

'For somebody whose mum never knitted anything for anybody as far as I could tell, you should think twice before you condemn other people,' Daisy told her smartly, knowing Aunt Rose wouldn't like hearing her censure a twelve-year-old who was far from home and well out of her normal environment. But sometimes this one was impossible.

They were all far from home in Aunt Rose's motley household, she thought suddenly. Though it was hardly very far for her youngest brother Teddy and herself, moving down to Weston from their Bristol home after their mother had died.

It was just temporary, of course – they still had their old home in Vicarage Street to go back to any time. Except that temporary had somehow become more permanent than any of them had planned. You had to thank Mr Hitler for some of that – but not all of it.

It had been sensible for Teddy to be sent away after their mother's terrible accident. He had been too young at five years old to take it all in properly, and Aunt Rose and Uncle Bert had been only too glad to give him a loving home. But it had been Daisy's choice to come here too.

Her older sisters were still in Bristol with their father, and Baz – well, Lord knew where her brother Baz was now, Daisy thought with a grin. Somewhere in mid-Atlantic for all she knew, with all his grand ideas of going to sea, but far more likely to be on a trawler in the Irish fishing grounds.

Her usual cheerful nature was returning fast after the little bust-up with the brats. Vanessa was sometimes the giddy limit, though, and Daisy had to keep reminding herself that she came from a broken home, as they called it. And if what the billeting officer said was true, it was unlikely there'd be a proper home for her to go back to at all, what with her flighty mother and her drunken father.

Which was *fine* if Aunt Rose had wanted her for a permanent lodger, but that wasn't really the plan. Daisy could more or less understand why her childless aunt and uncle had wanted to fill their house with children when the opportunity came, even if it had taken a war to give them what they had always been denied.

Evacuees weren't always welcome in every household, especially when you had to take them in whether you wanted to or not. Aunt Rose loved them all, though Lucy's parents hadn't been too keen when they had been allocated a brother and sister from London at their farm.

Privately, Daisy thought this might be a blessing for when IT happened. She thought about Lucy's prognosis in capital letters now, referring to it as IT, unable to bear putting it into actual words.

'What we having for tea then?' Vanessa asked her sullenly, when she had changed out of her uniform and returned to the parlour.

'Bread and scrape and think yourself lucky to get it,' Daisy said cheerfully, the way Uncle Bert usually did.

'Is that all?'

Daisy sighed. 'Vanessa, why can't you try to be pleasant

4

now and then? We all have to get along, whether we like it or not.'

'You're so sweet, aren't you?' the girl snapped at her. 'A proper blooming angel. Well, I'm not helping to get the tea and that's that. I'm not skivvying for nobody.'

'I'm not asking you to be a skivvy, you idiot. Just cut the bread and don't be so pathetic.'

'Why can't we ever have pie and mash like me mother used to buy down the pie and eel shop?'

Daisy shuddered. 'Because we can't. Now, are you going to cut the bread or do I tell Aunt Rose that you're being obstructive again?'

The girl stared her out. She was going to be a smasher when she grew up a bit, all high cheekbones and wide brown eyes like a blooming film star, Daisy thought, using one of the girl's favourite words.

'If I knew what blooming obstrucky meant, I might be bothered!' Vanessa said, flouncing towards the cutlery drawer and catching her finger on the edge of the carving knife.

She gave a piercing cry and clutched at her hand, wringing it up and down like a yo-yo.

'You really are a ninny, Vanessa . . .' Daisy began, and then she saw how the girl's face had paled.

'If there's blood I can't look,' she whimpered. 'Me old gran used to cough it up, and it was all bright red, like a lot of froth . . .'

'Sit down,' Daisy snapped, knowing she was referring to the TB her grandmother had died of, and not wanting to be reminded too graphically of the symptoms that she knew only too well on account of Lucy. 'Put your head between your knees, and let me look at that finger.'

She practically had to wrench the girl's hands apart, while Vanessa turned her head the other way. It was only a nick, but for somebody terrified at the sight of blood, Daisy knew it might as well have been a river.

5

'Don't move a muscle while I fetch some vaseline and sticking plaster from the medicine box, and you'll soon be as right as ninepence.'

'Don't tell them boys then,' Vanessa muttered next.

'Of course not. Girls have to stick together, don't they?'

She dared her to argue with that, and got the merest hint of a smile in response. But she really was deathly white by now.

'There's nothing to be ashamed of in being afraid of the sight of blood, Vanessa,' Daisy told her.

'I ain't afraid . . .'

'Everyone's afraid of something. It's natural.'

Vanessa glared at her. 'Oh yeah? What are you afraid of, then?'

'I'll tell you a secret. When I was a little girl I used to be afraid of clouds.'

Vanessa hooted. '*Clouds* can't hurt you. Who ever heard of anyone being afraid of clouds?'

'Well, you just heard it. I thought they were monsters in the sky, just waiting to come and gobble me up,' Daisy went on evenly. 'Until my mother told me differently. She could always see good things everywhere.'

She waited, knowing Vanessa wouldn't be able to resist asking.

'Go on then. What did your mother say? She sounds like a blooming saint.'

Daisy ignored that. 'She used to tell me that clouds were like castles in the sky, and if I looked at them for long enough I'd see them too. And she was right.'

'I think that's daft.'

'It's no more daft than being afraid of a little bit of blood from a cut finger. What would you do if you *really* hurt yourself?'

She saw the girl shudder as she finished taping the cut finger, and spoke more cheerfully. 'Oh well, it's one way to get out of slicing bread, I suppose, and I won't tell anyone

6

your secret if you don't tell mine. So don't go bragging that you got the better of me!'

'Would I ever?' Vanessa retorted as she flounced off, and they both knew very well that she would.

Daisy began savagely slicing the bread herself, knowing that Aunt Rose would be tired after her afternoon out – and more likely from an afternoon of cheerful gossiping.

It was a regular occasion that was part social and part war work, but one that Rose and the knitting circle hugely enjoyed as they put the world to rights far better than any politicians ever could, in their opinion.

Daisy caught sight of herself in the mirror over the mantelpiece, and paused to smile for a moment, remembering her appearance in her new uniform.

Not bad, Daisy Caldwell, she told herself mentally. Not bad at all. Even if there were some who had thought she would never stick at it, and that her fads had come and gone as frequently as changing her stockings. But she'd proved them all wrong, and she blooming well knew it!

Two other young ladies were also assessing themselves in a mirror that afternoon. Daisy's oldest sister Imogen and her best friend Helen Church were in Immy's bedroom in Vicarage Street, and scrutinising their appearance with less admiration than Daisy had done.

'Do you remember that night at my mother's fund-raising ball in Bath last year, Immy, when we both looked such a treat?' Helen said dolefully. 'Well, *you* looked like an absolute angel as usual, of course. Uniforms are such a miserable colour, and they don't do a single thing for my complexion.'

Immy laughed as her friend ruffled her hand through her blonde curls.

'You'd look a treat in anything, and you know it . . .'

'Oh well, you would say that, but it doesn't. Anyway, James will probably turn somersaults when he sees you, regardless of this beastly khaki. They say girls go dotty over men in uniform, so let's hope it applies the other way round as well.'

'I wish I could let him know what's happening,' Immy said wistfully; 'but since I haven't the faintest idea where he is right now . . .'

'He'll write when he can, you know that. You needn't fear that any French mam'selles will get their clutches into my brother, darling.'

'I hadn't given such a thing a second's thought, actually, so thank you for putting the idea in my head!'

Helen stared at her. 'Good Lord, you aren't taking me seriously, are you? Anyone with half an eye could see that James is totally besotted with you.'

'Anyone with half an eye can't see much of anything,' Immy replied smartly, pulling a comic face and crossing her eyes.

They both began to giggle, and then sobered up as they heard the creaking floorboards from the converted rooms above that had been turned into a self-contained flat for paying guests.

It no longer contained the two elderly widows who had lodged there for a year, since they'd both decided to get out of Bristol before Hitler's bombs made an unholy mess of it, as Immy's father put it. The flat was now the middle Caldwell sister's domain.

Immy still had to remind herself that Elsie was no longer a Caldwell, but a Preston, since she and Joe had married in haste at the very beginning of the war, six months ago. It wasn't *indecent* haste though, she insisted quickly, even though Elsie had become pregnant a few months later, raising a few eyebrows.

'And why not, when two people are as passionately in love as those two lucky stiffs?' Helen had said stoutly, sounding far more worldly than she really was, and knowing little about the mysteries of love-making or childbirth, for all her sophisticated outlook on life.

8

But together they had consulted the brown-paper-covered book that Immy's brother had failed to hand back to his school chum, to be read strictly beneath the bedclothes, and explaining things far more frankly than a young boy or an unmarried girl had the right to expect.

Or maybe not. To someone with a logical mind like Imogen's, it always seemed faintly bizarre that schoolteachers instructed people on dull old dates in history and expected you to recite them parrot-fashion, and yet never dreamed of telling pupils about the most fundamental thing of all . . .

'Where have you gone now, Immy?' she heard Helen say, as her eyes misted over. She brought them back into focus, and met the knowing gaze of her friend.

'Or do I need to ask?' Helen went on. 'Dreaming about James again, I suppose, and wishing he was coming home on leave soon, like Joe.' She gave a mischievous grin. 'Do they still *do* it, do you think? Are they *allowed* to, when she's expecting?'

'How should I know?' Immy said crossly. 'It's none of our business, anyway, so don't even think about it.'

'We could always ask Daisy. I never thought she'd be so knowledgeable about stuff like that, but I bet she even knows all about delivering babies by now.'

Immy laughed. 'I doubt it! Whatever else Daisy does in that hospital of hers, I'm sure she'd be far too squeamish to be present at a birth! I'm sure her best role is offering tea and sympathy to the wounded servicemen, and revelling in being a perfect little Miss Nightingale.'

Helen spoke shrewdly. 'You're proud of her though, aren't you?'

'Of course I am. We all are. Who ever thought Daisy would forget her flighty ideas of going on the stage and turn into a really dedicated nurse? Actually, I'm glad she didn't try to follow in Mother's footsteps. It would probably have broken Father's heart to support her in the theatre, which he would certainly have done, of course. But I know he

9

couldn't have borne watching her perform on the very stage where Mother used to.'

As she spoke, she was momentarily transported back to the halcyon days when their sweet-faced mother had danced and sung on stage, enchanting everyone who saw her. Frances Caldwell had been a star, beautiful and ethereal, and while her three daughters had inherited her beauty, no one could replace her in her children's eyes, nor their father's either. It had devastated the whole family when the cruel illness that had deprived her of her senses had driven her to the edge of the Avon Gorge and seen her plunge over to her death.

Even now, eighteen months later, the memory of the way she had almost floated towards the edge of the precipice in a weird kind of slow motion that no one had been able to stop could still make Imogen shiver with horror.

'So are we going to parade in front of your father, or shall we get out of uniform and pretend everything's back to normal?' Helen's bright voice broke in.

'Let's change,' Immy said swiftly. 'It will be soon enough to remind him when we have to report for duty after the weekend.'

Helen gave her a quick hug. 'I'm really going to miss you, Immy. Whatever happened to our plans of joining up together and staying together? It would have been such a lark. And now we're reporting to different units, and being sent Lord knows where.'

'Well, I'm sure *you* needn't worry. Your father's got influence, and I daresay you'll get a cushy job. Mine's just a shopkeeper . . .'

'But you've got the brains, darling,' Helen told her lightly. 'Just like that little sister of yours. And Elsie's got her man.'

Elsie Caldwell Preston wasn't feeling anything like as perky as everyone said you were supposed to feel when you were expecting. In fact, if anyone had bothered to ask her right now, she would have told them she felt decidedly wretched. Doctor Wolfe had told her she was definitely two months pregnant, if not a little more, and of course she was delighted about the fact – and more than a little scared.

If only Joe had been here to share this time with her – if only these were normal times, instead of months into a war that seemed to have been forecast for ages beforehand, and now seemed be going nowhere . . . but where people all around her were joining up and taking part, while all she had to do was sit and twiddle her thumbs and feel utterly frustrated . . .

She felt the weak tears fill her eyes, and told herself she was being a fool. It was also a little shaming, as if she resented the fact that she was going to have their baby, which of course she didn't. It was just that she had never felt this way before. She had never felt so helpless and so vulnerable – and so alone, without Joe's support.

Even here, in the little flat that her father had put at their disposal for as long as they wanted it, she was alone. She was terribly proud that Joe had enlisted the minute he could and hadn't waited for conscription, and of course she adored him and was deliriously happy to be married to him . . . but being married also meant that she couldn't do her bit for the war effort like her sisters and her brother Baz, and being pregnant meant she was going to grow fat and ugly . . .

Without thinking she put her hand protectively over her belly, where the uncomfortable stitch was starting to nag at her again. But with the thought of becoming fat and ugly came more of that swift shame, because it seemed to imply that she didn't want this baby.

And she did. Of course she did. It was something precious that belonged to her and Joe alone. Something they had made out of their love for one another. Some*one*. A real little person.

Sometimes, in the long hours of the night when she

couldn't sleep, she tried to imagine the baby's face. Tried to see herself bathing it and feeding it and dressing it. Tried to imagine it as that living, breathing little person, instead of the rather hideous diagrams the midwife had given her that showed a baby's progress inside a mother's womb.

She didn't want diagrams of that odd little froglike creature with its sightless eyes and half-formed limbs. She yearned to hold the real thing in her arms, to have it here and now, as a sort of living proof that Joe was still near, still beside her in his baby son or daughter, like a talisman . . .

She shivered, not wanting to admit to anyone how fearful she was for Joe. It wasn't the way women were supposed to behave in wartime. They were supposed to be strong and stoical and keep the home fires burning and all that stiff-upper-lipped patriotic business. But it wasn't so easy in the chill of the night when you remembered all you had read in the newspapers that day about the way the war was going, and the wireless bulletins that were so depressing.

She tried to be more positive, but she didn't have her sisters' capacity for it, and never had had. Elsie was quieter and more of a thinker than Daisy, who plunged into everything with equal enthusiasm. She was far less strong than Imogen, whom they all looked up to as the older, clever sister who could do no wrong.

Elsie was a failure in her own eyes, and even though Doctor Wolfe had told her these odd moods might trouble her at times, she knew none of it would be half so bad if only Joe was coming home for good instead of forty-eight-hour leave in a few weeks' time. If only Adolph Hitler hadn't started this hateful war . . .

She jumped as she heard the knock on her door and called out to someone to come in, her voice choking.

'For pity's sake, Elsie, what's wrong?' Immy said in concern, seeing how flushed her sister looked. 'You had a letter from Joe this morning, didn't you?' All must be well with him, or Elsie would have told them by now.

'I just feel so miserable without him,' Elsie burst out. 'I know I'm being a misery, and I'm not the only one to be left alone in wartime . . .'

'Far from it, darling,' Immy said drily.

'But I keep getting this wretched nausea all the time, and you know how I've always hated it.'

'Are you following the midwife's suggestions about sipping warm water before you get out of bed in the morning, and eating a dry biscuit or two?'

Elsie gave her a wan smile. 'Of course I am. And are you practising to take over her job now with all this new-found knowledge?'

'Not likely! I just want to help, and if she thinks it will work, you should try it, Elsie. If you have our old spirit stove by the bed you can heat up some water without moving a muscle. I'll find it for you.'

'Oh, I'm sure it was thrown out long ago,' Elsie said, still feeling contrary and not prepared to be pampered.

'No it wasn't. It's in the air-raid shelter with the rest of the emergency supplies, but right now I'd say your need is more urgent than waiting for one of Hitler's bombs to fall on Bristol.'

'And I hope you're crossing your fingers when you say that,' Elsie said.

13

Two

Daisy hadn't heard from Lucy for several weeks now, and she felt alternately guilty and annoyed with herself. Guilty because she didn't have the nerve to go to the Luckwell farm and ask Lucy's mother what the latest news was; and annoyed because she was a nurse and should be professional enough to deal with whatever she had to face.

She was capable enough when the wounded were brought in from the special trains, and had proved herself on more than one occasion, even when some of the older nurses were trying desperately not to retch at the sight of the men's suppurating wounds and the sickly-sweet gangrenous smells that came from some of the poor devils. But Daisy knew she wasn't completely professional yet. She hadn't had enough experience to be able to hide her feelings when it was her best friend involved in a horrible debilitating disease. She wondered how any normal seventeen-year-old girl coped with being in a sanatorium with old men and women dying of consumption. Being handed out regular sputum dishes and having the disgusting mess examined and assessed was humiliating enough, without watching the rest of them go through the same procedures, and knowing that, at the end of it all, most of them went out of there feet first.

Daisy shuddered; but she had decided that being a nurse was her vocation from the day when Lucy had been in danger of being crushed by her horse and Daisy had had such praise heaped on her for keeping her head in the midst

14

of a panic, knowing exactly what to do for her shock and sprained ankle.

Minor things, she thought now, dismissing them. Like taping up Nessa's cut finger, and reassuring the patient with her own childish tale of being afraid of clouds . . . which was perfectly true. They were all minor things that anyone could cope with who had an ounce of gumption.

But this was something else. Something that was tearing the Luckwell family apart, and Daisy too. Even Aunt Rose, who had known Lucy and her family far longer than Daisy had, usually came back from her visits to the farm with a grim face. At those times, Daisy guessed that even Lucy's no-nonsense mother had been unable to resist spilling out all her anguish to her old friend.

'It's just not fair!' she said out loud, forgetting where she was for the moment.

The young soldier whose leg she had been binding looked at her in astonishment, not knowing how her thoughts sometimes went off at a tangent while she did the routine jobs on the ward.

'Crikey, nursey, you've got a bee in your bonnet today, aincher? What ain't fair, for Gawd's sake? I mean, we all know this bleedin' war ain't fair, and my having half a leg on the port side ain't fair, but a pretty young miss like you shouldn't have anything troublin' you, unless it's the fact that you and me can't go dancin' tonight, what with my iffy leg and all . . .'

Daisy laughed at his nonsense. 'Stop it, Private Webb. There's nothing wrong with your leg that a few weeks' treatment won't cure, and you'll be up and dancing with the best of them in no time.'

'How about it then?' he asked slyly. 'There's nothing in the rules that says a nurse can't go dancin' with her patient, is there?'

'Not that I'm aware of . . .'

'Except that a bobby-dazzler like you is sure to have

a boy somewhere, I'll bet. Come on now, what's his name?'

'You're a terrible flirt, Private Webb, and I'm not telling you,' Daisy said with a giggle.

'Ah-hah, so there is somebody then! Just my luck when I'd found the girl of my dreams.' He put his hand over his heart dramatically.

'Stop it, for goodness' sake, or you'll have Sister after me,' Daisy told him, finishing off the leg-binding and admiring the neat job she had made of it.

'All right then, but remember to save the last dance for me,' he called out after her as she swished away.

She grimaced at the task the nurse at the next bed was performing, knowing that her patient wouldn't be dancing ever again, or doing anything else, for that matter. His number was well and truly up, and he hadn't even had a single visitor, Staff Nurse Hetty had said indignantly, even though they'd informed his relatives. Some of them just couldn't face it, she had added derisively.

Remembering those words, Daisy resolved to cycle over to the Luckwell farm as soon as she had finished her shift that day. The sanatorium in Wales was too far away for Lucy to receive regular visitors from home, and farming folk couldn't just go off whenever they wanted to.

There were always cows to be milked and livestock to be fed; and anyway, it was forbidden for Daisy to visit Lucy, when she was working in a hospital herself where patients had open wounds and were so susceptible to infection. But she owed it to the Luckwells to visit them as often as possible, as she had promised Lucy she would.

At least her friend was well away from any dangers of bombing, Daisy thought ironically, as she left the hospital on that blustery March afternoon, bending low over her handlebars as she cycled towards the rural part of the town beyond the miles of sand and seafront. She could have kept to the inland streets and avoided this always windy part of Weston, but she liked to come this way, because it was where she had literally bumped into Cal for the first time.

The stinging in her eyes now, as the sand was whipped up by a strong gust of wind, had as much to do with wondering where the dickens the air force was sending him, as with the saltiness of the sea air. Daisy was in love, and although she didn't exactly envy her sister Elsie for expecting a baby so soon after being married, she certainly envied her the closeness with Joe that had produced it.

You didn't say so to anyone, of course. Such thoughts were best kept private or else you might be thought of as fast. But when you were a nurse, you were privileged to witness sights and sounds that other people weren't; and she had listened to more than one soldier's confession about how much he loved his girl, and the things they did together, while wondering if they would ever be able to do them again. She had washed and dried every part of their bodies, and joked with them over sizes and shapes, and wept secretly at their desperation that things might never be the same again for many of them – and not only in the baby-making department, either, as Staff Nurse Hetty called it, but in losing confidence in regaining their old jobs, or in facing their families or going home a wreck of a man.

It was tragic in many ways, and Daisy had already vowed fiercely that if Cal came safely home again – which of course he *would* – if he asked her to give in to him, she would. She definitely *would*. Only a hard-hearted harpy would send a man away to war without giving him what he craved the most . . .

The fact that Cal had never been anything but the perfect gentleman made such a vow easy to keep, of course, and he had never even touched her bosom except very tentatively on the outside of all her clothes; but Daisy wouldn't think about that. She was a romantic – she was Guinevere to his Lancelot – and she loved him so much, she would give him anything.

'Here, watch where you're going, miss,' she heard some-one shout, and swerved to avoid the small column of air cadets marching along the seafront.

She heard them snigger and one of them made a rude gesture towards her, making her face burn. *Snot-rag*, she thought crudely, using one of Uncle Bert's least attractive expletives; but then her face softened as she watched them march away, with their leader barking orders at them. Cal had been one of them not so long ago, and they would all be sent far from home, the same as he had been. She and Lucy had taken a special delight in riding their horses as close to the Locking Camp periphery fence as they had dared, where they could watch the air cadets doing their training. It all seemed a very long time ago now. It seemed as if all of them had aged a hundred years instead of less than one.

'Daisy, my lamb, 'tis good to see you,' Mrs Luckwell exclaimed at once, when she arrived hot and breathless at the farm. 'Your auntie's always telling me how busy you are these days with your nursing, so I'm glad you can spare a bit of time to come and jaw with us.'

Daisy knew it wasn't meant as a reproach, but right now she was sensitive enough to see it that way.

'I've been meaning to come for ages,' she said quickly. 'I'm sorry it's been such a long time, Mrs Luckwell—'

'There now, you musn't think there's a need. Lucy wouldn't want to think you felt obligated to us on her account.'

'I haven't heard from her for a few weeks,' she said, when she had been given a large glass of home-made lemonade and a slice of Mrs Luckwell's seed cake. 'That's why I'm here really. What's the latest news?'

'Not so good, my dear.' She spoke without expression, which to Daisy's trained ear meant that 'not so good' meant 'pretty bad'. 'Some days I almost wish the Good Lord would

18

– but 'tis wrong to think that way. He'll choose her moment in His own good time.'

For a moment Daisy didn't follow. When she did, she was shocked.

'You don't mean you want her to . . . to . . .'

'To die? Daisy, love, you must have seen plenty of folk going from this world to the next by now, and 'tis often more of a blessing than a sadness.'

'But those are *old* people. Or badly wounded soldiers who haven't got a hope of surviving. Lucy's your daughter. My friend. She's only seventeen . . .'

'And she's dying slowly. By inches, you might say. If 'twere one of our beasts, we'd have it put down painlessly and there'd be an end to it.'

Daisy didn't know to answer her. Uncle Bert said often enough that farming folk had a different philosophy from the rest of them. Animals were part of their lives, to be fatted and slaughtered when necessary, and they couldn't afford to be sentimental over them. In farmers' eyes, people were not so different. Unless they were talking about a *daughter* . . .

'I've shocked you, haven't I, Daisy?' she heard Lucy's mother say quietly. 'But you musn't think we don't care. It's a kind of safety valve, see? And once it blows – well . . .'

Whatever else she was going to say was interrupted by the door being flung open and two small figures rushing inside, followed by one large one. The brother and sister stopped as soon as they saw the visitor with the bright-red hair that Daisy tried in vain to keep tidy at the hospital, while the older fellow's face split into a wide grin.

'We ain't seen you around here lately, Daisy. Ma was saying the same thing t'other day, weren't you, Ma?'

'*Ben!*' Mrs Luckwell chided her bumbling son. 'If you can't say something pleasant . . .'

Daisy saw how his face reddened. He wasn't the brightest of young men, and she had always felt a mite sorry for him. 'It's all right, Mrs Luckwell. I know it's been a

19

while. So how are you, Ben? Taking to baby-sitting, I see.'

'We ain't babies,' the boy with the cockney accent said indignantly. 'We've been doing a special job, feeding the pigs.'

'I can tell that by the smell. And who are you?' Daisy asked him, knowing very well that these were the evacuees Lucy's mother hadn't wanted, but whom she was fussing over now like the proverbial mother hen.

'I'm Cyril Jenkins and this is me sister Tess. Are you a nurse or summat?'

'That's right,' Daisy told him. 'You're a bright boy, aren't you?'

'Nah. Knew it by the uniform, didn't I? The nurse used to come to our 'ouse every day to stick a needle in me mum before she died.'

'Oh.' He said it so matter-of-factly Daisy didn't know what to say. He must be around seven-going-on-forty, she thought, seeing the wise old eyes in that so-young face. Tess looked even younger, but she spoke up suddenly.

'Our mum had the sugar, miss.'

'She means—' Mrs Luckwell began under her breath.

'I know what she means,' Daisy told her.

She knew that in the worst cases, sugar diabetes could bring on a coma and even death, and maybe this was what had happened to the Jenkins mother. She sympathised with these two, having lost her own mother, though in very different circumstances; and her little brother Teddy hadn't been much younger than them when it happened. She switched her thoughts abruptly.

'I'll have to be going, Mrs Luckwell,' she said next. 'But if you ever want these two off your hands for an afternoon sometime, shall I ask Aunt Rose if they can come to tea with our little crowd?'

'That would be nice,' Mrs Luckwell beamed. 'Providing young Vanessa don't put on her airs and graces. These little 'uns have had enough trouble in their short lives, what with their mum dying, and their dad wanting 'em out of the way for the duration.'

Everything had changed since the war began, Daisy thought, pedalling back towards the town and up to Aunt Rose and Uncle Bert's rambling old house. Families were being split up all the time, and if you didn't know the full circumstances – who could blame the Jenkins father for wanting his two little ones out of the way when bombs were falling? Most children were being sent to the country for safety, well away from London and the south-east counties.

It made her start thinking about how her own family had been split up, long before the war came. It had all begun with her mother's death, and the fact that her father's once proud business had been bought up by a northern emporium. What a disaster that had seemed at the time, and how it had all faded into far less importance now. Weirdly so, thought Daisy, especially since if it had never happened, then Elsie would never have met Joe and got married, and her father wouldn't have become the manager, if not the owner, of his shop once again, since all the young men had gone away to war anyway. It was definitely weird, the way things worked out.

Aunt Rose would have said there was an Almighty Design in all these things, of course, along with her churchy friends; but Daisy wasn't so sure of any of that any more. Not since her mother had died, and not since the war had started that nobody wanted, and definitely not since she had seen some of the hideous injuries she was faced with every single day.

A loving God shouldn't allow these things to happen, and Daisy wasn't sure she believed in anything except the need to survive. She dismissed all those moments that were almost like revelations when some poor dying soldier prayed to God to let him go . . . and more than one of them had

21

sworn that they glimpsed this long white tunnel and some heavenly light at the end of it . . .

It was all a myth, and you might as well believe in fairies. Daisy didn't believe any of it – nor the way some of the older nurses swore they had seen guardian angels hovering near their charges in the still of the night . . . It gave Daisy the shivers, though it was a non-belief she didn't dare to share with anyone else, least of all Aunt Rose, who would be horrified at such blasphemy.

When she heard the sounds of children's shrieks and laughter, she realised she had already reached the house. She opened the gate with relief, glad to put all these uneasy thoughts behind her. Aunt Rose told everyone approvingly that she was growing up into a sensible young lady. But Daisy wasn't at all sure she wanted to be sensible. Not if it meant facing things beyond her understanding.

She was basically an optimist, but there were also darker moments when she sometimes felt she spent far too much time with sick people who wanted help in moving from this world to the next, as they put it, instead of having fun, the way any normal seventeen-year-old should. And that was a fine way for a nurse to think, she thought in sudden anger – and not a little shame.

'We've got a visitor, and you'll never guess who it is,' Norman was yelling at her now, prancing around with his brother like two small whirling dervishes.

'Me mum's come to see us,' Ronnie shrieked. 'She's having a cuppa tea wiv Auntie Rose and Uncle Bert.'

'Good Lord,' was all Daisy could say.

She saw her brother Teddy playing with George in the corner of the garden, and the dog was going wild, leaping up and down after the yo-yo Teddy was teasing him with. There was no sign of Vanessa.

'Me mum's going to take us 'ome soon,' Ronnie said confidently.

'Is she?' Daisy said, doubting it. What kind of a crazy

22

woman would take her kids back to Kent, with its proximity to London, when they had the comparative peace and security of the south-west countryside?

She went inside the house, to find her aunt and uncle in the middle of a fine old harangue with a blowsy-looking woman in a shabby coat and down-at-heel shoes. She was shouting at Aunt Rose, whose face was getting redder by the minute, Daisy noted, and seemingly out of her depth for once.

'I know you've done your best for 'em, missus, but they're my kids, and they'd be far better off with me than with you. My sister's got a place in Wales with her young man's fam'ly now, and we can all go there for the duration.'

She glared at the older couple, daring them to dispute her words. But why would they? wondered Daisy. Unless the woman was lying, and there was no place in Wales for them at all. She certainly had a shifty look about her, and didn't ever meet anyone's eyes for more than seconds. The evacuee boys were often more like defensive little devils than angels, but Daisy knew her aunt wouldn't want to see them hawked around the countryside on a whim.

Without thinking twice, she put in her spoke while Aunt Rose was still drawing breath.

'Don't you have to go through the proper channels before settling the boys somewhere else, Mrs . . . uh . . . Turvey?' she said, groping in her mind to remember the boys' surname. 'I know that's what my aunt and uncle had to do when Vanessa came to stay with us. The billeting officers are very particular about checking each property to see that there's enough accommodation, and that there are suitable hosts for looking after the children.'

She knew she shouldn't be taking charge like this, and she didn't quite know where all the words came from. She only knew that she looked and sounded authoritative in her uniform with her usual tangle of curls tamed and swathed on top of her head for neatness and hygiene, since she'd gone straight from her hospital shift to the farm. Her uncle took his cue from her now.

'My niece is quite right, Mrs Turvey. It's good news that you've come to visit the boys, but we're responsible for them now, and we couldn't relinquish that care without checking firstly with our own billeting officers, and then they would refer the transfer request to the billeting people in Wales where your sister lives.

'I think you'll find that's the legal requirement,' he added, having no idea whether it was or not, and pretty sure that no such thing applied to any case where a child's own mother wanted to remove him. But he counted on the fact that Mrs Turvey wouldn't know that. It was obvious that she wasn't an educated woman, and heaven knew where her husband was in all this. She might want custody of her children back for some other reason, maybe to get extra housing assistance, or to plead poverty with her local council, or even to get extra rations.

The Lord knew her reasons, and He wasn't telling, Bert thought grimly, but there were plenty of devious goings-on these days. He also knew how attached Rose had got to all these children filling their empty old house, and he wasn't having two of them taken away from her without being sure the cause was genuine.

Besides, in all these months the Turvey woman had only written a couple of sketchy letters to her boys and not even sent them a Christmas card. He hardened his heart against what some would have seen as a loving mother's request, and then Rose spoke up crisply.

'So what do you think, Mrs Turvey?' she said, her equilibrium restored as she saw the indecision in the woman's eyes. 'Naturally, you must do as you think best, but Norman and Ronnie are quite settled now, and it would be a shame to disrupt them all over again. Of course, the bed-wetting did take quite a while to overcome,' she added, as if as an afterthought. 'But if it starts all over again,

24

I'm sure your sister and her young man's family will be understanding.'

Mrs Turvey gave a small shudder. 'P'raps I should think about this some more before I decide for sure. I'm told the house in Wales ain't very big, and it may not be so suitable.'

'I think that's a very wise decision,' Rose said. 'Now, another cup of tea before you go?'

It was inevitable that Ronnie would wet the bed that night. It hadn't happened for weeks now, but Daisy told Elsie on the telephone that weekend that you couldn't blame a mother for wanting to see her boys, even though it meant a certain amount of emotional disruption. Daisy had recently begun a course of instruction on emotional disturbance, though mainly with regard to servicemen having to face civvy life again, whether it was limbless or sightless – or even having a complete mental breakdown.

'Some of these poor kids don't know where they are these days,' Daisy went on, with seventeen-year-old wisdom.

'Ah, you're really enjoying playing Miss Nightingale, aren't you, Daisy?' she heard her sister say, with an unmistakable smile in her voice.

'It's what I do, isn't it? You'll be glad of someone like me in a few months' time, earth mother, so don't scoff.'

'Would I dare? I'm only teasing, darling, you know that. Actually, I'd be glad of someone like you right now, if you could tell me why I keep feeling so horribly nauseous all the time.'

'Have you told Doctor Wolfe?'

Elsie sighed. 'Oh, he has enough to do without a perfectly healthy expectant mother fretting over the slightest thing. Besides, I'm under the midwife's care now, and she says it's perfectly normal at this stage. And before you ask, I've done everything Immy suggested, including having the camping stove by my bed and sipping hot water every morning before

I get up. It works – but I'm sick at night too, so what's your diagnosis for that, oh great white doctor?'

Daisy grinned. 'I'd say Immy's missed her vocation, if she's advising you on morning sickness! How is she, by the way? More to the point, *where* is she?'

'Oh, somewhere in Oxford now, I believe,' Elsie said vaguely. 'All set to be a driver for some army bigwig.'

There was no mistaking the misery and frustration in Elsie's voice now. This was supposed to be one of the happiest times in a woman's life, wasn't it? Daisy thought. She tried to cheer her up.

'Never mind, Joe's coming home on leave any day, and I'm sure you won't be worrying too much about morning sickness then!' she added daringly.

'I hope not. It would be too awful – but I'm not going to talk about such things with you, little sister, so stop fishing!' she said with a laugh.

After they finished talking, Daisy set about tidying her room as she always did on a Sunday evening when the whole household had come back from church. They were quite a little crocodile now, she reflected, with the boys bellowing out the hymns, and Vanessa pooh-poohing the whole thing, despite the fact that she always joined in lustily, and had quite a sweet singing voice.

By now, Daisy's own voice had been discovered, courtesy of Aunt Rose's insistence, and she was in the choir, despite any feelings she may or may not have about the ethics of joining in a service in which she had no real belief; but she enjoyed the music so much that she went along anyway. It wasn't treading on her mother's professional toes, either, since Frances Caldwell had sung modern ditties on the stage and danced like an angel.

Daisy paused in the midst of her tidying, burying her nose for a moment in a soft mauve cardigan that reminded her of one of her mother's. It didn't do to dwell on the past these days, when they all had to get through difficult times, but when the past held the sweetest memories, it was hard not to yearn for them.

That must be the way Elsie would be yearning for her Joe right now. The thought was in Daisy's head before she could stop it. She didn't *want* to imagine what they did. She didn't *want* to admit to anyone that she knew very well how a man's body looked, because it was part of her job to know and understand the workings of bodily functions. She knew about sex. Not that she had ever experienced it, of course, but she knew the mechanics, which sounded so clinical; but that was the way the medical books explained it. Some of the older nurses were more explicit, though, she thought with a grin.

She didn't really *want* to wonder how it would be for her and Callum Monks, if he ever came back into her life again. But sometimes she did, however guiltily. Sometimes she just couldn't help thinking of those pleasures of the flesh, as they were referred to in the Bible, if only to take her mind off the awful things she had to do in the hospital, and to remind herself that she was young and in love, and a perfectly normal and healthy young woman.

'Daisy! What on earth are you doing up there?' she heard Aunt Rose's voice call out from the parlour below. 'We're all waiting to have a game of charades before the little ones go to bed.'

That just about summed up her life, she thought ruefully, feeling the heat in her face. Longing for something she couldn't have, without ever knowing quite what it was . . . and spending the next hour or so in the company of bawling, squabbling infants and her doting relatives, playing a game of charades.

Three

Imogen Caldwell, now Private Caldwell, reported for duty at the army unit just outside Oxford with a mixture of excitement and apprehension. It was one thing to drive to Weston and back in the big old family Rover car that was mostly relegated to standing in the road with no petrol in its tank now. It was quite another to have been assigned as official driver to a Captain Grayson Beckett, Royal Engineers, whom she was about to meet that morning. She couldn't deny that she was a little fearful. The last time James had been home on leave and she had told him of her intentions, his comical descriptions of officers had made them sound like ogres.

'They either have barking voices you can hear a mile away, or they talk with a mouthful of plums, don't-ya-know, and they look down their noses at you as if you've just crawled out from under a stone. You don't want to have any truck with officers, Immy!'

'I don't have much choice if I want the driving job, do I?' she had said, feeling ridiculously irked by his teasing words. 'Unless you think I should join you as a co-driver in your blessed tank?'

He had sobered at once, hearing the uncertainty in her normally strong voice. He gathered her to him, murmuring against her hair, glad that she couldn't see his eyes and the knowledge there.

'That's the last thing I want, darling. Bertha's a one-man tank, and you're a one-man woman – I hope.'

28

'Of course I am.' She had wrenched away from him. 'You know that, don't you? You don't think I shall start falling for a fancy officer's uniform, do you?'

James laughed softly, confident of her feelings for him. 'I do not. And I'm only teasing. I'm sure your officer will be a perfect gentleman, sweetheart, so let's forget him, and think about more important things – like you and me.'

She had capitulated at once. Safe in James's embrace then, with his kisses warm on her lips, it had been easy to forget her qualms. But now he was far away, and she was here, about to knock on the door of this office, not knowing what was awaiting her on the other side of it.

'So you're Private Caldwell,' the officer said with a smile. 'Do sit down, and don't look so scared. I'm not known for eating young ladies.'

Imogen sat. He wasn't at all like she had expected. For one thing, he wasn't young and he wasn't old. About her father's age, she guessed, which presumably meant he was a regular soldier and hadn't been conscripted because there was a war on. He had a round, jovial face, and the buttons on his jacket were slightly strained as if he had eaten too well lately.

'Well? Do I pass the test?' he asked, his well-bred voice having just a hint of the south-west in it that reassured her immensely.

'I'm sorry, sir. I didn't mean to stare,' she said, acutely embarrassed at knowing she had been doing exactly that.

'That's all right. Since we'll be spending plenty of time together, it would be a tragedy if we hated one another on sight, wouldn't it? Now then,' he went on more briskly, shuffling papers about on his desk. 'let's get down to business, Private Caldwell. You're from Bristol, I believe, which is not so far removed from my home in Devon, so we have something in common. And you're a competent driver, I take it?

'Yes, sir.' She was on safer ground now, sure of her

abilities. 'I'm also a typist and I'm good with figures,' she added for good measure.

'Good God, have I found myself an angel?' Grayson Beckett said with a smile. 'I have a secretary who sees to all my admin work, but there may be occasions when your other talents come in useful, Private.'

Immy's heart missed a beat at the word, but there was nothing in the least suggestive in his manner, and she was certain he meant exactly what he said. She hadn't realised she was still so sensitive over innuendoes – ever since her best friend Helen had been taken in by Joe's cousin Robert and nearly come to grief.

At the time Immy had stormed the hotel where Robert Preston was staying, and dealt with him very efficiently, but the legacy had left her wary of double meanings. Thankfully, she realised now that Captain Beckett hadn't meant any such thing. Her other talents were simply that.

He stood up with a smile and held out his hand to her.

'You'll want to settle in to your quarters today, Private, and I'll see you here at nine-thirty hours tomorrow morning.'

'Yes, sir,' Immy said smartly, shaking his hand and then stepping back a pace before saluting.

'Actually, it's a bit of a lark here,' she told her father on the telephone later that day. 'It doesn't feel as if we're in the middle of a war at all, though some of the other girls have heard rumours that the regiment's being sent to France soon. But you know what rumours are.'

Quentin Caldwell didn't take her levity so complacently. 'Just take care, Immy. Personally, I'd rather have all you girls safely home in Bristol.'

'I know, but we have to do our bit nowadays, don't we, Father? And I always wanted to travel, didn't I?'

She wasn't aware that she had, but it seemed as good a way as any to put his mind at rest. And to change the subject quickly. 'What about Baz? Have you heard from him lately?'

Her father snorted. 'He's talking about joining the Navy now, the young idiot. He's far too young, of course, and he's impatient for the war to last a few years so he can enlist. He doesn't know what he's talking about, and I've warned him not to push his age on so that they take him. He's working on a trawler now, and I even had to hear that news from the old ferryman he used to work for. His letter to me came a few days after I happened to meet old Enoch.'

Immy wasn't sure whether pride in his son's ingenuity or annoyance at his deceit was uppermost right then.

'He'll do all right, Father. Baz always did,' she said.

When they finished speaking, she put down the telephone carefully. If things had been different, she would have added, *Give my love to Mother*. But if things had been different, the country wouldn't have been at war with Germany, and she wouldn't have been wearing a khaki uniform and about to bunk in with five other girls in a communal barracks where there was little chance of privacy.

The thought of it gave her a small shiver, and she told herself she mustn't be snobbish. She was used to sharing life with her two sisters, and to a certain extent her close friend, Helen; but sharing with strangers was something that none of them had ever contemplated. The old saying that war made strange bedfellows was certainly true, she thought – not even sure that she had the words right, but they rang true enough, and that was all that mattered.

In the barracks, apart from her bed, she only had a locker for her clothes and personal things – somewhere to keep her precious letters from James, including the one that had come only that week that was heavily censored, but marked 'somewhere in France'. Which was one of the reasons she hoped the other girls were right, and that she too would be going to France.

'Fancy a game of dominoes before lights-out, Caldwell?'

31

one of them called to her. She didn't really, but she joined them, if only to be sociable.

In Weston-super-Mare that evening Bert Painter was finding it hard to be sociable to the three evacuees in his care. Rose could overlook their annoying little habits, but he didn't like lies and he couldn't abide the sneaking little tales they told on one another. The two Turvey boys were still young and impressionable, but the Brown girl should know better. And one of them had taken twopence from the mantelpiece. It wasn't so much the paltry amount, as the lies they were all intent on inventing about it.

'If one of you doesn't own up, then all three of you will have to be punished,' he snapped, wishing Rose was here to deal with this, instead of out at her church choir meeting with Daisy.

Teddy was snuggling in a corner, hugging George as if he would smother the dog, while the other three young-uns squabbled amongst themselves, each accusing the other.

'You're worse than bloomin' Hitler,' Vanessa burst out finally. 'I didn't take yer bloomin' money, so it must be one of them.'

'Well, it weren't me, pig-face,' yelled Norman. 'And if it weren't you and it weren't me, then it must be our Ronnie.'

His brother went a dull shade of puce, and they all saw the tell-tale dark stain begin to creep over his shorts in his fright at being accused.

'I ain't got it!' Ronnie shrieked. 'I ain't no pick-pocket.'

'Now look what he's gone and done!' Vanessa snapped. 'He's gone and peed himself again.'

'I hate you!' Ronnie screamed at her, tears bursting out of his eyes now, as he threw himself flat on the floor and banged it with his head.

'Silly little devil will end up with a head like a bloomin' hangover if he ain't careful,' Vanessa crowed knowledgeably.

'Be quiet, Vanessa, and leave him to me. You're just making things worse,' Bert shouted, hauling a bleating Ronnie to his feet as the door opened.

'What on earth's going on in here?' Rose gasped. 'Daisy and I could hear you all along the street. Has there been an accident?'

'Only the usual,' Vanessa said sulkily, unable to resist the barb.

As Ronnie looked imploringly towards Daisy for sympathy, she took him out of her uncle's grip and cuddled him, ignoring the bitter smells that wafted up from shorts that had known previous wettings and were never quite rid of them, no matter how many scrubbings they endured.

'Come on, sweetie, let's get you cleaned up and into your pyjamas, while Auntie Rose sorts out the rest of them,' she told him.

'Is she going to hit me?' he said fearfully.

'Of course not,' Daisy said quickly, wondering how often this had been the case in times past.

'Well, I didn't take the money . . .'

'What money is this?' Rose said at once.

'On the mantelpiece. The twopence that you always leave there for the newspaper boy,' Bert said shortly.

'I paid him before I left,' Rose said. 'Is that was all this rumpus was about?'

'*See*?' Vanessa yelled at Bert, her eyes flashing triumphantly.''Tweren't us at all. I *told* you it bloomin' well weren't!'

'And how was I supposed to know that?' he said angrily.

'You'd better say you're sorry, Uncle Bert,' Daisy said softly.

'Well, of course I'm sorry . . .'

'Not to me. To them.'

It wasn't her place to challenge him, and she didn't really know why she was doing so. She just knew how they must all feel, to be falsely accused when they were all so vulnerable; and from the way Ronnie was shuddering against her, dampening her frock in the process, she knew how hard he had taken all this fuss. He might like to appear like a little toughie, but he was only a baby . . .

'I'm sorry, children,' her uncle said to them all now, struggling to keep his dignity. 'I was wrong, but if we can all be all friends again, now is as good a time as any to tell you what we've got planned for tomorrow. Since the weather's so fine, we're all going to start on a project when you get home from school.'

'What's a project?' Norman asked suspiciously, as Teddy came out of the shadows, releasing a relieved George, and Ronnie stopped shuddering.

'We're going to dig for victory,' Bert declared. 'Auntie Rose and I have decided we're going to dig up the back garden and plant vegetables, and you can each have a little plot to grow your own.'

'Is that all?' Vanessa said scornfully. 'I hate vegetables anyway.'

'You'll go hungry then,' Bert told her.

He stared her out, and she finally shrugged and went back to the *Beano* she had been reading, while Daisy took Ronnie upstairs to get him cleaned up, told him he wasn't in disgrace, and that, if he wanted her to, she would help him dig his very own garden plot.

He threw his arms around her neck. 'I love you, Daisy,' he whispered.

'I love you too, Ronnie,' she told him.

Then, still snuffling, he hesitated before asking: 'Daisy, what's a plot?'

On days like these, Daisy decided she definitely wasn't going to have children. They were exhausting – and if she felt like that at seventeen, she thought weakly, heaven knew how older women coped with having them and looking after them. Heaven knew how Elsie was going to cope, but maybe it was different when it was a baby that you and your husband had made because you were so much in love. Just like her and Cal . . . or at least, how she believed it was for her and Cal.

Sometimes she wondered if it was all a fantasy. Maybe she was just enjoying the fact of being in love without thinking beyond the excitement of meeting him on the beach, and writing long letters, and hearing his voice on the telephone. And when none of that seemed to have happened for ages, even pining away for him had its own poignant charm.

Being a romantic, Daisy could see the sweet tragedy of it all, of being Juliet without her Romeo . . . but that was as far as the imagination went, because she certainly didn't want to end up like *them*. She and Cal weren't exactly star-crossed lovers . . . they weren't lovers at all, in the real sense of the word.

She pushed the erotic thought out of her head. Sometimes she wondered if her nature was too shallow for her to *really* be in love, the way Elsie and Joe were in love. The way Immy and James were in love. Sometimes she thought she was far more like Helen Church than either of her sisters – happy to flirt and play at being in love, but never seriously thinking of what settling down meant.

She pulled a face at her reflection now, as she pulled the confining pins out her hair and shook it loose. *Settling down* had such a middle-aged sound to it, and she was far from ready for that yet. Even though she was sure she did love Cal, and absence was supposed to make the heart grow fonder, she wasn't at all sure that her earlier thought of *giving in to him* was such a good idea now. At least not until she was much, much older. It was just too final a commitment, and once a person had carnal knowledge of another person, it would be going against all the Bible's teachings not to be true to him for ever.

Anyway, perhaps he wouldn't even ask her.

She turned away from the mirror, flopping down on her bed and staring up at the ceiling, and feeling more restless than she had any right to be. She was here in a loving home, full of people that she loved, doing a job that she loved, and yet something was missing. Not her darling mother or the rest of her family. Not even Cal. It was something else. Something that everybody else had, and she didn't. And she wasn't thinking of *that*, either.

After a long while, she sat up slowly, realising exactly what was missing. Since she had never been one to waste time wishing for something if she could do something about it, she knew exactly what she had to do.

'*No*, Daisy, you're far too young, and I forbid it,' her father said, when he came down to Weston to visit them that weekend, hot and bothered from taking the train in order to save precious petrol in the car.

Daisy looked up, flushed, from the patch of earth she was forking over for Ronnie, since he'd got fed up with the whole idea of making a vegetable plot for the moment, and had wandered indoors looking for Teddy and George.

'How can you say I'm too young! Baz is younger than me and he's already gone to sea.'

'And you know my feelings on that,' Quentin said grimly. 'But my dear girl, you're already doing a fine job of nursing in a hospital, and seeing sights no young girl should be subjected to, in my opinion. So why on earth would you want to join up and do exactly the same as you're doing now? I can't see the point, darling.'

'*I* can, Daddy. I know I'm a good nurse, but I'm stuck here, and I want to be in the thick of it . . .'

'Oh, for pity's sake, Daisy, listen to yourself,' Quentin said, quickly losing patience. 'War is not a game, my dear, and you're not Florence Nightingale.'

She flinched, hating him for belittling her, especially as the precocious Vanessa was probably skulking somewhere near, listening to every word.

'I'm not pretending to be any better than any other nurse,

Daddy,' she went on, struggling to keep calm. 'I just feel that I want to go farther afield. I never thought war was a game, and I see the evidence of it every day on the wards, remember.'

'And you just remember that you'd need my agreement before you did anything so foolish as enlisting, Daisy. If not legally, then out of respect for me.'

She wouldn't mind betting that Baz wouldn't wait for his father's approval. But boys seemed able to get away with anything.

She couldn't hide her anger and frustration now, but the idea had been growing inside her for days, and she hadn't even recognised it for what it was. Nor could she hide – except from everybody else – the other, more shameful reason for wanting to get away from here and everyone she knew. In the midst of the undoubted excitement and drama of wanting to be in the thick of it, despite all its dangers and heartbreaks, there was something far less noble lurking in the back of her mind.

If she was away from home – even out of the country – then when the inevitable news came through about Lucy, then maybe she wouldn't feel it quite so personally and emotionally. It was cowardly and she knew it, and it was something she would never have dared to admit to anyone else.

'I never imagined you wanting to be a boy, darling,' she heard her father say more whimsically, as if he realised how tense she had become, without ever guessing the truth of it. 'You're far too much your mother's daughter for that.'

She felt her eyes mist at once, knowing this was a kind of emotional blackmail, but loving him all the same for being able to talk about his wife in that calm manner, and for comparing her in any way to her delicate, beautiful mother.

She hugged his arm, and told him she certainly wouldn't want to be tossed about on the ocean, thank you very much! And resisting the thought that, to get anywhere out of England at all, it would mean going by ship, unless you were Cal, of course, and flew aeroplanes . . .

'So shall we just give ourselves time to think about it, Daisy?'

'All right. It was only an idea, anyway,' she mumbled, knowing it was more than that, but satisfied for the moment that he was even considering it.

'And at least I have one daughter safely at home,' he went on with a smile. 'Elsie's busy sewing for the baby now, and of course, with her skills, the child will have the best layette outside the royal family!'

Daisy laughed, sticking her garden fork into the little patch she had dug for Ronnie, and deciding that it was enough work for one day, especially as the little wretch had left most of it to her. She linked arms with her father as they strolled indoors to join the rest of the family.

'It's a far cry from creating hats for the city gentry though, isn't it, Daddy?'

'It is, but I doubt that Elsie thinks she's got a poorer bargain, my love. Joe's home on leave this weekend, which is why I decided that now would be a good time for me to let them have the whole house to themselves.'

Safe in her husband's arms during these precious few days and nights, Elsie wished that times like these could go on for ever. They couldn't, of course. There was a war on, even though it didn't seem much like it lately, and everyone was calling it the phoney war and wondering when anything was going to happen.

It was short-sighted to be having such thoughts, of course, because everyone also knew that war was very much a reality in Europe. Hitler's planes were bombing cities and towns, and by now, nearing April, the enemy's grip was being firmly felt all over Europe. Finland had capitulated to the mighty Russian Red Army, and all the Scandinavian countries were in imminent peril.

Elsie's geography had never been particularly good, but like everyone else she felt it her duty to know what was going on, and to follow the events of the war on the wireless and in the newspapers, even though it had hardly touched her personally. Apart from Joe going to war, and there was nothing more personal in her life than that . . .

'Come back, my love,' she heard Joe whisper in her ear as he felt her shudder. 'What were you thinking about?'

She swallowed her fears for him, in case saying them out loud was tempting fate. And although it wasn't patriotic, she didn't want him to go away, she thought passionately. She didn't want him to fight, nor even to be a hero. She wanted him here always, with her and their baby. It was where they all belonged. Soon – far too soon now – they would be saying goodbye again, and this time she was very sure he would be heading for France. If the fighting wasn't on their own English soil – and thank God it wasn't, she added silently – then the servicemen fighting for God and country had to go wherever the fighting led them. She knew it, but it didn't make it any easier.

As if his thoughts echoed hers, she felt him rest his hand lightly on the soft swell of her belly beneath the bedclothes on that sunny Sunday morning.

'You don't need to worry, you know,' he said softly. 'Didn't you know I've got a charmed life?'

She swivelled round in his arms to lie as close as possible to him, feeling his flesh warm against her own, almost as close as if they shared the same skin.

'Can you guarantee that?'

He bent his head to kiss her throat, and his mouth went lower, making her catch her breath with a rush of ecstasy, recognising the swiftly rising desire in him, matching her own. His voice was muffled as he spoke against her breast.

'How can it not be so, when I've got my darling wife to come home to?'

'And our baby,' Elsie breathed raggedly.

'And our baby,' Joe said, moving slowly downwards beneath the bedclothes to kiss the mound of the child growing there.

She gloried in his love-making, in his gentle, considerate approaches, and the unhurried manner in which he made her ready for him. He was everything she had ever dreamed of in a husband and lover, and each time he made love to her she wept a little, simply because it was all so perfect, and she adored him so much.

Sometimes she was almost afraid that such happiness couldn't last, and that some day there had to be a reckoning for it. But those were crazy, demonic thoughts that normally came in the dark sleepless hours before daylight when the baby was lying awkwardly, and the blissful dreams of Joe were interrupted by darker ones of tragedy and death.

But they were for another time. Not now, when Joe's hands were seeking her warm moist secret places, and she could feel him hard against her, and herself responding as she always did.

'Joe, I love you so much,' she gasped out, burying her face in his neck. 'I wish – oh, I wish . . .'

As she felt him enter her and start to move within her, he stilled her words with a deep and passionate kiss. Without the need for words, she knew her dearest wishes were the same as his, and that one day, God willing, they would be together for always.

Four

W ar might be raging in Europe, but as the phoney war in Britain seemed to be making people complacent, many evacuees were being taken back to London and the Home Counties, and causing disruption in more than one household.

'It's a big mistake,' Bert Painter said, reading aloud the latest newspaper account of the reversing trend. 'Old Adolph's got his sights set on England, sure as eggs are eggs, and when he's done with marching through Europe, he'll be looking to invade us. Stands to reason. Poor little kids won't know whether they're coming or going if they end up being sent back to the country all over again. And to different families, probably.'

'You don't really think that, do you, Bert?' his wife asked anxiously.

He looked at her sternly. 'Now look here, Rose, you know as well as I do that we've only borrowed these little tartars. They've got homes and families of their own to go back to, and it's foolish to get too fond of any of them.'

'Tell that to the fairies,' Rose scoffed. 'You're just as fond of them all as I am, so you don't fool me on that score, Bertie. You're the one who takes the boys out as often as possible, teaching them how to catch fish and playing sand football with them at the beach.'

'So I do,' he admitted. 'And it's something we all enjoy;

41

but they'll be different children by the time they go back to the big cities, won't they? They'll have learned our country ways. Pity it will all have to end.'

'Oh, you think it'll be a pity when the war ends, do you?' she said archly.

'I damn well do not, and you know it, woman,' he growled. 'I was thinking of you and how you've let yourself become far too attached to them, that's all.'

'And I suppose you haven't, you old softie?' she said with a laugh. 'Anyway, I doubt that ours will be taken back just yet, now that Mrs Turvey's given up the idea of taking her pair to Wales,' she added beneath her breath in case any of them was lurking near. But none of the children was up yet, and Teddy practically slept the sleep of the dead until somebody woke him.

'A good thing too. The woman looked no better than she should be,' Bert said in reponse, in what Rose always thought was the daftest statement ever. But it always made her lips twitch, and they were in a more harmonious mood by the time Norman and Ronnie came rushing into the room with a shock announcement.

'What do you mean – all her things have gone?' Rose demanded, as Norman hopped up and down with importance, and Ronnie crossed his legs desperately. Fear or excitement always had the same result with Ronnie.

'She's gone back 'ome,' Ronnie shrieked, his self-control finally giving up as the waterworks started at both ends. 'I wanter go 'ome as well.'

Daisy appeared in the doorway, still half-asleep after her night shift at the hospital and none too happy at seeing Ronnie's darkening trousers after all their efforts to get him dry.

'What's all the noise about?' she snapped.

As Rose rushed out of the room and up the stairs to find out the truth of it all, her uncle told her quickly.

'The boys say that Vanessa's things are missing, and she's gone home.'

Daisy stared at him. 'She can't have gone home,' she said, her thoughts still muddled from being woken up rudely by all the shouting. 'She's got no money and she wouldn't know where to go.'

But they all knew that she would. Vanessa's East End nous made her far more canny at twelve than many older girls. In her own self-opinionated words, *she knew what it was all about*. She had been doing odd jobs at a local corner shop after school, and saving her money for what she said her old gran always called a rainy day. This could just be it.

'The railway station,' Bert said now. 'She'll obviously have tried to catch a train to London.'

Rose came back to the room, her face white. 'It's true, Bert. All her clothes and comics are missing and her gas mask too. The little minx . . .'

'That's not what I'd call her,' he said, his face darkening furiously now. 'I'm getting down to the railway station now and then on to the police. Lord knows when she left the house and anything could have happened to her.'

Daisy was fully awake now, abandoning any thought of sleep. 'Shouldn't we let the billeting officers know as well? They'd have her home address and other contacts. I could do that, if you like.'

'You're right, my love,' Rose said. 'You see to that and I'll clean up Ronnie and get Teddy downstairs. Then we'll have some breakfast and get the house back to some kind of order. It's no use all of us panicking. She might not have gone very far at all and I'm sure she'll be back with us by dinner-time.'

She didn't believe it, but she said it to calm down the two young boys, who were looking terrified now that the first excitement had died down. Vanessa had been a thorn in all their flesh from the day she had arrived, but the thought of where she might be now was something Rose didn't care to think about. You heard such awful tales . . .

'Do you think Nessa's dead?' Norman whispered.

'Of course she's not dead,' Rose said briskly. 'What an idea! She's being a very silly girl and I'm sure her mother won't be at all pleased that she's given us such a fright.'

'Ain't we going 'ome then?' Ronnie howled in searing disappointment.

Rose gave him a hug. 'What, and miss Uncle Bert taking you out on Saturday? Uncle Quentin's coming here for the weekend as well, remember, so you'll have two uncles fussing over you.'

As she took him upstairs to wash and change him, she knew it wasn't much consolation. No matter what the potential danger, the poor little devils would have much preferred to be at home with their own families, instead of living with strangers. A few months away from home had done nothing to change that, and she was full of sympathy for them.

All the same, she thought more practically, she wished someone would give them a magic cure for Ronnie's evil-smelling undergarments . . .

Long before Vanessa's disappearance had been discovered, she was sitting beside a cheery driver in a long-distance lorry that was taking her back where she belonged, and even though she was a bit sorry for the fuss it would cause, she couldn't control her excitement at going home. She knew she could pass for much older than she was, especially with a bit of Daisy's lipstick that she'd borrowed, and she had invented a story for the driver about only visiting here for a week or so. She knew her mum would be glad to see her, and if they were short of money, she could always get a Saturday job at the market. Just thinking about it reminded her how much she had missed the jostling streets of home, and she was never going back to the bloomin' country again.

*   *   *

'If the girl's gone back to London, we'll find her,' the billeting officer told Daisy. 'I'll put a call through to the appropriate department at once, although if her mother accepts her back, you realise that will be the end of it. We don't force these children to come here, Miss Caldwell, and if they're unhappy, there's nothing we can do about it.'

'I hope you're not implying that she wasn't well treated at my aunt and uncle's home,' Daisy snapped, far too tired to play games with this frosty-faced woman. She should be in bed, not chasing about the town after the ungrateful Nessa Brown.

'Knowing Mr and Mrs Painter, I'm sure she was treated very well,' the woman conceded. 'But the fact remains, if these children and their parents want to stay together, there's nothing we can do about it.'

'But you'll be sure to let us know that she arrived back safely, won't you?' Daisy persisted.

'Naturally. Now, I suggest you go home and let us get on with our job. You'll be informed as soon as we know anything.'

Daisy left the Town Hall, feeling snubbed at the woman's unspoken criticism, but not without a sudden grudging admiration for Vanessa's self-confidence in even considering travelling all the way back to London on her own. It made her own move down to Weston with her aunt and uncle seem so much less of an adventure than it had seemed at the time.

Not that the evacuees had ever had any choice, she thought, pitying the smaller ones sent off to Lord-knew-where with their name labels pinned on their chests, and all their possessions in carrier bags or cardboard suitcases with their gas masks slung around their necks. Like a lot of unwanted parcels. Newspaper and cinema pictures of them, herded together on railway stations before the war had even begun, had been heartbreaking – and a major cause of Aunt Rose's determination to take some of them in.

Remembering Aunt Rose now, as she stood outside the Town Hall fuming, sent Daisy back to the house at once, to report her news. Her uncle had returned from the railway station, where no one had seen a young girl waiting for an early-morning train. Even if they had, they would probably not have registered that she was a runaway. Vanessa had the knack of self-composure, and the only time Daisy had seen it slip was at the sight of blood when she had cut her finger on the bread knife.

For a moment she felt a chill run through her. Vanessa was obviously making her way back home to the East End of London; and if the Germans broke through all the south coast defences and started bombing London, Vanessa might very well see a lot more blood than she had ever seen in her life before . . .

She stopped surmising and went to make a pot of tea for them all. Her tiredness had vanished for the moment, and it was more important to keep cheerful for the sake of the three small boys, especially Ronnie, who was still bitterly jealous of Vanessa, and didn't see why he and Norman couldn't go home too. They were going to have trouble with him if they weren't careful.

'Who wants a game of ludo?' she asked brightly.

Before they could answer, Daisy turned in relief as she heard her father arrive at the house, and the news was quickly related to him. The appearance of a new arrival was a diversion for the children, and while they all chattered noisily, Daisy left them all to it and went back to bed for a few hours.

Knowing they would find it hard to sleep, the boys had been allowed to stay up later that evening, and were still awake when the billeting officer telephoned to say that Vanessa Brown's mother had been in touch. Her daughter had come home, and although she'd given her a pasting, she was keeping her now, and it was no thanks to these country yokels for letting her wander about all over the place.

'I'm just repeating what was told to me, and I gather Mrs Brown is none too pleased at us for letting the girl make the journey on her own,' the woman said, as if Rose couldn't read between the lines. 'Just as if anyone would have allowed it if we had known her intentions! Some of these people have no gratitude, but I suppose we have to learn to put up with a lack of manners in wartime.'

'And that seems to be that,' Rose reported to Bert and her brother when she put down the telephone. 'Vanessa is back where she belongs, and it seems that we count for nothing after all.'

She was far too stoical to cry, though she felt remarkably near to doing it at that moment, partly out of an unnecessary feeling of failure, and partly with indignation at the girl's ingratitude. Her brother patted her hand.

'Now you know that's not true, Rosie. All these kids have got a good life with you, and if that little madam's foolish enough not to know it, then there's nothing more you can do about it, except to be sure you did your best.'

'Just what I've been telling her,' Bert agreed. 'So let's change the record, shall we? What about you, Quentin? Is the shop still doing good business?'

Quentin pulled a face. 'Hardly. Folk aren't buying much in the way of fancy goods these days, except for cloth for blackout curtains, of course, and tape to put across the windows to keep out bomb blasts. But even the demand for that has dwindled since we haven't had a whiff of any bombs.'

'My goodness, Quentin, you do sound gloomy!' his sister exclaimed. 'And it almost sounds as if you want the bombs to fall.'

'That I don't! But I can't pretend that it won't happen in time, just like we've always predicted, what with the docks at Avonmouth and the aircraft factories at Filton.

Sometimes I wish they'd just get on with it and let us do our bit, that's all. It's like a battle of nerves, wondering when it will happen. Oh, and did I tell you I've joined the AFS? In my spare time, of course.'

'What's the AFS?' came Teddy's curious voice from the fireside rug where he was quietly tickling the adoring George's ears.

'It's the Auxilliary Fire Service, son.'

Teddy perked up at once. 'Are you going to drive a fire engine?'

'Well, I probably won't drive it, but I'll be able to ride in one if there's a fire somewhere in the city.'

'Can I come with you?'

Quentin laughed, ruffling his hair. 'I don't think so. It won't be play-acting, Teddy, not like the little red fire engine I bought you for your birthday.'

If the enemy finally did set their sights on Bristol – as he knew in his heart they must – then none of them would be play-acting.

'So how is Elsie?' Rose said, changing the subject quickly.

'Blossoming, of course, since Joe came home on leave. And Imogen wrote to say she's now an official driver for a Captain Grayson Beckett.'

'My word. Who ever would have thought it? It's a far cry from all your girls working in the family business, isn't it, Quentin?' Bert said. 'And young Baz too – not that he was ever cut out to be a shopkeeper. I always said as much, didn't I?'

'You did,' Quentin said crisply. 'And as usual you were right. So what are we going to do with these three young-uns to keep them occupied tomorrow, Rose? What's the plan?'

'Well, to keep their little hands from digging up their vegetable seeds to see if they've started growing yet; and before we had all this fuss over Vanessa, Bert thought you and he could take them all to the beach.'

'Well, there's nothing stopping us now that we know she's all right. You should come too, Rose. There's no sense in staying indoors and moping. There'll be time enough for that when you've really got something to pipe your eyes for.'

He didn't say it with any real meaning – just to jolly her along – but for a moment his eyes clouded, as if seeing into a future he didn't want to acknowledge. There might be those who thought this war was going to be over soon, and that it wouldn't come home to England, but Quentin didn't believe that. Nor did any of them who had seen it all before . . .

'Let's all go,' Daisy put in quickly, seeing the strained look in her father's eyes. 'There's no point in brooding just because Vanessa Brown preferred to be in her own home than here with us, is there?'

'And there speaks a sensible girl,' Rose said approvingly.

Two weeks later a letter arrived addressed to Mr and Mrs Painter. Rose opened it, to find Vanessa's badly spelled apology inside.

'Dear Aunty Rose and Uncle Bert,' it said,

> I know I did wrong to run out like that, and me mum said I had to write and say sory for any upset. It weren't that I didn't like you all, I just wanted to come home where me frends are. I've got a Satday job down the market now and am earning a bit to help out. Mum says she's glad of it, even if she weren't too plesed when I turned up like a bad penny. The lorry driver had a bloomin' fit wen he knew how old I was too. That's all reely, excep mum says can you send me rashun book as soon as yesterday, cos she can't feed me proply without it.
>
> Yours respecfully,
> Vanessa Brown
> PS this is my address for the rashun book.

If Rose hadn't cried before, her eyes were decidedly moist now, though she dashed the tears away with an angry gesture as she thrust the letter under Bert's nose.

'The silly little girl,' she said, sniffing. 'But I suppose it's true that there's no place like home, even if it's a miserable-sounding place like 27 Hollis Mews.'

'You don't know that it's a miserable place. It might be very select.'

'And pigs might fly,' Rose said.

But she did as Vanessa asked, and packed up the precious ration book. She also bought her several of her favourite comic papers and film-star magazines, and told her she hoped she would enjoy them; and if ever she wanted to come back, she was to write to them direct, and not go through the billeting people again.

'You must be mad,' Bert said, when she told him what she had done. 'She's never been the easiest of children, and you're more soft-hearted than you like to admit, aren't you, Rosie?'

'Oh well, I doubt that we'll ever hear from her again, but I just wanted her to know that she's always welcome.'

'I suppose she was one of the family for a good few months, and they can't all be little angels,' he agreed. 'And you've still got the other three to fuss over.'

'Four,' she reminded him. 'Daisy's not too old to enjoy a bit of fussing.'

'Thank you, ma'am,' Daisy said with a grin and a genteel bob.

But Rose knew there was something bothering Daisy lately. She had an exuberant nature and was never happier than when she was busy. Her nursing career certainly saw to that, and when she was off duty she was still enough of a tomboy to enjoy a rough and tumble with the boys.

But in Daisy's quieter moments, Rose often thought she glimpsed a strange look in her brown eyes that was hard to define. It wasn't exactly fear; it was almost a resigned look, a look of waiting for something to happen; and if it didn't happen soon, Rose wondered if she was going to explode with apprehension.

If she had been able or willing to put it into words, Daisy could have told her aunt precisely what was wrong. But putting it into words meant bringing the fear out into the open, giving it shape and form as if it was some living, evil thing. Hanging over her like a death knell – which was exactly what it was, of course.

But not *her* death knell, nor even that of the poor wounded servicemen who were brought to the hospital by nearly every train now, until they were almost full to capacity, and couldn't take many more. War wasn't yet defiling the beautiful, burgeoning spring of the English countryside, but it was so near, almost within touching distance across the English Channel in France and the countries of Europe. And it was here in Weston General, where every time Daisy tended a wounded soldier or airman, and heard his halting, whispered words as she wrote a letter to his family on his behalf, she thought of another hospital, another sick bed, and of her friend Lucy Luckwell.

Some days her restlessness was worse than others. She wrote regularly to Lucy, but the replies were sketchy now, simply because Lucy had so little to say about the dullness of her life in the sanatorium. She had once been so full of life, so eager to excel at her riding skills and become an equestrian star, and now she had nothing at all to look forward to. Only the endless weeks and months to endure until this foul disease killed her.

At least the wounded servicemen in Weston General had had the chance to do something worthy in their lives, thought Daisy. Something that gave them dignity and a feeling of a job well done. Something for their country. Something to die for and to make their families proud of them.

'I'm going to the Luckwell farm,' she said suddenly to her aunt. 'I need to see Lucy's mother and find out how she is.'

'Do you want me to come with you?' Rose said.

'No. If you don't mind, I'd rather go alone.'

She didn't know why she felt the way she did. How did you explain a sense of foreboding, a premonition, a need to share pain? Unless it was because she felt that need so often on the wards and, young as she was, she knew she embraced it – absorbed it even – and was somehow able to give comfort.

A born nurse, some of the older ones called her, but she knew it wasn't just that. It was the legacy her sensitive, beautiful mother had given her. Frances had transmitted a rare sense of emotional giving from the stage, while Daisy used it to the best of her ability when holding a dying man's hand or smoothing his brow. Right now, she knew she needed to be with Lucy Luckwell's mother.

The farmer's wife met her at the door of the farmhouse, her eyes red and swollen with crying.

'I was going to phone you as soon as I felt able, and now you're here. I always said you must be one of them thought-readers, Daisy.'

She held out her arms, and Daisy went straight into them, each of them holding on tight, each supporting the other – the slender young girl and the buxom countrywoman. Behind her, Daisy glimpsed the shadowy figures of the men: Lucy's brother Ben, and her father, helpless as all grown men seemed to be at times of great emotion.

There was no sign of the evacuee children, but since it was halfway through the morning, Daisy remembered that they would be at school. It was odd how things became disconnected in the brain at times like these. The sun still shone, the grass grew, schoolchildren attended their classes, and somewhere in Europe a bitter war was raging. And none of it was as important as this moment in time, when she knew without being told that her friend was dead.

'It's happened then,' Daisy said, in a voice as wooden as if it was carved out of oak.

Mrs Luckwell nodded, releasing her. 'The people at the sanatorium phoned to tell us an hour ago. It was peaceful, they said. She just slipped away in her sleep. We have to be thankful for that, don't we, Daisy?'

Her eyes pleaded with Daisy to agree, not to strain these moments still more by being angry, and railing against a God who could let a vivacious young girl die like this, far from home, and without the chance to say goodbye to those who loved her most. Daisy bit back the bitter words she felt like saying, knowing she must keep them until later, and not distress this family still further.

But as she drank the endless cups of tea that Mrs Luckwell pressed on her, and listened to the awkwardness of the men's conversation, it dawned on her how doubly tragic it was that this was a family who couldn't truly reach one another when they needed one another most. They were all suffering, and they had all loved Lucy; but they found it impossible to express it in words. And it shouldn't be like that. The patients in the wards who faced death found it easier to speak of their fears to the nurses and, young as she was, she listened, sympathised, and held their hands. Who had held Lucy's hand, she wondered? Or had she died all alone, as her mother implied? If so, Daisy didn't want to know about it.

'You'll have arrangements to make,' she said awkwardly, when the stilted conversation dwindled to silence. 'I know my aunt will want to come and see you, Mrs Luckwell. May I tell her? And is there anything else I can do? Anyone I can inform?'

Lucy's mother shook herself. 'Oh no, my dear. Ben will see to all that, and the family doctor's coming soon, and he'll tell us what to do. We want Lucy brought home, of course, and we'll tell you when . . . when – well, anyway – yes, tell your auntie I'll be glad to see her whenever she can come.'

As her voice became more disjointed, Daisy swallowed hard.

'Would you like us to take the children off your hands for a few days?'

'Lord bless you, no! Their little lives have been disrupted enough, and they need us. I'll be meeting them from school, just like always.'

Privately, Daisy thought it was the Luckwells needing the evacuee children now, and she pedalled back home with tears blinding her eyes, to throw herself in her aunt's arms and sob her heart out.

Five

Two weeks later, the trauma and sadness of the funeral was all over. Lucy had been laid to rest in the town she loved, and to Daisy it seemed that her family was being remarkably strong. It sometimes seemed as if she was the only one still trying to make sense of it all. Why her? Why Lucy?

Anyone with a brain in their head knew there would be casualties in a war. You read about them in the newspapers every day. You heard the reports on the wireless, and if you were a nurse, you had to be prepared to deal with injuries that in peacetime would never have been within the scope of your abilities. Nursing was not the gentle activity of simply putting a cup of tea to a wounded soldier's lips – if it ever had been.

Daisy knew that only too well. War brought injuries and death. You had to steel yourself to deal with whatever the next trainload of wounded servicemen brought in. You did it because you were trained, and because they were strangers. Compassion and efficiency went hand in hand. But you weren't trained to deal with the death of a friend, who had done nothing worse than just get progressively sicker. You weren't trained to deal with your feelings in that situation. You didn't know how to handle them . . .

She read the words she had written in an impassioned letter to Cal Monks. Baring her soul, she thought dramatically, because she had vowed that between friends and lovers there should be no secrets festering away inside like a cancer. He

55

was her dearest friend, her best friend in all the world now that Lucy was dead. She had to keep saying it to believe it. Even though she hadn't seen Lucy for months, she had still been her best friend and confidante.

She would dearly have liked to share her feelings with her sisters, but it wasn't fair to burden Elsie with her misery, and Imogen seemed to be having quite a good time with her Captain Beckett too. By all accounts she was driving him here, there and everywhere, Daisy thought, in a small fit of jealousy, and making new friends. If she didn't get out of the bedroom that was stifling her, she was going to go quietly mad, and what good was that going to do Lucy or anyone?

She screwed up the letter to Cal and threw it in the waste-paper basket. It wouldn't be fair to him to write as emotionally as she had, when he would assuredly be having his own battles to fight. She had heard from him at last, and he seemed to be having a good time as well, from his wild descriptions of dogfights and zooming in and out of the sun. The letter was heavily censored, but although she could sense his enthusiasm, it made her feel more detached from him than ever. His obsession for the sheer exhilaration of soaring into the sky in a silver machine was comparable to her brother's about the sea.

Drying her eyes that seemed to be perpetually damp now, Daisy took a few deep breaths and told herself it was time to pull herself together. Life went on. She went downstairs and called out to the three boys messing about in the garden that she would race them down to the beach. Meeting her Aunt Rose's approving eyes, she knew she had already turned a corner, however tiny it felt.

Baz Caldwell's confidence was growing. From the day he had enjoyed ferrying passengers across the River Avon with old Enoch Bray, to his recklessness in running off to join the fishing fleet, he'd known he would never be happy doing anything else but going to sea. It was all he'd ever wanted, and after the first sticky moments with his father when he'd tried to explain how much it meant to him, he knew he had found his destiny. By now, life behind the counter of his father's shop seemed as if it belonged to another world. He had never been cut out for it. It was women's work, and even his sisters had eventually agreed to that. Of course, the war had changed everything. He wasn't surprised that his sister Elsie was already expecting a baby after her marriage to Joe Preston. They obviously *did* it, he thought, with the familiar stirring in his young loins. But he still marvelled that his older sister Imogen had been so keen to join up, and as for Daisy being a nurse – well, that was a turn up for the books and no mistake.

'What are you grinning at, Bazzer? Dreaming of some pretty little miss you've been toying with?' his mate asked him in the waterside pub that evening. Baz wasn't old enough to drink in pubs, but because of his hefty size and the company of his seafaring mates, few ever questioned his age.

The third man sniggered. 'Give the lad a chance, Duggie. He's still wet behind the ears. Don't know what he's got it for yet, do you, Caldwell?'

Baz snorted. 'Maybe I do and maybe I don't. In any case I ain't spreading it around like you two buggers and risking a dose,' he added daringly.

The others laughed. 'Quite right, kid,' Duggie said. 'You leave it to the experts. There's time enough for you to find out what's what. You do what you've got to do beneath the blankets.'

Baz felt his face flame now. Bastards, he thought furiously. He was the youngest on the trawler and their baiting didn't normally bother him, but tension was never far from the surface these days, and the North Sea waters where they fished weren't getting any warmer, despite the fact that it was springtime now. They weren't the safest place to be, either, what with the German U-boats a constant, stealthy underwater menace.

The three of them were weaving their unsteady way back along the waterfront towards their digs late that evening, all somewhat the worse for drink, when Duggie stopped suddenly, pointing dramatically out to sea.

'Look out there, kid. Iceberg ahead!'

As Baz's heart leapt, he gave a loud gasp, and Duggie chortled again.

'Oh sorry, my mistake – it's just a wave. Christ, you'd think we were on the *Titanic*, the way he reacted, wouldn't you, Harry? Here, kid, take another swig to calm your nerves.'

He handed over a half-drunk bottle of beer. Booze was officially forbidden on the boat, but once on shore they took advantage of the watered-down ale the pubs provided, and sneaked more than a few bottles on board, since no one took much notice of regulations when the temperature was freezing and they were wrapped up to the gills in heavy gear.

Baz felt Duggie sling his arm around his tense shoulders.

'Cheer up, boy; there's worse things at sea, ain't there? And are you sure you want to join the bloody Navy?' he slurred.

'If it means getting away from you buggers, I'm sure all right,' Baz snarled, wondering for a moment what his father would say if he could see him now, rolling along a waterfront with a pair of rogues for company, to sleep the sleep of the unjust in a seedy seamen's boarding house until they put to sea in the morning.

He found himself grinning as his two mates began telling bawdy stories to liven up the rest of the evening, and he felt the usual surge of excitement at their risqué jokes. To hell with what his father thought. This was what he'd always wanted, and if it wasn't exactly adventure on the grand scale, it was adventure such as he had never dreamed of; and who knew what the future held?

By the end of April it was clear that it was going to be an exceptionally warm spring. If anything was designed to cheer the spirits, despite the food rationing and miserable reports of Hitler's relentless march through Europe, at least the weather was fine, Rose Painter told her niece, with typical British optimism.

'And it's time you spent more time in the fresh air, stopped moping around and thinking about people who are worse off than yourself.'

'How can I?' Daisy said. 'I see them every day on the wards!'

'You don't live at that hospital, Daisy. You're young and healthy, and Lucy wouldn't thank you for turning yourself into a nun on her account. You're still allowed to have fun, you know.'

Daisy's first reaction – to snap that she didn't know what she was talking about – was tempered by her aunt's look of understanding.

'I know that,' she said slowly. 'It just seems wrong, that's all.'

'It's not wrong, darling. Look at those boys in the garden now. Teddy's adapted well to living here because we're his family; but even though the other two are far from home and missing their mother, they're having a wonderful time now with Bert and his chickens.'

Daisy looked, and nodded. 'It was the best thing Uncle Bert ever did, buying some chickens and letting everyone name their own.'

'*And* providing us with eggs for breakfast when they condescend to lay them,' Rose said. 'I swear they have minds of their own, though, and prefer waking us up at the crack of dawn to doing what nature intended them to do.'

Daisy was laughing now. 'Oh, Aunt Rose, you always did me good!'

'So do as I say, my love. Go out and have some fun.'

Daisy knew she was right, but before she did anything about it, she was going to do what she always did on Friday evenings, and that was to go and talk to Lucy. It didn't feel weird to crouch down by her grave and put some flowers in the little pot she'd bought especially – checking first with the Luckwells to see that they didn't object – and talk things over with Lucy.

'Aunt Rose thinks I should go out and have some fun,' she said, as she removed the dead flowers from last week and replaced them with daffodils.

Most of the garden at home was thriving with young cabbage plants and sprouting potatoes and the feathery tufts of carrot tops now, but they still kept the front and side garden bright with flowers. And these were special, for Lucy.

'I wouldn't go anywhere if you thought I shouldn't,' Daisy went on. 'Your parents are still having the annual gymkhana at the farm, and they say there's going to be a special prize in your memory this year, Lucy; but I couldn't bear to be there. You understand that, don't you?'

Her heart gave a stab as she remembered last year's event, when they had both been so excited and happy at performing, and Lucy had excelled in everything she did. Such a short time ago, and yet it seemed like a lifetime.

No, she definitely couldn't go this year. Maybe next year . . . she was sure Mrs Luckwell would understand.

'Is that you, Daisy?' she heard a voice call out. Her head jerked around at this intrusion into her private time with Lucy. Across the fragrant-smelling churchyard, she saw one of the other nurses from the hospital walking towards her.

'I thought it was you! Come to visit your friend, have you?'

Daisy had only ever spoken to this girl once or twice,

and didn't particularly want to speak to her now. She couldn't even remember her name for a few moments. It was Alice something-or-other. Alice Godfrey – that was it. She muttered that yes, she was visiting her friend, feeling rather absurd to be saying the words out loud, as if this was a social call for afternoon tea . . .

'I'm visiting my brother,' Alice said. 'It's about the only time he can't answer me back. I never thought I'd miss it so much. Daft, isn't it?'

'I didn't know you had a brother,' Daisy said, for want of something to say.

Alice shrugged her narrow shoulders. 'He was older than me, nearly twenty-two. He was in the RAF, and he bought it over France.'

Daisy's heart jumped again. 'Oh – how awful – how long ago was it?'

'More than six months now. Long enough for us to get used to it, and even be glad in a funny way that he's not coming back in the circumstances. He'd always been so good-looking in a Robert Donat sort of way, but he'd had half his face burned away in the crash,' she said, almost matter-of-factly. 'They brought him home after he died, and my dad and me went to see him, but my mum couldn't face it. I'm glad she didn't; then she doesn't have to keep remembering it.'

'But you do.'

''Fraid so,' Alice said. 'But you have to get on with things, don't you? I make it my business to be extra gentle with those boys who come into the hospital with burns, though, I can tell you.'

She took a deep breath. 'Anyway, I didn't mean to depress you still more. You'll be missing your friend, I daresay. I heard something about it and I'm sorry. Young, wasn't she?'

'Seventeen,' Daisy said, her head drooping. It still seemed cruel and unbelievable to even put it into words, but at least

Lucy had died peacefully, and didn't have half her face burned away . . .

'Look, Daisy, we all have to face up to these things. We don't have much choice, do we?' Alice said, with twenty-year-old wisdom. And then she perked up.

'I'll tell you what: there's a dance at the Methodist Church Hall to raise funds for servicemen tomorrow night, so why don't we go? A group of the other nurses were talking about it, and there's always safety in numbers, isn't there?'

As Daisy hesitated, she grinned. 'Oh, do say yes. There's sure to be a lot of young chaps keen to dance with a couple of smashers like us. There'll probably be quite a few from RAF Locking. What do you say?'

For a minute Daisy couldn't say anything at all. Locking Camp was so near to the Luckwell farm. It was also the place where Cal had done his training, and she missed him and Lucy so much . . . and this girl's words were bringing it all back to her. It was on the tip of her tongue to say she couldn't possibly go dancing, even if Aunt Rose permitted it . . . and then she remembered that Alice's family had gone through a terrible bereavement too, and they all had to get over it in the best way they could.

'I'll have to see if it's all right with my family first,' she said lamely.

'Well, I'll wait for you outside the Hall at half past seven then. Try and come, Daisy. It does help, believe me. And remember that it's all in a good cause.'

That's what she told Aunt Rose, half-hoping that her aunt would forbid it, and half-hoping that she wouldn't. It was Aunt Rose who had said she should have some fun, and that you couldn't let Adolph spoil everything. And she was sure Lucy wouldn't have objected. If Lucy had been here, she would have been eager to go too. But Daisy hadn't been at all sure it was what *she* really wanted, until she saw the doubt in her aunt's eyes.

'I'm not sure about this, Daisy. Dancing with young men – strangers . . .'

'Oh, Aunt Rose, I'm not a child! I do know how to behave, and I attend strangers every day, remember! And don't tell me you and Uncle Bert never tripped the light fantastic, or the black bottom, or whatever you called it!'

'We certainly did not dance the black bottom! I must admit we had our moments, but we were courting then, of course,' she added hastily. 'Young girls didn't go to dances unaccompanied in our day.'

'I won't be unaccompanied. I'll be with Alice Godfrey.'

'Do her parents own one of those small hotels on the seafront?'

'I don't know. Why? Do you know some people by that name?'

'There's a Mrs Godfrey who's just joined our knitting circle. I did hear that she had a son who'd been killed,' Rose said vaguely.

'There you are then. It's all perfectly respectable!' Daisy said, glossing over that bit of information. 'Oh Aunt Rose, please say I can go! You know how I used to love to dance when Mother was alive. Remember how I used to try to copy her footsteps when I was little, before Teddy was born? And Daddy used to stand me on his slippers and try to waltz me around the room with his two left feet and made us all laugh . . .'

She caught her breath, filled with the bittersweet memories of times past, and the imagery of her mother, still young and beautiful, at the height of her success, and of her family who adored her. How long ago it all seemed, and yet the imagery was as vivid in her mind as if it was only yesterday. The yearning to dance was as strong a passion in her now as it had been then. Dancing was like living in a dreamworld, floating on air, swaying to the music and blotting out the terrible things that were happening in the world today; and it was in her blood.

'I suppose you had better go and see if you've remembered anything your mother taught you, then,' Rose said, her eyes suspiciously moist. 'But your uncle will take you and he'll fetch you at ten thirty sharp.'

'Oh but—'

'No buts, Daisy. If you want to go dancing, you have to go on my terms.'

From the steely tone in her voice now, Daisy knew there was nothing more to be said; so her thoughts turned instead on what to wear. She had nothing remotely suitable, of course. She had never been to a grown-up dance before, and anticipation quickly turned to panic as she riffled through her wardrobe.

In the end she chose her Sunday-best pink-and-cream floral frock and her cream-coloured shoes with the smallest of heels, washed her hair and gave it a vinegar rinse to make it shine, and brushed it out to a shimmering sheen. She couldn't tame the shock of natural curls, but why should she? she thought defiantly. Her hair was her crowning glory, or so they said; and even though Cal wouldn't be there to see her, she wanted to look her best.

The rest of the family assessed her as she came into the parlour for their approval on Saturday evening, still nervous, but brimful of an excitement she couldn't deny. She was seventeen and she was going dancing . . .

'Cor, you look just like one of them film stars, Daisy!' Norman said, and Ronnie nodded in brotherly agreement, struck dumb for once.

She smiled on them benevolently.

'She don't look like a film star,' Teddy snapped. 'She just looks like our Daisy done up like a dog's dinner.'

'Well, thank you, Teddy dear,' Daisy snapped back. 'When I need approval from a baby I'll ask for it!'

'I'm not a baby! I'm nearly eight!'

'Oh yes, I was forgetting. You'll be joining up next, won't you?'

Rose intervened before the squabbling got serious.

'Daisy, if you don't stop scowling your face will stay like it, and you'll be cracking that make-up before you even reach the Methodist Church Hall,' she said meaningly, assuring Daisy that she knew very well she was wearing a touch of rouge and face powder and that her lips were several shades redder than usual.

'Anyway, I think she looks a real treat,' Bert said heartily. 'And a credit to her mother.'

'Thank you, Uncle Bert,' Daisy said with a lump in her throat, because it was the nicest compliment anyone could have paid her.

'So if you're ready, my lady, your chariot awaits you,' he went on grandly, holding out his arm to her.

She crooked her arm through his, feeling like a princess as they swept out of the house, even though the old Morris car took a bit of cranking to start and rather took the edge off it all as it wheezed down the hill towards the brightly lit church hall.

People were already going inside or waiting for friends to arrive and, with a feeling of relief, Daisy caught sight of Alice Godfrey as Bert stopped the car and pressed her hand for a moment.

'You have a good time, my love, and don't go fretting over your aunt's fussing. She cares for you, and it's just her way of showing it.'

'I know,' Daisy said. 'And you know I'd never let either of you down.'

She leaned forward and kissed him on the cheek before she got mopey again and ruined her spanking new look. She desperately hoped she had managed to wash all the vinegar out of her hair and cover the smell with a splash of eau de cologne so that it didn't waft into his nostrils, or those of any dance partner.

'You look lovely, Daisy,' Alice Godfrey said enviously, as if she had never seen her before. Nor had she, except in her nurse's uniform, and the cardigan she had worn over it at the churchyard on Friday evening.

'So do you,' Daisy said, realising that the cut of her new friend's clothes was far superior to her own. It took a haberdasher's daughter to know that, she thought, to cover any thought of embarrassment.

Alice pulled a face. 'Oh, I'm no beauty, and I know it. You are though. You could wear a sack and look nice. And your hair is such a gorgeous colour,' she added with a sigh.

Daisy started to laugh as they went inside the hall. 'Stop it, for goodness' sake. You'll make me swollen-headed. Anyway, my brothers and sisters have all got the same colour hair, so I'm used to being called a ginger-nut!'

'I would never call you anything so beastly,' Alice declared. 'But it makes me realise I don't know anything about you, Daisy. I didn't even know you had a big family. We must get to know one another properly if we're going to be friends. And I think we are – aren't we?'

Daisy realised they had linked arms as if to give each other courage as they went into the hall where the band was playing on a raised dais. Couples were already dancing, and there was a fair sprinkling of servicemen among the young girls and chaperones. There was also a large banner proclaiming that this evening's event was for fund-raising purposes for our brave boys in uniform.

For a moment Daisy thought wistfully how Lucy would have loved this if she'd ever had the chance to be here. But then her heart gave a lift. She knew she would never forget her, but Lucy wasn't here any more, and now there was someone new, if she wanted to give friendship a chance. It seemed more than coincidental that they had met in the churchyard where Lucy was buried, so near to the spot where Alice's brother lay too. It seemed like fate, and Daisy wasn't one to sneer at fate.

She smiled at Alice now. 'I think we could be very good friends,' she said.

*   *   *

She wrote in her diary that evening that today had been another turning-point in her life. She had a new friend, and she had danced with a boy called Jed.

Her fingers poised over her pencil as she wrote his name, seeing him in her mind's eye as she did so: tall and gangly in the army uniform that seemed far too big for his slight frame; remembering how he had asked her to dance – clumsily, awkwardly, almost apologising for being alive at all.

'You won't find me much good, I'm afraid,' he'd said. 'I've got a gammy leg from a shrapnel wound, but if you're willing to take a chance, we could always hop around slowly. Mind you, I don't know the steps either—'

'Oh, for pity's sake,' Daisy said, starting to laugh. 'Are you sure you want to do this?'

'Quite sure. I spotted you the minute you came in, and I've been plucking up courage to come over and ask you ever since.'

'Good heavens, have you?' Daisy said. 'Am I that frightening?'

'Not frightening at all. Just very pretty.' As he spoke, he went red with embarrassment. 'But if you don't want to dance with me, I'll understand . . .'

'I do,' she said, standing up at once. 'Of course I do. And don't worry if you don't know the steps. I can teach you.'

She held out her hand and, as he took it, he drew her on to the dance floor to mingle with all the other couples in a slow waltz.

Much later, when she had related all that she was going to about the evening to Aunt Rose and Uncle Bert, and she was out of her finery and snuggled up in bed, she continued writing in her diary that it was just like the romantic novelettes told you it would be.

A kind of electric shock had tingled through her the moment their fingers touched. It had almost made her faint for a moment, because she had been so certain she could never be attracted to anyone else but Cal. *He* was her young man, the one she had decided dreamily that she was going to marry one day – not this soldier with the intense brown eyes and the rather haunted expression on his face.

He wasn't even good-looking – not in a film-starry way, anyway – and in any case he was hoping to go back to France soon, once his leg healed. He clearly had plans of his own. He wasn't a patient at Weston General, but in a convalescent home nearby, which was why Daisy had never seen him before. But before the evening had ended, he'd said he wanted to see her again, and she didn't know what to do about it.

Six

On her next day off, Daisy took the train to Bristol, and walked to Vicarage Street from Temple Meads. She needed to talk to Elsie. Though quite what she was going to say to her, she didn't know. They had talked over many things in the past, but never anything as personal as how you knew if you were really in love. But Elsie was a married woman now, and must know some of the answers.

She saw Elsie watching out for her from the window of the upstairs flat she now occupied in the family home, and she waved wildly. It felt good to be home. She loved Aunt Rose and Uncle Bert, but this was where she really belonged, she thought with a surge of guilt for having decamped there so readily. Then she forgot any of it as her sister greeted her at the door with open arms, and the only thing Daisy could think of to say was:

'Good Lord, Elsie, what have you got beneath that pinny? A whale?'

Elsie laughed, pulling her inside. 'Well, I can see your education has advanced in more ways than one since you've been nursing, Daisy dear. Is everyone so frank about such things now?'

'Cripes, I'm sorry – I didn't mean to be rude . . .'

'It's all right, you goose; I'm just teasing. It's rather refreshing, actually. Father studiously ignores it when he can, but I have to admit that it's quite a bump for less than four months, isn't it?' she said, patting her stomach affectionately. 'I keep telling him if he doesn't stop growing at this rate, we won't be able to get through the front door by the time he's ready to be born.'

'You're sure it's going to be a boy then,' Daisy said, noting the cosiness of the rooms with their unmistakable mark of Elsie's tidiness and attention to detail.

'No, but I have to call him something, don't I? I can't think of him as just an *it*. There's a real little person growing in there, Daisy, and it's one of life's major miracles.'

Daisy forbore mentioning one of the cruder nurse's comments that anyone could do the necessary to produce a kid, and it was a bloody sight harder not to get caught. But anyone seeing the bloom on her sister now, and the glow in her eyes when she talked about her baby, could surely only think of it as the major miracle that she did.

'So let's have some tea and then you can tell me all the news,' Elsie said. 'Is everyone well? I told you about Immy driving an officer around, didn't I?'

'Yes. I wonder what James Church thinks about that.'

Elsie's face sobered. 'Oh Daisy, she had such a terrible letter from him recently. His tank regiment was involved in action, and one of them was blown up. Everyone inside it was blown to pieces too. James described it in graphic detail to Immy, which was a bit unfair, to upset her like that, I thought. I mean, she must realise it was something that could happen to James too.'

Daisy was shaking her head. 'It might seem unfair to you, Elsie, but they have to do that. They have to tell someone, or they would burst with the anguish of it all. It helps them to talk and to get it out of their systems. Believe me, I've heard plenty of harrowing tales on the wards, and if Daddy knew half of them – some gruesome, some downright intimate . . .'

She half-grinned, to take the seriousness out of her words, and Elsie paused in the little kitchen area, studying her sister thoughtfully.

'Is this really my flippant little sister talking? You've certainly grown up a bit, Daisy.'

'Well, for goodness' sake, I am almost eighteen, even though Aunt Rose seems to forget that sometimes. And that's rather what I wanted to talk to you about, in a roundabout kind of way.'

Now that the moment was here, she found herself floundering; but as Elsie put the tray of tea on the table and poured them both a cup, her sister looked at her with more concern.

'There's no trouble between you, is there? You know Aunt Rose means well, Daisy. Remember how Mother always used to say we should put that on her headstone some day?'

'And we never thought Mother would be the first one to have a headstone, did we?' Daisy murmured. 'The Luckwells are going to get one made for Lucy soon, but apparently the ground has to settle first.'

She bit her lip, not wanting to be discussing headstones and churchyards and all that went with them, and not really knowing how the conversation had veered that way.

'Well, this is turning out to be a jolly day, isn't it?' Elsie said briskly. 'If you've got something dire to tell me, Daisy, let's get it over and done with; otherwise let's talk about something more cheerful, shall we?'

Daisy took a long drink of tea, weaker than they used to have it, because they all knew tea would be one of the next things to be rationed. Tea was precious now, and what was already in the store cupboard had to be hoarded and couldn't be wasted. She took a deep breath.

'It's nothing dire at all. It's probably a silly question, anyway, and I can feel myself getting all hot and bothered at even asking it. It's – well – it's how do you know if you're really in love, Elsie?' she finished in a rush.

'Is that all?' Elsie said in some relief. 'Oh, I'm sorry, darling; I can see this is important to you, and it's not silly

71

at all. But how can anyone answer such a question? You just *know*.'

'Well, that's no answer at all,' Daisy said crossly. 'How did you know for certain that you were in love with Joe – or is that too personal a question?'

Elsie gave a long sigh, her eyes faraway with remembering. 'It's not too personal, since it obviously means so much to you – and we'll get around to just *why* in a moment or two. I knew, because my heart began to pound every time I saw him, and even the anticipation that we were going to be together could start it racing. I knew, because I couldn't imagine being without him ever again. I couldn't even bear the thought of it. Does that make sense?'

'I think so.' It made it all the more emotive, because Elsie had always been quieter and more reserved than Immy or Daisy, and she had never opened her heart to her so frankly before.

'So come clean, little sister' – Elsie was more assertive now – 'who is this paragon of virtue you think you're in love with? He *is* a paragon of virtue, I hope? And I think you know what I mean.'

'Don't worry, I'm not about to besmirch the family honour, Elsie. But I really did think I was falling in love with Cal. I told you about him, didn't I? And then Aunt Rose let me go to a dance last Saturday, and I met someone called Jed, and I'm not sure about anything any more.'

'Aunt Rose let you go to a dance on your own?'

'Of course not. I went with another nurse, and it was for fund-raising purposes, so it was all very proper, and Uncle Bert took me there and back – and just telling you all that makes me feel about six years old, 'she added crossly.

'You rather look like it, sitting there with your arms folded and that mutinous expression on your face. So who is this Jed?'

'He's a soldier on convalescent leave, and I really *liked* him, Elsie, and he says he'd like to see me again – and to write to me when he rejoins his unit. So do you think it would be disloyal to Cal if I agreed to it?'

Elsie leaned across and kissed her cheek. 'I think it would be a lovely thing to do to write to a soldier and give him news of home. I know how Joe appreciates my letters. And where's the harm in being friendly to two young men? Providing you keep them both as friends, of course.'

It wasn't what Daisy had once had in mind regarding Cal, but that wasn't something she wanted to keep reminding her family of, least of all Elsie, who had only ever had eyes for one man. She wasn't so sure about Immy. Her oldest sister had always thought her too young and scatty to confide in, and Daisy had never known about any young man in her life before she had fallen in love with James Church. They always seemed such a perfect couple, and it was so romantic to realise that someone you had known all your life was someone so special . . .

They heard the outer door open downstairs, and to the relief of both, the time for confidences was over. The next minute Quentin Caldwell had knocked on the door of his daughter's flat and poked his head inside.

'Well, this is a rare treat,' he said heartily. 'Two beautiful daughters at one fell swoop. We only need Imogen to surprise us and we'd have the full set.'

Daisy laughed, giving him a quick kiss. 'How are you, Daddy? And how's the fire-fighting? Adolph's not sending anything to keep you busy yet, is he?'

'Don't be too complacent, my dear. Being prepared is not only the Boy Scouts' motto, and we'll be ready for whatever comes our way.'

'Nothing, I hope,' Elsie said quickly, crossing her fingers.

'Don't you believe it, my love.' Then he turned to Daisy as he saw Elsie's face pucker. 'Has your uncle got around to building that air-raid shelter yet?'

'Not yet. He doesn't think any bombs will come our way.

73

He calls Weston a soft target, whatever that means. Probably all that mud and sand,' she added.

Quentin shook his head. 'What he really means is that it doesn't have the same risk as Bristol has, darling. No docks or aircraft factories.'

'Well, how do the Germans know about that?'

'Of course they know it, just as we know which cities to target when we send our aircraft over there. Warfare has become far more sophisticated these days, and they'll know where and when to strike, believe me.'

Daisy shivered, and she couldn't help seeing how this conversation was upsetting Elsie. Men saw war on a different level from women, she thought shrewdly. They only saw the need to fight, and to win at all costs, while women saw the pain that war inflicted.

'If the danger of bombing is so much worse in Bristol, then why don't you both come down to Weston with the rest of us, Daddy?' she said impulsively. 'There's still plenty of room in that old house of Aunt Rose's, and I know she'd love to have you both, and Teddy would adore it . . .'

They answered simultaneously.

'I can't do that, Daisy. I'm still the manager of Preston's Emporium, and with so many young men away in the services, it would be like deserting a sinking ship. I have my AFS work to think about too . . .'

And Elsie: 'I'm not leaving here! Joe and I have made this our home for the duration, and he'll want to be sure he has me to come back to . . .'

'Gosh, I'm sorry I spoke!' Daisy said.

'Actually, Joe keeps suggesting I should go north to stay with his family,' Elsie went on. 'But I only met them once, when we had a few brief days there on his Christmas leave, as you know. I'll want to get to know them properly some day, of course – and they'll want to see their grandchild. But Immy made an even dafter suggestion. You remember that housing agent she used to work for, who got stage fright even before the war began and left Bristol in a blue funk?'

'Mr Harris – yes,' Daisy said. 'I thought he was a rather sweet old boy, in a roly-poly sort of way.'

'Not so much of the old boy, if you please, Daisy,' her father said with a laugh. 'He was younger than me!'

'Anyway,' Elsie put in, 'Immy keeps in touch with him for some strange reason that I can't fathom. He went to Cornwall to live with his brother who has a market garden somewhere near Penzance. Only now they've gone into partnership with a small boarding house as well.'

'Is this conversation getting anywhere?' Daisy enquired.

Her sister smiled at her impatience. 'Yes. Apparently Kenneth Harris says that any time any of Immy's family feel they should get away from Bristol, he would make room for us at his boarding house. Immy told me to think about it, but why on earth would I want to move so far away from my family?'

Daisy agreed. The family had been to Cornwall years ago, and it was quaint and pretty, full of old tin-mine chimneys and china-clay workings – and miles from anywhere. The beaches were lovely, though, she remembered in an unexpected burst of recollection. There were such tales of smuggling and magic and mystery that had enchanted them as children. But you wouldn't want to *live* there!

Quentin cleared his throat, as if he too had been remembering the past.

'I'm sure Imogen meant it for the best, Elsie, and it was certainly a nice gesture from Harris. But we all have to do things in our own way. Now, how about some tea for your father, or am I already being rationed?'

Daisy was almost glad to get on the crowded train back to Weston. Her visit hadn't really solved anything, except that she'd decided she owed it to Cal to write and let him know that one of her patients had asked her to write to him as a friendly gesture. It wasn't *quite* the truth, but putting it like that didn't make it sound too bad – or too personal. That was what she would do.

There was one thing that scared her, though. All the time Elsie was talking about Joe, it was clear that she was seeing his face in her mind. She had been with him very recently, Daisy reminded herself, and it was how it should be . . . but she sometimes found it hard to visualise Cal, and not only Cal. Sometimes she couldn't even visualise Lucy's face either. She didn't want to lose the image or the memory of either of them, but it was happening, and she couldn't seem to stop it.

Now there was Jed, who was very nice, but who didn't make her heart pound the way Elsie's heart pounded whenever she thought of Joe. He didn't make her starry-eyed at the thought of seeing him again, and that scared her too. Maybe she wasn't destined to fall deeply in love with anyone . . . or maybe she simply hadn't met the right one yet after all.

When she arrived at the Weston house in the early evening, it was to find them all in an uproar. Teddy was covered in spots, and the other two boys were scratching themselves in sympathy, with Aunt Rose trying vainly to plaster them all in calamine lotion and ignoring their squeals at the coldness of it.

'Chickenpox,' Rose announced to Daisy. 'Teddy's quite bad with it, and I'm sure the others are going down with it too. Have you had it, Daisy?'

'Yes. I think we all did when we were little, and it's beastly.'

'They'll have to stay away from school, of course, and you'd better see what the position is at the hospital, Daisy. It's very infectious and you can't risk giving it to the patients. We must keep to ourselves until all risk of infection has gone.'

'I'll telephone right away,' Daisy said with a groan, thinking that the infection had probably spread already. But with three fractious little boys in her care, Aunt Rose would need all the help she could get.

There was another sneaking little thought in her mind too. Fate had a strange way of sorting things out sometimes. She obviously couldn't see Jed now. She must also telephone the convalescent home and get a message passed on to him. It was the only decent thing to do before he tried to get in touch with her.

But half an hour later, when she had made the calls, including one to Elsie, who assured her that she also had had chickenpox, she had heard the matron of the convalescent home give her the news that Private Jed Williams had already been sent home to make room for more patients. Without even contacting her, thought Daisy. So much for romantic dreams that meant nothing . . .

A week later she received a letter from him, sent to her via the hospital.

Dear Daisy,

I thought I was going to be in Weston for a few more weeks, but all in a rush they bundled me off to convalesce at home with no time to let you know. So I'm back in Folkestone with my parents until I'm fit. It's not the best place to be, as we can hear the bombing from the other side of the Channel and the air seems to be constantly full of searchlights looking out for enemy aircraft, but so far we haven't seen any. I'll be glad to get back in the thick of things myself. Still, it could be worse, and I've got hardly a limp now.

I just wanted to say I'm sorry we didn't meet again but if you'd like to start writing to me, I'd love to hear from you sometime.

I thought you were a really smashing girl, and maybe one of these days I'll get the chance to say 'save the last dance for me', if you don't think that's being too forward.

Yours sincerely,
Jed

Daisy sat back and read the letter all over again. It could hardly be called a love letter, but she liked him all the more for that. He was nice. A nice young man. One that her father would approve of. And even though he didn't say as much, the town where he lived was obviously so much more dangerous a place than here.

All the same she knew she shouldn't let sympathy cloud her judgement. She would definitely write to him, but Cal was still her young man, and she would do as she intended and let him know about Jed. It would salve her conscience.

It was tedious being at home all the time for the next couple of weeks, and attending to the ever more demanding needs of three bored children. Daisy found herself hoping Elsie knew what she was in for, but presumably one little baby wouldn't cause as much disruption as these three. She also found herself reading the newspapers and listening to the wireless more avidly than before, and as April slid into May, everyone anticipated the sound of air-raid sirens, even if nothing seemed to be happening yet.

But the awful reports of what the European countries were suffering brought the reality of war in this lovely spring ever nearer. It wasn't only buildings that were being destroyed, it was thousands of people too; and Hitler's boast of invading England was no longer to be dismissed as the dreams of a madman, but a real possibility. Every wireless bulletin made it sound graver.

'It looks very bad,' Uncle Bert told his wife and niece, after listening intently to the latest one. 'I fear for all of us, my dears, and this ineffectual government is doing nothing to relieve the situation. Chamberlain will have to go.'

'There's no doubt about that,' Rose said, 'and the sooner the better. The poor little countries in Europe stand no chance against a dictator like Hitler, and if he has his way, we'll be next.'

'Of course we will. Britain is his goal, and he has to

78

overrun all the others before he can get to us.'

'Do you really think it will happen?' Daisy said fearfully. 'I don't want to have to think of myself as a German. I'm English!'

'We'll always be English, my love,' her aunt told her stoutly. 'He may rule our country, but he'll never rule our hearts and minds. I'm sure the people in those other countries all feel the same.'

'He'll never rule our country, Rose, so get that notion out of your head. We'll win in the end because we have right on our side.'

Daisy wasn't so sure any more – she wasn't sure of anything – and when the news came through that Hitler's army had taken Holland and Belgium, it looked as if the whole world was teetering on the brink of a massive Nazi triumph. Only France stood in the way of the invasion of Britain. If that fell, Germany's long-range aircraft would be able to bomb every corner of Britain.

But what looked like the beginning of the end took a dramatic twist. As Hitler's relentless march proceeded, the Prime Minister resigned at the end of a disastrous reign in parliament, and by the Whitsun weekend of May the tenth, Winston Churchill was ready to form a new coalition government. It seemed as if the whole country breathed a collective sigh of relief.

'It doesn't change the fact that our boys are still being sent to France, and many of them are coming home maimed or worse,' Bert said grimly. 'Elsie must feel constant anxiety over her husband, and the Good Lord only knows where young Baz is nowadays.'

Daisy could have added that Immy would be full of anxiety about James Church too, just as *she* was about Cal – and Jed.

She found it a relief to be finally back at work after the stress of caring for the three bored little boys, and the enforced insularity of home life. But when she came home from her first day back at the hospital, she had news of her own to impart. She took a deep breath.

'Please take a look at this leaflet, Aunt Rose. They're asking for volunteers to join a special unit of nurses for the hospital ships bringing the wounded home from France, and I need you to persuade Daddy to let me go. I know he'll say I'm too young, but I'll be eighteen next month, and people younger than me are risking their lives every day, so please support me,' she finished quickly.

'Oh no, Daisy; France is such a dangerous place these days . . .'

'It's no more dangerous than London, or Kent, or Sussex will be very soon,' Daisy said, dragging up her knowledge of the south-east counties. 'And even Bristol, if what you've all been surmising is correct. I really want to do this, Aunt Rose. You do see that, don't you? If Mother were here, I'm sure she'd understand.'

She didn't often use her mother's name to gain a point, and she wasn't even sure that Frances *would* have sanctioned her joining the special unit, or agreed with her need to do something. But it was more than a growing need now. The restlessness inside her was stronger than the need to stay in safe surroundings, even doing such a vital and necessary job in Weston General.

'What about your fellow nurses? I doubt whether many of them have this sudden urge to be in the midst of such danger,' Rose said, not rising to the bait of being no more than a surrogate mother to the Caldwell progeny.

'At least four that I know of as yet, and one of them is Alice Godfrey. You remember – the nurse I went to the dance with. You said you knew her mother.'

'And is Alice Godfrey's mother willing for her to join this special unit?'

'Yes, she is. In any case, Alice is twenty, and very sensible, Aunt Rose. I'd like you to meet her.'

'I think I should, since she seems to have such influence

over you,' Rose said decisively. 'You had better invite her to tea on Sunday afternoon.'

'And you'll think about what I've said – about persuading Daddy that I really do need to do this?' she persisted.

'Perhaps. But first of all I'll have to persuade myself that I don't think it's the maddest idea you've ever had,' Rose said drily.

'She'll do it,' Daisy told Alice confidently next morning when they were having a welcome break in their shift. 'We always relied on Aunt Rose to get around Daddy when we wanted anything. My mother used to say she was as immovable as the Rock of Gibraltar. She's Daddy's older sister and she always had influence over him, but in a very sensible and logical way.'

'She sounds pretty formidable to me! My mother said so after meeting her at their knitting circle afternoons, but she seems to like her.'

'And so will you. She can be tough, but she's also the sanest and kindest person you ever met. So please say you'll come to tea and further our cause.'

Alice looked at her curiously. 'You really are set on this, aren't you, Daisy? I keep having second and even third thoughts, although I know I'll do it in the end. But you're different. It might sound sugary and pathetic, but I'd say you have a real burning light in your eyes. You're not a descendent of old Florrie, by any chance?'

Daisy laughed. 'Not that I'm aware of, but thanks for the compliment – if it *is* a compliment. Or are you just implying that I'm jumping in with both feet because I'm still a juvenile?'

'You're anything but that, sweetie,' Alice said lightly. 'I think you're someone to be admired, if you must know – and at such a tender age too,' she added teasingly.

Seven

Quentin Caldwell's voice was loud enough to make his sister hold the telephone well away from her ear.

'Of course I object. The girl's far too young, Rose, and I expect you to make her see that!'

'And what if she simply joins this special unit, anyway?'

'How can she, without my permission?'

Rose sighed, knowing this was going to be a sticky conversation. But she had been in the habit of getting her own way for far too long to be beaten now. Contrary to what Daisy had expected, she now admired the girl for being determined to follow her heart, if not her head.

'Quentin, I'm not at all sure that she *will* need your permission. You agreed she could train to be a nurse, and if she's required to do a certain job, I think she's obliged to do it.'

She didn't quite believe it, but she hoped he would. But when he didn't answer immediately, she plunged on before he remembered that this was a voluntary unit.

'You have to let them go, Quentin,' she said gently. 'Daisy's a young woman now, and you should be proud of her.'

'I am proud of her, woman. You don't need to tell me to be proud of my own children.'

'Frances would be proud of the way she's grown into a responsible young woman too.'

She heard him sigh heavily, and knew she had won.

'Then tell her she has my blessing,' he said, before he

put down the phone, then went on to report this latest development to Elsie, the only one of his children he still had at home.

Even she didn't belong to him any more, but to Joe Preston.

In his heart Quentin still felt it wasn't right for women and children to go to war. It was against the nature of things. Man was traditionally the hunter and woman the homemaker, however old-fashioned the idea was nowadays. In the last war they had lost thousands of their young people, and it looked poised to happen all over again. Logically, it *must* happen again, because no war ever ended without casualties and tragedies.

In fact, for all the preparations, which sometimes seemed as unreal and ineffectual as some of Frances's old stage sets, he felt uneasily that Bristol itself was holding its breath. Like many cities, it was merely awaiting the inevitable. Once France fell – *if* it fell – *when* it fell – there would be no stopping the enemy.

Elsie could see at once that he was troubled. He told her of Daisy's plans, and saw the matching mixture of worry and pride in her eyes. He cherished Elsie's placid company in the family home, but he knew he finally had to say what was simmering away in his mind. It had to be said.

'Elsie, my love, I've been thinking about that suggestion of Immy's for you to go to Penzance and stay at Kenneth Harris's boarding house for a while. And before you start objecting, just hear me out.'

'He agreed to let me go without any fuss?' Daisy said in astonishment, when her aunt relayed most of the conversation with her father. 'I always said you were a marvel, Aunt Rose!'

'I wouldn't say that, nor am I entirely convinced I did the right thing, even now; but I know your heart is set on it.'

'You've always known the right things to say to Daddy, though,' Daisy said, her mind already winging ahead with all that it meant.

'I've always known how to get around my brother, you mean. So what's the next move?'

As if only just realising how much she was going to miss her niece and also just what she was giving her blessing to, she cleared her throat awkwardly. Daisy put her arms around her and kissed her.

'I have to sign up for the special unit, and then we just await orders. Alice has already done it. We're going to stick together, so each of us will take care of the other. You don't need to worry.'

'You can be sure of that, can you?'

'I just believe it, that's all,' Daisy said candidly, refusing to be dampened by her aunt's genuine unease now that the deed was done. 'Of course, I shall expect you to say an extra prayer at church on Sundays from now on to keep the whole unit safe.'

'You can rely on that,' Rose said. 'And I hope you're a good sailor.'

Alice Godfrey said the same thing when Daisy told her in delight that she had put her name down for the new venture. Alice's father had a small boat and Alice had been used to the choppiness of the Bristol Channel from an early age. Daisy had only had a few trips on a Bristol pleasure boat or on the river ferry when her brother Baz showed her his ferrying skills, but she wasn't going to let a little thing like boating inexperience put her off. What was there to worry about, anyway?

Two weeks later she had rather different thoughts. They left Folkestone on what had once been a cross-Channel ferry, now painted white with a large red cross on it to identify it as a hospital ship. She had been excited to find they would be based at Folkestone, and had tried to contact Jed immediately, only to find that he had already returned to his regiment. If he had tried to let her know, the letter must have crossed with her coming here.

But right now, with the boat heaving up and down in the heavy swell of the English Channel, and her stomach trying hard to mimic it, Jed was the last thing on her mind.

'Keep your eyes on the horizon, Daisy,' Alice advised her. 'Actually, this is reasonably calm, so you'll soon get used to it. Don't look at the water whatever you do.'

'I'm trying not to,' she gasped.

'And don't turn your face into the wind,' a less sympathetic nurse remarked alongside her.

Daisy made a superhuman effort to keep the contents of her stomach intact and failed. You didn't need food rationing to streamline your figure, she thought wildly. All you needed to do was step on a boat and let the elements do it for you.

She realised Alice was holding her tightly while she dispatched the rest of her breakfast to the fishes.

'You'll feel better now,' she was told. 'And once you get your sea-legs it won't bother you at all, however rough it gets.'

'Tell that to the fairies,' Daisy muttered. 'My brother said one of his mates was always seasick, and he'd been at sea for years on a North Sea trawler.'

'Oh well, I daresay the North Sea's different,' Alice said, dismissing it. 'But you'll be as right as rain soon, Daisy. You'd better be, otherwise we'll be putting you in a bunk alongside the patients.'

'Maybe that's what she's got in mind. Is that it, Caldwell?' the other nurse said with a knowing smirk.

Alice turned on her. 'If you haven't got anything else to do, Nichols, go and see if they've got any ginger in the galley. Chewing on that can help. Or a drink of ginger cordial.'

'Am I her nursemaid now?' Nurse Nichols said at once.

'Oh, just *do* it, for pity's sake, and don't be a grouch all your life!'

The girl marched off, and Daisy grinned, feeling marginally better now.

'She doesn't like being told what to do, Alice.'

'She'd better get used to it then, because none of us really knows what we're in for. It's not going to be as cosy as dealing with patients on the wards, with all the proper equipment at our disposal. In desperate situations, we'll probably have to improvise.'

'Like hacking off a leg with a kitchen knife?' Daisy said, without thinking.

'Something like that,' Alice said solemnly, at which Daisy heaved violently again and spent the next ten minutes leaning over the side, while the waves and spume sped by below her.

When she finally raised her head, to find a glass of ginger cordial thrust in her hand from the uncompromising Nurse Nichols, she saw the coastline of France in the distance. As she saw it, still grey and hazy beneath a dull sky, they all realised they could hear the sound of distant gunfire, and the bile in her mouth turned to the first real taste of fear.

'Alice,' she said hesitantly.

'I know. I'm scared too. But we're here to do a job, and we're bloody well going to do it, aren't we?'

Daisy hadn't heard her swear before, though she was well used to hearing cuss-words and blasphemy from the hospital patients. Who could blame them, when it was the only way to relieve their feelings? It never bothered her. It didn't bother her to hear Alice swear so calmly now, because it all seemed to fit in with the determined mood they were feeling.

They were here to bring their boys home, to patch them up as best they could and send them back to fight again . . . and they were bloody well going to do it, she thought daringly.

'You're right,' she said. 'We're bloody well going to do it.'

As Alice laughed and squeezed her hand, she suddenly

felt weirdly calmer. Not that she thought she was never going to throw up again – she was sure she would – but it wasn't going to bloody well stop her doing her job. And that was enough, she told herself severely. Aunt Rose would have a fit if she could read her thoughts. So it was a b– jolly good job she couldn't!

The job of the hospital ships was to act as shuttle ferries, the administrator had told them officiously. They all had to think of the ship they were on as an extension of their base hospital. The nurses wouldn't be expected to set foot on French soil except in emergencies. The stretcher-bearers and orderlies would bring the wounded on board, where they would be quickly assessed and sent to various sections of the ship. It would all be done with quiet efficiency, just as if the nurses were working on the wards at Weston General and other hospitals from which the nurses had been recruited.

Daisy remembered those words when the ship eased into the dockside of the strange French town and the first wave of patients was brought on board. There was nothing of the quiet efficiency they had been led to expect. A dark cloud of uniforms seemed to rise up at their approach – those who could stand at all – and the rush to get on board would have seemed an ungodly scramble, had it not been for the distress of the majority, and the uninhibited screams of those who could no longer hold them in.

There was complete chaos for an hour while they were all admitted on board; but the initial helplessness at not knowing what to do was overtaken by swift realisation that the really helpless ones were these once strong young men who seemed so pitiful now, and who needed help from the even younger, stronger, but so-called weaker female sex.

Daisy found strengths she didn't know she had as she helped to ease patients tenderly from stretcher to bunk or was advised to simply leave them where they were, as their needs were quickly affirmed. There wasn't time to blanch at open, gaping wounds as the call for bandages rang out time and again, bleeding was staunched, and doctors snapped for assistance in minor stitching operations and morphine injections.

But fumbling fingers became more efficient as they began the reverse journey back to Folkestone. Eyes and ears were sharper in the intensity of patient care. There was no time to think. All Daisy's concentration was on the patient she was tending at the moment . . . and then the next one . . . and the next.

In some cases the wounded had travelled miles on foot and farm carts, and any other way they could. It was raw, instant nursing, creating a bond between the members of the voluntary unit like none of them had experienced before.

'You did well, Caldwell,' Daisy heard a voice say as she straightened up her back from holding together the ragged pieces of a soldier's arm while the surgeon sewed it together temporarily. He had moved on now, but the older nurse beside her gave her shoulder a pat.

'Thanks,' Daisy muttered, not sure whether or not to risk saying more, in case it resulted in her spewing all over the patient, now that reaction was setting in.

'She did, didn't she?' the husky voice whispered from the bunk. 'What's your name, girlie? Just so I can tell my old woman it weren't really no angel who helped me. And t'other one as well.'

'Daisy,' she murmured.

'And I'm June. June Nichols,' the voice beside her went on.

Daisy hadn't even noticed who had been working beside her so efficiently, but now she saw that it was the nurse neither she nor Alice had cared for very much. She didn't look so severe now, and she certainly wasn't crowing over Daisy's seasickness any more. All of them were dishevelled, their uniforms spattered with blood, and in some cases drenched with it; but they had all worked together as a team, respecting each other without the need to say as much.

'Come on,' June said brusquely. 'We've got more patients to see to. We'll come back and see you again in a while, soldier.'

'I'll be here,' he said hoarsely. 'And the name's Tom. How about a date?'

'Oh yes, and what's your old woman going to say about that?' June said cheekily. They heard him chuckling weakly as the nurses moved away.

'It doesn't hurt to humour them,' June said. 'Poor devil probably isn't going to get much more use out of that arm when he gets back to Blighty, even if they save it.'

'Do you think it's that bad?' Daisy said, shocked. 'I thought not, since the surgeon had patched it up . . .'

June shrugged. 'It'll do for now, but my guess is he'll be invalided out soon. Don't let it get you down, kid. You'll see plenty more like that on these trips; but if we keep smiling, so will they.'

'Have you done this before then? I know you're not from the same hospital as my group . . .'

'I've been on it for a couple of weeks, and due for a few days off soon, thank God. You can't go on for ever, so when you get the chance, take my tip and have some fun, Daisy Caldwell. Remember: you're a long time dead.'

Daisy shivered, and then had to forget Nurse Nichols's advice, as they were needed urgently. She may be a cynic, Daisy thought, but she had plenty of compassion too, and she respected her more by the time they had done a second trip that day. By the time she almost fell into their assigned billet in Folkestone late that evening, she was more tired than she had ever been in her life before.

'I lost sight of you hours ago,' Alice said, when they were both stretched out in their beds, tenderly flexing muscles they hardly knew they'd had. 'Were you working with the dreadful Nichols?'

'I was, and she's not so dreadful once you get to know her.'

'That's good,' Alice murmured, too tired to discuss it.

'She says we should have some fun on our days off, because we're a long time dead.'

'Is she a philosopher or something?'

'No, but I think she's right. Maybe we can find a local dance or the flicks, Alice. What do you say? There's no Aunt Rose around to tell me not to go!'

Alice was wider awake now. 'Why, Daisy Caldwell, I'm surprised at you,' she teased. 'But I'm all for it. I heard there's a Canadian Air Force unit based near here. How do you fancy dancing with a mountie? They're supposed to always get their man – or woman!'

When Daisy didn't answer, she half sat up.

'What's up now?'

'Can you tell me if this billet is moving about, or am I still on that bloody ship?' she said weakly.

'It happens when you've been at sea for a while. Breathe deeply and try to sleep and it'll pass. We have to do it all over again tomorrow, remember.'

'Oh, I remember,' Daisy muttered.

They were to be given one day off every week; and remembering what June Nichols had recommended, on the following Saturday they sought out the nearest dance hall, if only to get the smell and sight of blood and bodies out of their memories for a little while. The stories some of the soldiers told were too horrific to keep in mind for more than a few minutes, or they might have been in danger of losing their nerve completely, and asking to be transferred back to Weston General on the next train. There were also rumours of a huge retreat in the offing, in which case the little town of Dunkirk would be even more chaotic.

It wasn't only Daisy who was affected by seasickness. Alice was often greener by the end of a mercy voyage than she was at the beginning. But on that Saturday evening they scrubbed their hands with carbolic soap, washed their hair and set it with Amami setting lotion to make it smell sweeter, dabbed eau de cologne profusely behind their ears, and donned their prettiest summer dresses.

Alice said daringly that if she knew what a brothel smelled like, they must smell just like one by now. Daisy laughed, adding jokingly that she had no wish to know what a brothel smelled like anyway!

Like all the streets and buildings in the town, the dance hall was all in darkness because of blackout regulations, but once they were inside the double inner doors, it was so brilliantly lit, it hurt their eyes for a few moments.

Alice linked her arm inside Daisy's. 'There's nobody to tell us what to do now except the dragon sister-in-charge, and she's not likely to pop up and tell us how to spend our evening off, so let's enjoy it.'

'Right-oh,' Daisy said, aware that she was having more freedom right now than she had ever had before.

She might be almost eighteen years old, but she was still cosseted to a degree and treated as one of the children by Aunt Rose and Uncle Bert. She had never been away from home like this before, and while the nurses had been more or less chaperoned and regimented on the hospital ship, with a serious job to do, now they could let their hair down.

The release of tension was suddenly enormous. Almost at once she realised the grip on her arm was lessening too, as a young sailor headed straight for Alice and asked her to dance.

'You don't mind, do you, Daisy?' Alice murmured.

'Of course not . . .' she began, but she was talking to thin air, as the sailor whisked Alice away and on to the crowded dance floor.

Daisy stood uncertainly for a moment or two, and then edged towards a vacant chair, vainly trying to recall how her sister Imogen's friend, Helen Church, had a remedy for feeling at a loss.

Helen was far more sophisticated than any of the Caldwell

girls, what with her parents being so well off, and her father a solicitor and everything. Helen said you should always behave like royalty: never fiddle with your hands or your hair, always think serene thoughts and try to be calm and composed at all times. If you feel confident, you'll look confident . . .

'May I have this dance, ma'am?' she heard a voice say, while she was still deciding to tell Helen Church a thing or two about trying to feel calm and composed when everyone else seemed to be having a good time, and you felt suddenly abandoned by your only friend . . .

She jerked up her head. A tall young man in an air force uniform was standing in front of her, leaning towards her so that his features were momentarily shadowed. He held out his hand, and she automatically put hers into his as he drew her to her feet.

'I'm sorry. I know you people prefer to have the introductions made first, but there didn't seem anyone around to do it. So allow me. Flight-Officer Glenn Fraser, originally from Toronto, now attached to the RAF, and recently deployed to somewhere in the south-east, as they say, at your service,' he finished with a small bow.

'Oh!' Daisy said. 'Well, uh, how do you do, Flight-Officer Fraser . . .'

'It's Glenn, please. And you are?'

'Daisy Caldwell. Nurse. Originally from Bristol and Weston-super-Mare, currently attached to one of the hospital ships based in Folkestone.'

The lengthy introductions suddenly seemed ridiculously formal when everyone around them was blatantly determined to have a good time. The war seemed a million miles away, and without warning they laughed simultaneously.

'So shall we dance, Daisy Caldwell? Or are we going to stand here looking at one another all evening? Not that I have any objection to that, either.'

'I'd love to dance,' she said, more breathless than she meant to be.

His smile was warm and admiring, and Daisy felt her heartbeats quicken. She liked his voice, and she liked his style and his politeness, and as he guided her on to the dance floor and she went into his arms, she reminded herself that she would probably never see him again – that mounties may always get their man, but it didn't necessarily apply to women too.

'You're amazingly light on your feet, Daisy,' he told her, when they had circled the floor several times, adroitly missing the clumsier dancers. 'Were you training to be a dancer before you became a nurse?'

'No, but my mother was a dancer, and it always came easily to me. My sisters aren't bad, either,' she added.

'You mean there's more than one of you? I can't believe it.'

'What can't you believe?' she asked, smiling at him more provocatively than usual, because she felt safe in this atmosphere where people were desperate to make the most of evenings like these – while they lasted. And because she already liked him a lot.

'I can't believe any man could be fortunate enough to have more than one daughter with the looks of an angel,' he said, the pressure of his hand on the small of her back increasing slightly. Just enough to make her skin tingle at his closeness. The floor was packed, so it might have been just an involuntary movement. They were already pressed close together, and she could sense every part of him, and she knew it must be the same for him. Before she knew it, she took fright.

'You're the second person to say that to me lately, but he was half-delirious at the time and I didn't believe him either.' She spoke lightly to cover her nervousness, since the atmosphere between them had suddenly become rather too intimate, too soon.

He laughed softly, just as if could read her mind, and he leaned forward so that his cheek touched hers for a moment.

'Not everyone's just throwing you a line, Daisy, though you must hear plenty of them in your business. Some of us are actually sincere.'

'I'm sorry,' she said, embarrassed now that she might have offended him. 'But you're right. Some of the patients do say the daftest things, and it would be silly to believe all of them, wouldn't it?'

'It surely would. You need to be selective.'

The band finished playing the tune, and reluctantly they broke apart.

'Thank you,' he said gravely. 'Perhaps we can have another dance later.'

'Possibly. But I have to find my friend now. It was very nice meeting you,' she said, and rushed away from him.

Now he would think her a complete idiot, she thought, fuming, as she found her way to the ladies' cloakroom for a breather, away from too many prying eyes on her blazing cheeks. But the cloakroom was so crowded that she couldn't hide away, and Alice was already there, dabbing powder on her cheeks.

'Good Lord, Daisy, you look like a whirling dervish. I saw you dancing with that good-looking fellow. Lucky you! I got stuck with a boring rating. So how did you get on? Did he ask you for a date?'

Daisy looked at her dumbly. No, he hadn't asked her for a date, because she hadn't stayed around long enough for him to make such a move. And if he had, what would she have said? That she couldn't go out with strangers because her Aunt Rose wouldn't approve? That she wasn't sure when her next day off was?

Or that she already had a young man in the RAF who never wrote to her, and there was another boy on the horizon whom she couldn't contact?

'No,' she said crossly. 'But he's asked me for another dance, so that's something, isn't it? I think.'

'Well, don't bite my head off. I thought he looked smashing, so why are you so jumpy? He didn't make a pass at you, did he? You know what I mean, I suppose,' she said, lowering her voice.

To Daisy, the delicacy of the question implied that Alice suspected she didn't know what was what.

'He was very nice and very polite. And if he does ask me for a date, I shall probably say yes.'

'Well, he's not going to ask you if you stay in here all evening, is he? So we'd better go back to the fray – unless you've got cold feet.'

Eight

B y the end of May the general complacency that still
lingered, to some degree, gave way to total panic as the
threat of invasion became very real. As the Germans overran
Belgium and parts of France, newspaper and wireless reports
couldn't hide the news that the British Expeditionary Force,
which had fought such valiant battles in France, was being
inexorably herded into a corner on the twenty-mile stretch of
beach in and around Dunkirk. The Germans were surrounding them on all sides, and there was no way out except by
sea or surrender.

Bert Painter, self-styled eyes and ears for the family now,
with his addictive attention to whatever the newspapers and
wireless announcers had to say, reported the latest facts to
his wife once the boys had gone to bed.

'It looks bloody grim, Rose,' he said, 'and our Daisy's
in the thick of it. We should never have let her go on those
hospital ships.'

'We couldn't have stopped her,' Rose retorted, knowing
she had played her part in Daisy's departure, but knowing
too that her niece had too much self-will not to have gone
anyway. 'But it's too late for second thoughts now. She's
doing her bit as she always wanted, and we can be proud
of her.'

'I am proud of her, woman, but it doesn't stop me
worrying about her.'

'And you think I don't?'

She stared at him in resentment, wondering why they

were bickering like this, when by all accounts there was an army of men waiting to be evacuated from somewhere called Dunkirk, which to Rose was no more than a dot on a map on the northern part of France.

'So what do the papers say will happen next?' she went on less aggressively.

'Whatever it is, they won't give us the full facts,' Bert said. 'Churchill's got a hell of a lot to deal with after only three weeks in office, so let's hope he's got the guts for it. And you'd better say a few extra prayers at church on Sunday.'

The fact that he didn't set as much store by such things as Rose did made his words all the more ominous, and she found herself wishing she had a crystal ball to see just how her niece was faring; and just as instantly, she was guiltily glad that she didn't.

Daisy was terrified. It was like a nightmare. Theirs was only one hospital ship among many large craft waiting offshore, and what seemed to be hundreds of smaller craft of all descriptions – fishing boats, pleasure steamers, trawlers – all ferrying men out to the bigger ships to take them home to England. The hospital ships had been doing a necessary job of work before, receiving the wounded off the French beaches. Now, it seemed as if the whole world was trying to cram into the fleet of ships awaiting them.

The town of Dunkirk itself was burning and a pall of smoke hung over the port, enhanced by the sickly smell of rotting corpses of horses and men. The beaches had quickly became choked with the swelling numbers of starving, weary soldiers, and word had quickly gone out from Whitehall that any ship that could float was to be sent to the French coast to get the men out. A vast flotilla of little boats of all descriptions had set to sea at once.

As the men were rescued, the harrowing tales they told were of burning lorries, abandoned vehicles, and men and horses mown down by German bombers and left dying and stinking by the roadside. Some had walked for days to reach the coast without food or water, and were literally starving.

The bigger ships, including the hospital ships, were obliged to stay away from the beaches near the breakwater known as East Mole, while the smaller ships made day and night rescue sorties and brought the men out to them in batches. And all the time they were being bombed by German aeroplanes, intercepted by the swooping RAF Spitfires, so that the air was filled with noise and the bitter smell of burning oil and white-hot metal. Nearby a huge fire was raging in a refinery, adding to the chaos and sending clouds of acrid smoke over the entire area.

'It's like something out of hell,' Daisy Caldwell whispered to her friend Alice, both of them white-faced, their hearts pumping as the whine of enemy aeroplanes and screaming shells split the air.

They held each other's hand tightly, wondering if their own distinctive hospital ship was going to be defence enough against an enemy who cared little for human life. And Daisy, aware of the incongruousness of the little ships moving like a tidal wave in and out of the beaches with their precious cargo, wondered desperately if her brother Baz was among them.

The two girls strained their eyes in the gloom of evening, but all they could see in the light of the German flares were the thousands of black dots that were men, trying to reach a boat that would bring them nearer home. Some of them never made it at all. Some were trampled by their companions; some overfilled the small boats and were lost in the stampede; some found themselves in a small boat that took a direct hit from a German bomb. Larger vessels had already been sunk by German U-boats, including the destroyers *Wakeful* and *Grafton*. Even though there was a cordon of British submarines guarding the evacuation ships, the might of the German forces seemed invincible as word filtered through that the two destroyers were only two among the many British ships that had been sunk.

'You two nurses, stop gawping and see to these men!' they heard someone bellow behind them. They jerked backwards, aware that they had been so awestruck and horrified by what they were seeing that they had momentarily forgotten what they were here to do.

Half-sobbing with fear and nerves, Daisy and Alice rushed to do the medical officer's bidding as several small boats coasted near to them, and the men were hauled aboard, ragged and hollow-eyed after trekking for miles on foot to reach the coast.

'Let's pray for bad weather tomorrow so the German planes can't fly,' Alice said grimly, as she and Daisy both tried to staunch a soldier's badly wounded leg, both being horribly sprayed by the bubbling, sweet-smelling blood of an artery.

'Oh God, I can't stand it,' Daisy babbled in a sudden panic, knowing that it was hopeless, completely hopeless. He was so obviously about to die. To her horror, the soldier suddenly looked her straight in the eyes and gave a weird smile.

'That makes two of us, girlie,' he said, before he choked on his vomit and slumped backwards.

'Leave him,' they heard an officer say behind them. 'He's beyond help, but there are others who need you nurses. Now *move*!'

Like automatons they leapt to obey him, thankful for the orders, for without them they knew they would probably slink away into a corner like terrified animals. There were always others to be helped, others to be bandaged and given a cigarette or drink of water, or held tightly as a surgeon performed an impromptu operation, while desperately trying to be oblivious to their screams . . .

*　　*　　*

Joe Preston had lost sight of his unit hours ago. He'd lost his rifle and all his ammunition, and his boots as well. God knew where they had gone, but the pain in his feet now was so bad he didn't know where it began or ended. He couldn't even be sure if he had caught a bullet in one of them; he only knew that if he didn't keep moving towards the beaches of Dunkirk he'd be trampled underfoot by the crawling army of men pushing him forward.

But by now he was so exhausted and so disorientated he knew he had to stumble out of the ragged column and sit by the dusty roadside for a while to gather his senses. He fell over an arm that had once held a rifle and was now separated from the rest of its owner, and almost gagged with the horror of it all. He was a strong man, but men had never been born to deal with this, nor to be reduced to unmanly weeping. The taste of dust and death was in his mouth and the sight seared his eyes; he staggered farther into the fields and lay there panting to get some strength back before going on.

In desperation he tried to think of home, of his parents, and especially of his sweet Elsie and their coming baby, because if he had to die here, then it was Elsie's image he wanted to take with him to his Maker.

It was hard to think of anything but the stink in his nostrils and the steady drone of the German bombers overhead. He was light-headed from lack of food, and he carefully raised his head, dream-like, as he saw the column of men ahead of him scatter in an almost beautiful slow-motion formation when one of the enemy bombers bore down on them, screaming death from the skies. The next minute the group of men were no more than corpses as the bomb made a direct hit. And but for his need to breathe clean air for a few moments, Joe would have been one of them.

As it was, his senses were shattered, his hearing blasted. The shame of not being one of his dead travelling companions was a tormenting pain in his mind, and he staggered forward again, sobbing, shouting, unable to hear his own voice, except in his head, raging at a God who could let this happen. He hadn't known those men, but they were all his brothers, and he hadn't been man enough to share their final moments. And then, with an almost fiendish need for survival, the next thought in his head was that maybe somewhere among the corpses he might find a pair of boots that would fit him, allowing him to go on . . .

He didn't hear the sound of a vehicle right behind him as he staggered back on to the road. He couldn't hear the driver shouting at him. He hardly felt the pair of arms that lifted him into the field ambulance and laid him on a stretcher, although he was aware that there were people surrounding him who were still alive, still breathing. He was conscious of the fact that at least he was not going to die alone, and the last thing he saw before he closed his gritty, bloodshot eyes and let it happen, was the sight of the sand dunes in the distance.

As if the gods were taking pity on the evacuation forces, there was a thick sea fog on May the thirtieth, making it impossible for the German bombers to take to the skies, and on that day thousands of men were transported to the ships. One of them was Joe Preston, courtesy of the field ambulance that had miraculously found him wandering about half-crazed the night before.

'Here's another batch for you ladies,' the driver said cheerfully to the nurses on the hospital ship waiting to receive the wounded. 'It'll do their poor eyes good to see a few pretty faces, so give 'em a smile. This unlucky bastard's in danger of losing a foot – pardon my language – and needs a surgeon pretty damn quick . . .'

'Joe? *Joe*?' Daisy stuttered, finding it hard to recognise the emaciated man with the blackened face on the stretcher, muttering and pulling at the covering blanket incessantly. 'It is you?'

'Do you know this one?' said the stretcher-bearer. 'You

won't get any sense out of him. He can't hear you. Shell-shocked, I reckon, and hasn't said a word since we picked him up. Just keeps mumbling Elsie, or Esther, or some such name. That's not you, is it?'

'No. It's Elsie. My sister. Joe's her husband. Oh my God, Joe . . .'

As her voice threatened to rise hysterically, she was pushed out of the way by a medical orderly.

'You're no use to me here, Caldwell,' he snapped. 'Go and pull yourself together and send me someone who isn't going to fall to pieces at the sight of a gangrenous foot.'

'I'm sorry,' she stammered again, humiliated. 'But he's my brother-in-law – and you don't really mean it about his foot, do you?'

Her pity for Joe overcame her panic for a few seconds, but then she realised he was trying to say something, and she bent low over him in order to hear the mumbled words.

'Caldwell . . . Elsie . . .'

'He must have heard my name,' Daisy said, but the orderly shook his head as Joe's eyes resumed their wild look.

'I doubt that. Probably read my lips. Now do as you're told and get out of here. There are others who need you, and this one's going straight to the theatre.'

Daisy scuttled away, knowing that the theatre was a grand name for the cabin they used as a makeshift operating room. She prayed that Joe's foot would be saved, even though she had the guilty feeling that if it wasn't, then at least Elsie would have him home. Joe's war would be over.

There was nothing she could do for him now, but when they returned to base for a few hours off she must telephone home at once to let Elsie know that Joe was safe. She wouldn't give any more details, since he would assuredly be sent to a British hospital as soon as they landed, no matter what happened here.

The orderly was right. There were others who needed her. By the time the ship reached Folkestone, to the usual accompanying cheers and placards of what seemed like hundreds of onlookers at all the south-east ports, waiting to welcome their boys back home, no matter what the hour, it began to look more hopeful that Joe wasn't going to lose his foot. The bullet had gone straight through, but the infection hadn't turned gangrenous after all and was responding to treatment. He was still in dire need of nourishment, but although his hearing hadn't yet returned, he was conscious enough to recognise Daisy.

'Who'd have thought . . . Elsie's little sister . . . would turn out to be . . . such an efficient nurse?' he said haltingly.

'Not so efficient,' she murmured, knowing he couldn't hear, but not wanting to let him know how awful she had felt at letting him down. She wasn't much of a nurse after all, she thought, if she couldn't even help her own brother-in-law. The shame of it didn't escape her as Joe squeezed her hand. She mouthed the words at him slowly so that he could read her lips.

'I'll let Elsie know you're safe, Joe, but I don't know where they'll be sending you yet.'

He nodded, and then closed his eyes in weariness, so there was no point in saying any more. But if she knew him, then once his foot had healed, his war wouldn't be over at all. With a fervour she hadn't felt in weeks, Daisy wished that hers was. She wished she could go back to being what she was before – scatty Daisy Caldwell, not putting her mind to anything serious, just enjoying being who she was, with an indulgent family all around her; and for the first time in ages, she felt a sob tear at her throat, knowing that nothing could ever be like that again.

The evacuation went on for several more days, and was pronounced a huge success. The enormousness of the numbers filtering through to the newspapers had civilians reeling. Thousands upon thousands of British and French troops had been rescued in little over four days. Returning soldiers with little or nothing to write on had thrown slips of paper out of lorry and train windows taking them to British hospitals, and the cheering crowds had promised to send them on to waiting wives and sweethearts. Quentin Caldwell had received one such note from his son.

'My God, has the boy gone completely mad?' he roared to his daughter Elsie, his leonine expression belying the emotion he felt.

By now Elsie knew that Joe was safe, and in a military hospital somewhere in Essex. But this small scrap of paper inside an envelope from Baz, sent from Dover, was something his father had never expected.

What a lark, Father, ferrying our boys back and forth from France. Hope to see you soon. Your loving son, Baz.

Quentin's mouth worked as he finished reading it out to Elsie. As if it wasn't enough that his eldest daughter Immy was God-knew-where, and his youngest was doing dangerous work on the hospital ship. Now this. Did God mean to test him by sending all his children to war? Thank God Teddy was far too young ever to be involved, and Elsie too pregnant.

'You should be proud of him, Daddy,' he heard her say softly. 'It was a pretty fair bet that when Mr Churchill asked for anything that could float to take to sea, Baz and his mates wouldn't hesitate.'

'Of course I'm proud of him. I just don't want to lose him,' he said abruptly.

'I'm sure you won't. He's like a bad penny. He'll always turn up just when you least expect him.'

But she said it with a smile because she didn't think Baz was a bad penny at all, and she was enormously proud of what both he and Daisy were doing. For Daisy to have actually been on the hospital ship that brought Joe home was a good omen that she was doggedly not going to ignore.

'You're a good girl, Elsie.'

'No, I'm not. I'm a useless one. All I can do is sit around waiting for my baby to be born while everyone else is being brave and useful,' she said, frustrated all over again at her inability to do anything for the war effort. She had tentatively offered to go to the shop for a few hours each day, since most of the young men had enlisted now; but Quentin wouldn't hear of it in her condition. It simply wasn't done. So she sat at home and knitted comforts for the troops, feeling as matronly as her Aunt Rose and her knitting circle.

'Elsie, I think you should think seriously now about going to Cornwall to stay at the boarding house run by Immy's old boss,' Quentin said next, glad to have something else to think about besides his son's reckless behaviour.

'Why now? And why on earth should I, when Joe's back home and likely to get convalescent leave?' she exclaimed.

'Because, my darling,' her father said carefully, 'I think the threat of invasion is becoming imminent, and I would rather know you were safely out of harm's way when Hitler decides to start bombing us. Now that he has no opposing army standing in his way, his bombers will be able to reach every part of Britain.'

Elsie stared at him, her stomach gnawing at his words. For so long now, they had believed Bristol's docks and aircraft factories would be a prime target for bombing, but the planes had never reached here. Already, town and city signposts were being removed, so that if the invasion came, the Germans wouldn't know where they were. It all seemed so farcical, since why on earth would the victors care which town they overran?

'I won't leave here, Daddy,' Elsie said stubbornly. 'Not unless Joe insists on it.'

'Or Hitler does,' her father said.

On June the fourth Winston Churchill's speech to the House of Commons was later broadcast to the nation. By then, Daisy and Alice and their companions were crowded around the wireless set in their billet, listening to the measured words of the orator. He pronounced the evacuation a resounding success, praising everyone who had taken part, from the nurses and medical staff to civilians who had welcomed the brave soldiers back home; and above all Churchill praised the RAF for their part in the proceedings. He emphasised that without them casualties would have been far higher than they were, and that no one should underestimate the skill and devotion of our airmen.

'I wonder if your dashing Canadian's listening,' Alice whispered to Daisy. And Cal, thought Daisy, with a catch in her throat. And Cal . . .

But Alice was shushed at once as Churchill's voice continued. His final words made them all fall silent, with emotions running high.

'We shall go on to the end; we shall fight in France, we shall fight on the seas and oceans, we shall fight with growing confidence and growing strength in the air, we shall defend our island, whatever the cost may be; we shall fight on the beaches, we shall fight on the landing grounds, we shall fight in the fields and in the streets, we shall fight in the hills; we shall never surrender.'

'Well,' said Alice, when the broadcast was finished. 'I'll say this for him: he has a way with words, if nothing else.'

'I thought it was perfectly thrilling,' Daisy said, choked. 'If anyone can lift the nation's morale, it's him.'

'So now we've heard him, and we're all feeling better for it,' one of the other girls said practically. 'So what do we do now that we've got a few days off? I say let's go into town and see if there's a dance anywhere. After dealing with so many half-deads all this time, a bit of live, red-blooded male to whisk me around the dance floor is just what I need.'

At any other time it might have sounded callous and heartless, but they were all weary, and longing to get the lingering smell of blood from their skin and clothes, and they were all in full agreement. What possible harm could it do to enjoy themselves? It was hardly going to stop the war effort.

'We'd better check with the CO first,' Alice said.

But as expected, there was no objection, and an hour later, when they had somehow all managed a bath in the regulation five inches of water, scrubbed every inch of themselves and changed out of uniform into something more feminine and sweet-smelling, they marched in a small convoy with their arms linked, down to the centre of town, looking for anything to wash away the memories of the last few days, for a little while at least.

It was almost a replica of another night that wasn't so long ago in reality, and yet that seemed like a lifetime ago in many respects. The dance hall was open and crowded with girls and servicemen, and the music was in full swing when they entered. There was no RAF contingent from Biggin Hill that night, but there were plenty of willing partners for six reckless young ladies intent on enjoying themselves.

They didn't talk too much about where they had been. They were conscious of careless talk costing lives, as the posters put it, in case there were German spies among the friendliest and most admiring of young men; and now, with talk of invasion more glibly on everyone's lips than before, the danger of careless words seemed even more of a threat. Daisy didn't quite know how it could be, but she stuck to the rules anyway.

The evening did something to settle the nerves that were still very much in evidence in all of them. Earlier, Daisy had managed to phone her father to tell him she was safe, and heard the news about Baz. She was very proud of her little brother, and could just imagine how his adventurous soul had relished the chance of beating the Germans at their own game, and fishing soldiers out of the sea right under their dive-bombing noses.

She thought of it in Baz's terms, and found herself

grinning at the melodrama of it all, though she was careful not to make too much of it to her father, and just said how thankful she was that they had both come out of it unscathed – was able to reassure him about Joe too.

'I should think he'll be in hospital for quite some time, but with any luck they'll transfer him somewhere nearer home,' she told a tearful Elsie, when she too came on the line. 'But I'm sure he'll be writing to you as soon as he can.'

She had crossed her fingers when she said it, because when she had last seen him he hadn't seemed capable of holding a pen, let alone writing a sensible letter. But there were always nurses willing to write letters for soldiers who couldn't do it for themselves. She had done it enough times. But she had also seen what shell-shock did to people. It went deeper than anyone realised, and she only prayed that Joe would be restored to full health again, for her sister's sake as well as his own.

'Wake up, Daisy; it's time to go back to base unless you want to get a rollicking,' Alice urged her at the end of her evening, as her thoughts wandered.

'Sorry, I was dreaming,' she said hastily.

Alice grinned. 'I know. You were wishing your Canadian had been here instead of that sweaty-palmed sailor who was jigging you about.'

'Something like that,' Daisy told her, wondering why Alice persisted in mentioning Glenn at all. It was hardly likely she would ever meet him again.

That was another thing about war. You met, you fell in love – or not – and then you were parted for ever. Unless, by some miracle, something happened like Joe Preston being brought to her hospital ship. That was a coincidence, if you like. But coincidences did happen, and she had the proof of that, even if she didn't care to think about her own behaviour too often. She had simply gone to pieces at seeing someone close to her, and that was something she *wasn't* proud of.

The next morning, as they idly awaited orders for their

next assignment, the daily batch of mail brought a letter addressed to her. She didn't recognise the handwriting, and the original postmark was blotted out. She took it back to the billet, empty for once, and for a moment her heart leapt, wondering if it could possibly be from Glenn, knowing she hadn't forgotten him at all, despite her airy-fairy reactions whenever Alice mentioned him.

Her heart began to beat faster, instantly recalling the deeply attractive Canadian voice. Then she realised that it couldn't possibly be from Glenn, since the overwritten address on the letter told her it had been forwarded from Weston General Hospital, and her heartbeats became more sickeningly agitated now as she tore open the envelope and took out the single sheet of paper.

For a few seconds she stared disbelievingly at the tortured words, unable to take in the sense of them immediately as they danced in front of her eyes. *Unwilling* to take them in at all, as she let her gaze slip down to the end of the letter and the scrawled signature at the end.

Sheilagh Monks. Cal's mother.

Nine

Alice had some news. She found Daisy alone in the billet, hunched over a screwed-up letter in her hand. It was obvious that something was very wrong.

'What's happened?' she asked at once, sitting beside Daisy on her bed, and taking her cold hand in hers.

Daisy looked at her vacantly.

'I wish you had known my mother,' she said finally. 'Did I ever tell you she was quite a famous dancer? She had the voice of an angel too. We all loved to watch her perform on the stage.'

'I know. You told me,' Alice said, trying not to show her alarm at this apparent retreat into the past.

Daisy took a deep breath. 'It's all right; I'm not going mad. I'm just trying to put into practice some of the things she told me, and it's difficult.'

Her mouth trembled before she went on. 'I even told the problem child Vanessa how my mother got me over my fear of clouds by saying they were castles in the sky when I thought they were monsters. What kind of a blithering idiot would think clouds were monsters anyway?'

'I suppose some might,' Alice murmured, not having the faintest idea who Vanessa was. 'Is that what's troubling you now?'

'Of course not. But she also said that if there was something bad – really bad – in your life, then sometimes it helped to try putting it aside for a little while and coming back to it later. Think of something pleasant, she always said

110

– if only for a few moments – but it doesn't work, does it? Because all I can think of is . . . is . . .'

Alice put her arms around her, seriously alarmed now.

'Is it something to do with that letter?' she asked, knowing it had to be. A family thing, perhaps. One of her sisters was expecting a baby, and it was her husband they had just brought back from France. Surely they hadn't had to amputate his foot after all . . . The letter fell to the floor, and Alice picked it up.

'Read it,' Daisy said in a choked voice. 'Read it out loud, then perhaps I'll start to believe it.'

Alice uncreased the crumpled letter, which Daisy had presumably screwed up in order to deny its existence. But she couldn't deny it for ever, and Alice started to read it aloud, slowly and deliberately, as if reading to a child.

> Dear Miss Daisy Caldwell,
> I'm sorry to have to write to you since I don't know you at all, but I thought my Callum would want me to. The telegram came three weeks and two days ago, and a parcel of Callum's belongings was sent home a little later.

Alice swallowed. The preciseness of the timing was heartbreaking, as if the letter-writer was counting every day since the telegram came. She knew that feeling. And everyone knew what telegrams meant these days.

> The telegram said my Callum had been killed in action. A letter came from his squadron-leader a week ago, saying that he had died heroically in the course of duty, so that was a comfort.
> Your name and the address of the hospital where you worked was in Callum's notebook, so I thought you would want to know the news. I'm very sorry to

be the bearer of bad tidings, Miss Caldwell.
Yours truly,
Sheilagh Monks (Mrs)

'Oh Daisy, I'm so sorry! This was the young man you met in Weston doing his air force training, wasn't it?'

Daisy's voice was clipped now. 'Yes. Cal. I thought I was going to marry him one day. But it's all a waste of time, isn't it?'

'What is?'

'Falling in love. Getting to know someone. Thinking you might have a future together. It's all a waste of time and energy, because if the TB doesn't get you, then bloody Hitler will. We all lose people in the end.'

For a minute Alice didn't connect the two, and then she remembered Daisy's friend Lucy, who had died in a TB sanatorium far from home; and seeing how Daisy was shivering uncontrollably now, she knew she had to say something positive to shake her out of her depression.

'How can you say that? Was it a waste of time knowing Cal? Would you have missed one second of the time you shared with him? And your friend Lucy too. Wasn't she your very first best friend – and the one you shared your very first secrets with, I'll bet? Of course we lose people in the end, Daisy, because that's how life is and we can't stop it or change it. I lost my brother too, but no one can take away my memories of him, and you'll think the same way about Cal when you've had time to adjust to losing him.'

'Oh really. And will I adjust to my guilt over not being so sure I loved him after all? And thinking about writing to Jed – and dancing with Glenn . . .'

'For pity's sake, Daisy, you're making me really angry now. Grow up and stop being so self-centred. Think about how Cal's mother is grieving. Her loss is far greater than yours. I know how my mother felt when we heard about Roy, and Cal was still his mother's baby, however much of a hero he was.'

112

She didn't say what they all suspected: that the glib remarks about every one of them dying a hero were no more than words to soften the blow and give the bereaved a semblance of pride – and the deceased some dignity.

Daisy didn't say anything for a few minutes, but her face began to show a little more colour. She finally replied slowly, as if it was a great effort.

'Oh, I know you're right. And I know I'll have to write back to Mrs Monks, though I can't think what on earth to say. It won't help me, but I suppose it might help her, and I can hardly ignore her letter. It would seem as if I didn't care.'

'That's my girl,' Alice said, giving her shoulder a squeeze. 'And it *will* help you, believe me. And I didn't come in here just to pry . . .'

'You didn't pry. I don't know what I'd have done without you.'

'You'd have coped. You're stronger than you look, Daisy Caldwell,' Alice told her with a glimmer of a smile. 'Anyway, let me say what I came to tell you. We're being disbanded.'

'What?' Daisy frowned, unable to switch her thoughts so quickly after the enormity of the letter.

'Well, not all the hospital ships, of course. But the special units – which means us, my sweet – are being sent home for a week's leave now that the evacuation's over, and then we have to report back to our own hospitals again.'

'Just when I was getting used to my sea-legs,' Daisy replied, with the first *almost* hint at a joke she had made since hearing from Cal's mother.

Alice found herself breathing a small sigh of relief. Daisy was one of the resilient kind, thank God, though they were all going to find it strange to be back on the wards again after the excitement – if that was the word – of being at the sharp end, as they called it.

'You're not to fuss over Daisy when she comes home,' Aunt Rose told the three small boys sternly. 'She'll be feeling very

tired, and she's coming home for a rest before she goes back
to work at the hospital again.'

'Ain't she going to tell us about her boat, and all the
operations she did, and the *blood*?' Norman said at once.

'She won't want to talk about any of that, so you just keep
your gory little thoughts to yourself,' Rose said sharply.

She hesitated, but decided not to mention the letter that
Daisy had told her about on the telephone the previous night.
It was obvious by the way she had said it and then gone on
all in a rush to say what time she expected to be home that she
didn't want any questions about Cal either. Not yet, anyway.

Although, in Rose's opinion, the sooner you spoke about
such things, the sooner you came to terms with them, she knew
Daisy had to deal with her young man's death in her own way.

It was more than likely that she would want to spend a
few days at home in Bristol too. Her father would want to
see for himself that his youngest girl was all right, and Elsie
would want to hear about her husband at first hand.

'Our Daisy's coming home! Our Daisy's coming home!'
Teddy began chanting. 'Will she be bringing presents?'

'Of course she won't, you loony,' Norman honked at him.
'She's been fixing up army blokes with broken bones and
legs hanging off. She won't have been buying presents for
babies . . .'

'I'm not a baby,' Teddy howled, red-faced, throwing a
cushion at him, and getting it hurled right back.

Rose ignored their usual antics, more concerned with
how Norman's younger brother had paled. Ronnie was not
the robust character his brother was, and the chickenpox
had hit him far harder than any of the others. He had a
persistent cough that reminded her all too well of Lucy,
though the family doctor had assured her that it was nothing
remotely like consumption, and that Ronnie was merely a
more delicate child than some.

Being a foster-mother was not always the easiest of
occupations, thought Rose, wondering for the umpteenth

time how Vanessa was getting on these days. They had heard nothing since that one letter, but she supposed it was to be expected. As Bert constantly reminded her, the children were only borrowed. One day they would all go home, and there would be just the two of them again.

It was only right and proper, she thought stalwartly, but it would be a wrench all the same. She was being a selfish and wicked old woman, because when they all went home again, it would mean the war was over, and nobody could deny how they would all rejoice at that.

'Who's going to help me get Daisy's room ready for her then?' she asked, and was predictably talking to thin air as the boys all scuttled out of the house to feed their chickens.

For Daisy, it felt weird to be going home again. Everything seemed to be happening at a slower pace and a far lower level than in the furious days of Dunkirk. It was strange to see people going about their everyday lives, queueing for food, discussing the weather, gossiping with neighbours about the price of fish or the latest on who had done what with whom . . . If it hadn't been for the glaring newspaper reports, it would have been just as if Dunkirk had never happened at all.

Daisy found it hard to deal with. She had been in the thick of something more horrendous than in her worst nightmares, and now there was nothing to do but spend time at home and wait for the days to pass before she reported back to Weston General. It was an awful anticlimax, and a shameful one too, because it implied that she had *wanted* the trauma to go on – that she had *enjoyed* being thought of as some poor wretch's guardian angel, his little Miss Nightingale – and she knew such feelings weren't worthy of her.

'There's to be a special service at church on Sunday, to give thanks for all the soldiers who were brought home safely,' Aunt Rose told her when she had been listless and uncommunicative for two days. 'You'll come with us, of course.'

'Must I?'

'Certainly you must. I'm sure Alice Godfrey and her family will be there as well, and Teddy's very proud of you, you know.'

'Oh well, *Teddy*,' Daisy said, dismissing him. 'He's just a baby. What does he know about anything?'

'He knows you did a very brave thing, and he doesn't understand why you won't talk to him. And he's not a baby; he's an intelligent child, if only you'd give him half a chance. In fact, all the boys are dying to hear about your experiences whenever you feel ready to tell them, and we can't creep about the house for ever for fear of upsetting you. Don't shut us all out, Daisy.'

It was the first time Rose had come near to criticising her.

'Is that what I'm doing?'

'Well, isn't it?'

Daisy spoke abruptly. 'I'll think about it. Right now I need some fresh air, Aunt Rose. I'm going to see Alice. Is that all right?'

'Darling, whatever you want to do is all right with me,' Rose said gently. 'You know that.'

Sometime soon Daisy knew she would have to talk about Cal. That was something else she had kept bottled up inside. Only with Alice could she seem to talk freely about anything these days, and half an hour later the two girls were walking along the wide stretch of sands, watching the rippling tide wash it clean.

'Will they put barbed wire along our beach, do you think?' Daisy said dully. 'Spoiling everything.'

'I doubt it. I can't imagine the Germans will bother coming ashore in the Bristol Channel when they've got the whole of the south coast to invade,' Alice said cheerfully.

Daisy scuffed at the sand with the toe of her shoe,

resentful that Alice seemed to be coping with the aftermath of Dunkirk far better than she was. Even *thinking* about the Germans invading England was enough to send cold shivers down Daisy's spine, let alone talking about it so calmly.

'Doesn't it bother you?'

'Don't be stupid, Daisy. Of course it bothers me, but I'm not going to let it take over my life, and nor should you. We just have to get on with things, like Mr Churchill said.' She hesitated. 'Have you written to Mrs Monks yet?'

'No. I don't know what to say.'

'Say how you feel. Say what's in your heart.'

'That's a bit difficult, since there's nothing there at all any more. It's just a great big empty void.'

Alice stepped right in front of Daisy, stopping her in her tracks, and shaking her by the arms.

'You've got to stop this, Daisy. You're not the only one to have lost someone, you know. You're not the first and you won't be the last, and a fine sort of nurse you're going to be if you can't cope with the fact that people are going to die in a war. If you're thinking of reporting to the hospital with that attitude and that gloomy face next week, you'd do better to stay away.'

'Well, thank you for that! You don't understand how I feel—'

'Yes, I *do*. I understand very well, but Daisy darling, we all have to go on. Would Cal want you to fall apart because he was killed? Wouldn't he want you to go on helping others with your lovely smile and your chirpy nature that cheers everybody up? You know darned well he would.'

Daisy didn't say anything for a while, and they automatically resumed walking again while she digested her friend's words. She wished she could hate her for saying them, but in her heart she knew it was the best piece of common sense she'd heard yet.

'We met just about here,' she said slowly. 'Me and Cal, I mean. I was just as miserable then – and I had every right to be, because Lucy had just told me about her TB. Cal cheered me up with his nonsense.' She felt herself give a half-smile, remembering.

'There you are then,' Alice said. 'Isn't that just what I told you? Think about the good times you had and be glad of them.'

'I'll try,' Daisy said, taking a long breath. 'I really will.'

Even when they heard a squadron of aeroplanes flying low overhead, she wouldn't let the pain rush in. If Alice could bear it, so could she; and although she felt a mite better by the time she got back to the house, her new resolve was immediately tested as Norman and Ronnie came hurtling in from the garden.

'Norman says your boy was prob'ly flying one of them planes,' Ronnie shrieked, 'and I said he wouldn't still be here, 'cos he'd be shooting down Jerries by now, wouldn't he, Daisy?'

She heard Aunt Rose draw in her breath and start to scold the pair of them, shooing them out of the room; but Daisy stopped her.

'No, don't be cross with them, Aunt Rose. I can't hide it for ever.'

It was sad that little boys had to hear of death and destruction and come to terms with it, as they all did. Taking away their innocence, because of a madman. But she didn't know how to tell them without breaking down. Then, like a bolt from the blue, she tried to imagine how her mother would have handled this, and somehow she found the words.

'Sit down, boys, and Teddy, come here too,' she said, seeing him in his usual corner, curled up with George. 'Remember all those pictures in your comics with the aeroplanes and their brave pilots zooming about the skies?'

'Yeah,' said Norman, his eyes lighting up. 'That's what I'm going to be when I grow up too.'

'Are you?' Daisy said, momentarily diverted, but glad of

the small lead. 'It can be quite dangerous, you know. You know how the comic pictures show some of the planes going down in flames, don't you?'

'Oh yeah, but they're not our planes,' Norman said confidently.

'It's not only the enemy planes that get shot down, Norman. It's our planes as well, and sometimes it's our pilots and our airmen who get killed.'

Ronnie started to snivel, while Teddy continued to clutch George until he whimpered in protest. But Norman, with uncanny insight, stared into her eyes, reminding her of Vanessa, who had had that kind of directness too.

'Has that happened to your boy?'

'I'm afraid so, Norman. Cal's mother wrote to tell me. She said he was a hero, and she especially wanted me to know that.'

Ronnie rushed out of the room with Teddy following. Norman continued to stare at Daisy, while she desperately tried to remain unblinking and dry-eyed.

'That's good, isn't it?' he said at last. 'That he was a hero, I mean.'

She gave him a weak smile.

'I think it's the finest thing any man could have said about him, Norman. My Cal was a hero, and we must always remember that and try not to be too sad about it. Now, if you don't mind, I'm just going to change my shoes before Aunt Rose tells me off for bringing all this sand indoors.'

She just managed to get out of the room with her head held high, seeing the small nod of approval in her aunt's eyes before she rushed upstairs, kicked off her shoes and threw herself on to her bed to sob her heart out for Cal, with healing, wrenching tears.

'Well, what do you think of our Daisy?' Imogen asked Helen.

They had managed to get a forty-eight-hour pass together

at last, and had decided to spend it in London rather than going home. What the folks didn't know about wouldn't hurt them – and there might not be too many more chances like this once Hitler started bombing them.

There was a feeling of recklessness about them as they checked into the small hotel that weekend, shared with most other people intent on having a good time while it lasted.

'I think she's marvellous,' Helen said. 'And young Baz too.'

'Oh, *Baz*,' Immy said, finding it easy to push her daredevil brother out of her mind. 'It was always on the cards that he'd be in at the deep end, pardon the pun. But I never expected Daisy to end up such a dedicated nurse, *nor* go to sea.'

'You never did give her credit for knowing her own mind, did you, darling?' Helen said airily, as they unpacked their small suitcases and hung up their frocks in the minuscule wardrobe. *Real* civvy summer frocks, she thought with satisfaction, not the beastly uniforms that had become almost a second skin now.

Immy laughed. 'That's because she so rarely *did* know her own mind, and you know it. I must admit, though, I feel rather proud of her.'

'And so you should. But don't let's spend all weekend thinking about Daisy or anything to do with the war. It's such gorgeous weather, and there are plenty of young men around, so let's just concentrate on having *fun*, Immy.'

'All right. Just as long as you remember I'm practically engaged to your brother, so I've got no intention of doing anything awful!'

'And you think I have?' Helen said innocently.

'Given half a chance, yes! Though not too awful. Just a little bit daring to liven up our dull lives.'

Helen sighed. 'I must say the war's not giving us anything spectacular to do so far, is it? I'm stuck in the catering corps, and my mother seems to think the experience will be terribly useful for when I marry and give dinner parties

– though she should visit the army canteen before she says that!'

'And I'm not going to set the world on fire, either!' Immy said, before going on casually:. 'By the way, have I told you we're moving to London shortly? Captain Beckett's being transferred to the War Office, and he's requested that I go with him as his official driver, promoted to lance-corporal.'

Helen squealed. 'You lucky stiff. You'll be right in the thick of all the excitement here and I'll still be stuck in Bedfordshire.'

'You might not think I'm so lucky when the bombs start falling.'

'And what about your Captain Beckett?' Helen said, ignoring that. 'He's not falling for you, is he, Immy?'

'Good Lord, no. He's got a wife and three children.'

'What difference did that ever make to anything?'

Immy laughed. 'None, I suppose, except that he's very much a family man, and I'm in love with James.'

Her face was pink as she whirled around in her floral cotton dress and fluffed up her distinctive red hair.

'So what do you think? Will I do for this stroll in the park we're going to take this afternoon if you can *ever* make up your mind what to wear!'

'All right. Providing we go looking for somewhere to go dancing tonight. I'm sure James would have no objection to your making some far-from-home soldier happy for a few minutes while you trip the light fantastic with him.'

Probably not, Immy thought, *but in my dreams it will still be James's arms I'm dancing in . . . and I miss him so much . . .*

'Helen, there's something I haven't told you,' she said more soberly.

'Good God, don't tell me your Captain Beckett really *has* made a pass at you? I was joking, Immy!'

'Of course he hasn't, and please be serious for a minute.

It's about Daisy. You remember the young airman she was mad about?'

'Go on. What about him?'

'He was shot down. You know the form – killed in action.'

'Oh Lord, I'm so sorry. Poor boy – and poor Daisy.' She shuddered. 'It makes me glad I'm not attached to anyone. How's she taking it?'

'How do you think? I haven't spoken to her myself, and I know I must, but it's hard to know what to say, isn't it? I had a letter from Aunt Rose a few days ago, and Daisy's shocked and grieving, naturally. Cal's mother wrote and told her the news just before she went back to Weston on leave, so I gather the poor darling's still pretty numb from everything.'

She looked at Helen, wishing she hadn't had to say anything to mar their few days off, but unable to keep it to herself for this entire weekend. Besides, what affected one of the Caldwell girls affected them all, and she grieved for Daisy too. But since Helen clearly didn't quite know how to handle this situation, she squeezed her arm and managed to put a bright smile on her face.

'Oh, let's cheer up. Are we going out to paint this town or aren't we? We'll find a dance hall this evening, raise a glass or two of lemonade in Cal's memory and be extra nice to some other baby-faced air force erks. What do you say?'

'I say Daisy's damn lucky to have a sister like you,' Helen said with a catch in her throat.

'What rot you do talk sometimes, Helen!'

But she felt a deal of pleasure at the words all the same.

Ten

After half a dozen stilted attempts, Daisy wrote a short letter to Cal's mother, saying how very sorry she was to hear the news, and that she would always remember Cal with love. It seemed little enough to say, but she simply couldn't eulogise about him. She remembered his bright and breezy personality, and still couldn't come to terms with the fact that he no longer existed.

It was one of the horrible things you learned when you were a nurse. One minute you were there, and the next you weren't. It seemed inevitable when people were old and had lived a long life, and died peacefully in their sleep. You could deal with that because it was a dignified and expected ending. But being blown out of the sky as if you were of no more importance than a fly being swatted out of existence was something else.

She didn't tell anybody about the night sweats when she awoke in terror, imagining the scream of the German plane homing in on Cal's; trying not to imagine the terrifying moment when the crew knew the inevitable, split seconds before they were hit; wondering if Cal, with his Irish Catholic background had had time to make whatever peace those people did, before the agonising burning began, and his skin shrivelled and fried . . .

Daisy wished desperately that she could blot it out of her mind. For a nurse in wartime, who had already experienced more that most girls her age, there was the added dread of going back on the wards and seeing those broken young men who would remind her all too vividly of Cal.

She was called into Matron's office on her second day back.

'I've been hearing reports about you, Nurse Caldwell.'

Daisy flinched at the shrewd look in the older woman's eyes.

'You're not doing too well, are you?' she went on briskly.

'I'm sorry, Matron,' Daisy murmured.

'I'm sure you are, but being sorry's not really enough, is it? There's no place in my hospital for nurses with only half their minds on their work.'

Daisy felt a surge of fright at her words.

'I don't want to leave! Please don't make me!'

'Sit down, Daisy,' Matron said. 'Please don't think I don't understand. I know that being involved in the Dunkirk evacuation must make our routine work seem very tame . . .'

'I would never say such a thing, nor think it.'

She didn't think of the work as tame. She just seemed to be in some kind of never-never land, going about her tasks like an automaton . . .

'I also know that you've had some personal bad news recently, and in view of this, I'm going to suggest that you take a little more time to adjust. Two more weeks won't go amiss.'

Daisy was aghast. 'But I won't know what to do with myself. Please, Matron, I'd far rather come to work.'

'And I would far rather have a nurse who gives herself wholly to her patients, and right now you're not doing that, are you? Think of these two weeks as a temporary reprieve, and we'll assess you again when you return.'

Daisy's mouth trembled and she swallowed hard. But she wouldn't break down. Her chin lifted. To be thrown out of the job she loved would be shaming and terrible, and if she had to see this as a temporary reprieve then somehow she would come back well and strong, even if she didn't know how . . .

'So what do you plan to do with yourself?' Aunt Rose asked, when she had reported home with the news, thankful that the boys were all at school and couldn't see how upset she was.

'I don't know. What do you suggest? Not join your knitting circle, I hope,' Daisy said dully.

'I wouldn't dream of suggesting it. We have some very lively afternoons, and we certainly wouldn't want a gloomy face putting a damper on our gossip.'

Daisy gave a wan smile. 'I know what you're trying to do, Aunt Rose, and it won't work. I'd put a damper on everyone right now.'

'Then go home for a few days. You may not have noticed, but the boys are creeping about the house, afraid to say a word for fear of you snapping at them. You're not being fair to them, Daisy.'

'Oh, thank you! And they have such gigantic problems to deal with compared with mine, don't they!'

Rose looked at her thoughtfully before she spoke again. 'Well, I suppose you can discount Teddy's trauma of seeing his mother fall over a cliff to her death, which is why he clings so tightly to George for security. And Norman and Ronnie are far from home and still being tormented about the way they talk by the local schoolchildren. Added to which, they don't even know if they'll have a home to go back to if Hitler starts dropping his bombs on London. And Elsie's husband is shell-shocked and still having treatment for his injured foot. This isn't just your war, Daisy. Other people have a few little problems, wouldn't you say?'

'I'm going to my room,' Daisy said abruptly, flouncing off in a way that would have done credit to Vanessa.

'A good idea. It will give you time to think.'

They so rarely quarrelled, and Rose watched her go, grieving for her insecurity, when she had always been so strong. But she was still very young, and young girls weren't meant to see the things they did nowadays. She turned thankfully to Bert as he came stumping in from the garden, for once ignoring the mess he brought in with him.

'I know now why I was never meant to be a mother,' she stated.

Astonished at such an announcement, Bert put his arms around her. He smelled of earth and the freshness of the outdoors, solid and dependable, always her rock. As the words slipped into her mind, she felt a weird sense of premonition, because nothing was solid and dependable in these dark days.

'What's up, old girl? And why are you shivering on this lovely warm day?' Bert said gently.

'A goose walking over my grave, perhaps,' she replied. And then: 'I always wonder why people say that. Did you ever see geese walking over graves?'

'Come and sit down and tell me what's happened,' Bert said, knowing this prevarication hid the real problem. 'It's Daisy, I suppose. You didn't expect her to get over the news about her young man so quickly, did you?'

'I didn't expect her to be given two weeks' extra leave from the hospital because she's not pulling her weight, either.'

'Ah. Is she here?'

'Don't *ah* me like that,' Rose said with an irritated gesture, slipping into the usual format for one of their spats. 'She's in her room and I don't know if what I said to her has done any good or not. Probably made it worse.'

'And all this is why you don't think you were cut out to be a mother?'

'Yes. No. Oh, I don't know. You can't change what the Good Lord intended for you, anyway, so what do you want for your dinner?'

Bert chuckled, well used to her quick-fire change of tactics. 'Anything you want to serve up, my love – even a bit of tongue pie, since it will tell me you're back on form. Meanwhile, I'll go and have a word with Daisy.'

'It won't do any good . . .'

But he had already gone, padding through the house in his socks now, and she didn't have the heart to scold him for not finding his slippers. George probably had them anyway . . .

Half an hour later Bert and Daisy came downstairs together. Daisy was red-eyed by now, and she flung her arms around her aunt.

'I'm sorry for being so beastly to everyone,' she whispered.

'Daisy, my love, you couldn't be beastly if you tried. Now then, are you hungry? It's only toast and spam, I'm afraid.'

'I love spam. And Aunt Rose, I think I'll do what you said – go home, I mean. Just for a few days. I think I need a bit of space to think about things. Providing you don't think I'm not grateful for being here.'

'Don't be silly; of course I don't think that. Sometimes we need to go back to our roots to find out who we really are – and that's enough of me being the amateur philosopher for one day, so let's eat, and afterwards you can phone your father and tell him to meet you from the train.'

'I'm really glad you're here,' Elsie told her, when they had hugged one another, and Daisy had exclaimed again at her sister's blossoming shape. 'At least I will be as long as you don't keep making disparaging remarks about my infant!'

'You know I'm only teasing, don't you?' Daisy said. 'I didn't mean anything by it, Elsie, truly.'

'I know that – and since when did you take every remark so seriously?'

'Since Cal died,' she said simply.

Elsie folded her arms over her bump, seeing the misery in her sister's eyes, and she felt a huge burst of sympathy for her. It wasn't right that any of them had to go through these things, she thought fiercely. It wasn't right, and it wasn't fair. What had ordinary people done to deserve being maimed and killed?

'Oh Daisy, I was so sorry to hear about Cal. I never knew him, but I felt as though I did, and I know he meant a lot to you.'

Daisy looked down at her hands, held tightly together in her lap. 'Maybe not as much as I thought he did, and that's the awful thing about it. I did love him, Elsie, but I know it wasn't the kind of love you and Joe have. And he died believing it *was* that kind of love, while I was out dancing with other people and having fun . . .'

'It didn't sound much like fun being on that hospital ship, darling!'

Daisy shrugged. 'Well, of course not. It was like something out of hell when we were taking the men off the beaches. But in between times . . .'

'In between times, you have to have some fun, or you would go mad. There's no shame in that, Daisy. Do you think Cal never had any fun when he couldn't see you? Didn't he ever go out for a few drinks with his mates, or chat to some other pretty girl? I'm sure he did, unless he was a saint, and it didn't mean he thought any less of you.'

'I never thought of any such thing!'

'Well, think of it now. How does it make you feel? Better, or worse?'

'Jealous,' Daisy said spontaneously.

Without warning, they were both laughing, until Elsie clutched at her side where the baby was starting to press uncomfortably against her. At six months now, it was certainly making its presence felt.

'Are you all right?' Daisy asked her.

'I'm fine. And so will you be. That was the first touch of the old fiery Daisy I've heard in a long time. Don't lose it, darling. Remember Cal with loving affection and let him go, the way we had to let Mother go.'

It was so rare for any of them to speak about their mother nowadays that Daisy felt her heart jump.

'Do you think about her, Elsie?'

'Quite often, actually, and especially at night when this babe won't let me sleep, and I wish she was here to give me advice. Not that she could have told me anything sensible in her last years, of course. But I remember her before Teddy was born and the illness began. I could have gone to her with any problem then.'

Daisy felt an unreasoning jealousy that her older sisters had known their mother for longer than she had – that they had had those extra years with her.

That was the second stab of jealousy in five minutes, she found herself thinking. The second real feeling inside her numbed body in ages.

'What do you want to do while you're here?' she heard Elsie ask more briskly. 'Father's still busy at the shop, of course, so we'll be left to ourselves during the daytime; but he's terribly glad you've come home, Daisy.'

'Is he?'

'Well, of course he is! He doesn't show his feelings, and never did, except to Mother, but he misses you all. That's one of the reasons I won't leave him, even though Joe still wants me to go and stay with his parents in Yorkshire for the duration, or at least until the baby's born. But how can I? I hardly know them.'

Daisy only heard the things she wanted to hear. 'Elsie, you can't stay with Daddy just because he misses the rest of us. That's piling the guilt on to us. And besides, don't you owe it to Joe to go along with his wishes? You must have said as much at your wedding, with all that love, honouring and obeying rot.'

'My goodness, you really are getting back on form, aren't you, sweetie? And of course I want to do as Joe wishes, but

I'm not leaving Bristol and that's flat. If I did, I'd rather go to Cornwall, anyway.'

She looked at Daisy, her eyes lighting up. 'That's an idea! Why don't we both go there for a few days, and take a look at this boarding house Immy's old boss has taken over? Just the two of us, Daisy – well, three if you count my bump, and he's not big enough to argue yet.'

'I think I've done enough travelling lately . . .'

'Oh, nonsense. Anyway, I'm supposed to be the stop-at-home, not you! For someone who once wanted to follow in Mother's footsteps, I don't know why you're hesitating. She wouldn't have hesitated for a minute. You know how she always loved Cornwall, and so did we, remember?'

'Of course I remember,' Daisy said, cross at being considered such a stick-in-the-mud. 'But what about Daddy? Didn't you say he was glad I was here?'

'Daisy, you're really making me angry now, and it's not good for my blood pressure,' Elsie said, to take the sting out of her words. 'He wouldn't object for a few days, and I'm sure Mother wouldn't. Let's talk it over with her.'

Daisy's heart jolted. It was one thing to talk to Lucy in the privacy of the small Weston churchyard, but it was something you had to do alone; and she had never associated Elsie with such a thing. But perhaps everyone did. Perhaps she wasn't as unique – or as crazy – as she had thought. Alice talked things over with her brother too, she remembered.

'I'm not mad, Daisy. I sometimes like to walk over the Downs and stand at the place where Mother fell, that's all. I remember the picnic we had on that perfect day, and how happy we all were. And I remember Mother in one of the lovely, floaty dresses she always wore, and how she almost danced towards the edge of the cliff, still happy, not knowing what was facing her—'

'Stop it! I don't want to hear this.'

'Well, you should. It was a lovely day for all of us, and

130

when I go there and think about her, it gives me a kind of peace. It would do the same for you.'

Daisy didn't believe it, but in the end she agreed to leave the house and walk to the Downs on this lovely June day. The grass was sweet and young, and the trees were in full leaf. People were sitting in the sun and enjoying picnics; others were walking their dogs as usual and, apart from the many uniforms in evidence, it was easy to forget that somewhere in Europe the war was raging, and people were dying. And if the news was to believed, since so much of France was occupied now, that war was coming ever nearer to themselves.

Daisy hadn't come to the Downs since her mother had died, unable to bear being reminded so painfully. But until now, it hadn't occurred to her that she had shunned this place where the Caldwell family and their friends used to come so often. The thought flashed into her mind that there was more than one kind of war. There was the one that threatened so much of the world now, and there was the inner war within a person. Daisy's war.

'Let's walk towards the edge,' Elsie said. 'There's nothing here to hurt us.'

'I'm not sure if I can . . .'

Elsie linked her arm through her sister's. 'Darling, you've already proved that you can do anything you want to. I'm proud of you, and she would be too.'

They walked slowly and deliberately across the springy grass to where the Avon Gorge plunged down to the silvery ribbon of river far below. It looked beautiful today with sunlight glinting on it, and no hint of the many tragedies it had witnessed over the years, both on the graceful span of the Clifton suspension bridge – that favourite haunt of suicides – and at the jagged cliff edge that Frances Caldwell had seemed to float towards, her arms outstretched as if in some kind of slow-motion embrace, mistakenly thinking that a straying child was her own darling Teddy.

Daisy shuddered, remembering as clearly as if it was happening now. It was cruel of Elsie to bring her here, and yet she knew in her heart that it was something everyone had to do. She had felt she same way over saying goodbye to Lucy, with the sense of needing to finalise something. Perhaps wise old Aunt Rose had meant exactly this in saying that Daisy needed to go back to her roots.

'It sounds silly, but I wish I had some of Mother's favourite roses to throw over the edge right now,' she said slowly. 'She loved them so much, didn't she?'

'They would last longer if we put them on her grave, darling. We can go there tomorrow if you're up to it.' Her eyes challenged Daisy's, knowing her sister had only visited their mother's grave a very few times.

'Perhaps. And *then* perhaps – *perhaps* – I'll think about Cornwall.'

Their heads jerked round as they both heard the cheerful shout at once.

'The Caldwell girls, by all that's wonderful! Two out of three isn't bad, though naturally I'd have preferred the third one, if you don't mind my saying so.'

They saw the tall young man in the army uniform striding towards them, and they broke into relieved smiles, both glad to be free of the unbearable tension of the last few minutes.

'James!' Daisy said in genuine delight. 'How lovely to see you. And if you didn't prefer Immy to either of us, we'd have thought there was something seriously wrong with you. How is she, by the way? I presume you've heard from her since we have?'

James Church laughed easily. 'The last I heard, she and Helen were taking a weekend's leave, living it up in London—'

'*What?* Instead of coming home?' Elsie said at once.

'And you don't mind?' Daisy broke in.

'Of course not. Our leaves didn't coincide, anyway. War's

not much fun, Daisy, whether you're driving a tank in the thick of the action, or chauffeuring some pompous officer about. As for poor old Helen stuck with the catering corps, I should think she's bored witless. I don't begrudge them a few hours' fun, and besides, I'm sure they'll keep one another in order.'

It seemed to underline what Elsie had told her, thought Daisy. War wasn't fun for anyone, and providing you remembered where your loyalties lay, what did it matter if you let your hair down now and then? The fact that James and Immy obviously trusted one another implicitly made her momentarily ashamed. But she knew she was thinking more of herself than Immy right then. She had never physically let Cal down, and if she had toyed with writing to Jed, and danced with Glenn, it hadn't fundamentally changed her feelings for Cal.

'I heard your news, Daisy, and I'm sorry,' James said more soberly.

'Thanks.'

'But I gather you're something of a Dunkirk heroine now,' he went on. 'Who would ever have thought it of our young carrot-top?'

'Oh, stop it, for pity's sake,' she said, starting to grin at the teasing look in his eyes. 'I only did what I was asked to do.'

'Well, there speaks a real heroine; but I won't embarrass you any more. And since it's rare for me to have two pretty girls to escort, how about if I buy you a both a sticky bun at the Whiteladies Tea Rooms? Or even two sticky buns for Elsie, if that's not an indelicate remark to make.'

'If you weren't my sometime-in-the-future brother-in-law, I'd take offence at that,' she said, laughing. 'But since I'm sure Daisy and I could both manage two sticky buns, I won't.'

'Come on then.'

They crooked their arms through his and set off across the Downs with far lighter hearts than when they had arrived there. The sun shone brilliantly in a clear blue sky, and somewhere high above a lone seabird wheeled and dived with all the grace and fluency of a dancer, as protective as a guardian angel. As the thought soared into her head, Daisy felt extraordinarily uplifted.

Afterwards, she couldn't have said what had changed her. It might have been simply Elsie's ever-calm influence and sensible approach to life. Or her insistence on retracing their footsteps to the Downs and facing their dragon, which was how Daisy had always viewed the scene of her mother's death.

Or maybe it was James Church and his teasing, friendly manner, treating Daisy as the little sister she would be when he and Immy were married, and the fact that he restored a continuity to their lives that had been missing for so long.

Whatever it was, she began to think of that day as a turning point in her life. It was the day she rediscovered her roots, and knew that some things were constant after all. The following day she and Elsie picked a bouquet of their own garden roses and placed them on Frances's grave.

'So have you decided, Daisy?' Elsie asked her quietly in that peaceful place. 'Do we go to Cornwall for a few days and see what Immy's Mr Harris is doing with his life?'

Daisy looked at the inscription on the headstone for a long moment. Apart from the date they would never forget, it said simply:

FRANCES CALDWELL
BELOVED WIFE AND MOTHER
SAFE IN THE ARMS OF JESUS

Daisy nodded slowly. 'I think Mother would approve, don't you?'

Elsie put her arm around her and hugged her close. 'I'm sure she would, darling. So we'll break the news to Father tonight.'

'And then we'll have to get in touch with this Mr Harris

and see if he's got room for us,' she said more practically, when they were walking back to Vicarage Street. 'It would be too bad if the boarding house was filled up after we'd started making our plans.'

'It won't be. Immy said he'd always make room for the Caldwell family,' Daisy said, with the ultimate confidence of youth.

Elsie blessed her intuition that had led them to the Downs that day, and in particular she blessed James Church's healthy male optimism. No wonder Immy loved him. Not that he could hold a candle to her Joe, of course, she thought at once. Not in *her* heart, anyway.

As if her thoughts were in tune with Elsie's, as they so often were when they were together, Daisy asked if she had had any recent news of Joe, knowing guiltily that she should have asked long before this if she hadn't been so consumed with her own misery.

'They're keeping him in that military hospital in Essex for the time being. The shell-shock has affected his hearing, but they hope it will only be temporary,' Elsie told her. 'Thank goodness his foot is responding to treatment, and I know Joe. Once it's completely healed, he'll be eager to get back to his regiment.'

She gave a half-smile and her words couldn't disguise her pride in her husband. 'You'd never have thought a mild-mannered shop manager would be so aggressively patriotic, would you?'

'I never thought Joe was mild-mannered – not in a soppy way, anyway. He must have been pretty persuasive to get you to elope and get married without Father's consent.'

'Oh, I didn't need much persuading, darling,' Elsie said softly, remembering. 'I knew Joe was going to enlist the moment war was declared, and I simply couldn't bear to live without him.'

'But isn't that just what you're having to do now?'

Elsie pressed her hand lightly over the mound of her belly.

'Not while I have this little one to keep me company. Nor while I have the memories of all that we've been to one another. And that's quite enough intimate information for an unmarried young lady to be told,' she added teasingly.

'Oh pooh,' Daisy retorted. 'You forget that I'm a nurse. We have privileged information about lots of intimate things.'

'Well, not *my* intimate life you don't!'

Daisy laughed, hugging her arm as they approached the tall house in Vicarage Street that had seen all the Caldwell children born. Solid and welcoming, as always; the flowers in the front garden were in full bloom now, scenting the air with Frances's favourite roses and bringing her presence very close for one breathtaking, ethereal moment. As if she only had to turn around and her mother would be there, dancing in the wonderful, legendary way that had entranced everyone who saw her, her feet hardly seeming to touch the ground, her delicate features making everyone adore her. Daisy gave a small, secret smile as she heard the soft sigh of the breeze rustle through the trees, as sweet and tremulous as her mother's voice, and felt more at ease with herself than she had felt for a very long time.

The feeling wouldn't last, and Daisy knew it; but for now, it was enough.

Eleven

The trains travelling to the south-west from Paddington disgorged hundreds of servicemen returning from France at Stapleton Road and Temple Meads stations, where willing hands were ready to receive them and despatch them in trucks to the various hospitals and reception centres.

Most of them had nothing but what they stood up in, and there was now a tented inner city for the able-bodied, while they were assessed. The Red Cross, WVS and other organisations were in the forefront now, as well as ordinary civilians, ready to help where they could.

'I've offered to take in several soldiers while you girls are away,' Quentin Caldwell told his daughters. 'There's plenty of room here, and they'll be more comfortable than sleeping in a tent until further orders. Mrs Meakin, our old housekeeper, is coming in to supervise and make our meals. Her son was killed in France, so she thinks it's the least she can do to help some other mothers' sons.'

'I think that's very brave of her,' said Elsie.

'And it will help her too,' Daisy said more practically.

'So now there's nothing to stop you two enjoying your few days in Cornwall,' Quentin went on. 'I've spoken to Kenneth Harris on the telephone, and there's a room all ready prepared for you. You can stay for a week, if you like, and you're not to worry about paying him, because it's all been taken care of.'

'Father, that wasn't necessary!' Elsie said at once.

'Maybe not, but it's done.'

137

'Thank you, Daddy,' Daisy said. She kissed his cheek, her instinct telling her more than Elsie's did how much he wanted to do this for them. As if by sending his girls to Cornwall, to the place where the whole family had always been so happy in days gone by, he too could recapture some small sense of those halcyon times.

'Yes, well,' he said now, reverting to his usual brusqueness, 'just enjoy yourselves, and remember to send me a postcard. Nothing too saucy, mind!'

'We'll telephone you the minute we get there,' Elsie promised.

'And you're sure the midwife said it's all right for you to travel?'

Elsie laughed. 'For the tenth time, *yes*! And you're the one who's been urging me to get away from Bristol all this time! Providing we're not too squashed up in the train, I'm sure I shall be perfectly all right.'

The kind of leisurely ride to Cornwall they used to enjoy was very unlikely. With fewer private motor cars on the roads owing to the precious hoarding of petrol, every train was hot and crowded. But with a panache that took Daisy by surprise, Elsie blatantly flaunted her pregnancy, which got them seats all the way to Marazion station, near the much larger resort of Penzance. The last couple of miles excited them as always, as the line meandered along the beach, reminding them that they were actually there at last.

They finally emerged on to the platform, stiff and exhausted from the long journey, immediately assaulted by the smell of sea and sand and the screech of seagulls as the one ancient remaining taxi took them to Kenneth Harris's seaside boarding house in Marazion.

They smiled at one another. Frances had always said that if her heart had had a spiritual home, this was the place. Neither of them said it today, but Daisy knew they were both remembering it.

'We did right to come here, didn't we?' she said softly.

Before Elsie could answer, the green-painted front door opened, and a portly, middled-aged man emerged to greet them, arms outstretched.

'Oh Lord, he's not going to kiss us, is he?' Daisy whispered in alarm.

'My dear young ladies, how good it is to see you,' Kenneth Harris said, beaming. 'And you both grow more like my dear Imogen every day. Come in, come in do, and have some tea. You must be parched after that ghastly journey.'

He was as quaintly fussy as ever, and when had her sister ever been his 'dear Imogen'? Daisy thought darkly. Immy had only been his assistant in his housing agency, for heaven's sake; but perhaps he had had delusions of making her more than that. She stifled a giggle, unable to imagine her beautiful older sister in the arms of the rotund and slightly perspiring Kenneth.

All the same, the bizarre image settled her stomach, which she hadn't realised until now was churning ever so slightly at the end of this long train journey. Elsie, too, looked paler than usual, and needed to get indoors and relax. Her training took over.

'We'd love a cup of tea, Mr Harris, but I think we would appreciate seeing our room first and having a short rest,' she said firmly. 'Perhaps we could come down for the tea in about half an hour.'

'Of course, my dear; but there's no need for that. For my honoured guests, tea shall be brought to your room on this occasion.'

He spoke with all the pomposity of the overlord of his domain, and Daisy didn't dare glance at Elsie, sure that the two of them would burst out laughing. They managed to contain themselves until they reached their room and were alone.

'Isn't he priceless?' Elsie gasped, tears streaming down

her face. 'How on earth did Immy work with him every day without falling apart?'

'Lord knows. He's straight out of Charles Dickens. Mr Micawber?'

They convulsed again, until Elsie held her side and begged Daisy to stop, because it wasn't doing the baby any good at all.

'Yes, it is,' Daisy told her positively. 'At least he'll come out smiling!'

She flopped down on the second bed while they roared with laughter again.

'We'd better stop this, or Mr Harris will think he's got two hooligans in here,' Elsie said finally, wiping her eyes.

'Agreed. So why don't you lie down for ten minutes, and I'll go and see if I can telephone Daddy to tell him we've arrived safely,' Daisy said. 'He'll only fret himself silly until we do.'

It wasn't a bad idea to separate for a short while either, she thought, as she went downstairs to enquire about the telephone, since the minute they looked at one another now they started laughing. But it felt so good to laugh again. Daisy felt better than she had in ages, being able to laugh at inconsequential things – to feel young and scatty again and forget all their worries for a little while.

She knew they were already absorbing some of their mother's delight in this corner of the world that Frances had always said was full of Merlin and mystery, and where she had instilled a love of all things fey and magical in her children, and none of the fear.

The boarding house overlooked the long stretch of sands known as Mount's Bay on the outskirts of the village. The fairy-tale castle of St Michael's Mount soared into the sky, as breathtakingly beautiful as they remembered it as children, and whether by accident or design, they had been given a room facing the sea, with a perfect view of the bay and its castle. A narrow causeway separated the mainland from the castle and its island, which could be reached on foot at low tide.

'What absolute bliss,' Daisy said later, kicking off her shoes and standing by the window looking out. By then she had telephoned her father, and Kenneth Harris had personally brought them a tray of tea and biscuits. 'Do you think it was fate that dear old Kenny decided to settle here, just so the Caldwell girls could renew their acquaintance with Mother's favourite haunts?'

'Probably,' Elsie said lazily. 'Mother was a great believer in fate.'

'She was, wasn't she?' Daisy said with a feeling that was more than satisfaction, and more like a glorious sense of continuity. 'Do you remember the tales she used to tell us? I liked the one about Joseph of Arimathea coming here. Oh, and the lost land of Lyonesse, stretching from Penzance all the way to the Scilly Isles. Oh, and Dozmary Pool, and Merlin's sword . . .'

Elsie was laughing at her again. 'You're such a romantic, Daisy! And we always thought you were such a scatterbrain; but you really think deeply about things, don't you?'

'You have to when you're a nurse,' Daisy said, her face clouding over for just a moment.

'Well, you're not a nurse for the next week, and I don't need nursing,' Elsie told her firmly. 'We're going to enjoy ourselves and spend every morning walking on the beach looking for fossils and pebbles.'

'Just like we always did,' Daisy said happily. Finding their roots. Being children again – providing you could disregard the bump beneath Elsie's dress – and forgetting that a war existed.

Not that Elsie could forget it for very long, and almost the first thing she did was to write a letter to Joe. She sat in the window seat, describing the view to him, wishing he was here to share it with her, wishing she could stay here for ever.

141

She drew in her breath as the thought entered her head. Because, of course, she could. Or at least, for the duration. Her father was always urging her to do so for her own safety – but how could she desert him?

They joined the other residents in the dining room that evening, mostly elderly folk, some of whom were permanent boarders, and a few holidaymakers. Kenneth had told them he didn't advertise too much, because there was always a select clientele happy to enjoy the quiet life he offered.

'It's strange to find somewhere so peaceful, isn't it?' Daisy commented the next morning as they took their first walk along the sands. Without warning, she reflected that Cal was at peace too. No more fighting. No more war. Thoughts of him were usually painful, but in that instant she realised she had begun to accept his death, and come to terms with it, as she had to.

'I think it's perfectly lovely,' Elsie said. 'It relaxes the mind and gives you time to think – and the best thing is, there's no overwhelming talk of war in the dining room. I suspect Kenneth has banned it.'

Daisy took her seriously. 'He can't do that, and Cornishmen have joined up the same as everybody else. There are plenty of servicemen about.'

'I know that, Daisy, and I was just teasing. Cornwall does give you a lovely sense of peace, though, doesn't it? And did I tell you that Kenneth's promised to take us to have a look at his brother's market garden one evening after supper?'

'Oh joy! What excitement!'

Elsie laughed. 'It's enough excitement for me and the babe, Daisy. I don't want to go rushing around for the next few months, nor dancing the night away.'

'You want to stay, don't you?' Daisy asked her baldly.

'Good Lord, no! I couldn't leave Father on his own, could I?'

But she didn't meet Daisy's eyes as she spoke, and she

should have known that her sister was shrewd enough to have noticed it.

'You know it's what Daddy wants for you, Elsie. And Joe too, since you've brushed off his offer of spending time with his parents.'

'I haven't brushed it off, as you so charmingly put it. I just wouldn't want to be there without him. There's a difference.'

'Oh well, don't let's quarrel about it. I'd race you to the causeway if it wasn't a foregone conclusion that I'd win,' she said airily.

She knew the mild and gentle air was having the desired effect, though it wasn't the way a lively seventeen-year-old expected to feel for very long. And she would be *eighteen* in a couple of weeks, she reminded herself, realising that she had almost forgotten her birthday with all that had been going on lately.

Uncannily, Elsie tuned in. 'So what delights do you want for your birthday, little sister?' she asked.

Cal, Daisy thought instantly. *Lucy*. And to be rid of her guilt at knowing she had danced and flirted with Jed and Glenn while she was still in love with Cal. For everything to be the way it used to be. No more war, no irritating little evacuees getting under everyone's feet, and her mother. Most of all, her mother.

'I daresay Aunt Rose will manage to make me a cake if the rations run to it,' she said, swallowing the futility of her thoughts. 'The infants will expect it, though I'm not sure I want to blow out eighteen candles!'

'Of course not. It's so *old*, isn't it?' Elsie said with a grin.

Daisy playfully scuffed sand at her feet and got a shoeful back. Right then she felt about six years old, and it was a good feeling. She knew she would miss Elsie dreadfully if she did decide to stay.

'You and Daddy will come down to Weston for my

birthday, won't you? Unless you've taken up residence here, of course.'

'Darling, it's not going to happen,' Elsie said slowly. 'This is an interlude, no more. It's a place to come back to, the way we always have in the past, but not to stay; so let's say no more about it, please. In any case, of course we'll be in Weston for your birthday, and I don't think I care to be travelling up and down the country too many times in my condition!'

Daisy knew she had come to a momentous decision, without really knowing why. She guessed it must have something to do with feeling even farther away from Joe in this isolated corner of England. Whatever the reason, it was their business, and for once she held her tongue, and didn't ask.

They arrived back in Bristol on June the fourteenth, two days before Daisy's birthday and four days after the news broke that Italy, having joined forces with Germany, had declared war on Britain and France. The little Italian restaurant that had been part of the row of shops including Preston's Emporium, where Quentin was manager, had been closed at once, and the owners immediately interned.

'How awful!' Daisy exclaimed, when they had been welcomed back to Vicarage Street and their father had told them the news. 'You mean that nice Mr Bertorelli and both his sons are in prison? And his wife too?'

'All of them, I'm afraid, since they're now officially our enemies. All Italians in this country will have suffered the same fate.'

There were many Italian families in business in the south-west, and it seemed barbaric to round them all up as if they had suddenly become the enemy overnight. But that was what they were now, Daisy realised.

'I can't believe it. Mrs Bertorelli was such a nice lady, and they had lived here for years. How can they be considered a threat to anyone?'

'Such things are under government control, Daisy, and it would be the same for British citizens living in Italy or Germany, and in any of the occupied countries. They would want to get out as soon as possible, or risk imprisonment.'

'Well, I think it stinks,' she said, not having appreciated this angle of war until now. Going back and forth to Dunkirk on the hospital ship had been a daring adventure, despite all they had had to see and do; but this was an insidious way of taking away people's liberty, and it frightened her.

'That's not the worst of it,' Quentin went on grimly. 'Anti-Italian riots have broke out in London, according to the newspapers. Windows have been smashed and Italian shopkeepers threatened with violence. So far there haven't been any reports of it here, but swift internment is the best answer, for their own safety.'

'Daisy, there's nothing we can do about it, however much we sympathise with the Bertorelli family,' she heard Elsie say. 'Come and help me unpack my things, and then we'll tell Father what we did in Cornwall, and how Kenneth Harris is lording it over his residents.'

Daisy knew she was right, but it didn't stop her disgust that people she knew were being imprisoned in their own adopted country, just for where they had come from.

'I suppose we'll be allowed to send them things; or will they be put in the condemned cell?'

'You're getting this all out of proportion, Daisy,' her father said sharply. 'Elsie's right. There's nothing we can do about it, and if we raise our voices in favour of the Italian immigrants, we risk being vilified ourselves. You would do well to remember that.'

'So we just sit back and let it happen, do we?'

'That is exactly what we do, because we can't do anything else.' Knowing better than to continue the futile argument with her father, she marched out of the sitting room and upstairs to Elsie's flat ahead of her sister. Elsie took a little longer to climb the stairs, but when she had closed the door behind her, she turned on Daisy.

'You're being very short-sighted, you know, and Father's right: internment is for the Italians' own safety as much as anything else.'

'I know,' Daisy said miserably. 'I just feel so sorry for them, that's all. It's hardly their war, any more than it's yours or mine; but we all have to pay in one way or another, don't we?'

'If you've realised that, then you've grown up a lot, darling.'

'You have to grow up when you're faced with death every day and your young man's been blown to bits, wouldn't you say? Oh Lord, I'm sorry, Elsie; I know you've got your own worries over Joe, and I shouldn't be making you feel unhappy when we've just had such a lovely time, but it never goes away does it? You can't really escape from what's happening in the world, because there's nowhere far enough.'

Elsie spoke calmly. 'So let's just concentrate on doing something very ordinary instead of trying to sort out the world's problems. And if you want to do something *really* ordinary, I'll show you the baby's layette and you can coo over the thought of becoming an auntie.'

Daisy gave her a reluctant smile and tried to put the shock of what her father had told her out of her mind. The crazy temptation to march through the streets waving banners and announcing their friendly neighbourhood Italians' innocence in all this madness, as if she was some latter-day suffragette, flitted into her head and disappeared as quickly as it had come. As her father said, it would no good, and such stupidity would only bring the wrath of warring Bristolians down on their heads. He was right. There was nothing they could do.

'Auntie Daisy! Now that does make me feel old!' she

said instead. 'All right, let's get unpacked, and then I'll put up with being shown this wonderful layette for the most wonderful superbabe yet to be born.'

'Was there ever any doubt about that?'

'So Elsie wasn't tempted to move down to Cornwall for the duration, and she's staying in Bristol, just as I always thought she would,' Rose told Bert, putting down the telephone.

Daisy had just let them know that they'd had a lovely time, and they would be with them on Sunday, Daisy's birthday. Since there were no trains on that day, they were to use the car, with the petrol Quentin had been hoarding for just such an important occasion. You couldn't let a daughter's eighteenth birthday go by without travelling in style.

Teddy began jumping up and down with excitement.

'Our Daisy's coming home on Sunday,' he chanted, repeating everything for confirmation as usual; and then he frowned. 'I can't always remember what our Elsie looks like, though.'

'Well, you goose, she looks just like Daisy, only older,' Bert reminded him. 'Your sisters were always like three peas in a pod.'

He had only been a little one when his mother died and he and Rose had taken him in, Bert remembered. Teddy hadn't seen much of any of the others since, except Daisy, and the war had separated all of them, the way it had separated so many families. It sometimes made him a little uneasy to think how he and Rose had absorbed two of the Caldwell children into their lives, when they still had their own home, and their father, and siblings of their own. As he reminded Rose now and then, all these children were only borrowed, and that went for Teddy and Daisy as well as the evacuees. He didn't care to look too far ahead and think how it would affect her when they all went home again.

'What are you looking so gloomy about, Bert?' she scolded him.

'Nothing that need concern you, my love. But if I'm going to get that bookcase finished for Daisy's birthday present, I'd better get on with it.'

'And Teddy and I are going to make Daisy's cake, aren't we, love?' she asked him brightly, seeing the puckered look still on his face as he tried to remember what the rest of his family looked like. Rose resolved to get out the old family photo albums soon.

Bert deliberately avoided mentioning the Italian situation. It was bad enough that all the newspaper headlines were black and heavy, predicting the worst, now that Mussolini's navy was at Hitler's disposal. *Newspaper reporters*, Bert thought, with a scowl. Scandalmongers, most of 'em, and what they didn't know, they invented. Right now they were inventing all kinds of things about the most innocent of folk.

One of Rose's knitting circle was the wife of a small restaurant-owner on the seafront, and neither of them had been seen or heard of for several days. Everyone knew what must have happened, but putting it into words made it seem a hundred times worse, and speculation never helped anyone.

Besides, he and Rose had three young boys to care for, and every new mention of the war's progress had Ronnie wetting his bed, while Norman became ever more angry and wanted to go home. It was for their sakes that Bert tried to keep everything as normal as possible. Daisy's birthday, and the small family party that would bring most of them together again for a short while, was the best boost any of them could have right now.

'You boys can come and help me,' he called out to Norman and Ronnie as he went down to the shed at the bottom of his garden. The bookcase was no more than three open shelves, but he knew she would welcome it for all her nursing manuals. He was staining the shelves this afternoon, and it should be thoroughly dry by the time she arrived home on Sunday.

'Our Mum don't believe in birthday presents,' Norman said with a sniff. 'She says she ain't got no money for daft stuff nobody wants.'

'It's always better to give people something they want,' he agreed. 'Now that I've got into my stride with the woodworking, I might make you and Ronnie a box with a lift-up lid next, to keep your comics in. What do you think of that?'

Norman shrugged. ''S all right, I daresay.'

'I think you're nice,' Ronnie said suddenly.

'Well, thank you, Ronnie. I think you're nice too,' Bert said.

''Cept when he pees himself,' Norman hooted.

Bert ignored that, concentrating instead on the fair job he'd made of Daisy's bookcase. He was pleased with it, and he hoped she would be too. Teddy would be up to his elbows in flour now, he guessed, helping Rose make the cake for Daisy's birthday tea, and these two were engrossed in watching him stain the old wood to a deep gloss.

If they were able to ignore the occasional sounds of planes going off in formation from RAF Locking, they could almost think this was an ordinary summer's day with nothing sinister to threaten their world.

'Did you finish your drawings for Daisy's birthday?' he asked the boys. Norman was no mean artist when he tried, and Ronnie had an eye for colour.

'Course we did,' Norman said. 'Ronnie can get them and show you.'

He glared as his brother started to protest, and then gave in as he usually did. They would never get on, Bert thought, but presumably that was the way brothers close in age behaved. Give them a real problem to cope with, and they stuck together, close as clams.

Ronnie came back five minutes later with their birthday drawings. Ronnie's was a crayon sketch of Daisy, her bright hair tumbling around a smiling face. Norman's was a picture of the house seen from the front, where there were still borders of flowers in the garden. It was bright and cheerful, and seeing it through a child's eyes brought a daft lump to Bert's throat.

'I know Daisy will love them both,' he told them. 'Take them back inside now, Ronnie, and put them somewhere safe until tomorrow.'

'Can I show them to Aunt Rose first?' he said.

'Of course you can.'

He wasn't really a clinging child, but he had become attached to Rose, which sometimes caused friction between him and Teddy, since Teddy considered Rose his property, she being his real aunt and not just a pretend one. He sighed, glad that Rose understood them better than he did, even without having had children of her own. It was the female instinct, he supposed, and then gave up thinking about anything at all except the more pressing need to get his handiwork done.

Twelve

Being eighteen years old was quite a milestone, Daisy thought, and although it would have been perfect if her mother and Lucy had been here to share it, she was determined to let nothing cloud this beautiful day. She wasn't so grand that she couldn't be as excited as a child again, wondering what gifts she was going to receive when her father joined his daughters for breakfast.

Elsie had made her a silk scarf from a piece of material Daisy had admired for a long time in her sister's box of fabrics, which she'd once thought was like an Aladdin's Cave; and Quentin presented her with a small silver locket that opened. Inside was a tiny photo of Daisy's mother.

'You always liked that particular photo, and I thought you might like to have it as a keepsake,' he said gruffly.

'It's the most perfect gift you could have given me,' Daisy said, finding it hard not to cry, but determined to resist, for all their sakes.

'So now let's have our toast and porridge, and then we'll get started,' Quentin said briskly. 'Elsie and I will want to get back here in good time this evening, so we'll want to spend as much of the day in Weston as we can.'

The soldiers who had been given temporary accommodation in the Caldwell house had been efficiently moved on before the girls arrived home from Cornwall, much to their relief. Neither of them had relished the thought of having to make conversation with strangers, while hearing about their experiences would have revived too many

memories of Dunkirk for Daisy, and of Joe's injuries for
Elsie.

So once they were ready they set off in the big old Rover,
determined to feel as carefree as anyone could in the middle
of a war. Rose had already telephoned to wish Daisy a
happy birthday, and to let them know she was making a
rabbit-and-vegetable pie for their dinner, so she hoped they
would all have good appetites. Daisy managed not to groan
out loud until she had heard Teddy's excited squeals at the
other end, and had put down the phone to report.

'She'd have you all looking as well fed as me,' Elsie
laughed, patting her stomach. 'But she shouldn't go to so
much trouble, nor try to stretch the rations.'

'Oh, you'll never stop your aunt trying to feed the five
thousand, no matter how meagre the rations; and I daresay
those farming friends of hers supplied the rabbit, so there's
no need to feel guilty,' Quentin said complacently. 'Now,
who's for a song to speed us on our way?'

It was what they had always done when they set out in the
car on a family occasion. They sang until they were hoarse,
and then they played I-Spy, leaving Daisy with the feeling
that she should be eight years old again, not eighteen. If she
had been, Frances would have been sitting in the front seat,
Immy and Baz would have been here with them, and Teddy
wouldn't even have been born yet . . .

'A penny for them, Daisy,' Quentin said suddenly, noting
her silence.

She drew in her breath, but she wouldn't cast a shadow
over this lovely day by making them aware of a small sad
moment. She spoke cheerfully.

'I was just thinking how lucky we are to have each other,
that's all.'

'Well, we all know that,' Elsie said, giving her hand a
squeeze. 'So let's have another song now that we've all got
our breath back.'

It certainly helped to make the journey go faster, and

when they drew up outside Rose and Bert's house in Weston, Daisy looked at it with real affection, knowing with a little shock that this was more truly her home now than the one in Vicarage Street, and Aunt Rose had been the one to make it so.

Then she couldn't think of anything else but the three small boys rushing out of the front door to greet them, followed by the adults. Teddy flung himself into his father's arms, and as the evacuee boys hopped up and down from one foot to the other, Daisy thought briefly that she hoped this didn't presage an accident on Ronnie's part. Then everyone was talking at once.

'We've got presents for you, Daisy,' Teddy shrieked.

'We made them ourselves,' Norman shouted, eyeing Elsie's bump somewhat suspiciously, but deciding to ignore it for the moment.

'How wonderful!' Daisy said.

'And Elsie, my love, you're really looking in the pink,' Bert said, beaming.

'Thank you, Uncle Bert, and it's marvellous to see you all again,' Elsie said, as she was embraced by her aunt and uncle in a great bear hug.

'And you had a lovely holiday? You both look very well!' Rose said.

'They do, don't they?' Quentin put in, the proud father, with Teddy in his arms now, and valiantly resisting the urge to scoop the excitedly yapping George away from his feet. 'The Cornish air was just what they needed.'

'So let's all go inside, shall we?' Rose said more practically. 'We'll have the neighbours wondering what's going on, and I'm sure they already think of us as a completely mad household.'

But she was smiling as she spoke, since nothing gave Rose more pleasure than to be surrounded by children and family. For now, all thoughts of whatever else was going on in the world could be put aside, especially the news that Alice Godfrey's mother had passed on to her that week.

They had a mutual friend, an American lady by the glamorous name of Gloria Feinstein, who had owned a dress shop in Weston for many years. But now, with the tragic events in France and wide concern by America and the neutral countries over Italy's involvement, the American government was urging all its citizens to leave Britain at the first opportunity.

So with her typical impulsiveness, Gloria had done exactly as her government advised and had already left Weston, leaving her affairs in the hands of her solicitors until further notice, Mrs Godfrey had told Rose tearfully. It was as if the American government had already decided there was no hope for Britain, and that invasion was imminent. It had taken a long while and quite a few cups of tea for Rose to calm her down, and another long chat with Bert that night to calm herself down.

If Daisy hadn't been enjoying a well-earned holiday in Cornwall at the time, Rose knew she would have spilled it all out to her long before now. But not today. This was Daisy's day.

'Come and see what I made for you,' Teddy was shrieking wildly now.

'And me!' yelled Norman, echoed by Ronnie.

'Now come on, boys; let's all calm down a little and get our breath back,' Rose ordered. 'We'll go inside and have some lemonade, and then we'll all give Daisy our presents, one by one. Youngest first,' she added, before they could clamour over who was to get priority.

They all knew that Teddy would have yelled that he had to go first anyway, since Daisy was his real sister, and only a tacked-on one for the other two; but Rose's words saved any argument, and Daisy was delighted with the primrose plant Teddy had dug up from his own patch of garden and put into a pot for her bedroom, tied with a scrap of yellow ribbon.

'It's lovely' she told him. 'Just what I wanted.'

The pictures Norman and Ronnie had done were produced next, which Daisy admired and promised would go on her bedroom wall. Then it was Bert's turn. He was no more than an amateur carpenter, but the bookcase had been made with love, and was truly just what Daisy needed. She threw her arms around him, hugging him close.

'I love you,' she whispered in his ear so that only he could hear.

'I love you too,' he whispered back.

'And if you two can tear yourselves apart, there's one more present to come,' Rose said, unexpectedly touched by the sight of them. If she'd ever been lucky enough to have a daughter, she would have wanted one just like Daisy, she found herself thinking . . .

She went to the sideboard and produced an envelope. She could see by the boys' faces that they didn't think it looked like much, and hoped Daisy wouldn't think the same.

'Gloria Feinstein has gone back to America, Daisy,' she said. 'All the stock at her dress shop is being sold off at bargain prices, and since you always loved her fancy supply of clothes, I thought I should have your pick of it. So there's a little money to make the shopping expedition worthwhile. At my age I've got plenty of clothes to see me out.'

Daisy opened the envelope and gasped at the crisp notes inside it. It was a totally unexpected gift, and she felt a rush of tears in her eyes, thinking how dear her aunt was, and how her occasional brusqueness hid a genuinely kind heart.

It was Rose's turn to get a huge hug now, and stammering thanks that Rose quickly brushed aside.

'You can thank me best of all by doing justice to your dinner and putting on a bit of weight. You don't want to follow those film stars and end up looking like a stick.

Oh, and I nearly forgot – there's a letter for you on the mantelpiece. It looks like Immy's writing.'

There was no reason for Daisy's heart to jump, thinking it might have been from someone else. Not from Cal, of course . . . unlikely to be from Jed, since he seemed to have forgotten all about her . . . and not from Glenn, who didn't know her address. She tore open the envelope, thankful that her family couldn't see how her thoughts had immediately gone to three young men. But why not? She was young and healthy and . . .

'Oh! Immy's sent me some money for my birthday too!' she exclaimed, fingering the two crisp pound notes inside the letter and card. 'She says I'm to do what I like with it, within reason.' She started to laugh. 'What does she think I'll do? Book my passage to America!'

She immediately wished she hadn't said that, remembering Aunt Rose's friend who had taken fright and gone home when she had thought Britain was about to be invaded; but Aunt Rose was busy in the kitchen by now and hadn't heard.

'Our Daisy's rich now,' Teddy chanted.

'Well, hardly! But it was very nice of her, wasn't it, Daddy?'

'Very thoughtful,' he said, touched that his oldest girl had taken over the role of Daisy's mother in that instance, whether or not it was intentional. Eighteen was definitely a milestone, and Frances would certainly have thought so too.

'What does Immy say in her letter?' he asked.

Daisy skimmed it. 'Just that she and Helen had an enjoyable weekend in London recently, and now she and her Captain Beckett are based there, so she doubts she'll be seeing Helen too often. But the good news is that James is due for a forty-eight-hour pass soon, and he plans to stay in London so they can see one another.'

She folded up the letter carefully, her head full of dreams, imagining what it must be like to be sharing a clandestine weekend far away from home and family with the man you were going to marry. It might not be clandestine at all, of course, she thought hastily, but then again, it might . . . and the dreams took shape so swiftly she was almost scared that the others might see them in her eyes.

But the boys were squabbling on the hearthrug as usual, fighting over who was going to hug George, until the poor dog squealed and yapped in protest at such devotion. Her father and uncle were already deep in quiet conversation about the progress of the war, and Aunt Rose was producing the most glorious smell of cooking that was making her mouth water . . . Even though it was the middle of a lovely summer's day, Daisy was somewhere in dreamland, in the arms of an unknown lover whose kisses were sweeter than wine, and who was telling her passionately that he adored her . . .

'Who's for rabbit pie then?' Aunt Rose announced. 'Go and wash your hands, boys, and then come and sit at the table, all of you, before it gets cold.'

If anything was designed to bring a dreamer down to earth, that was it.

They had heard nothing from Baz, though Daisy had hardly expected to. Younger brothers were not in the business of remembering birthdays without a mother to remind them. In any case Baz was too busily involved in saving his skin to be thinking of such trivial matters. The ageing fishing trawler had finally been put out of action in the Dunkirk evacuation and he had parted company with his mates. Somehow he had found himself stranded on the French side of the Channel, and in the general confusion everywhere he had decided that he might as well become the adventurer he had always wanted to be.

While most of the BEF was struggling to make its way to the coast, in the next few days Baz was scrabbling about

157

through fields and hedgerows and making his way west. His aim was to get back home, and he reasoned that there had to be other British ships in the vicinity ready to pick up servicemen. There were plenty of others doing the same as himself, but in his flight from Dunkirk he had somehow found himself alone.

Being an adventurer, living on his wits and what he could find to eat, wasn't as exciting as he had once imagined. He quickly became disorientated as he kept his head down and dug himself in every time he heard the whine and roar of enemy planes overhead, and the spatter of machine-gun fire.

A week later he was filthy and starving when he lifted his head cautiously from a ditch where he had been cramming down what he hoped were edible purple berries, and met the eyes of a young girl gazing down at him.

'Where am I?' he croaked.

She didn't answer, but continued with that cold wide stare. He wished he'd bothered to learn a few words of French, but there had never seemed the need, for a Bristol ferryman or a fisherman. In desperation he pointed to his mouth, making a gesture that he was hungry and thirsty too, since the berries seemed to have dried up the inside of his lips. He suddenly panicked, wondering if he had been poisoned by them.

The girl continued to stare, and then they both heard a shout, and she turned and fled, screaming out something that he couldn't understand but which certainly seemed to indicate that the best thing he could do was to run. And run like hell.

Weren't the French supposed to be their allies . . . ? Before he could even move, he was suddenly hauled to his feet by a large and aggressive farmer with a pitchfork in his hand. My God, he was going to be stabbed to death here and now, Baz thought in a wild panic. Maybe the farmer thought he was German. He had dodged several columns of German soldiers marching this way, and the rumble of tanks had frequently shaken the ground. He had no idea where he was and he bellowed out the first thing that came into his head.

'I'm English!' He shouted, the way people did when speaking to foreigners. '*English*. You understand? I need to find a ship. A boat.'

The man spoke rapidly to the girl, who sped away from him towards the farmhouse Baz could now see across the fields. He'd obviously wandered inland well away from the coast – and that was that, then. The farmer didn't understand him, and he either thought he was a thief or a runaway, and he was going to turn him in.

'You want food?' the farmer said.

Baz felt his legs turn to water and, in his relief, he had a job not to let the hot gush of piss fill his pants.

'Thank God. You speak English,' he gasped.

The man shrugged. 'And you want a boat.'

'No. Well, *yes*,' Baz said. Of course he bloody well wanted a boat. He wanted to get home. He had never wanted it more. They were slightly at cross purposes, but the end result was the same.

He grabbed a handful of the berries he had eaten, feeling their purple juice squeeze through his fingers. Now that he realised he wasn't going to die by the pitchfork, his belly clenched with the thought that he might have poisoned himself.

'Are these good?' he stuttered, gesturing towards his mouth again.

Without answering, the farmed picked another handful, put them in his own mouth, and began to chuckle.

'*Oui*. Good, eh?' he asked. The grin faded. 'You know what happens?'

'What happens?' Baz croaked. Whatever it was, he didn't want to know. Couldn't the bastard see that he needed something solid in his guts before he passed out completely?

'France has surrendered,' the man snarled. 'The German

pigs' – he turned and spat on the ground – 'they our masters now.'

Baz stared at him in cold horror. His head seemed to float on his shoulders from the lack of food, but his brain was still active enough to tell him that this wasn't a game any more. He was in occupied France, in what was virtual enemy territory, and while these people had no choice but to put up with the invaders, he knew *he* would be considered the enemy if he was caught.

He would be shot. And he would also be putting this farmer and his family in danger if they were seen to be helping him. He knew that too.

'The coast,' he said urgently. 'Which way?'

He swayed as he spoke, and the farmer gripped his arm.'You go nowhere. You come to farm and eat, and then we think about boat.'

Baz could have wept then as he almost dragged himself along beside the farmer. It wasn't far across the fields, but with the sore and bleeding blisters on his feet that he'd hardly noticed until now, it seemed like a mountain to climb before they were safely inside the stone-flagged farmhouse. And he still didn't know the details of France's collapse. The farmer's wife didn't speak English, and the daughter was either too young or too frightened to try.

But from the way they gabbled to each other in French, with many arm-wavings and glares his way, it was painfully clear that the woman wanted to get him away from there as quickly as possible, and he couldn't blame her for that. He wanted it too. But eventually the farmer made it obvious to her that Baz needed food, and he greedily ate the bowl of stew she finally slapped down in front of him, and downed several glasses of water, before he felt in any way human again.

'You rest now,' the farmer ordered.

More alert now, Baz looked at him suspiciously. How did he know he could trust any of these people? The farmer had seemed affable enough, but his wife was decidedly unfriendly. They could easily turn him in to win favour with the Germans, and for the first time he knew how it felt to be hunted, and to trust no one. He started to protest, but the farmer spoke again, pointing to the stairs.

'You rest here for one hour.'

'I'm grateful, but I think I should leave right away,' Baz said uneasily. 'You may be in danger if I stay.'

The man shook his head vigorously. 'We leave after dark. Now, you rest!'

The aggression had returned, and Baz knew he had little option. He was so tired he was almost collapsing where he stood, and he winced as he put one foot in front of the other on the creaking wooden staircase. He was shown into a white-painted boxroom with a narrow bed and various Catholic artefacts on the small chest of drawers. He couldn't be sure, but as he sank on to the bed and heard the door close, he thought he also heard a key turn in the lock. But he was too weary to care any more, and the last thing he saw before his eyes closed was the face of the Virgin Mary on a painting above him.

The creaking on the stairs woke him with a start of fear. He had no idea how long he had been asleep, but he was sure it had been more than an hour. It had still been daylight when he reached the farm, and through the tiny square of window he could see the dark blue of the night sky, dotted with stars. He heard the key turn in the lock, and knew his earlier thought had been right. They had locked him in, and now he was about to learn his fate.

His heart drummed sickeningly, and he stared hard at the door, wondering if it was about to be kicked in by jackboots, and if a machine gun would spray him with bullets. It would be a bloody shame to splatter this nice, clinically white room with blood, he found himself thinking incoherently.

For some wild reason he found himself thinking it must

be how his sister Daisy felt in her nice, clinically white hospital ward: defiling all the nice, clinically white wards with blood – he couldn't seem to get the bastard words out of his head now.

He was very tempted to scream that he was willing to surrender, even though he knew it was the coward's way out, but his mouth and throat were so dry he couldn't utter a sound. The walls seemed to be revolving, and he knew he must be hallucinating, so the farmer's wife had probably slipped something into his stew to make sure he remained docile until the Germans came . . .

The door opened and two men came inside as he cowered in terror on the narrow bed. His only hope was that if they were going to kill him they would do it quickly. He wasn't cut out to be a hero, and his only consolation was that when he met his sweet mother in heaven – if he went to heaven – she would understand and forgive him the way she always had.

'We go now,' the farmer said.

Baz blinked in the patch of light showing through the door.

'Go?' he croaked. 'Go where?'

'To boat. This man takes you.'

He swung his legs off the bed, forcing himself not to vomit with relief that he wasn't about to be killed, and feeling a surge of shame at his momentary willingness to surrender. It would never happen again, he vowed. But he was finding it hard to walk, and he knew he was in no state to go anywhere.

'I can't,' he said finally. 'My feet are too swollen.'

The other man spoke rapidly in French, and the farmer nodded.

'You not walk. You ride in cart. Please – go now.'

Baz swallowed, sensing that the wife's fears had been transmitted to her husband. He hobbled to the door and down the stairs as carefully as he could. There was no sign of the wife and daughter, and he tried to thank the farmer as he went outside into the cool of the evening, and saw the horse and cart outside. He had nothing to give the family, but he scribbled his name and address on a piece of paper, just in case they should ever need help.

Then he was bundled inside the cart, covered with a blanket and bundles of straw, and he realised that this journey was a hazardous one for the man taking him to the coast. Baz hardly thought such a move was a good idea at night, but presumably it was preferable to doing it in daylight. He gave up speculating, and settled down to the most uncomfortable and stifling journey of his life.

He had no idea which part of the coast they were heading to, but at last the cart stopped, and as he lifted his head he saw the hazy outline of the sea ahead, with several large ships tied up in the harbour. The driver removed the straw and blanket, and Baz drew in great gulps of air, as the man pointed to the harbour. Baz realised now that the dark, moving shadows ahead of him weren't bushes, but the shuffling figures of men.

Without saying a word, his saviour got back into the cart and turned it around, leaving Baz to hobble away, to merge in with the small army of servicemen all as bent as he as on reaching the ships. He was just one among hundreds now, and no one questioned his dishevelled appearance.

'Come on, you buggers, get a move on,' a raucous English voice roared at them from the quay. 'Get on board as quick as you can and find yourselves a space. We'll be out of here in the morning, but you can bet your boots the Jerries will be bombing at first light, so I hope you've got a few prayers up your sleeves.'

His bloody cheerfulness set Baz's teeth on edge. He thought himself a survivor, and he hadn't come all this way to be bombed by Jerry planes; but nor had any of these. There were plenty worse off than he was, and with no hospital ship to tend to them either, just the rough handling of a ship's medico. His blistered feet were the least of their worries.

He squatted down on deck, wedged between a dozen soldiers, all as exhausted and stinking as himself, and waited for daylight to come. He knew that he was on a large ship, one of several in the harbour, but theirs didn't finally get under way until mid-morning. By then the whine of air-raid sirens was constantly filling the air, the smell of burning was acrid, and the cloud of enemy aircraft was blotting out the sky, bearing down on them out of the morning sunlight like angry wasps, but with far more lethal intent. Bombs were falling like rain, and there was no chance of avoiding the inevitable. A bomb struck them amidships, rocking the entire ship, throwing men and lifeboats into the sea.

'Anyone still standing, grab a lifejacket and jump,' the crew were screaming now. 'You'll be safer in the sea than waiting for these bastards to blow us to bits.'

It was like something out of hell as lifejackets were tossed between them, many literally torn from the next man's grasp as each fought for his own. Someone thrust one at Baz.

'Here, kid, put this on and jump for it,' the man yelled.

He did as he was told and rushed to the side of the ship, instinctively drawing back as he saw how very far below the water looked. There was oil spilling out of the ship now, and a thick black sludge was spreading over the sea's surface, raw and pungent. Baz was too terrified to jump and the hard cork of the lifejacket was throttling him. But the ship was tilting badly now, and the sheer volume of men behind him was pushing him, taking away his decision to leap over the side. It was one heaving mass of men and cumbersome lifejackets.

Then, with one last strangled gasp for survival, he found himself hurtling overboard in the midst of them, and as he hit the water the lifejacket became his killer, breaking his neck on impact.

Thirteen

'I never thought I'd say this, but I really envy my sister,' Daisy said to Alice Godfrey, in a welcome ten-minute break from their ward duties.

'What? Having a baby!' Alice said in disbelief.

'No, of course not. I wouldn't want one until I've been married for years, anyway. I didn't mean Elsie. I meant Immy. It must be exciting to drive an officer around all the time, and be in on everything that's going on in London.'

'You wouldn't think that if you were in the middle of an air raid!'

'All the same, it's very romantic to think of her and her young man spending a weekend's leave together, even in the middle of an air raid. I shouldn't even think they'd notice the bombs falling.'

Alice laughed. 'Daisy, you're such an idiot. People get killed and wounded in air raids, or haven't you noticed? It's what keeps us working too,' she added, as Daisy's brow puckered.

'I know, but I'm sure Immy will be all right, and the rest of us too. Did I ever tell you I sometimes think of my mother as our guardian angel keeping us all safe?' She felt her face grow hot as she saw Alice's astonished look. 'Oh, forget I said that. I don't really know why I did. It's not something I tell everyone.'

'Then I'm honoured that you told me. And I don't actually think you're an idiot at all. I think you're a rather special person, if you must know.'

Daisy squirmed. 'Well, now you're *really* making me feel soppy. And we'd better get back to work, or Sister will be after us.'

It made her feel good all the same, to know that someone as sophisticated as Alice Godfrey thought of her as someone rather special.

Since she and Elsie had come back from Cornwall, and her eighteenth birthday had come and gone, she was feeling more relaxed in one way, and more restless in another. Part of her relished the knowledge that she was still doing the job she loved, and another part said it wasn't enough to be stuck here in her local hospital when other people were out there in the midst of danger, doing *really* worthwhile jobs.

She was old enough now to volunteer. Each time the thought entered her head it gave her a shivery feeling of anticipation. She wasn't Florence Nightingale, but Florence had gone out to where she was needed, and to Daisy that was what heroines were made of. But she could just imagine the hue and cry if she dared to suggest such a thing. So although she did nothing about it, it was a thought that wouldn't go away.

It wasn't such a comfortable thought to know that there were ships still trying to get servicemen out of France that were being bombed and sunk before they even left the French ports. It wasn't safe to be on the sea nowadays, any more than it was safe to be in one of the key cities that were likely to be German targets.

She wondered where her brother was now. They hadn't heard from Baz in weeks, but since that was nothing unusual, she gave up thinking about him and got on with the business of writing a letter home for the patient in her care.

This was something she enjoyed doing, because it always gave someone at the other end a bit of hope. A wife or a mother was going to get a letter written in her neat hand on behalf of their loved one; and she encouraged all her patients to let her do this for them, carefully putting the words in their heads if they were too reticent or inarticulate to think of them for themselves, but making sure the sentiments seemed exactly right for each man to have said.

'Right-oh then, Private Stokes. If you're ready to dictate, I'm ready to write. And nothing too saucy this time, if you don't mind!'

He laughed back at her, trying not to cough and start his wretched wheezing again, and winking with the one good eye that wasn't heavily bandaged. Both arms were bandaged too, and it had been touch and go whether or not he lost his right hand in the shell blast.

It was a good thing he hadn't, since it was the one he used to lift his pint, he'd told the doctors chirpily at the time.

'Now, Nursie, you know a little bit of sauce never did anyone any harm!' he answered in reply to her comment.

'Well, I prefer to save it for putting on my chips,' Daisy said smartly, knowing some of them liked to include a bit of spice in their letters, even if it meant shocking her. It didn't actually. She was only acting as a mediator, and in the end they were *their* words, not hers, even the more intimate ones.

'All right,' Private Stokes said. 'Let's start with "My dear Hilda", as usual, and ask how she is. And the kids too. Then tell her I'm as well as can be expected, and hoping to get out of here very soon, though I shall miss my pretty nurse and her warm hands.'

'Are you sure you want to say that bit?' Daisy said, pausing. 'Wouldn't it be nicer to say you're missing your wife's warm hands?'

She knew he'd led her into this the minute she heard him chuckle again.

'Oh, much better. Now, you're good at anatomy, aren't you, Nursie? So where shall we say I'd like to feel them?'

'How about holding yours?' she said innocently.

'My what?'

'Hands, of course,' Daisy said, seeing the ward sister

approaching, and knowing there would be no nonsense out
of her if she heard this one's cheek. But if it did them good
and raised their morale, where was the harm in it?

Though she knew very well that if it wasn't wartime,
when people were becoming far more liberal than they ever
had been before, her parents would have been scandalised
to hear her speak in such a provocative manner to a virtual
stranger. Even her mother, with her more flamboyant life,
being a stage artiste . . .

'Now then, we've asked your wife how she is, and
enquired after the children,' she said more briskly. 'Do
you want to tell her how well you're doing?'

Private Stokes scowled. 'You can tell her that the treatment hurts a bloody sight more than nearly getting my hand
blown off, if you like. Bloody doctors. More like effing
butchers, if you ask me.'

Daisy waited patiently, knowing this was one of Private
Stokes's expected reactions. He was actually doing very well
indeed, but with the usual impatience of the regular soldier,
he couldn't stand any kind of inactivity. She folded her arms,
and his scowl gradually turned into a grin.

'Shocked you, did I, ducks? I restrained meself from
ekchually saying the word, of course, for fear of offending
them delicate little ears of yours—'

Daisy snapped at him before she had time to think.

'Oh, shut up, Stokesey, and let's get on with this letter.
I've heard worse than that in my time, so don't think you're
anything special! And there's plenty in here far worse off
than you too, so stop feeling sorry for yourself. It's your
wife I feel sorry for, if you're going home to her with your
bad temper.'

His mouth dropped open with shock at her sharp retort.
Daisy surprised herself, but sometimes shock tactics were
better than tip-toeing around. Anyway, she did feel sorry
for the families who had to put up with them on their return
home when they still weren't fully fit, especially those who

played on the extent of their injuries, which she knew very well some of them did. There was a lot to be said for supervised convalescent homes with properly trained staff until they were restored to full health, rather than inflicting them on their long-suffering wives.

'Ever thought of being a female prison warder, have you, Nursie?' Private Stokes snarled. But then his eyes twinkled and his voice lowered to a more lecherous tone. 'Not that I'd object to a bit of nightly bullying from the likes of you, mind, if you know what I mean.'

'I haven't the slightest idea,' Daisy said airily. 'Now then, should I write all that to your darling Hilda, or do you have something nicer to say to her?'

He chuckled at her then. 'Just tell her I hope to be getting out of here soon and then she can give me my bed-bath instead of the wicked nurse with fingernails like talons digging into my backside.'

'I hope to be getting out of here soon,' Daisy dictated as she wrote down her own interpretation, 'and I'm looking forward to having some of your loving care instead of these nurses. They do their best, but they're not you, dear.'

She looked at him. 'How does that sound to you?'

'Perfect,' he said, with the surprising glint of a tear in his eye. 'My old woman will love that. You wouldn't care to be my personal secretary, I suppose?'

Daisy laughed, closing the notepad before copying it out properly for him to check and then having it posted.

'If the choice is between a female prison warder and personal secretary to a wicked old rogue like you, Private Stokes, I think I'll stick where I am!'

She moved on to the next man on the ward who wanted her services, knowing she had cheered his day, just as he had cheered hers. She enjoyed writing their letters for them, and the men appreciated having a young and pretty nurse to do it for them, especially one who wasn't so starchy that she couldn't indulge in a bit of banter now and then. And it wasn't going unnoticed.

She was called into the ward sister's office later on that day, and her heart skipped a beat, knowing this was never a good sign. Daisy tried frantically to remember any misdemeanours she might have committed.

'Sit down, Daisy,' Sister Macintosh said, 'and there's no need to look alarmed. I'm not about to give you your marching orders.'

'Thank you, Sister,' Daisy murmured. But she must have done something wrong, otherwise why would she be here?

'Several of your patients have shown me the letters you've written for them, and I must say you have a way with words. I don't imagine it's always exactly the way they're told to you, is it?'

'I never try to alter the sense of them, Sister, but sometimes they find it difficult to say what they mean. Sometimes the words don't come out quite right, and I just try to tidy them up a little bit.'

Her own words weren't coming out quite right at that moment, Daisy thought in a panic. Had someone complained? Maybe someone's wife had thought she was putting a little too much sentimentality into a letter from a normally tough-talking soldier . . .

'My dear girl, don't look so flustered. I'm not condemning you for what you're doing. On the contrary. You have a rare sensitivity for one so young, especially when writing letters for some of the older patients.'

Daisy felt herself blush. If Sister knew what some of those older patients dictated to her – and the younger ones – just to tease her. But a compliment couldn't be the sole reason for being called into Sister's office. She waited, knowing there had to be more.

'Your mother was once a talented entertainer, I believe,' Sister went on, taking Daisy off guard.

'Why yes, she was. Frances Caldwell. She was a singer and dancer.'

Sister nodded. 'I seem to remember. And that must be where you get your own artistic talents from. There is a real art in writing letters, and not everyone has it. So I have the details of an opening that might interest you.'

Even though she was dying to discuss it with someone, she knew it was only right to tell her family first. She had already been invited to have supper with Alice at the Godfreys' home that evening, so by the time she went home, she could hardly contain herself, and she went straight into the parlour where Aunt Rose and Uncle Bert were listening to the wireless, and thankfully the boys were already in bed.

'You'll never guess what's happened today. You could have knocked me down with the proverbial feather,' she burst out.

'It must have been something monumental then,' Rose said, laughing at her excitement. 'Have you been promoted to chief surgeon? If so, remind me never to have my tonsils out.'

'Oh, Aunt Rose, it's nothing so unlikely! Though the whole thing seems unlikely to me. Well, perhaps not, considering what brought the suggestion about; but fancy her bringing Mother into it. That was a surprise, I can tell you.'

She started giggling, her voice rising almost hysterically.

'Are you going to tell us *anything*, or is this a guessing game?' Rose said.

'I'm *trying*,' she gulped. 'I've been offered a post in Norfolk if I want to take it. Well, not actually *offered* it, but I've been invited to apply for it, as Sister thinks I'll be so well suited to it. I have two weeks to think about it—'

'I think you'd better slow down for a start,' Bert said, in his usual placid manner. 'Let's see what we've learned so far. You've been offered a new job – or almost – and your mother comes into it in some way. And if you don't stop babbling and giggling, we shall start to think you've been breathing in some of that laughing gas we're always hearing about. Now take some deep breaths, and start from the beginning.'

Daisy tried. But hadn't she told them everything already? What more was there to tell? The post was being advertised, and Sister Macintosh thought she would be well suited to it.

The only obstacle was that it was somewhere in Norfolk, which was still little more than a bulge on the map to Daisy, and also a very long way from home. It was also much nearer to the east coast, and together with the south it was the area most likely for the Germans to invade, and start their most intensive bombing campaign. She could be putting herself right in the heart of danger.

Her small *frisson* of nerves was replaced by a stab of shame. Hadn't she just traversed the English Channel a couple of dozen times in a hospital ship, helping to bring back those very patients who would hopefully be recovering now in the Norfolk military convalescent home, and other places like it? The lucky ones, anyway. The ones who had survived.

'Daisy, I don't think this is a good idea,' Aunt Rose said at once, when she had finally slowed down enough to outline it properly.

'Why not? I thought I'd have you on my side, anyway, since you didn't oppose my going on the hospital ship.' She was startled at this reaction, knowing very well that she needed everyone's approval, especially her father's, and that approval all started here, with Rose and Bert.

'Darling, that was different.'

'How was it different? It was far more dangerous that just sitting about in a hospital ward or a military convalescent home holding some soldier's hand and writing a letter for him!'

172

Rose gave a slight smile. 'And is that really going to satisfy your restless heart? Think about what you've just said, Daisy.'

Stubbornly, she refused to be put off. 'Writing letters wouldn't be my only job, and I never thought it would be. They need trained hospital staff in these places, and I'll still be using my nursing skills, so I don't see why you should object. Anyway, if I were to volunteer for one of the services like Immy, I could be sent anywhere.'

'You're not thinking about that, I hope,' Bert said sharply.

'I've thought about it quite a lot, as a matter of fact,' she muttered.

'And I think your father would have something to say about that, Daisy,' Rose said, just as sharply.

'I daresay, but I'm not a child any longer. I *am* eighteen now, and able to make decisions of my own. And right now, my decision is to go to bed and think about it, so please excuse me if I say goodnight.'

'Just a minute, young lady,' her aunt said more aggressively. 'Aren't you forgetting something?'

'Am I?'

'You're not a fully trained nurse yet, no matter what title you give yourself, and you won't be properly qualified for a good many years. You haven't really applied yourself to lectures, have you? I sometimes think the *idea* of being a nurse is what attracted you first of all, Daisy, and I'm not saying that you haven't become someone we're all proud of; but I do wonder if it really is a vocation.'

Daisy resisted the temptation to rush out of the room, upset by this censure that she hadn't wanted and hadn't expected. She was so sure Aunt Rose had been right behind her longing to be a nurse, and knew she had made a good job of it so far. But Aunt Rose was right, of course, and she was still only a probationer, with choices to be made. She didn't intend to say anything more about volunteering for the forces, which would only underline the family's opinion of her butterfly mind. But the more she thought about it, the more alluring it became.

Without knowing it, her aunt had already begun to squash the idea of working at a convalescent home, prompting Daisy into questioning the static occupation of being no more than a sympathetic helper while she wrote letters for strangers. She knew very well it wouldn't be just like that, nor only that. But the questioning had made it all sound flat and unexciting, despite the fact that every unknown soldier would be grateful for her help, just as Private Stokes had been.

The pros and cons went round and round in her head, but in the end she admitted that Aunt Rose was right abut one thing. It wouldn't satisfy her restless heart, at least not for ever. It had been good of Sister Macintosh to think she was well suited to it, but there were other things she could do. And that posed other questions. Was Sister Macintosh hinting tactfully that perhaps hospital nursing wasn't the right job for Daisy? And was she really satisfied exactly where she was? Working in a familiar environment, where she could go home each day?

She lay fully dressed on her bed, her hands behind her head, thinking of all the people she knew, who weren't doing just that. Elsie . . . well, Elsie had never been as adventurous as the rest of them, and she had found her destiny with Joe Preston. Joe had enlisted just before the war began, and Immy's young man, James Church, had been a soldier for much longer. She thought about Immy, her beautiful oldest sister whom she had always looked up to so much, and who hadn't wasted a precious minute in joining up with that friend of hers.

Even Baz – risking their father's anger by refusing to stand behind a shop counter in their one-time family business, and doing just what he wanted from the minute he had started working for the old ferryman on the River Avon, to going to sea on a fishing trawler. With Baz's cheek and thirst for adventure, he would probably end up as Admiral of the Fleet, Daisy thought with a grin.

So that left her. Yes, she was doing a worthwhile job, and yes, she had a way with words and an artistic talent bestowed on her by her mother, if Sister Macintosh's awkward compliment was to be believed. But she knew that, anyway, Daisy thought immediately, with a touch of her old confidence. She had inherited some of her mother's performing talent and her self-assurance, and once she had desperately wanted to follow her on to the stage, until Lucy's accident had decided her on a nursing career.

God! she was so shallow . . . did she really know *what* she wanted? She had wanted Cal – she still thought of Jed and Glenn with guilty affection . . . She turned her head on the pillow, momentarily caught by the brilliance of the moon through her window throwing playful shadows over the bed as a small breeze ruffled the leaves of the trees outside. She heard it sighing through the branches, as sweetly as a whispering voice. Telling her to go where her heart took her.

She sat up slowly, hugging her knees. Despite all the time she had worked at the hospital, she knew some thought she was only playing at it, because she hadn't done much of the formal and rigid training that was required. She was still not a *proper* nurse, as young Norman had once taunted her. It took years to be properly qualified, and even though she had once had the fanciful notion of possessing healing hands, it wasn't enough. And if she could waver like this, then she wasn't dedicated enough.

She saw the moonlit shadows dancing on her bedroom wall, as light and ethereal as fairy dancers. As light and beautiful as her mother, with the voice of an angel. Her guardian angel.

'Is that what you wanted me to do all along, Mother?' she whispered slowly. 'To be like you?'

Her eyes misted with tears, knowing she could never,

ever emulate the stardom of her mother. She could only be herself; but she was well aware that the women's army catered for all kinds of personnel. Even entertainers had their place. Only her father could be the one to advise her now. If he was absolutely horrified at the thought, then she would abandon it for ever.

Since her aunt and uncle seemed determined to avoid the issue, and she couldn't see her father until the following weekend, Daisy decided to talk it over with Alice Godfrey, telling her about the proposed transfer first. They walked along the beach, breathing in the salt air with some relief after a day on the wards.

'It's up to you, Daisy, but I have to say I've also had the feeling that you've become restless lately. So if you're getting the opportunity to move on and work in this convalescent home, perhaps you should take it.'

'Yes, but is it what I want? It won't be the same, anyway. I'll be doing far less real nursing, and more *caring* – which is all very noble, of course, but perhaps more suited to . . . well . . . to someone older,' she finished lamely.

'You think our wounded boys won't be happy to see a young and pretty face when they're convalescing?'

'Oh Lord, now you're putting me in the wrong. I knew you would!'

'Daisy, you have to make up your own mind on this. It seems to me you've reached a bit of a crossroads, anyway. You don't really want to stay at Weston General, and you're not relishing the prospect of this new job in darkest Norfolk or wherever it is. So what do you want to do?'

'I'd quite like to entertain the troops,' she said in a rush. 'And now that I've said it I know you'll think that's a really daft idea!'

'No I don't. I can't sing for toffee, but you were wonderful when we did the carol-singing for the patients at Christmas. Everyone said you were a star in the making, so why not?'

Daisy shook her head. 'I'm not a great singer. I can dance

far better. And I don't want to be a star. My mother was a star. I just want to be useful.'

Alice gave her shoulder an affectionate squeeze. 'Well, that may be so, but I reckon you'll be a star whatever you do, Daisy.'

She still hadn't mentioned any of it to her aunt and uncle before she went home on Saturday, and she was anxiously trying to think how to tell her father.

She was glad Elsie was there too, because she needed her moral support. It was an important decision she was about to make, and if either of them had their doubts – well, she wouldn't think that far ahead.

'So when are you going to tell us what's troubling you, Daisy? Out with it, girl,' Quentin said, when they had finally made enough small talk.

She took a deep breath. 'Several things, actually. But firstly I wanted to ask what you'd think if I was to give up nursing, Would it upset you too much?'

'It all depended on what else you wanted to do,' he said, knowing her too well. 'But I also think you're old enough to make your own decisions now. Something tells me you've already done that, and that this is just a formal gesture to keep your father happy.'

'No, it's more than that, truly. I want your approval, both of you.'

'Do I take it that you don't have your aunt's?' Quentin asked shrewdly.

'Not exactly,' Daisy said carefully. 'She doesn't know all of it, though.'

'Then wouldn't it be a good idea if we were to hear all of it?'

Elsie intervened quickly. 'Daisy, what's changed your mind about nursing? You were so keen, and I always thought it was something you wanted to do because of Lucy.'

'Perhaps that's all it was, and I *did* enjoy doing it and helping people, even though some of the things I have to

177

do are too ghastly to even think about. And I never told you everything about how awful it was on the hospital ship, and seeing those poor men brought on board – I'm sorry, Elsie, I know Joe was one of them – but you had to be there to know how terrible it was – how sickeningly terrible . . .'

'All right, Daisy,' her father said, seeing how Elsie's face had blanched. 'So you've had second thoughts about your choice of career, is that it?'

'Sister Macintosh says I could apply for a post in a Norfolk convalescent home. She seems to think I'm overflowing with sensitivity, but I got the distinct idea that what she really means is I don't have what it takes to make a good nurse.'

'I'm sure that's not the case, darling,' Elsie said at once.

'Well, I'm beginning to think it is. And ever since she put the thought into my head, I know I don't want to spend my time writing letters for wounded soldiers, or being at everyone's beck and call like a glorified maid. I'm sorry if that sounds awful, but I've been seriously thinking about something else, and now that I've got all of that off my chest, that's really what I wanted to talk to you about.'

She realised she was breathing erratically. It was crazy to feel so inhibited when she was with her own family, but she *needed* their approval. She needed their blessing. Her voice was high and quick as she blurted it all out.

'I'm old enough to volunteer for the ATS, Daddy, and they have all kinds of opportunities for women in the services now. I wouldn't want to go into the catering corps like Helen Church. I'm hopeless at cooking, anyway, and I can't drive, so I couldn't do what Immy's doing. But there are other things.'

As she paused, Quentin looked at her young and beautiful face, so like her mother's, the eyes the same wide velvety brown as Frances's were, the hair a mass of titian curls. He heard the breathy quality of her voice in her uncertainty, and saw the upward tilt of her chin and the natural grace with which she moved.

And he knew.

Fourteen

D aisy had the distinct feeling that her father didn't want to hear any of this, so that in the end she told him she was still making up her mind about joining up, and said nothing about trying to follow in her mother's footsteps. On Monday morning she still hadn't made up her mind what to do.

'Sister Macintosh didn't even try to persuade me one way or the other,' Daisy reported to Alice in a bit of a rage.'It's obvious she doesn't care what I do.'

'I wouldn't let her worry you. Anyway, you're going to do what you wanted, aren't you? But how about your family? I bet they had something to say.'

'My father had already telephoned Aunt Rose before I got home from Bristol, so she was prepared.' Daisy gave a wry grin. 'And there I was, all the way home in the train, wondering how I was going to break it to her that I was thinking of joining the ATS, and she didn't turn a single blessed hair!'

'Your auntie's a very progressive woman.'

Daisy laughed uneasily. 'Well, that's one word for it. But now what?'

'Go to an enlistment centre?'Alice said vaguely. 'Tell them you're ready and waiting to dance for the troops, and available for stage and screen.'

'I didn't say I was *that* good, although I knew most of my mother's routines, and after she got ill and couldn't remember half of them my father used to encourage me to do them at home to make her smile.'

She wasn't smiling now, remembering. It seemed such a long time ago, and yet she could remember as if it was yesterday, how the whole family – even Baz, before he got so cocky – used to applaud her efforts to copy her mother's dances and bring some of the glittering memories back to her.

'I shall miss you, Daisy,' Alice said. 'I wonder where they'll send you.'

'Lord knows. I've got to volunteer first, then be accepted.'

'Oh, you will be. They take anyone these days.'

She laughed at Daisy's indignant expression. 'I'm *teasing*, you idiot. Of course they'll take you, and be glad of your talents.'

Daisy nodded, although she felt far less confident now than before. It would almost have been a relief if someone had opposed her idea, she thought, with a silly burst of resentment against the whole world. But nobody had. The evacuee boys were already squabbling about who was going to have her bedroom, and Teddy was boasting that his sister was going to be a film star.

'Nobody's going to have Daisy's bedroom,' Aunt Rose told them firmly. 'It will always be ready for Daisy when she comes home on leave.'

The word had struck a note of caution in her. If she had thought she was being regimented before, she was going to be even more so now. She knew everyone at the hospital, and she was planning to work among strangers in a very grown-up world. She had a sudden attack of nerves.

Aunt Rose sensed it, following her up to the bedroom that night as she prepared for bed. 'This has to be your decision, Daisy, but please think very carefully about it. And always remember your mother's motto,' she advised. 'No matter how much you quake inside, keep your chin up and never show it.'

'I never thought Mother ever quaked before a performance!'

181

'That proves how clever she was, doesn't it?'

Whether it was true, or just something that Aunt Rose knew would make her feel better, she resolved to remember it. But a week later she was still dithering, feeling more unsure of herself than ever before.

By then the whole country was reeling because France had been doubly humiliated in defeat, being forced to sign the armistice with Germany in the same railway carriage in the forest of Compiègne where they themselves had been the victors in 1918. It was a cruel piece of diplomacy on Hitler's part; and to add to the threat of the British invasion being seriously felt by everyone now, the news came that German forces had occupied the Channel Islands. It seemed it could only be a matter of time before Britain, too, was overwhelmed by the enemy.

The thought of Daisy Caldwell performing a balletic dance routine for a bunch of war-toughened soldiers who just wanted to get home seemed pathetic.

She finally decided to talk things over with their Methodist minister, by whom Aunt Rose always set such store, and who knew the family well. She didn't have to take his advice, but he would be an independent observer, and it was better than rushing into things as she usually did.

He listened sympathetically, as always; and because she was nervous, she spoke more quickly than usual.

'Once I tell the recruitment people what I've been doing, I'm sure they'll put me straight into a medical unit, but that's not what I want to do. In fact, I'm not at all sure that I'm suited to nursing after all.'

'I doubt that anyone else would say that, Daisy. I always hear glowing reports of you from your aunt. Do you think you're more suited to being under enemy fire should the need arise? or would you go to pieces the moment you heard a German shell overhead?'

Daisy's face burned. 'I'm not a coward, Mr Penfold. You know I worked for several weeks on a hospital ship. I don't think I would go to pieces in a crisis, but I feel I can do other things to help the war effort.'

'And what would those things be?'

She bit her lip, knowing how feeble it would sound to say she could dance quite well, and she could sing a bit, and she had inherited her mother's talent; therefore she thought she could entertain the troops to keep up their morale. But she remembered what Aunt Rose had told her, stuck her chin in the air, looked him straight in the eyes, and said it anyway.

His voice held a tinge of amusement. 'So you would be no use as an ambulance-driver, or a trainee motor mechanic, or—'

'No, of course not! I believe I would be of most use as an entertainer. You know my mother's reputation, Mr Penfold, and in all modesty I do think I have a little of her talent. I thought I could be a dancer,' she finished lamely.

'I see. But you don't have any professional performing experience, do you, my dear? Stop and think what that means for a moment. I doubt that a well-brought-up young lady dancing in front of a crowd of battle-scarred soldiers would get away without a great deal of cat-calling and probably a whole lot worse. Could you deal with that?'

When she didn't answer, he went on more gently: 'Apart from which, Daisy, I don't think the army is in the business of hiring unknown entertainers in the middle of a war, nor letting you pick and choose what you want to do! And you're still very young. If you really want to change direction from nursing, have you thought about working in a munitions factory, for instance?'

Daisy held on to her temper, knowing he was being calm and sensible, but making her feel a child at the same time. She tried not to react angrily, knowing you didn't do such things in front of a minister of the church.

'I've thought about it,' she said evenly. 'But my sister

Imogen is in the ATS and I've heard good things about it, so I wanted to do my bit there too.'

'Is your sister an entertainer as well?'

From his sceptical tone now, Daisy guessed that he wondered if the entire Caldwell family was about to dance its way into the war effort.

'No. She used to work for a housing agent before he left Bristol and went to live in Cornwall when the war began. Immy's a lance-corporal now. She's the official driver for a Captain Beckett, and I believe they're attached to the War Office. It's all pretty hush-hush, of course, so all I know is that my sister is based in London now.'

If it was stretching it a bit to wave Immy's credentials in front of him, Daisy had no qualms about it. *Look them straight in the eye and keep your nerve*, she remembered . . . and she was doing just that.

He leaned forward and patted her hand like a Dutch uncle. 'Daisy, why don't you give this a little more thought before you do anything at all? But I'm very glad you came to me before doing anything rash, and I want you to know that my door is always open if you want to come and talk to me about it some more.'

'Thank you, Mr Penfold,' she murmured.

She knew this was his way of dismissing her, and that she had really got nowhere at all. If she had expected easy answers, she hadn't got them. In fact, it had complicated matters. It had all seemed so simple when she had first thought about it, and now she didn't know where she was.

'Don't thank me. But young girls who think that wearing a uniform is glamorous won't get very far. You'll be expected to muck in with everyone else, and you won't get any favours by passing yourself off as an entertainer, nor by mentioning your mother's name as a password to fame and glory. I also suspect that her style of dancing, however beautiful in its day, is somewhat passé now.'

Daisy felt a little shock at this sting in the tail, just when she thought he was being his usual benevolent self. And he could be right . . . but she wasn't going to let his disapproval put her off just yet. She had once thought that dancing was going to be her destiny. But she had also thought the same thing about nursing, when she'd come to Lucy's rescue at the Luckwells' annual gymkhana and known what to do about her sprained foot. Right now she was blowing hot and cold like the wind, she thought angrily.

Alice grinned knowingly when she told her she had gone to see the minister.

'So you decided against marching straight to the recruitment office and telling them that dancing was the only job you would consider?'

Daisy was tempted to say airily that that was exactly what she had planned to do, but she couldn't quite bring herself to lie so blatantly.

'I thought it was prudent to talk it over with Mr Penfold first, but for all the good it did me I might as well have consulted Teddy,' she snapped. 'Or *you*!'

'Oh well, pardon me, and the best of luck, whatever you choose to do,' Alice said, deciding to retreat out of an argument she couldn't win, and clearly thinking Daisy had about as much chance of getting her own way as of persuading Adolph to clear out of France and let everyone get back to normal. As it was, they parted on chilly terms.

Daisy had already written to Immy, and she was longing to get a letter back to tell her she wasn't being entirely crazy; but instead of a letter she got a telephone call from her early that evening.

'I hope you know what you're doing, Daisy,' Immy said. 'I always thought you were happy being a nurse.'

'So I was, but not enough to do it for life.'

'You'd hardly be in the ATS for life – at least, I hope not. We all hope it will be over soon, but from the sound of it . . . well, never mind about all that now. I gather the family doesn't object.'

From the way she said it Daisy knew she had already discussed it with everyone else, and it didn't improve her feeling of being a grown-up.

'Oh Immy, I thought you'd understand! You joined up the minute you could, so why shouldn't I?'

'No reason at all, darling,' Immy said, after a brief pause. 'But you know the army has a habit of sending people to the opposite ends of the country from where they belong, and giving them the least likely jobs. You might just end up as a wireless operator.'

'I doubt it. I don't know one end of a battery from the other.' But it was exactly as Mr Penfold had said, she fumed. She could end up doing anything.

'They'd jolly well soon teach you if they thought you had the aptitude for it; but knowing you, little sister, you'll probably come up smiling. You and Baz usually do,' she added. 'Good luck, anyway, and keep me posted.'

Immy kept the smile in her voice until she had replaced the receiver in the draughty hall of the small hotel, not wanting to put a damper on what Daisy obviously thought was her new vocation. Not wanting to tell her how London and the south-east were being seriously prepared for the invasion, with barbed wire in the streets, railway station signs blacked out and sandbags piled up around the most precious and vulnerable buildings.

The evacuation of children, which had been suspended during the early months of the year in what had been dubbed the phoney war, was in full swing again now, including the transportation of many of them to Canada. Immy couldn't imagine how terrifying it must be to be sent far away from everything that was familiar when you were so young and bewildered by it all.

As she heard James's voice behind her, she swung round into his arms, regardless of whether or not the hotel landlady might be in the vicinity.

'Are you going to stand there staring at that telephone for ever, sweetheart, or are we going out to do the town?'

She raised the smile to her lips again. This was the start of their precious forty-eight-hour pass. She knew now that it was also James's embarkation leave – that in a few days' time he would be setting sail with his regiment – and both of them were desperate not to waste a moment of their time together, having no idea when the next time might be.

'We're going out on the town,' she said huskily.

And afterwards, when they came back after dark, fumbling their way through the blacked-out streets after an evening of reckless laughter and dancing at the Hammersmith Palais, what then? *What then . . . ?* Immy didn't dare to think that far ahead, but the thought that these two days and nights might be all they had was never far from her mind. She knew it couldn't be far from James's mind too.

He was a red-blooded young man who loved her passionately, and she adored him in return. And they weren't children. They knew what could and did happen in a war. Daisy's young man had been killed when his aircraft had been shot out of the sky, and one of James's friends had died when his tank had been blown up. Elsie's husband had been in danger of losing his foot after Dunkirk. Such things were part of the sacrifice of war. It was a knowledge that drove people to make the most of the moment, knowing it might never come again.

For all Immy and James knew, tonight, and tomorrow night, might be all the nights they would ever share.

'What are you thinking about now?' James saw the way she ran her tongue around her bottom lip as she always did when she was thinking deeply.

'Just that I love you,' she said softly. 'And that I don't want to waste a minute of these two days. So what shall we do tomorrow?'

'Let's decide that after tonight,' he answered, his voice telling her nothing.

'You're right. So now that I've tried to put Daisy right, I'm going to see if there's any hot water, have a good wash, then go to my room and change into my dancing frock. Then you can tell me how beautiful I look!'

'You always look beautiful to me. You know that, Immy.'

'Well, we'd better not stand here in the hall admiring one another any longer, or people will definitely start looking at us oddly,' she said with a laugh, because when his voice deepened like that she felt a rush of love for him that almost overwhelmed her, making her weak, making her long for the kind of fulfilment she knew could only come one way. And as yet, she hadn't known it.

When they left the hotel later that evening, there were predictably no taxis to be had, but it wasn't far to walk, and as they made their way carefully to the Palais, arms around one another for safety, Immy had the certain feeling that tonight was going to be a turning point in her life.

He had once called their love his talisman. When they had realised the miracle of having fallen in love after years of being no more than friends, he had asked nothing more than to know that she belonged to him. But she didn't, not fully, not yet. Not in the biblical sense. In her mother's, and certainly in her grandmother's day, it would have been thought of as another kind of sacrifice.

Even though she was very aware that he wanted her as much as she wanted him, it was something she and James had never yet discussed, and he had never asked anything more of her than she was willing to give. A special touch, an extra caress, a deeper kiss . . . but tonight she was going to give him all of herself. She knew it as surely as she breathed.

Inside the dance hall, the myriad lights from the revolving chandelier were dazzling after the darkness outside, and the orchestra was already playing a waltz as she floated into his arms. No enemy threats could diminish the pleasure they found in one another. Nor even the distant sound of air-raid sirens and the dull thud of shell-fire that frequently rocked the ground like an earthquake waiting to happen.

This was their night, and when, leaving the Palais several hours later, they saw the indigo of the sky criss-crossed with searchlights seeking out enemy planes and the occasional silver flash as one of them was caught in their beams, it only added to the urgency and wantonness of scurrying back to their hotel, urged on by an air-raid warden, suggesting that they might want to get down to the shelters or the Underground for safety.

'What do you want to do, Immy? Do you fancy sharing the night with a few hundred others crammed into the Underground?'

'I do not! I only want to share this night with you!'

She spoke as recklessly as Daisy at that moment, the words leaving her lips before she could think properly, and she felt his arm tighten around her waist as she prayed that he wouldn't think her too brazen.

'My thoughts exactly, Immy darling.'

She felt her heart beat faster at his words. She wanted him so much, but she was nervous that she wouldn't be all that he expected of her. She was twenty-one years old and she didn't know how to behave with a man in the most intimate situation of all. Her mind blotted out her brief fling with a brash young man who had worked on a Bristol newspaper.

Morgan Raine had wanted her too, and had been so very seductive in pursuing her, awakening her to her first heady taste of young love . . . and she had been so near to giving in to him, until she found out that she wasn't the only girl in his life. She had thought herself in love then, but that was before she had found the true love of her life.

How you actually behaved in that most intimate situation of all was something they never taught you at school, and she had no one to advise her. Elsie would have known, but Elsie was far away in Bristol, and besides, you couldn't ask a younger sister such basic things. It was too humiliating. It wasn't the right order of things.

She was gasping by the time they reached the hotel. She was out of breath from racing through the streets as carefully as they could, considering the black-out, but with their way partially lit by the brightness of the moon and the weaving searchlights. And she was out of breath with nerves.

'Immy,' James said, catching her to him, seconds before they went indoors. 'You know I would never hurt you, don't you? And you know – you do know – what I want . . .'

She realised that the longing in his voice was mixed with uncertainty and a kind of desperation, and she was suddenly aware that he was nervous too. Not in the same way that she was, perhaps, but nervous of her reaction.

She felt an acute sense of tenderness towards him then, realising that a man could feel this way too. That it wasn't all just rush and fumble, the way Morgan Raine had tried to seduce her on a Bristol hillside. She leaned forward and kissed James's lips, suddenly calm, and in control of her destiny.

'I know, James. And I want it too,' she whispered against his mouth.

Immy was required to leave details of her whereabouts at all times, in case she should be needed urgently for any reason. Even a forty-eight-hour pass wasn't excluded, and when the hotel landlady told her over breakfast that there had been a message for her to call Captain Beckett, she flew into a panic at once.

'He didn't say it was urgent,' the woman said. 'But I suppose you never know these days, do you?' she added, eyeing her and James with a professional and experienced look.

Not that she had any objection to what they did, providing they didn't wake up the rest of her lodgers . . . besides, these two were a particularly handsome couple, and she'd had a bit of a fling with a fellow or two in her time. She didn't begrudge them their fun.

'James, I'll have to call him straight away,' Immy said. She was totally flustered, as gauche and guilty as a child caught stealing apples, and desperately hoping the landlady didn't think Captain Beckett was her husband or father.

'Calm down, darling. I'll come to the telephone with you,' he said, having no more appetite for breakfast, and knowing that this call could only mean that their leave was going to be cut short. They had had just one night – one spectacular night – and who knew how long it was going to have to last them?

Immy asked the operator for Captain Beckett's private number and waited for what seemed like an age before she got through.

'It's Lance-Corporal Caldwell answering your call, sir,' she remembered to say formally, even though her heart was jumping and her teeth seemed too big for her mouth.

'Imogen, I wouldn't have interrupted your leave unless it was important, but I thought you would want to know the news right away. Word came through just after midnight that Bristol has been bombed.'

'*What?*' For a moment she couldn't take in what he was saying. Her eyes glazed, and she couldn't seem to hold the receiver. She felt James take it out of her hand and heard him speak rapidly into it.

'Captain Beckett, this is James Church, Imogen's fiancé. She's feeling rather unwell, so can you tell me what's happened? I gather it's something to do with Bristol, and we both have families there.'

Immy grabbed the phone from him, her face on fire. She knew he had called her his fiancée for the sake of her reputation, although they weren't officially engaged yet; but such details were hardly important now. A fine soldier she would appear if she crumbled at a piece of news over a telephone. She drew a deep breath and spoke as crisply as she could, holding the receiver away from her ear so that James could hear every word clearly too.

'I'm sorry about that, sir. Can you give me the details?'

'There have been some casualties,' he said cautiously, 'and buildings have been flattened. I gather much of it was around the railway station area, but other than that the reports are still sketchy. But I thought you would want to check with your family, Lance-Corporal, and then contact me again.'

'Thank you, sir,' she said, choked. What he meant was that if her family was in any way involved, she could take a few more days' compassionate leave.

She knew the form. She knew the unspoken words. And right now, the thought whirling around in her head was that while she and James had been making love, their beloved city was being devastated by the enemy. Their families could have died. It was a reckoning – and she knew she was letting her panic take her to ridiculous places. It wasn't their fault. It wasn't their penance.

'I'll see about a train right away,' James said tensely. 'If not, I know some people who might find us some transport going west.'

'Yes, but first of all I have to phone my father to see if he and Elsie are all right,' she stammered.

His voice was strong and reassuring. 'I'm sure they will be. Vicarage Street is miles away from Temple Meads, and so is Clifton.'

She was dumb for a moment, and then she was flooded with guilt. His home was in Clifton, and he'd be frantic too, and she had thought only of herself.

'But James, you can't get to Bristol and back in your short embarkation leave,' she almost wept, wondering how these precious few days had suddenly gone so terribly wrong. And through no fault of their own.

'I'll manage,' he said grimly. 'Now, do your telephoning, darling, and let me see about transport.'

He was gone while she was still dithering, but when

she tried to get through to their home number and then the number of Preston's Emporium, all the lines were clogged. In desperation, she called Aunt Rose's number instead, praying that someone would be there. The voice that answered was small and scared.

'Oh, Immy, thank God,' Daisy gasped. 'We wanted to get hold of you, but we didn't know where you were, and it's just so awful!'

Fifteen

'Daisy, keep calm, and tell me exactly what's happened,' Immy said sharply, aware that the landlady was hovering behind her with a cup of tea.

As if warm weak tea was going to solve everything, when everyone knew it should be hot and strong for shock – and also very sweet, if only there hadn't been a sugar shortage. She pulled herself together, and listened to her sister's babbling words.

'It was so frightening, Immy. We could hear the bombing from here and everything was shaking. Every time we heard the sound of enemy planes the boys started screaming, and Norman was yelling that he was going home, and of course Ronnie wet the bed, and we were changing sheets in the middle of the night, and Uncle Bert was shouting at us not to panic, and Aunt Rose was practically crying and snapping at him that he should have done as Daddy always said and built a shelter in the garden, but he never would because we had the cellar here, and eventually we all went down there, and we've been up for hours—'

'For God's sake, Daisy,' Immy practically screamed at her. 'Stop blithering on about what you were all doing. I can't get through to Bristol on the phone, and I'm desperate to know if Daddy and Elsie are safe.'

She heard Daisy's audibly deep breath before she spoke more huffily. 'Well, I'm sorry, but I'm trying to tell you! Elsie phoned a couple of hours ago. She was still a bit shaky because she'd been in the house alone when the air raid started, and she had to go down to that miserable shelter in the garden that she hates. Daddy was out on fire-fighting duty and he's got a nasty gash on his forehead from some flying glass and had to have it treated, but apart from that he's all right.'

Immy felt her heart clench. Even though she was in uniform, this war had seemed so far away until now. It had been a war that was mostly happening in Europe, and now it was on their own doorstep. Not just here in London and the vulnerable south-east counties, but at home in Bristol. She felt as young and confused as Daisy as that moment. No, even younger, as vulnerable as a baby.

'Where did the bombs fall, Daisy?' she asked, knowing she had to know. Even saying it felt so unreal. It was their beautiful city . . .

'It's all been on the wireless. Haven't you been listening?'

No. I've been in bed with my lover . . .

'No. So just tell me, will you? James and I are coming home as soon as we can get on a train, by the way. He's gone to see about it now.'

'Oh, I forgot you were spending your leave with James.'

There was a tiny pause, and Immy gritted her teeth, guessing that her little sister would be putting all kinds of interpretations on that statement, and knowing that she would be right.

'Daisy!'

'Sorry. Lower Maudlin Street was hit first, and then the bombs fell all around Temple Meads station – oh, I wonder if the trains will get through? I don't think the lines were hit, but it's all a bit bloody, isn't it? Sorry again, but you know what I mean. They say some people have been killed and there are lots of wounded, and a lot of building damage too. Daddy was out all night, and Elsie said he's exhausted, but he still went to open the shop this morning as usual.'

'Is Elsie all right?' Immy said anxiously, remembering her condition.

'She says so, but I know Joe will start making her think seriously about going to his family in Yorkshire after this. I doubt that she'd leave Daddy though.'

'That's up to them to sort out,' Immy said. 'Look, darling, I'll have to go and pack my things, but please let Elsie know I hope to see her very soon.'

'All right. Oh, and Immy – I just want to tell you that as far as I'm concerned, this changes everything, of course.'

'Does it? What about?' Immy said with a frown.

She couldn't think about anything else but relief that their house was still standing and her family was safe. At least, for now. And if that was selfish, she couldn't help it. When it came right down to it, they all had to think of themselves and the people they loved.

Daisy reverted to her usual rushing words.'Well, I'm not leaving the hospital now. I can't, can I? Who knows when it might be our turn? So I've decided to stay where I am and get some proper qualifications. I may not be the world's best nurse, but I know where I'm needed.'

She hung up, fighting back the tears, not wanting to hear any platitudes from Immy, whatever her feelings were on her choice. It wasn't just the bombing that had decided her, anyway; because before all the horror of learning that Bristol had been hit last night, Private Stokes had died.

War was bloody, bloody, bloody, but Stokesey had been progressing nicely, and there had been no indication of the massive ulcer that had finally burst and killed him. Daisy had just posted his last cheerful letter to his wife, and now she had voluntarily offered to write another one, which would be more sensitive and personal than the one Mrs Stokes would eventually receive from Stokesey's CO. Daisy was definitely needed here, in however small a way.

'Who was on the phone?' she heard Aunt Rose say as

she went back to bundling Ronnie's soiled sheets into the copper and lighting the gas beneath it.

'It was Immy. She'd heard the news, and she and James Church are trying to get to Bristol sometime today.'

'Good,' Rose said, with only half her mind on what Daisy was saying.

It was only natural that Imogen would be anxious about her family, but privately she thought it a shame that her eldest niece had to curtail her few days' leave like this, especially with that nice young man of hers whom Rose liked enormously. Rose was far more canny about what went on in the world than her nieces might believe. Her generation had already been through one war in their lifetime, and she knew how intense passions could be when you never knew what tomorrow might bring.

Last night was undoubtedly a foretaste of what they could expect from now on. They were far away from the capital, but Rose had never believed they would be safe from Hitler's bombs. Bristol's docks and aircraft industry were too vital a target for the enemy to ignore. She had her own ideas about what she was going to suggest to her brother. If she and Bert could accommodate various children and dogs in this big old house, they could surely accommodate Elsie – and a baby, in due course, she reminded herself. It wouldn't be all beer and skittles, as they said, but a baby in the house would surely cheer everybody up.

She realised Daisy was fiddling with the copper stick, and asked her mildly if she intended standing about all day, or if she was ever going to get on with it and tip some soap suds into the water. And then, Rose thought grimly, before she set out for the hospital Daisy could help her create a proper shelter in the cellar, instead of the makeshift arrangements they had used last night. It was time to prepare for the unimaginable.

'I've been trying to think how to tell you something,' Daisy said at last. 'And I don't quite know how to do it. I know you've always thought I could never make up my mind about anything, chopping and changing like the wind—'

Her aunt broke in with a small smile. 'And now you've decided that perhaps you made the right choice after all, all that time ago when you told us you wanted to be a nurse.'

'Sometimes I think you're a mind-reader!' Daisy said, confused and relieved, because her aunt had spoken so calmly, instead of thinking her an irresponsible idiot who couldn't think sensibly about anything.

'No, my love, I'm no mind-reader. I just had a feeling that all the passion you put into it couldn't have been a waste of time. But you had to see it for yourself. It's your life, and you can't live anyone else's.'

'Not even my mother's,' Daisy said, knowing it at last.

'So are we going to sweep out the cellar and get some blankets down there ready for emergencies?' Rose said briskly. 'At least the boys enjoyed camping down there last night, and seemed to think of it as an adventure.'

'Some adventure! But I really haven't got time, Aunt Rose, honestly!'

Her aunt let her go, knowing she still had to inform Sister Macintosh of her decision, hoping that she still had a job at Weston General. She also had to make her peace with Alice, who had been decidedly stuffy towards her lately. But all such petty squabbles were forgotten in the shock news that Bristol had been bombed.

'Daisy, have you heard from your father and sister? Are they all right?' Alice greeted her anxiously.

'Yes, thank heavens. And Alice – we are still friends, aren't we?'

'Of course we are,' the older girl said, giving her arm a squeeze. 'It was a rum do last night thought, wasn't it? Were you scared?'

Daisy was tempted to say no, and then caught the knowing look on Alice's face. 'Of course I was scared. Weren't you?'

'Of course. So now we've both admitted that we're human, let's see what we have to do today.'

'I know what I have to do,' Daisy said, as the memory of yesterday's happenings rushed in on her. 'I have to compose a letter to Private Stokes's wife.'

'It's not really your job, Daisy. You shouldn't get too attached to the patients, and you don't owe him anything.'

'I think I do. And anyway, it's something I want to do – well, sort of. I've told Sister Macintosh I intend to do it, anyway, and I'm not backing out of it.'

'You're a good kid, aren't you, Daisy?'

Daisy shrugged. 'Not so as you'd notice! Anyway, I'd better go and see Sister before she catches us standing around gossiping.'

She went off with her chin in the air. She wasn't a kid any more, and she'd done her best to calm down the three terrified young boys last night when they'd firmly believed that Adolph himself was going to come goose-stepping into the cellar and kill them all.

Sister Macintosh listened coolly to all that Daisy had to say.

'So now you've decided your place is here with us, have you, Nurse?'

'If you'll still have me,' Daisy said humbly, fixing her eyes somewhere between the woman's massive shelf of a bosom and her starched collar.

'Well, I suppose we'll have to, since you've proved yourself so far,' Sister said with the glimmer of a smile on her lips.

Then the smile faded. 'In any case, we're expecting casualties from last night's air raid, and since this is more than likely to be a regular occurence from now on, I can't afford to let any of my nurses go. I know you've been restless on the ward lately, so I'm going to recommend that you do a spell on ambulance duty. There will be fully trained medical staff on board, of course, but it will give you useful experience in seeing how to deal with real emergencies.'

She was dismissed, feeling unsure what to make of this latest change. It was one thing to deal with changing bandages and taking temperatures, and mopping up various kinds of disgusting messes, but she had never been called to the scene of an accident before. Or the aftermath of an air raid.

Then common sense took over. Hadn't she already seen chaos in action on the hospital ship, where you never knew what you might see next? Hadn't she already observed emergency treatments without the clinical comfort of a hospital theatre, performed in crowded conditions on a rolling ship where the skill of the surgeon's hands was vital? This was one more challenge to test whether or not she really had the makings of a nurse.

She went home at the end of the afternoon to a new kind of chaos. Norman and Ronnie's mother had arrived from Wales with a very large man with a weather-beaten face, whom the boys were being urged to call Uncle Ivor.

'They're coming wiv us, anyway, missus,' their mother was shouting to Aunt Rose. 'Me sister in Cardiff don't really have room for us, but my gentleman's got a big enough place for us all, and now that the kids are in more danger 'ere than they were back in London, we might as well have 'em wiv us.'

'But Mrs Turvey, it's not Weston that's been bombed,' Rose said impatiently. 'I assure you we're quite safe here—'

'Oh ah, for the time being! But I ain't taking any chances wiv my kids, and Ivor wants to 'ave 'em safe wiv us, don't you, Ivor?'

'That's right, love,' he said in his thick Welsh accent. 'We've got plenty of room on the farm and the boys will love the animals, I'm sure. It's up in mid-Wales, see, so well away from any risk of air raids.'

'And don't tell me any of that other stuff about having to check with the billeting people,' Mrs Turvey went on. 'Ivor's already phoned the woman at the Town Hall, and she says they're my kids and I can do what I like wiv 'em. And you want to come and live wiv me, don't you, kids?'

'*Yes!* We want to go wiv our mum!' they shouted in unison, though Ronnie still hung back suspiciously at this new uncle. He could hardly remember his dad, but he knew he didn't talk a bit like this one. But if Norman thought he was all right, he supposed he did too.

'You can't take them away just like this without giving us any warning,' Bert said angrily. 'It's too much of an upheaval for them.'

'Yes we can. We're staying at a B & B that Ivor knows in Sand Bay for tonight, and they can bunk in wiv us,' the woman said. 'So they can go and get all their things and we won't be bothering you no more.'

'They're no bother, and I think you're making a big mistake,' Rose said stiffly, ignoring Bert's restraining hand on her arm.

Mrs Turvey stared her out defiantly, as large and blowsy as ever.

'No, I ain't. If I was taking 'em back to London it would be a big mistake, but we ain't going back there. We're staying wiv Ivor on his farm from now on.'

Daisy knew better than to join in this argument. She'd tried once before, but now, with the big, burly farmer folding his arms and forming a more than solid unit with the boys' mother, she held her tongue. They all knew Mrs Turvey was in the right, anyway. They were her children, and personally, Daisy sometimes thought they had been more trouble than they were worth.

But of course, Aunt Rose had got fond of them – and so had Teddy, she realised, seeing how he was snivelling in a corner, with his arms clutching George. It would be a real blow to her brother to lose his ready-made companions like this. While they continued arguing she managed to get him out of the room by bribing him with a drink of lemonade and a slice of cake in the kitchen.

'Do you want to come and have a game of snap in my room? George can come too, if you like,' she went on, making a rare concession.

He glared at her, not taken in for a minute by her tactics. 'Are Norman and Ronnie going to be taken away by that lady and man?'

Daisy sighed. 'The lady is their mother, Teddy, and it's only natural that they want to go and live with her.'

'They've got us, so why do they want to live with her? I don't live with my mother,' he said baldly, his lips starting to quiver.

'I know you don't, darling, but that's different. None of us can do that, but I'm sure you'd want to if you could. We all would.'

She was on delicate ground, and she wasn't sure that she was making things any better, but she hardly knew how to deal with this. Teddy rarely mentioned their mother, and she didn't want to revive his last memory of her hurtling over the cliffs into the Avon Gorge. She never wanted to think of that terrible day – as bad in all their minds as anything Hitler could deliver.

'Can me and George sleep in your bed tonight then?' Teddy said next.

Daisy stared, forcing her mind away from her mother's death to the sudden perversity of this question.

'Why on earth would you want to do that?' she said.

His bottom lip jutted out. 'I might cry all night if Norman and Ronnie aren't in the house; but if me and George can cuddle you, I prob'ly won't feel so bad.'

The devious little devil, Daisy thought at once. So much for caring what happened to the other boys. Kids were so bloody selfish – and she certainly didn't relish the thought of having George in her bed, filling the bedroom with his doggy smells and snuffling and snorting and twitching all night . . . but she saw how warily Teddy was watching her now, and knew the little blighter would create all kinds of fuss if she didn't agree to this, and Aunt Rose would be upset enough at losing two of her ewe lambs . . .

'Just this once, then,' she said firmly. 'One night only, do you understand?'

By the time Mrs Turvey and her Ivor had done exactly what they wanted to do and packed up everything belonging to her boys, it was time for them to say goodbye. By now, Teddy had gone back downstairs and was beginning to get tearful about their departure again.

'You can have some of my old comics,' Norman told him. 'I've left 'em in the bedroom, and you can cut 'em up if you like.'

'Will you take care of Jemima too?' Ronnie asked, sniffing anxiously.

'Who the blazes is Jemima?' his mother said, pausing as she rummaged through their cardboard suitcases to check that they had everything they had come with. 'You're a bit young to be takin' up with girls, ain't you, Ronnie boy?'

She dug Ivor in the ribs as she spoke, roaring with laughter as if she had said something funny, and Ronnie's face turned crimson.

'Jemima's my hen that lays brown eggs,' he shouted.

'Don't you worry, Ronnie,' Uncle Bert said, seeing how important this was to him. 'We'll take care of everything, and if you ever want to come and see us again, I'm sure you'll find that Jemima will remember you.'

'Yes, well, I doubt that that will happen,' his mother replied. 'What with these air raids now, we want to get the boys as far away from here as possible.'

'We shall miss you both,' Aunt Rose said suddenly, having hardly said a word for the last ten minutes as she

203

watched the preparations for departure. 'You've been good boys—'

She couldn't say any more as Ronnie suddenly threw himself into her arms and hugged her, burying his face in her shoulder.

'Go on now,' she said with a great effort. 'You'll have your mum to tuck you up in bed tonight, and I bet there are lots more hens on the farm where you're going to live.'

She silently begged Farmer Ivor to say that there were, and to her relief he wasn't slow to brag.

'Course there are, and ducks too, and lots of sheep. And there's always rabbits in the fields for your mam to make a stew.'

'Auntie Rose makes rabbit pies,' Ronnie muttered.

'Well, we'll make them as well,' his mother said impatiently. 'Now come on, you two, say goodbye nicely to the folks for looking after you, before we change our minds about taking you at all.'

The house was very quiet after they had all gone. Daisy was still stunned at the speed with which their busy and noisy household had suddenly become so depleted. Her Uncle Bert had gone down to his shed, unable to think of anything useful to say, and needing to adjust in his own way. Rose did the only thing she could think of to keep her hands busy. Plunging them into flour and lard and then kneading the dough was always a good way to vent off anger or frustration.

'Do you want to help me make some jam tarts, Teddy?' she said, seeing his wan face. 'And we'll make some fairy cakes too, if you like,' she added.

'Can I lick the spoon?' he asked hopefully, knowing he wouldn't have to share the delicious scrapings in the bowl with anyone else now.

'Of course you can, darling. It'll be all yours.'

The phone rang while she was up to her elbows in flour. 'I'll answer it,' Daisy called. It was Imogen.

'Where are you?' Daisy said at once.

'At home, and everything's all right with us and with James's parents. Father's preparing to go out on fire-fighting duty again tonight, so we shall stay here with Elsie. We both have to go back to London tomorrow, I'm afraid, but I think we've almost persuaded Elsie to come down to Weston to move in with you all. She really thinks it's her duty to stay here with Father, but we've told her it's completely ridiculous when he's on call, and likely to be more so in the future. What do you think? Will Aunt Rose have any objection?'

Daisy stared at the phone, feeling the most ridiculous urge to laugh hysterically. She couldn't think that Aunt Rose would have any objection at all, since her sole aim in life seemed to be care for other people's children.

'Is everything all right?' she heard her aunt say anxiously from the kitchen.

'Hold on a minute, Immy,' Daisy said. She called out the message, asking if there would be any objection to taking in another lodger.

She paused then, as the most extraordinary sound came from her aunt. For a second, it didn't register, and then she realised it was laughter. And Teddy, being Teddy, immediately joined in, clapping his hands and spraying flour around the kitchen until they were both wreathed in a fine white cloud.

'Oh, Daisy, of course it's all right. And isn't it just as I always said? The Good Lord giveth and the Good Lord taketh away. Only this time, bless His generous heart, He's done it in reverse.'

'Aunt Rose says of course it's all right, Immy,' Daisy repeated hastily into the phone, wondering uneasily if it always took church-minded folk like this, and if religion was finally going to her head.

'Well, you all seem to be having a jolly good time there, considering what happened here last night,' she heard

Immy say, a little indignantly. 'Are you having a party or something?'

'Not exactly. We've just lost the last of our evacuees today, so you can tell Elsie it'll be marvellous for us to be just family again.'

'I didn't say it was definite,' Immy said, with what Daisy thought was complete contrariness. 'I only said we think we've *almost* persuaded her. You know how long she takes to make up her mind about anything. Well, except marrying Joe. She's heard he's being sent to a convalescent home near Oxford, by the way; then he hopes to get some leave before rejoining his regiment.'

'And he'll persuade her to get out of Bristol if anybody can.'

'Well, he hasn't done it yet, has he? Anyway, James and I are going to see his parents now, so I'll have to go, Daisy. Take care of yourself.'

'And you too,' Daisy said automatically.

Immy had been unusually impatient with her, she registered. But she supposed it was reasonable, when she had had to cut short her little holiday with James to come flying down here to check that everyone was all right. They hadn't *had* to, of course – unless it was a touch of guilty conscience that had pushed them into it, she thought with a suspicious thrill.

For a moment, Daisy wondered exactly when it was that they had heard the news of the Bristol bombing and, more importantly, just what they had been doing at the time. It was so *daring* for them to have spent their few days' leave together, and although Daisy was perfectly sure they would have booked separate rooms, as any respectable couple would in a respectable hotel, it didn't mean they had to *stay* separate at all times, did it?

Since she had never actually experienced such excitement herself, she couldn't really think *what* they had been doing, and she gave up imagining, and went back to the kitchen, where Teddy's face was already plastered with pastry and jam.

It didn't take much to cheer you up when you were only eight years old, she thought, though it might be a different matter tonight when he started missing Norman and Ronnie properly; and she resigned herself to sharing her bed with him and the exuberant George.

Soon, if all went according to Sister Macintosh's suggestion, she was going to start a new phase in her nursing career, when she went out on rescue patrol in the ambulance.

Sixteen

One of Aunt Rose's favourite sayings was that one swallow didn't make a summer – and it was just as obvious that one air raid didn't make a war. Bristol became used to the almost nightly sound of the air-raid sirens, even when little came of them. Reading the local newspaper reports, Bert said caustically that he reckoned Hitler was just trying out his planes to see how far into England they could get over the Channel before dropping their bombs wildly.

Besides which, the swift retaliation of the RAF and the south-east defences were doing a sterling job in warding off the enemy attacks. When they reached the south-west, some of their bombs fell harmlessly into fields and ditches and only scared the cattle, and whenever such events were reported people cheered and jeered and said it only showed the incompetence of the German air force.

'That's not such a good thing,' Rose reminded Bert. 'If they start dropping bombs indiscriminately because they can't find their targets, then next time it could be a school or a row of houses. If they're aiming for the docks and know what the target is supposed to be, they're not so likely to hit ordinary people going about their daily business, are they?'

'That's true, Aunt Rose,' Daisy put in, the night before she finally started her new duties, feeling more than a touch of unease at wondering just how many ordinary people were going to become part of her rescue routine in future.

Bert went on doggedly, refusing to let them stop his flow.

'And you women have got blinkers on if you think it's the same for both sides, and that our boys in blue always know where to drop their bombs. We're all potential casualties in a war, Rose—'

'Well, I know that—'

'It's not just the chaps in uniform who are going to come a cropper, and we don't fight with bows and arrows any more, either. It's far more lethal these days. Anyway, I've decided I'm going to do my bit.'

Rose started to laugh. '*You!* What do you think you can do at your age! You're a bit rusty on the old pins for marching, Bertie love.'

'I'm not thinking of marching anywhere, but I'm not too old for joining the Civil Defence. Now that things are hotting up, it's time I did something about it.'

'I think that's very patriotic, Uncle Bert,' Daisy said.

'It's stupid,' Rose snapped. 'Your eyesight's not too good lately, and you couldn't run to catch a bus, let alone see off a few German parachutists invading Weston. Not that I think such a thing will ever happen; but really, Bert, do you honestly think you're up to staying out all night watching for enemy planes?'

'Is that all you think the CD does? Lord give me patience!'

'Well, I know they do that sort of thing, because one of our ladies at the knitting circle told me so. Her husband's in the Civil Defence, but he's twenty years younger than you, Bert. You did your bit in the last war, so you should leave this one to the younger ones.'

'And I think you should stop talking as if I've got one foot in the grave! What's got into you, woman? Did you think I'd be satisfied with digging up the garden and planting vegetables for ever?'

Daisy left them to it, knowing that when they began one of their wrangling arguments it could go on for a very long time. It was part bickering, part exhilaration; but whatever mood it took, she didn't want to get involved.

Besides, she had promised that as soon as Teddy got home
from school they would cycle over to the Luckwell farm,
which they had done a few times now since Norman and
Ronnie had gone, just to keep her brother happy.

Lucy's family always made a fuss of Teddy, letting him
help with the animal feeding, and since the Luckwells still
had their evacuees, it provided a sort of tiny link with
his old pals. Though Daisy had to admit that Teddy had
got over their departure extremely quickly, and the little
wretch was revelling in the fact that he was now Aunt
Rose's pet and didn't have to share her with anyone. Still,
it was better than having him moping around, she thought
cheerfully.

They spent an hour tramping around the farm, by which
time Teddy was smelling decidedly whiffy, and was due for
a bath as soon as they got back home, she told him, knowing
that Rose wouldn't let him sit at the supper table until he was
scrubbed spotless.

Daisy knew something was wrong the moment she stepped
inside the front door, saw her aunt's white face, and heard
the way her uncle continually cleared his throat, the way he
did when he was lost for words. For these two, that in itself
was an ominous sign.

'Shall I get Teddy straight into the bath?' she said
quickly.

'Yes, please, Daisy; and then come back down here,
please.'

Once in the bathroom she filled the bath with warm water
to the line that was marked around it now, for the permitted
level. Though what help it was to the war effort to restrict
bathwater, Daisy had no idea. She tried to keep her thoughts
on inane things while she helped Teddy undress and got
him in, warning him to wash himself properly or Aunt
Rose would be up to scrub him. Then she went back to
the parlour, her heart thumping.

'What's happened? I know it must be something awful, so please don't keep me in suspense.'

'Your father called us while you were out, Daisy . . .'

'Is it Elsie? Has something happened to the baby?'

'It's not Elsie,' Rose said in a strangled voice. 'It's Baz – at least, we must assume that it's Baz. There's no real proof, of course . . .'

'Rose, don't build up your hopes,' Bert cut in gruffly. 'I don't think these people would have contacted Quentin unless they'd been sure.'

'Well, I'm not giving up hope yet!'

'Will you please stop talking as if I'm not here and tell me what's happened to Baz? I have a right to know!' Daisy said, white-faced. It couldn't be anything bad. Not to Baz, the survivor . . .

They both looked at her, as if delaying the moment as long as possible, and then Bert nodded.

'You're right, my love. Your father has had a letter from a farmer in France. He couldn't read it himself, so he took it to someone who can speak the language. It said . . . it said . . .'

Rose continued in a monotone as Bert's voice cracked.

'It seems that Baz had been stranded in France after Dunkirk and found his way to this farm. He was taken to the coast and on to a ship at night, along with hundreds of others still trying to get out of France. The Germans were bombing the ships, and the one Baz was on was sunk before it got very far out of the harbour. Men were jumping overboard in lifejackets, but the water was very deep and oil was spilling into it and burning, and there were no survivors. Thankfully he'd left his address with the French farmer, or we might never have known.'

Daisy listened in horror as her aunt's voice went on in that strange flat tone, as if it was the only way she could say it all without breaking down. She swallowed the huge lump in her throat, unable to believe that her big, brash brother, so young and yet so full of self-confidence, could have perished in this way. She *wouldn't* believe it.

'We don't know for sure, do we? He might have got away. He could swim like a fish, and he'd know what to do . . .'

'Not even a fish could swim in thick oil pumping out of a broken ship, Daisy,' Bert said harshly. 'The farmhand who took Baz to the coast watched it all from a ditch on the shore, too scared to move while the Germans were bombing, and the ship was hit for a second time before it went down. Eventually they had the news that there were no survivors, and we have to believe it.'

So now there were four . . . Daisy pushed the silly words out of her head, but she couldn't push out the fear of wondering who was going to be next. Teddy was too young to be involved in a war, thank God, but Immy was in the greatest danger in London. There was also Elsie, who was too stubborn to move out of Bristol unless she was forced into it, and even she herself might be heading into danger with the ambulance people, if they were called to the scene of an air raid.

'Put your head between your knees, Daisy,' she heard her aunt's voice say sharply, and she did as she was told without question, realising she was starting to feel light-headed. She recovered quickly, though, ashamed of herself for letting go like that, when they were all feeling the shock of what had happened. A nurse should be able to rise above such panic, but right now she felt less like a nurse than like someone very young, facing a death in the family for the second time . . .

'Sorry,' she almost gasped. 'Do you think I should phone Daddy myself?'

'Not just now,' Aunt Rose said. 'He'll be busy on the telephone trying to contact Imogen, and then trying to find out more information from the naval authorities. I'm sure he'll call us again when he has any more news, and in the meantime I'm going to see Mr Penfold. Do you want to come with me, Daisy?'

'What for?' she asked blankly.

'To arrange for a small memorial service for Baz. I'm going to speak to your father about it, naturally; but it's the least we can do. In fact, my love, it's all anyone can do now. You do see that, don't you?'

'I think you could wait until you get proper confirmation before you have him dead and buried! And I don't want to talk to Mr Penfold, thank you very much. I'll go and get Teddy out of the bath before his skin is completely wrinkled, and then I'm going to my room,' she said in a fury.

She bolted out of there, unable to stay and listen to her aunt's calm belief that having a small memorial service for her brother would make everything right. It wouldn't, and besides, she wasn't at all sure he had gone to his Maker, which Aunt Rose would also be firmly believing now.

Such blind belief was starting to disintegrate as far as Daisy was concerned. It was worse than that. It was almost obscene. How could any benevolent God let this happen to a young boy who wasn't yet a man, however much he thought he was? It was too cruel . . .

Teddy looked up enquiringly as she slammed the bathroom door behind her and leaned against it with tears flooding her eyes.

'I'm turning all white,' he complained, 'and there's a hole in my boat and it's sunk. When I'm bigger I'm going out in a proper boat by the pier and learn to catch fish. Is that what Baz does?' he added vaguely.

Daisy hauled him out, wrapping him in a large bath towel, and almost smothering him in the process as she hugged him close, practically cocooning them both inside it.

'Oh darling, I hope you do!' she said almost hysterically. 'I hope that's the only thing you'll ever have to worry about.'

'You're hurting me,' he howled, and she reluctantly released him, wishing she could keep him safe like this for ever.

He would have to be told, of course. He couldn't be kept in ignorance, and it was impossible to think that they would never mention Baz's name again. When he was safely tucked up in bed that night, and she had stopped shaking, she queried it with her uncle, since Aunt Rose was still away consulting the minister.

'Should I tell him, do you think? Not that I know how to do it, but someone has to, don't they, Uncle Bert? Or to prepare him, at least. We could say that Baz was missing, and we weren't sure what had happened.'

She stopped, because even that sounded so impossible. If the French farmer's story was to be believed, they knew only too well what had happened. The ship that was meant to be bringing Baz safely home to England had been bombed by the Germans, and he had drowned in a sea of burning oil. She shuddered, not wanting to picture it, and willing the images away from her mind.

'I think that, of all people, you're the right one to do it, Daisy love,' her uncle said. 'You write your letters for the hospital patients, and if you can't find the words to tell Teddy to his face, then why don't you write it all down in a letter or a little story that he can understand without becoming too frightened or upset?'

'It's different when I write letters for people I don't know,' she said, and then stopped abruptly. Because she had just done the very same thing for Private Stokes's wife, and she had come to know the man over the weeks he had been in her care.

'Think about it, Daisy. Meanwhile, how about a cup of cocoa and a dash of sugar to calm your nerves?'

She gave a wan smile. 'Didn't you know that nurses aren't supposed to have nerves, Uncle Bert?'

'Maybe so,' he agreed, dropping an affectionate kiss on

the top of her head as he went to the kitchen. 'But nice young girls who care about their families are.'

Aunt Rose came home that evening with a bundle of pamphlets from the minister, supposedly to help the bereaved come to terms with their loss. Daisy refused to look at them, knowing she had to come to terms with this in her own way. By then she had ignored her aunt's advice and telephoned her father, anyway. He had sounded grim, saying he hadn't found out any more yet, but that they must believe the worst.

Then Elsie had spoken to her, clearly upset about Baz, desperately trying to hold down her own sense of excitement in the circumstances, because she was going to Oxford to see Joe at the convalescent home in a week's time, and then they were going to spend his leave together in a small country hotel nearby.

'I know it's ghastly news about Baz, Daisy, and I probably shouldn't leave Father alone at this time, but life has to go on. And I can't help thinking it might have been Joe, so I can't refuse to do what he's arranged, can I?'

'Of course you can't,' Daisy said. 'I'm sure Daddy will understand.'

'He's actually urging me to go. I honestly don't think he wants anyone around him at the moment, and I know he's thinking of Mother too.'

'I'm sure he is,' Daisy murmured. 'We all are. Well, keep in touch, Elsie, and let me know if you get any more news.'

Without knowing it, Elsie had given her the lead for her small story for Teddy, which she had now decided to write. A letter was too personal, and she knew she couldn't do it. Aunt Rose was still out, but she would approve, even if Daisy herself was having serious doubts about God being in His heaven and all being right with the world, when it bloody well wasn't.

Despite her undoubted grief over Baz, Aunt Rose would

be quite certain that he was now somewhere with his mother in heaven, and Daisy knew that that was the only way she could explain it to a vulnerable eight-year-old boy without letting him fear that everyone he loved was being taken away from him.

It wasn't as easy as she had thought to put it into words that were at the same time deeply personal to all of them, yet as detached as she could make them for Teddy's sake. It took her more than an hour to get it right, but she had to admit it was something of a catharsis for herself to write it all out. Then she went to Teddy's bedroom and gave him the pages to read.

'What's this for? I'm reading my comic.' He glared at her suspiciously, obviously sensing that something was wrong.

'This is important, Teddy. I could wait with you while you read it – or would you rather I read it aloud to you?'

'If you like,' he said sullenly.

'It's a story that's a bit sad. You know that sad things happen in a war, don't you?' She swallowed. 'You know about Cal.'

'He got blown out of the sky in his airplane, didn't he? I told my teacher,' he said, almost crowing with importance.

The horrible little *wretch* . . . Daisy gritted her teeth, but when you were only eight, she supposed, such things gave you a bit of status among your little friends. Knowing a dead hero was far better than not knowing one at all. She took a deep breath and tried again.

'Do you remember Baz when we lived in Bristol, Teddy?'

'Course I do. Well, only a bit,' he said with a frown. 'I can't remember his face very well, but I know he liked boats and fishing, and he used to work on the ferryboat a long time ago, didn't he?'

Oh God, this is so difficult . . . but it dawned on her that it was a very long time since Teddy had seen his brother,

216

so perhaps the news wouldn't be so traumatic for him as it was for the rest of them.

'Is he dead as well?' Teddy said, half his attention still on his comic, and making her heart stop for a moment before it raced on.

'Teddy, leave that comic alone for a minute, will you?' she said gently. 'What would you say if I told you something very sad had happened to Baz?'

She knew she was making an awful hash of this, when she was meant to be doing the opposite; but somehow she just couldn't say the words.

'If he's dead, perhaps I can work on the ferryboat when I'm bigger,' Teddy went on hopefully when she said nothing.

Oh *God* . . .

'Perhaps you can, darling,' she said in a muffled voice.

She stared at him, seeing the eagerness in his face, his little innocent face that was a miniature of Baz's face at that moment, knowing nothing of war and death, except for the thrill of it all – and the importance of telling a teacher and his friends that he knew someone who had been blown out of the sky in an airplane.

'You go back to your comic now, love,' she said, choked, 'and Aunt Rose will be up soon to tuck you in.'

'All right.' Then he paused, his face puckered. 'Daisy, when I say my prayers do I have to ask God to look after Baz as well as Mummy?'

'Yes, love, I think you should, and I'm sure they're looking after one another right now.'

Somehow she got out of the room, her eyes flooded with tears. She leaned against the door with a feeling of utter helplessness, wishing she still had the blind faith of a small child. Wishing she had Aunt Rose's faith.

Once she felt more composed she went downstairs and told her aunt and uncle what had happened.

'You handled it very well, my love.'

'No I didn't! It was Teddy who somehow saw through my clumsy attempt to tell him, and even then I couldn't actually say it. How could I, when we don't really *know*?'

Aunt Rose was sharper than usual. 'We know it in our hearts, Daisy, and you'll only make things worse by trying to keep hope alive.'

'And what have you got, if you don't have hope?' she said bitterly. 'Oh, I know you mean it for the best, but I can't keep on believing – about anything.'

'Don't you think we all feel like that at times? It's God's way of testing our faith and our strength.'

'Well, it's a pretty awful way, by killing everyone we love,' Daisy muttered.

'I don't want to hear more of this,' Rose said. 'I'm going to tuck Teddy in and hear his prayers, and your uncle can tell you what Mr Penfold has suggested. I've spoken to your father about it, and he's in full agreement.'

Daisy grimaced at her uncle when they were alone. 'I suppose I'm in disgrace now,' she said. 'But I can't help how I feel, can I, Uncle Bert?'

'None of us can, and you musn't think too harshly of your auntie's ways, love. She wants to do her best for everyone.'

'I know that. So what has Mr Penfold suggested that Daddy agrees to?' she muttered, trying to be rational, and knowing she wasn't going to like it.

'It won't be a memorial service, but a small family service of dedication for Baz and a celebration of his life. It won't be a burial service either, Daisy, because – well, it can't be, can it?' he added delicately. 'It will just be all of us, saying our private goodbyes to Baz within the blessing of the Church.'

Daisy was indignant. 'And when is this service going to be? It's all happening too soon, Uncle Bert. It's too hasty, as if we can't wait to wipe him out of our lives. As if we can't wait to say goodbye!'

They were still discussing it when Rose came downstairs again, her eyes slightly damp.

'It's not going to happen yet, Daisy. We all feel the same about that, and in any case we want to be sure Elsie feels up to it, and that Immy can be here too. Mr Penfold suggested we wait a while, possibly even until Elsie's baby has been born. We want Baz to feel the presence of all his family's love.'

Daisy hardly knew what to say now. She could see that Aunt Rose thought this was a perfectly logical suggestion, and it was certainly a relief to think they weren't going to have the service immediately. In Daisy's opinion it would have been in almost indecent haste.

'We all want to do what we think is best for everyone, Daisy,' Rose went on, echoing Bert's words. 'You do see that, don't you?'

'I suppose so,' she said grudgingly. 'And if Daddy and Elsie think it's a sensible idea, then I suppose I'll have to, won't I?'

'I still think it's weird,' she said to Alice Godfrey, when they had got over the necessary embarrassment of explanations and commiserations.

'You won't,' Alice told her. 'We had that kind of service for my brother, although we knew what had happened to him, of course. It was just for my parents, my aunts and grandmother, and me. And it did help. It made us all feel close, and that Roy was still part of us. It sort of brings it all to a proper conclusion. You'll feel the same when the time comes, Daisy.'

She took a deep breath. 'Well, I might and I might not. In any case, I don't want to talk about it any more. I feel as if I'm being choked with all this talk of churches and memorial services and people dying or not dying! Elsie's going to see Joe in the convalescent home; then they're going to take a short holiday together while he's on leave, and a good thing too. What's the point of being married if you can't spend time together?'

She went on babbling determinedly, trying to pull herself back into the land of the living, instead of some frightening, alien place where people died – or simply disappeared without trace, which was worse.

'I'd like to have some fun too! So before you think I'm being absolutely wicked to say such a thing, Aunt Rose told me I shouldn't sit around uselessly moping. She said I should even go to the pictures if I felt like it – and if you would come with me. So will you – please, Alice? What do you say?'

'I say your aunt is a very wise woman. But we already know that, don't we?'

Seventeen

In one way, Daisy thought, it was a good thing that Norman and Ronnie had gone to live in Welsh Wales with their mother and her fancy-man farmer. They would have been asking far too many questions about Baz's fate – especially Norman, with his ghoulish interest in death – and scaring Teddy out of his wits in the process. But in another way, she wished they were still here, to give them all less time to think. When the boisterous East End boys had been around, nobody had had time to think about anything but what they were getting up to; and Teddy certainly missed them.

It was true what they said, though: keeping busy stopped you thinking, at least for a while. And Sister Macintosh had been true to her word and arranged for Daisy to join the ambulance crew for a spell of road experience, as she called it. She was now assigned as general helper to the driver, Thomas Peterson, and his assistant, Luke Forbes. Thomas was a burly, jovial man about her uncle's age, while Luke was more serious, and in his mid-thirties, Daisy guessed.

If there were air-raid casualties, there would also be a senior nurse on board, and a doctor in real emergencies. Otherwise, Thomas told her cheerfully, he and Luke were thoroughly trained in dealing with general care needs.

'You've never had to deliver a baby, I hope,' she said cheekily, to cover her nervousness on that first morning, and thinking of Elsie.

'Not yet, but there's always a first time,' he said with

a wink. 'My old lady has had three herself, so I know what's involved; but I reckon Luke here would probably faint right off, so we generally leave all that kind of thing to the professionals. Most ladies have the midwife at home for their confinement, of course, unless there are any complications.'

'Good,' Daisy muttered, wishing she had never asked, never having thought about Elsie having complications. She immediately resolved to read up a little more about midwifery.

'Got a young man, have you, Daisy?' Thomas went on, as he explained the various bits of equipment in the ambulance to her. 'Thinking of getting married and having babies yourself, are you?'

'No. I'm never getting married,' she snapped, unaccountably annoyed at the question. 'It's not worth the trouble.'

Thomas stopped showing her where the bandages and TCP were kept and stared at her in astonishment.

'Well, that's a fine thing for a pretty young lady to say, if you'll pardon my being so personal. I thought you all wanted to walk down the aisle with the man of your dreams, like them Hollywood flicks are always telling us!'

'Not when the man of your dreams has been . . .'

She stopped, suddenly realising what she was saying, and that her two new companions were looking at her with great interest like two old gossips. She certainly didn't intend telling them that Cal had been shot down, nor that she was still in a huge amount of confusion over her brother and refusing to give into mourning like the rest of her family. It was none of their business.

Besides, she still hadn't given up hope for Baz. She kept her feelings to herself, knowing that her family would call her completely foolish; but she still hoped that somehow he had got out of that terrible burning sea, and that some kindly French farmer's wife was helping him back to strength. Especially if some pretty young farmer's daughter was doing her bit to help him back to normality as well. Knowing Baz, it would be the best of all aids to his recovery.

As she felt her mouth quirk into a half-smile, Daisy was mildly shocked at her own thoughts, even though she had decided by now that this was going to be her way of dealing with losing her brother. If she made herself assume that he was merely missing, instead of being sucked under, then choked and drowned in that dreadful sticky black abyss, then she could cope.

'You lose somebody, did you, Daisy?' Luke, the younger ambulance man was saying now. 'There ain't many families now that didn't, and they say it will get worse before it gets better. We just have to go on the best we can, don't we?'

'And there's your thought for today, Daisy girl,' Thomas added. 'So now that Luke's done his best to cheer everybody up, let's get started and see where we've got to go this morning.'

The ambulance contained various information pamphlets for the use of patients and crew. Daisy's attention was drawn to the one on procedure if a pregnant woman went into labour en route to the hospital. It didn't make comfortable reading for someone who had never gone into it in any detail, but after reading the pamphlet Daisy could only think of what lay ahead of Elsie.

She tried to imagine how it must feel to be carrying a baby inside you, and even more, with a shudder, how it must feel to have to get the baby out. Thomas caught her studying it while they waited for their instructions.

'For a young lady who ain't never getting married, so she says, you don't want to be worried about none of that!' he said with a chuckle.

'I'm reading it on a professional level,' she said defensively. 'I might need to help – though I sincerely hope I don't! Actually, my sister's expecting a baby, so naturally I'm interested.'

'Oh ah. Where's she then?'

'At our home in Bristol with my father, though at the moment she's visiting her husband. He's about to be discharged from a military convalescent home in Oxford; then they're spending his leave together,' she said briefly.

'He'll soon be back to being fighting fodder then,' Luke put in. 'They don't keep 'em out of the firing line any longer than they can help these days.'

Well, thanks for that little bit of hope, thought Daisy, deciding that of the two, she much preferred Thomas with his cheerful outlook on life, to Luke, the eternal pessimist.

'It's quite routine work in a way,' Daisy reported to Aunt Rose later. 'We had to collect some old people from their homes and take them to the hospital for their regular physiotherapy. And somebody from Bleadon had a broken leg and had to be brought in to have his plaster taken off. Things like that.'

'You sound disappointed. Did you expect dramatics all day long?'

'No, but I didn't expect it to be quite so dull! Even though Thomas reckoned I was a sight for sore eyes for the old folk. He talks like that all the time, but I quite like him,' she said with a grin. 'He's got three children, and to hear him talk about them, you'd think they were still babies. One of them's in the army, and the other two are still at school. His wife's a semi-invalid too.'

'You seem to have learned a lot about him in one day,' Bert said. 'Have you told him all your family history too?'

'Not much,' Daisy said. 'I was entertaining the patients in the ambulance.'

'What, singing to them, do you mean?'

'Of course not. Just chatting, that's all, and trying to reassure them. Some of them were nervous about their treatment.'

'And you'd be a sight for a lot of sore eyes, I bet,' Bert said slyly, echoing Thomas's words.

Daisy shrugged. 'I'm not even sure if I'm going to like

this job. It doesn't feel like real nursing, just riding around in an ambulance all day.'

'It's all good experience, Daisy,' Rose told her. 'And you won't feel like that when you're called out to an emergency.'

'Like an air raid, you mean? Or bringing an expectant mother into the hospital with complications,' she added, remembering Thomas's words.

'Well, let's hope you don't get any of those. It's enough of a trial bringing a baby into the world without complications,' Aunt Rose, who had never had any babies of her own, said shrewdly.

Her words gave Daisy a real stab of anxiety for Elsie, who was only two months away from her confinement now. Elsie was being extraordinarily stubborn about leaving Bristol, no matter what anyone said. Even Joe. But that could all change when they spent their few weeks together, she supposed. What a lovely thought for them. Daisy liked her brother-in-law enormously, despite his clipped northern accent, though she could never imagine him as a husband and lover . . . which was probably just as well, seeing as he was both to her sister!

At that moment Elsie was travelling on a train to Oxford to be with Joe, and trying to contain her emotions at the thought of being with him again, even though she knew his recuperation would be complete as soon as these few weeks were over, and he would then be rejoining his regiment; which was why she was determined not to let the terrible thing that had happened to her brother overshadow this time with Joe. This precious time, which might be all they had.

But she wouldn't think in that way either, she thought, with savage determination. As she sat in the train, crowded with servicemen and women, she allowed her hand to rest protectively over her belly beneath her cotton coat. Her talisman, her hope for the future that she and Joe would share. Her only regret was that he would probably be far away when the time for her confinement arrived.

She caught the glance of a hefty young woman in khaki uniform sitting opposite her, and gave her a little smile.

'You're very brave to be travelling,' the woman said.

'I don't think bravery comes into it, compared with what you're doing.'

Her companion laughed. 'Oh, I'm just in the catering corps, and there's not much danger involved in preparing food for the troops!'

'That's quite a coincidence. My sister's best friend is in the catering corps too. Helen Church. I don't suppose you know her.'

''Fraid not, love. It's a big army.'

Elsie nodded, feeling foolish for even asking. The two of them occupied the seats nearest the train window, which virtually isolated them from the rest of the people chatting together in the compartment, and impulsively she spoke again.

'I'm going to join my husband for a short time. He's about to leave a convalescent home after being at Dunkirk.' She couldn't resist saying it with pride.

'Good for him. So is this your first?' she asked, nodding at the bump beneath Elsie's voluminous cotton coat that nobody could miss seeing.

'Oh yes, and possibly my last, if the way he keeps kicking me is anything to go by,' she said conspiratorially.

The woman laughed agreeably in return. 'Are you so sure it's going to be a he?'

'Not at all, but you have to call him something, don't you? I always feel it's a bit undignified to refer to a baby as it!'

'So what are you going to call him or her?'

Elsie shook her head. 'We haven't decided. We thought it was bad luck to anticipate, and neither of us minds which we have. Just as long as he's healthy.'

'Amen to that,' the woman said with a smile, and turned back to the magazine she had been reading.

Elsie wasn't too sorry. She had the feeling that this conversation with a stranger was soon going to descend into aimless trivialities, and she knew she didn't have the social skills for small talk that her sisters did. Anyway, she would far rather think about Joe, and she also had her own book to read. She brought it out of her bag and smiled briefly at her travelling companion before pretending to concentrate on the pages.

The jolting movement of the train and the rhythmic clatter of the wheels made her eyelids droop, and she drifted off into a sleep where no wars existed, and the sound of babies cooing was the sweetest sound around. It was only when the book slid off her lap and on to the floor some time later that she awoke with a jerk to find that the train was pulling into a station.

'Is this Oxford?' she asked at once, and then felt her face flush as the servicewoman put her finger to her lips in a teasing hush-hush movement. Which was perfectly ridiculous, as far as Elsie was concerned, because if you didn't know where you were, how the dickens could you know when to get out of the train? She felt every bit as aggressive as Daisy might have been at that moment, since it was hardly likely that any German spies were going to be in the compartment taking notes!

'Yes, this is it, love,' the woman went on, taking pity on her, and hauling down her kitbag from the overhead rack. Then she handed Elsie's case down to her as well, as everyone made bustling movements to leave the train. 'Good luck, dear, and I hope you and your husband have a lovely time.'

Which was enough to make Elsie forgive her anything. And then she forgot everything but making her way down the crowded platform, craning her neck to see a familiar figure, and forgetting for the moment that of course he wouldn't be there. She was to take a taxi to the convalescent home, and once the formalities were over, they would go to the small country hotel where Joe had already booked them in.

For a moment, Elsie felt unexpected qualms. She felt so bulky now, so much more clumsy in her movements than when she and Joe had first met, when she had been determined never to set foot again in the shop where her father had once been king, and where now the mighty Preston's Emporium had taken over. She had been so defensive, and so resistant to the reputed Preston charm.

It had certainly been easy to resist Robert Preston's so-called charm, the son of the mighty Preston himself. She hadn't liked him at all. But then the nephew had arrived in Bristol with his northern accent that they had all found so amusing, taking over as manager and quietly offering her a job – and with it his heart.

A surge of excitement filled her veins. Joe had adored her from the start, and she had no reason to think any of that had changed because she was carrying his child – their child that she carried so proudly and lovingly. It was just – she felt her face grow hot as the thought crept into her head – just that it was not going to be so easy in the circumstances to demonstrate their physical love for one another; and she wanted that intimacy every bit as much as Joe did.

'Are you wanting a taxi, ma'am?' she heard a voice say. 'They're few and far between, but if you care to sit a while, me and my buddies will be happy to see what we can do for you.'

She realised the speaker was one of a group of men in RAF uniform, a Canadian by the sound of him, she registered swiftly. Daisy had said there were many Canadian airmen in the country now, and she murmured her thanks as this one indicated a bench seat for her. She was more tired than she had expected after simply sitting in a train for several hours, and she didn't want to be so tired that she couldn't enjoy being with Joe.

'Do you live here or are you just visiting?' the Canadian went on.

'Just visiting – the Oxford military convalescent home, as a matter of fact. My husband is there.'

'Well, say, you're really in luck. We go right past there, so if you're willing to trust yourself to our driver, we can give you a ride. Our truck should be along in a few minutes.'

'Oh, I don't think that's a good idea,' Elsie said in a mild panic.

'Sure it is. Anything's better than waiting around here for an hour, isn't it? I bet your husband will be mighty glad to see you.'

She hardly knew what to say in reply. Her father wouldn't approve of her accepting a ride from strangers, though she knew that both Imogen and Daisy would have had no such fears. They lived in the real world now, while she was stuck at home, twiddling her thumbs while awaiting the birth of her baby.

And that was an *awful* thought to have! The moment it entered her head, she was angry at being so wicked on account of the baby, and so insipid on her own account. She accepted the airman's offer at once, and within minutes the truck had arrived. The group of men ushered her carefully on board as if she was made of Dresden china. She revised the tiniest thought that she might be being abducted, deciding that their Canadian cousins were the nicest and most gallant men she had ever met. Apart from Joe, of course.

She was taken right through the grounds of the convalescent home, and when they stopped at the front door of the grand-looking house, she was helped down again with great courtesy. While she was thanking them for their kindness, she saw Joe watching her through the large picture window that was criss-crossed with tape to ward off bomb-blasts, his arms folded.

'Oh dear,' she murmured, as she was handed her suitcase. 'I'm afraid this is not the best way for a lady in my condition to arrive to visit her husband, is it?'

But surrounded as she was now by large men in air force uniforms, the situation struck her as so comical that she began to laugh, and seconds later Joe came striding out of the front door.

'Joe, darling, what do you think of this for an escort?' she said at once, half-wondering if he was going to be irate.

But before he had a chance to say anything, the Canadian who had first spoken to Elsie had come to attention and saluted him.

'We were only too glad to be of service to your little lady, sir, and we admire all you fellows tremendously. Best of luck to you both.'

They had got back into the truck and were on their way before Elsie could stammer out any more thanks; and then she turned to Joe, thankful to see that by now he was starting to laugh too.

'Well, they're certainly polite, I'll give them that,' he said. 'We've got a couple of them in here, as a matter of fact, so I wasn't surprised!'

'So is that all we're going to talk about?' Elsie asked him mildly.

Then she was in his arms, as close as he could reasonably get, considering her size, and uncaring of who might be watching. His mouth was kissing hers; she could feel his heartbeats, and knew that he was wholly hers again.

'God, how I've missed you, sweetheart,' he said huskily. 'Both of you.'

Elsie laughed shakily, sure of him at last, sure that any fears were unfounded, because all the love in the world was theirs for the keeping.

'We've missed you too, Joe,' she whispered, bringing him into the enclosed world that still belonged only to her and the baby.

'Right then,' he said more briskly. 'Let's go inside and have some tea, and once I've been formally discharged we'll be on our way. I'm anxious to get to the hotel and have you all to myself. The resident bus is going to take us there since it's not too far out of the town. It's all part of the service.'

He didn't add how much he had bribed the officials to do it, knowing Elsie would be exhausted from the travelling by the time they arrived. He could see it already by the mauve shadows beneath her beautiful eyes, and the slight slump in her shoulders; but tonight he was going to kiss all the tiredness away, he thought, with a surge of pleasure in his loins that had nothing to do with fighting off fatigue and more to do with the healthy lust of a man for his wife.

Only a fool would have assumed that the Luftwaffe would concentrate solely on the south-east coastal towns. Bristol was clearly destined to be a target, and although the air raids continued spasmodically in the early months after Dunkirk, everyone knew that sooner or later they were going to get the big one. Like most locals, Bert Painter was quite sure that this was only the beginning.

'We won't be completely safe down here either,' he warned Rose. 'They're talking about lighting decoy fires out on the moors to try and fool the Jerries, but they're not daft. They'll have done their homework and they'll know the difference between decoy fires and a city, especially by moonlight. So we'll make sure the cellar is as cosy as can be in case any stray bombs come our way.'

'Are the Jerries going to bomb us then?' Teddy said half-hopefully.

'Not *us*, Teddy,' Rose told him with a glare at Bert. 'But sometimes they may lose their way, so we have to be prepared. Anyway, didn't I hear you telling George the cellar was your own special cave?'

'Yes, George liked it down there,' Teddy said, perking up. 'Daisy showed me what to do with a bandage in case anybody got hurt, and I practised tying up George's leg, but he chewed the bandage off again.'

'That's because dogs don't understand about bandages,' Bert told him solemnly. 'You can practise on me if you like.'

He rolled up his sleeve and to Teddy's delight he pretended to groan in pain. As he rushed off to find a bandage, Rose thought, as she had thought so many times, what a wonderful father Bert would have made.

'You should have been a teacher, love,' she said instead.

'I know,' he said, and they both knew what she really meant.

He glanced towards the parlour, where Teddy had gone to fetch the first-aid box, and lowered his voice carefully. 'He's taken the news about Baz very well, hasn't he?'

Rose's eyes clouded. 'That's because he simply doesn't remember him properly, which is very sad, but a blessing as far as he's concerned, I suppose. It's not so good for the rest of us though, is it?'

'We can't dispute it now that Quentin has had official confirmation from the authorities though, Rose. It was just as that French farmer said: the ship has been named, and there were no survivors after it went down. It's a tragedy for all of us, but even Daisy has to accept it now.'

He said no more as Teddy came back to the kitchen, trailing the bandage behind him, and Rose tut-tutted at once, telling him it was no way for a nurse to handle it, especially as George began barking excitedly, clearly thinking this was a new game they were playing. At least it veered their thoughts away from Baz for the moment.

Rose firmly believed that grief was best expressed privately, but that everyone's public role was to bolster one another up. They all cared for one another, but they all had their own ways of dealing with things, and she was thankful that her brother Quentin and the two older Caldwell girls seemed to be doing just that.

* * *

Daisy wasn't taking it so well, and she had found an unexpected ally in Thomas Peterson when she had snapped at him, and then found herself weeping on his shoulder. She hadn't told anyone about Baz except Alice, as if by the words not actually being spoken out loud, it hadn't happened at all. But now they all knew that it had, and the minister had even come to the house and talked to them, and she had hated having to sit there po-faced while he rattled on in his pious manner. She knew he meant well, but she simply couldn't take it.

She finally burst out everything on the ambulance-driver's shoulder, when she had hardly said anything at all about her family until now. She had been what some folk called 'keeping herself to herself' and what Aunt Rose would have called 'uppity'.

It had been a particularly harrowing day when they had been called out to a suspected heart attack on the seafront. A crowd had gathered around the elderly man out walking his dog, and they reported having seen him stagger and fall, crashing his head against an iron girder beneath the pier. The man's face had become the colour of parchment, his lips blue. There was also a lot of blood seeping into the sand, and the odious sight of the dog pathetically licking at the blood, as if to staunch it for his master, made Daisy want to vomit.

She knew she mustn't. She had seen far worse sights than a bleeding head in the hospital when the casualties had come in, but somehow this was different. This was just a man walking on the beach with his dog, and a tragic accident had led to something far worse. The man's breathing was barely perceptible, and she stood helplessly by while Luke fastened the oxygen mask around his mouth and nose, shaking his head briefly at Thomas.

For a moment Daisy thought it meant that they were giving up on the man, but then Thomas barked at the two of them to bring the stretcher from the ambulance, and her feet were slipping into the soft warm sand as fast as they would go as she raced after Luke.

'You don't think he'll make it, do you?' she panted.

'He'll be a goner before we get him back to the hospital,' he replied. 'I've seen 'em like this before; but we'll go through the motions anyway.'

Daisy hated him passionately at that moment. This could have been her uncle, or her father, or any one of the elderly patients they regularly transported to and from the hospital for treatment. But she clamped her lips together and said nothing as they hauled the stretcher out of the ambulance and rushed back towards the pier with it.

As they reached it, Thomas shook his head.

'Too late, I'm afraid. There's a woman here who knows him. She'll take his dog home and inform his sister what's happened, so we'll just get him back to the hospital and let them do the business.'

Daisy looked on, horrified. Seconds ago the man had been alive and now he was dead, and the crowd had scattered, leaving them to get on with their job. It was what they did, and this part of it was a harsh and clinical job. At least the man had what her brother hadn't. His family would be shocked, but at least they could give him a proper burial and a proper goodbye.

She moved like an automaton on the short journey back to the hospital, and it was only when they had delivered the man to the side ward to be attended to that she stumbled outside, tears blinding her eyes. That was where Thomas Peterson found her, and spoke sharply.

'Come on now, Daisy; don't let me down. You've done well so far, and I didn't expect you to give way like this.'

'Didn't you?' she snapped back, almost hysterical. 'But you don't know – you don't know . . .'

And then she was blabbing out all the hurt and the pain in his accommodating arms.

Eighteen

By the weekend she couldn't stay away from home any longer: it had been a long, long week. She needed to be with her father, and she knew he needed to be with someone, despite what Elsie might have thought, or Aunt Rose advised, or the kindly Thomas Peterson offered in his own brand of counselling.

If her father had decided that his shop and his fire-fighting duties were more important than spending time with his youngest daughter, he was about to find out differently. Daisy was up in arms, she had some time off, and on Friday afternoon she caught the train to Bristol and went straight to Preston's Emporium.

Quentin turned from serving his last customer of the day and gaped in astonishment at the sight of his daughter, clearly distraught.

'Daisy, what's wrong?' he said at once.

'Does something have to be wrong before I can come to see you now, Daddy?' and then the irony of what she had said swept over her, and the weak tears started to her eyes again. If it hadn't been so melodramatic she would have stamped her foot in frustration. 'Oh, of course something's wrong! What could be more wrong than knowing for certain that my brother's been drowned?'

Through her tears she saw the several shop assistants shuffling awkwardly and begin muttering between themselves, and then her father came around the counter and took her in his arms.

'Come through to the back room, darling, where we can talk sensibly. Or would you rather we went home? Millie can close up the shop.'

'I'd rather go home,' she mumbled.

She felt suddenly tongue-tied, desperately wishing she could say how much she longed to be at home with her family all around her, the way they had always been. Her father and mother, Immy and Elsie, Baz and Teddy . . . They both knew those days could never come again, and she didn't know how much it would upset him to hear her say it. However close you were to someone, it was sometimes hard to say what was really in your heart, and Quentin had never invited such intimacies. It wasn't that he didn't care. It was simply that he found it hard to express his feelings in words.

They walked in silence to Vicarage Street, where the family home still stood as solid and welcoming as ever, a symbol of times past. Daisy felt a rush of nostalgia, imagining, just for a moment, that her mother was about to come running down the path to greet her with a smile and a kiss.

'I do miss her, Daddy,' she said, without intending to.

He tucked her hand in the crook of his arm and squeezed it hard, not needing any explanation. 'So do I, my darling. So do I.'

They went inside, and to Daisy's relief everything looked the same and smelled the same, thanks to the local woman they called Mrs down-the-road who came in once a day during the week to 'do' for her father and prepare a hot meal for him. They had long since dispensed with a proper cook and housekeeper and the additional help that had been needed for Frances as her illness progressed.

They had been a decidedly middle-class family then, but largely thanks to the war, everyone seemed to be merging into the same mould nowadays, and if it was being an out and out snob to think that way, Daisy thought defiantly, then she just didn't care.

'Now then,' Quentin said, when they had taken a tray of tea and biscuits into the garden on that late midsummer afternoon. 'To what do I owe the delight of this visit? And it really *is* a delight to see you, darling. Your mother isn't the only one to be missed.'

He forced himself to say the words, aware of how alone he must seem to them all, but alone in an aloof, self-sufficient way, when the truth was anything but that. He wasn't self-sufficient at all, except in the way that a man was supposed to be. He could still keep the stiff upper lip of the Englishman in public, and like his sister Rose, he kept his private feelings very private.

He had especially urged Elsie to join Joe instead of staying here and moping over Baz. It was her rightful place to be with her husband, and besides which, there had been a personal reason for his urging. He had needed time to be alone to grieve over his son. No man cared to let a daughter see his grief, not even this delightful one, who resembled Frances so much that it had almost made his heart stop to see her walk into the shop that afternoon.

'I keep thinking about that day when Baz came home to see us after joining the fishing fleet, Daddy,' Daisy said slowly. 'He was so proud of his new life, and so fearful of what you were going to say to him. We were all out here in the garden then, do you remember?'

'I remember,' Quentin answered. 'It was like a rite of passage for the boy, wanting to find his own feet without any assistance from me. And certainly opposing my wishes for him to join the family business in the shop.' He gave a faint smile. 'As it happened, it hardly mattered, since the shop was about to be taken over by Preston's.'

'He'd never have been happy standing behind a shop counter all his life, would he?' Daisy said, as much for herself as for her father. It had been obvious to everyone but Quentin at the time. Or rather, he had just refused to see it.

'That he wouldn't,' he agreed now. 'He was never happier than being near the water, and preferably being on it in some way or other. He could never have foreseen that the life he loved would eventually kill him, though.'

Daisy heard the bitterness in his voice and ached for him.

'None of us can foresee what fate has in store for us, Daddy. And if there's any comfort at all to come from this, then at least we know that Baz spent the last few years of his life doing what he really loved. How many of us can truly say that, Daddy? Only two that I can think of, and they're together now.'

She felt her lips tremble, because never until that moment had she been able to share Aunt Rose's conviction that her mother and Baz were somewhere in heaven together. Maybe she still didn't truly believe it in her heart, but she had to admit that there was a great comfort in having such a belief, and if it helped her father to believe it too . . .

Her heart gave a sudden, frightening lurch at a sound she had never heard before. It came from her father, and he was crying. Just as swiftly, she remembered that she *had* heard it before, just once, after her mother died. It had been as appalling then as it was now, those great, racking sobs from a strong man. She had heard other men sob in the hospital, but they were strangers, wounded, and needing emotional as well as physical support. She had helped them cope. Now, she didn't know what to do. And then she simply put her arms around her father and pressed him close to her, as though she were the parent and he the child.

After a while the shaking finally stopped, and he moved away from her, embarrassed and alone again. He busied himself with pouring more tea, until Daisy felt that she would be awash with it. But she knew it gave his hands something to do, and she took the cup dutifully.

'You'll stay here tonight, won't you?' he said at last. 'We can have a proper meal later, providing you're happy with spam and mash. Mrs down-the-road leaves me to it on Fridays and Saturdays.'

'Well, I . . .' She hadn't intended to stay, but now she saw that she must. He needed her. And the odd thing was, she could never remember a time in her life before when he had done so. It had always been Immy who had shared his confidences, being the oldest daughter; and more lately, Elsie. But now he needed *her*, his youngest. 'Of course I'll stay, Daddy.'

She had to let Aunt Rose know, and she spoke cautiously into the phone, knowing her father was within earshot, and not wanting to admit how desperately sorry she felt for him. She had learned from her nursing experience that it was far better to be able to let your emotions out than to keep them bottled up inside you, and thank God he had been able to do just that.

She couldn't help wondering if it was the first time, and if she had been the one to trigger it all off. If so, then she was glad, she thought fiercely, pushing down any guilt at witnessing his distress.

Emotional upsets had a habit of making you hungry, and preparing food gave you something else to think about. They decided to have their meal of spam and mash quite early in the evening, and it tasted surprisingly good.

'You're becoming a dab hand at cooking now, Daddy,' Daisy told him. 'Not that there's too much skill in bashing to death a few boiled potatoes with a drop of milk and a lick of margarine, is there?' she teased.

He laughed back. He actually laughed, Daisy thought gladly, and she determined to keep up this light-hearted tone, however much of a strain it was. For now, they had done their crying.

The summer nights were long and warm, and they didn't need to put up the blackout curtains until much later. By dusk they had already heard the whine of aircraft overhead. Searchlights were scanning the skies by the time Daisy went to bed in her old room, and she realised that the night was going to be very different here in Bristol from the comparative quiet of Weston.

'If you hear the siren,' Quentin said matter-of-factly, 'put on a warm coat or dressing gown and we'll go down to the shelter. I don't bother when I'm on my own, but I always insist that Elsie and I do so.'

'What does Elsie do when you're on your fire duties?'

'Elsie's stubborn, like the rest of you,' he said with a small smile. 'She doesn't like being in there on her own, but I finally persuaded her to be sensible for the baby's sake. It's not too bad – just a bit earthy, that's all. I'm sure Teddy would love it, and if Baz were here, he'd probably say it was like going camping.'

She caught her breath in her teeth, knowing what an effort it must have been for him to bring Baz's name into it so casually, and she knew, too, that it was part of the healing process not to ignore him as if he had never existed. It was something they must all do.

She leaned forward and kissed him. 'Goodnight, Daddy,' she said softly. 'It's good to be home.'

Some of her clothes were still in her wardrobe, including an old favourite dressing gown that should have been sent to the rag-bag long ago; but it was a link with the past, and although it was a warm night, she snuggled into it on top of the bedclothes and listened to the familiarity of the house and garden settling into darkness. She hadn't drawn her curtains, since the bedroom was half-moonlit, and through the window she could see the beams of the searchlights seeking enemy aircraft; but the night remained quiet, and the siren didn't sound. It was almost an anticlimax, Daisy thought. It would have been quite something to tell Alice that she had stayed in Bristol for the night, and their street had been bombed, and that she'd been on a *real* rescue mission right here in her own back yard . . .

It was wicked to even think such a thing. The newspaper and wireless reports were full of praise for the spectacular way the RAF was holding off the German Luftwaffe in their dogfights now, and keeping them out over the English Channel as much as possible. Even though it gave her anguish to remember that it wouldn't be Cal coming home to her from one of his RAF sorties, she kept the thought of his bravery in her heart.

Next morning her father looked decidedly better for having her in the house, and she made up her mind.

'I'd really like to stay another night if you'll have me, Daddy. I'd like to visit Mother's grave, and to take a walk down to the waterfront where Immy and Elsie and I used to go so often. I might even look in on old Enoch Bray too. Do you think that's a good idea?' she asked carefully.

'It's a very good idea, darling. I'm afraid I haven't found it in me to go and see him, and I know I should. Are you sure about this?'

'Of course I am.' She could see the relief in his face, knowing he couldn't deal with telling the news to the old ferryman, who had been such a mentor and friend to Baz. But she wanted to do this. She wanted to retrace old steps where they had all been so happy in times past, and she wanted to feel that this was still home, where her mother's aura still lingered in the walls, in the stones. Just for a while.

'Oh Lord, I'd better let Aunt Rose know I'm staying until Sunday,' she remembered, before her father left for the shop as usual on a busy Saturday morning. 'Uncle Bert keeps saying he wants to bring Teddy to see you sometime while he's still got some petrol, so shall I suggest that they come to fetch me? If I know Aunt Rose, she'll want to bring one of her famous pies for our dinner. What do you say, Daddy?'

She willed him to say yes. It would be like old times . . .

almost. To her surprise he wrapped his arms around her and hugged her tight.

'I say yes, of course. What more could a grateful father say to such a loving daughter?'

She watched him leave the house, her eyes troubled. He was still a comparatively young man, still upright and vital, despite all the blows that life had dealt him. He should be married – and the thought was so swift, so alien and so disloyal to her mother's memory that Daisy gasped with the shock of it. But it was true: he was never meant to be alone.

She went back inside the house, her hands shaking, wondering how she could even think of such a thing. It was this house, this lovely house that her parents had come to when they had married, and where all the Caldwell children had been born, that had always been such a happy house. It had known laughter and joy, and even when Frances had lost the ability to dance and sing in the way that had entranced her stage audiences, there had still been so much love. It was filled with memories; and love was still here, waiting to be revived.

Daisy stormed through the rooms, tidying things that didn't need tidying, furious at her own wayward thoughts. How could she even think of someone taking her mother's place? There had been two paying lady lodgers in the upper floor of the house once, when they had decided to convert it into a self-contained flat. They had both been widows, both called Mary, which was why the girls had taken to referring to them as the Marys – and one of them had developed a special rapport with Quentin.

Daisy tried to think of her name. Mary Yard, that was it. Though where she was now Daisy didn't know – and she certainly didn't want to think of her as a possible candidate for stepmother, thank you very much! She dismissed her from her mind, along with every other uneasy thought.

She telephoned her aunt and got the expected response.

'You must be psychic, Daisy! Your uncle and I were thinking exactly the same thing, and I know Teddy will be excited to be having a ride out. And tell your father not to worry about food, because I'll make one of my pies and bring it in time for dinner.'

Daisy smiled into the phone. She was so predictable at times. So endearingly predictable!

'That sounds wonderful, Aunt Rose. We'll see you tomorrow then.'

She began to feel more light-hearted, despite knowing just what she was going to do today. It was as she had told her father, but with a little something extra. Firstly, she was going to visit her mother's grave, talk to her the way she sometimes still talked to Lucy, and ask her what she would think if Quentin were ever to marry again. She didn't expect an answer, of course, except in feelings.

'Oh, Aunt Rose,' she murmured, 'perhaps there's more of you in me than I thought, if I'm starting to imagine the afterlife after all.' But how could she not believe that there was something there, when she had seen it in the faces of the dying patients more than once?

She shivered, brushing aside all these noble, if slightly spooky thoughts. She was young and alive, and she had things to do today.

The first thing she did was to cut a bunch of roses from the garden to put on Frances's grave. They had always been her favourite flowers, and she had planted them herself years ago. Today, the scent of them in full bloom was almost overpowering, thought Daisy. And then she went to the small churchyard where her mother was buried and where the granite headstone said it all.

FRANCES CALDWELL
BELOVED WIFE AND MOTHER
SAFE IN THE ARMS OF JESUS

There was no indication of the tragic way she had plunged to her death nearly two years ago. Quentin had wanted no reminders of that terrible day, nor ghoulish onlookers remembering it. Daisy swallowed, arranging the roses in the pot she had filled with water; then she stared at the headstone, as if to find inspiration from it as she had so often found it in her mother.

'Do you know what I was thinking about last night, Mother?' she said in a very low voice. 'I worry about Daddy being lonely without us all – without you – and if it would be right for him to . . . well . . . to . . .'

But she couldn't say the words. How could you ask your mother if she approved of your father marrying again, finding love again, finding happiness again? *And how could you not want that for him?* she asked herself.

The words stayed in her head, and as she slowly turned to leave, a small breeze blew through the quiet headstones, rustling leaves as sweetly as a sigh, and wafting a heavenly scent of roses into her nostrils. She turned back quickly, and a shaft of sunlight lit her mother's name for a moment before it was gone.

To Daisy it seemed symbolic. The bright light that was Frances Caldwell had faded, and perhaps it really was time to make room for someone else. It was the way she was gradually starting to feel about Cal, and the guilt that had bothered her so much over Jed, and especially Glenn, was also starting to fade. A strange sense of calm settled around her as she walked away, a sense that Frances had given her blessing to whatever future there was for all of them . . .

She must be going mad to let her imagination run away with her like this, Daisy thought angrily, as her ebullient nature returned. She was sane and sensible, not one of Aunt Rose's mad friends who went to seances and suchlike! In any case, the feeling of serenity was rudely interrupted as she bumped into someone outside the iron gates of the churchyard.

'Good God, by all that's holy! it's one of the Caldwell girls, isn't it?'

Daisy blinked at having her mood shattered so abruptly, and by a stranger with black curly hair and a strong Welsh voice. He stood in front of her, blocking her path as if he owned the world, and despite his arrogant good looks, she took an instant and unreasonable dislike to him.

'Do I know you?' she asked pointedly, as haughty as Helen Church.

He laughed. 'Well, I used to know your sister very well, and you're the spitting image of her, my lovely, so you must be one of the younger ones. I don't think it's Elsie, so it must be Daisy. Am I right?'

Daisy stared at him, trying to place him. She didn't like the way he was looking her up and down, and she couldn't ever remember Immy having a young man before James – certainly not one as brash and coarse as this one. She was certainly *not* his lovely! But she was more than curious to know just how well he had known Immy!

'Why aren't you in uniform?' she asked inanely, simply because she couldn't think of anything else to say.

He laughed again. 'The army wouldn't take me because of a heart murmur. Why? Do you fancy curing me? I could do with a bit of pampering, and I think I heard that one of you girls was a nurse. Is that you?'

'Perhaps it is and perhaps it isn't.' She really didn't want to stand here gossiping with him all day. He obviously got bored with her just as quickly.

'Well, never mind. Just say hello to Immy for me the next time you see her, will you? Tell her Morgan Raine was asking after her. We were *very* friendly once, if you know what I mean,' he added, winking one eye.

Daisy strode past him, disliking him even more for his smutty innuendo. She couldn't believe Immy would ever have consorted with such a rough fellow, and she intended asking her about him the first opportunity she got. She felt his gaze following her as she went down the hill to the water-front. She had things to do that were more important than chatting with a Welshman. She had to see Enoch Bray.

The smells of fish and salt and other unmentionables assaulted her long before she neared the waterfront. They used to come here often, the Caldwell girls and their brother, Baz. He was the one who always lingered, revelling in the tales of the old fishermen, and declaring his intention of going to sea one day, filled with the adventure of it. He'd got his wish too. He'd got his adventures, including the greatest adventure of all, as the minister referred to it. To Daisy it was death, plain and simple. She deliberately avoided looking at the small groups of seamen hanging about, knowing from of old that if she once made eye contact, she was likely to get some ribald remarks.

She heard them anyway, but while she looked straight ahead to the old fishermen's cottages she could ignore them; and it wasn't far to the small cottage where old Enoch lived with his wife. She knocked on the door and when it was opened a fraction, she saw the old ferryman.

He was just as gnarled and weather-beaten as ever from his years on the river, never seeming to change as the years went on; and after a moment staring at her as if she was a vision, his old eyes lit up in recognition.

'Bless my soul, if it ain't young Baz's sister. I can't recall which of you 'tis, my pretty maid, but you'd best come inside and tell me the news.'

'I'm Daisy, Mr Bray,' she said. 'Daisy Caldwell.'

She followed him inside the one small room of the cottage, evil-smelling with his pipe and his lingering cooking odours, and she was struck dumb. This old man had been like a father to Baz and given him his first job on the ferry, and she was about to tell him the worst news of all.

'Now then, 'tis bad news, ain't it?' Enoch said calmly. 'I can't think of no other reason why you'd come all this way to visit me. Now that my old woman's passed on I don't get any visitors, so out with it, Daisy Caldwell. Bad news never did improve by being kept inside.'

'It's Baz,' she blurted out.

He nodded. 'Of course 'tis Baz, and you've come to tell me he's dead. Why else would you want to see me? So how'd it happen?'

She thanked God that he seemed to be a mind-reader, although she supposed the look on her face must have warned him. She told him as concisely as she could, considering she hadn't been there to see it, thank God, and realised that she seemed to be thanking Him quite a lot these days.

Relating the contents of the letter her father had received from the French farmer was a trial, but by now she had discovered that the more you said it, the more believable it became. It didn't stop the hurt, but the hurt became familiar. Enoch said nothing during the telling, just nodding now and then, and then repeated what she herself had said, but putting it so much better in his simple way.

'He won't have minded going down with the fishes. It was all he lived for, so you just remember that when you're crying over him. He wouldn't have wanted to be blown up or shot at. If he had to go at all, he'd have chosen this way.'

Daisy couldn't imagine that anyone would have chosen to drown in a sea of burning oil, but she couldn't argue with this simple man who had also lost his wife and got no visitors. So when he offered her some tea she accepted, while trying not to keep her nose pinched at the cottage's aroma, or notice the dingy state of the cup she was offered.

'I must go, Mr Bray,' she was able to say at last. 'It's been a comfort to talk to you, and I'm only sorry it was with such bad news. Oh, and I'm sorry about your wife too,' she remembered to add.

'These things happen, my duck, but we can't dwell on 'em, or we'd go daft, wouldn't we? You just remember that, and don't waste your pretty life mourning Baz. He wouldn't want that.'

Daisy left him at last, pondering on his words, and knowing he was right. Everyone had their own opinion on how to handle a bereavement, but in the end you had to handle it in your own way. She walked back along the waterfront, and when a couple of the lounging sailors whistled at her, she held her head up high and squared her shoulders; unable to resist a smile, she knew she must be coming through the mist at last.

Nineteen

A week later Daisy decided she just might be psychic after all. She had managed to resist calling her father every evening, because she knew he wouldn't appreciate being made to feel he was in need of too much attention with Elsie being away. But the following Friday evening he called her.

'You'll never guess who came into the shop today!'

She registered that he sounded cheerful, so it couldn't be bad news.

'Helen's mother?' she asked with a grin, remembering the way she had deigned to visit their 'little shop' in the past. But she was being ungenerous, and Mrs Church was a very worthy lady, involved in fund-raising and Good Works.

'Mary Yard,' her father said.

Daisy felt her mouth drop open. 'Good Lord, I was only thinking about her the other day. Isn't that odd?' It was the only thing she could think of to say at that moment, but she was never speechless for long. 'What was she doing in Bristol?'

'She's here for a few days for the funeral of an old friend and just called in to say hello. She didn't know about Elsie expecting, of course – nor about Baz.'

He paused, and Daisy finished it for him. 'I'm sure she was shocked. About Baz, I mean. Not Elsie.'

She bit her lip, hoping she hadn't sounded frivolous at

that moment. But Mary Yard, of all people, when they had never expected to hear anything of her again, and who had come into her own thoughts only last week.

'Yes, she was upset to hear about Baz,' her father went on. 'We're going to have a long talk about it all tomorrow evening.'

'Oh.'

'It was good to see Mary again, Daisy, and it made me realise how much I've missed talking to my contemporaries. She's invited me to have dinner with her at the hotel where she's staying.'

'Oh,' Daisy said again.

'Is that all you can say, darling?' Quentin said, amused. 'In case you're worried, we are both over twenty-one, you know.'

'I'm sorry. I was just surprised, that's all. It'll be good for you to have someone to talk over old times with, Daddy. Remember me to her, won't you?'

'I will. And give my love to all.'

The call ended; Daisy went back to the parlour where Uncle Bert was playing snakes and ladders with Teddy before his bedtime, and Aunt Rose was knitting yet another pair of socks for the soldiers' benevolent fund.

'Daddy sends his love to us all,' she told them, 'and he sounds much brighter, thank heavens.'

'I'm glad,' Rose said. 'You can't go around with a gloomy face for ever, no matter how you feel inside.'

Daisy hesitated. 'Aunt Rose, do you remember the Marys who used to have the upstairs rooms in our house?'

'Of course I do. I liked them both. Widows, weren't they?'

'Yes. One of them – Mary Yard – is in Bristol for a few days, and she and Daddy are having dinner together tomorrow evening.'

She was watching Teddy's progress on the snakes and ladders board at that moment, but she was perfectly aware

of Rose's gaze on her, and she felt her face and neck go hot.
Rose could usually guess what she was thinking, no matter
how obtuse she tried to be.

'Well, as I said, you can't go around with a gloomy face
for ever, no matter how you feel inside. And you can't
mourn someone for ever, either. Baz certainly wouldn't
want that.'

And they both knew she wasn't just speaking about
Baz.

Later, when Teddy was in bed and Bert had gone down
to his shed for half an hour before his nightly civil defence
duties, it was Rose who brought up the subject again. This
time she was her usual blunt self.

'Daisy, have you ever thought about your father marrying again?'

Daisy flinched. 'Well, I – I don't know . . .'

'I didn't ask if you approved. I asked if you had ever
thought about it.'

'Not seriously. It may have crossed my mind once or
twice, but I always managed to ignore it,' she said defensively, since she had no idea whether or not her aunt would
approve.

'I don't think your mother would ignore it, if she was
here.'

'If she was here, there'd be no need to think of any
such thing!'

Rose nodded. 'Perhaps that wasn't the cleverest way to
put it. What I mean is, I'm perfectly sure Frances wouldn't
want your father to spend the rest of his life feeling lonely.'

'He's not lonely. He's got his work, and he's got us.'

'Nobody could deny that he thinks the world of his
children, but if you think any of it compares with the
comfort and company of being married,' she said, choosing
her words more carefully now, 'then you've still got a lot of
growing up to do, Daisy.'

'That's not fair,' she muttered. 'I've seen a bit of the

world now, Aunt Rose, and I'm not in the nursery any more.'

She could hardly say that she knew physical desire didn't end when the hair grew white or the teeth fell out, because she had written too many impassioned letters for her patients to be in any doubt about that! And Quentin Caldwell was nowhere near either of those states yet.

'Then you'll know what I'm saying,' Rose went on more briskly. 'Let's leave it there, shall we? Go and make some cocoa, there's a love.'

She did as she was told, unable to forget the conversation, and trying to imagine how she would feel if her father did ever marry again. How any of them would feel. It was obvious that her aunt – her father's sister – wouldn't think it a bad thing at all. And Rose had loved her mother as much as any of them. But what about Imogen and Elsie?

It was too big a problem to solve on her own, and who said it was going to be a problem anyway? she asked herself crossly. One dinner didn't foretell a marriage. She shivered, but Aunt Rose had made her think about it seriously now. Did any of them want their father to be lonely? And *was* he lonely? She guessed that he often was, especially while Elsie was away and he was in that big house all on his own, and perhaps all of them had been selfish in not staying there to give him moral support.

It had been the sensible thing for Rose and Bert to bring Teddy to Weston after their mother died. He'd been too young and bewildered to cope with the aftermath of that terrible time. Baz had already virtually left home . . . and nobody could prevent a war, which meant Immy had wanted to do her bit. Elsie had married Joe, so it was convenient for her to stay in Bristol and take over the upstairs flat after he had enlisted. But Daisy hadn't needed to flee down to Weston herself, had she? She could have stayed. She had truly deserted her father.

'Daisy, what on earth are you doing?' Bert's voice said

close behind her as she stood rigidly in the kitchen, clasping the kettle as if it was a lifeline.

'Oh Lord, I'm sorry,' she almost gasped. 'I was miles away, Uncle Bert. I haven't even filled the kettle yet.'

He took it out of her hands. 'What's wrong, my love?'

She took a deep breath. 'Will you tell me something honestly? I know it's an awful imposition of me to ask – and I know I shouldn't . . .'

'Well, I'll never be able to give you an answer unless you do,' he said mildly, as she floundered.

'Supposing something happened to you or Aunt Rose, and one of you was left behind . . .'

'You mean if one of us died. There's no need to be afraid of the word, Daisy. It's something we all have to face sooner or later. So go on.'

'Would you expect the one who's left to remain on their own for the rest of their life? I mean, it happens to so many people in the war, doesn't it?' she said, trying desperately to make this less personal than it had been to begin with. 'I was thinking about our old lodgers, the Marys. They were both widowed in the last war, and it's an awful long time to be alone, isn't it? Do you think it would have been disloyal to their husbands if they'd married someone else? It just made me think about these things, that's all,' she finished lamely.

'I think it's up to each person to decide for themselves. There's no right or wrong about it, Daisy, but the marriage service mentions "till death us do part", so if it's death that has brought about the separation, then I don't think it's disloyal to the first partner to think of marrying again. Not that I could imagine anyone else putting up with Rose or me, mind! Does that answer your question?'

'I think so. Yes, of course it does. Thank you, Uncle Bert.'

She didn't quite know what she was thanking him for, but she kissed him impulsively. He was a dear . . . and although it didn't really answer anything regarding her father and Mary Yard, she decided she was probably getting things all out of proportion. It was best to forget all about it. For now, anyway.

In any case, things were becoming too hectic to think of anything but work. She was only scheduled to have four weeks with the ambulance crew, but it was far less routine now with a spate of accidents due to the black-out regulations.

'It's not so bad when there's a full moon at night,' Thomas told her, 'but when it's pitch-black some of these old boys out on the razzle at the local pubs can't see their way past a lamp-post. We get a lot of sore heads, especially when they miss the edge of the pavement and go crashing into the road. Next morning is when we're called out, when their old ladies have done nagging them, and realise they might have done some real damage to themselves.'

'You're having me on, aren't you?'

'I am not!' He glanced at her. 'Anyway, girl, I don't want to worry you, but after last night's raid on Bristol, we've been called out to bring some of the injured to Weston, since their hospitals need to be ready for more casualties soon.'

'It's all right; I heard about it on the wireless,' she said quickly. 'My father phoned us to let us know it was over Sea Mills way and nowhere near us.'

And even if it was, she had a job to do . . .

'Is your sister back home yet?' he went on conversationally.

'Her husband's bringing her home at the weekend; then he's got to report back to his regiment.'

It would be awful for Elsie, thought Daisy. After spending these few weeks with Joe, they would be parted at an anxious time for her sister, with only weeks to go until her baby was born. She resolved to see her whenever she could, and also to find out if anything had come of her father's meeting with Mary Yard.

Luke said it was routine work to bring back some of the injured who had been caught up in the bombing raid. It was nothing to worry about . . . but she was more than thankful to have a senior nurse on board as well as herself, and even more relieved to discover that Alice Godfrey had asked for the job.

'I volunteered,' Alice said. 'I didn't see why you should have all the fun, gallivanting about with two fellows!'

'I'm not sure that's what I'd call it, but I can't tell you how glad I am that you're here,' she said fervently. It would be the first time they had seen the real evidence of a German bombing raid, and they had to go through the city and report to the nearest hospital where most of the casualties had been taken for temporary treatment.

Thomas spoke sternly. 'You'll both be fine, but this is a new situation to all of us, remember. It's not just dealing with someone who's come into hospital to have their tonsils out. Every day is going to be different from now on.'

'But not so much for you,' Daisy pointed out. 'You're used to being called out to emergencies, aren't you?' And she had already learned to respect them for their way of dealing with everything that came their way.

Before they reached the bombed area they could see the pall of grey smoke ahead, and smell the stench of burning. There was also a lingering whiff of gas in the air, and people still milled around, civilians searching for precious bits of property and missing animals, and the Civil Defence workers trying to keep everyone back until it was all made safe. They could see the skeletons of buildings in a small street that had once been family homes and businesses. Even from this one isolated attack, there was dust and rubble everywhere, and suddenly, frighteningly, the war was right here, in front of them.

According to the pompous wireless announcer that morning, it hadn't been a serious raid, just enough to flatten a few buildings and claim about thirty casualties. There hadn't been any major damage and the docks hadn't been affected – as if that was all that mattered, and these little suburban houses and shops were of far lesser importance. Daisy had hated the complacency of the man, sitting in his cosy little studio reciting the news into the microphone.

'All right, girls, let's get on with it,' Thomas said, as Daisy stared into space, and she realised they had already stopped at the Casualty entrance of the hospital. 'We've got work to do, and these folk would prefer to see a cheerful face to a miserable one, Miss Daisy, so *smile*!'

She tried, but it was hard to smile as she helped an old man and his wife with head wounds into the ambulance, clearly still in shock, and distraught over the loss of their home. She couldn't smile at a young couple frantic at the sight of their baby with a badly cut face from flying glass. She couldn't smile at watching Thomas and Luke carefully place a hysterical young boy on a stretcher into the ambulance, seeing from his notes that he had broken his leg in several places, and trying to block her ears to his weeping mother.

Alice was marvellous, Daisy noted. She was calm and efficient, while still showing overwhelming tenderness towards the patients. Hadn't they both done the same on the hospital ship, in a far more dangerous situation than this one, and with far worse injuries? But Daisy was beginning to wonder if she was losing her nerve, and it wasn't something she wanted to admit to anyone.

As soon as all the necessary paperwork had been done, and the patients' notes handed over, they were ready to return to Weston.

'It'll get worse before it gets better, you know,' Alice said, glancing at Daisy's white face as they got into the back of the ambulance with the patients.

'I know it will,' she muttered. 'I'm just wondering if I was really cut out for this after all.'

'Of course you are. Don't be stupid, Daisy. Everyone gets panic attacks from time to time, and you're no different from anyone else. It'll pass. Remember what we're here to do, and make sure Mr and Mrs Sage are comfortable.'

Daisy glanced at the elderly couple who were sitting patients, huddled close together in blankets. They still looked dazed and bewildered, and there was dried blood and rubble in their sparse hair, but they were talking together a bit more sensibly now. She tried to smile at them encouragingly, and the old man managed a cheeky smile in return.

'That's a smile to cheer anybody up, my lover. We was just saying as how you mind my missis and me of a lady dancer we once saw on the stage years back. Can't recall her name, but she were a real smasher.'

'Sam, behave yourself,' his wife said. 'The nurse don't want to hear none of your saucy talk.'

'Was her name Frances Caldwell?' Daisy asked, her voice catching.

Sam's old eyes lit up. 'By jingo, that was the name, weren't it, Mother?' he asked his wife. 'Sang and danced like an angel, she did. Begging your pardon, nurse, but you've got quite a look of her about you, see?'

'I suppose I should,' Daisy said. 'She was my mother.'

'Well, I never,' the old woman exclaimed, perking up. 'We never expected to be riding to hospital with a celebrity, did we, Sam?'

Daisy hardly knew what to say to that, but listening to the little exchange, she saw that the young couple were looking mildly interested at well. It was taking their minds off their injuries, and only the mother with the young boy was paying no attention. Alice gave her a meaningful nod and a nudge, and before she knew what she was doing, Daisy was elaborating on the times her mother had performed on the stage in front of big audiences in Bristol and beyond.

Minutes before, she had felt so helpless, as if she was little more than a bystander as the ambulancemen and Alice went about their business; but now she saw that her stories were really helping these people who had gone through such trauma last night. It was as good as a shot in the arm, Alice whispered to her, and if they thought Daisy was halfway to being a celebrity herself, it did no harm.

It made her think fleetingly about her one-time desire to follow in her mother's footsteps. It was a dream that would never have come true – she knew that now. She no longer wanted to leave nursing to go on the stage, nor even to join up and be one of a concert party. But she knew the hospital patients had a dreary time of it, especially those who had no family or friends near enough to visit them, and they all looked forward to the Christmas carol-singing by the nurses and the magic and puppet acts that several of the porters did.

Crazy thoughts began to whirl around in her mind as the ambulance rumbled on through the countryside between Bristol and Weston. Why should such treats for the patients just be confined to Christmas? Why not a more regular bit of entertainment? She wondered if she dared mention it to Sister Macintosh.

'My friend here sings a bit too,' she heard Alice tell Sam next, just as if she was a mind-reader.

She gasped, glaring at her friend. She didn't mean here and now, for heaven's sake! It was hardly the time and place.

'Give us a song then, love,' Sam's missis said.

'Oh I don't think so. These people don't want to hear me . . .'

'We don't mind,' said the young woman, jiggling the baby up and down. 'It might stop our Lucy-Belle snivelling.'

'The baby's called Lucy?' Daisy exclaimed, feeling her heart lurch at hearing the name so unexpectedly. She flushed as they looked at her in surprise. 'I had a friend called Lucy once. I always thought it was a pretty name.'

'So what's yours then, Nursie?' old Sam asked her.

'It's Daisy.'

'Come on then, give us a tune to cheer us all up,' his

wife encouraged, and then began a wavering tune herself. 'Daisy, Daisy, give us your answer do . . .'

With a little laugh, Daisy took up the song. Alice joined in, and even the young woman began crooning it softly to her baby while her husband sat silently and awkwardly, the way young husbands did, until he muttered a few of the words to keep her company.

Only the woman with the young boy who was going to have his leg set in plaster of Paris remained silent, but she gave Daisy a fleeting smile at the end of the song, and nodded towards her boy, who was dozing now from his pain-killing injections and sheer exhaustion.

Thomas called out to her: 'Give us another one, Daisy. You're good on the ears as well as being a sight for sore eyes. I always said we'd picked a good 'un.'

Her eyes prickled at the unexpected praise. It was her mother's talent, not hers, she thought fiercely, but if a little of it had rubbed off on her, she was eternally grateful.

She sang several more songs on the way back to Weston, and the old couple did their best to join in, though by now she could see that the small burst of excitement had tired them out. The baby and the young boy were asleep by now, and she decided that enough was enough.

'I'll come and see you on the ward,' she told Sam and his missis. 'And you never know – we might be able to have a sing-song then.'

'What are you up to, Daisy?' Alice said quietly when they were all settled.

'You'll have to wait and see, won't you?' she said with a grin, feeling considerably brighter than she had all day.

'It's having a purpose that does it every time,' she told her aunt and uncle that evening. 'It was awful going into Bristol and having to deal with those poor people and seeing how the houses had been demolished. I really felt useless, though Alice was being perfectly wonderful as usual, of course, and when Thomas told me to smile I could have hit him. But he was quite right. The patients wanted to see a cheerful smiling face, and it was just so strange that the elderly couple remembered seeing Mother on the stage.'

'I don't think it was strange at all. Half of Bristol must have seen her at one time or other, so why wouldn't they have seen the likeness in you? Old people retain things in their memories far more than you might think, Daisy.'

'Well, in the end it was rather a special journey back to Weston,' she said. 'Did I tell you the baby was called Lucy? Now *that* was a coincidence if you like!'

'Yes, it was,' Rose agreed. 'So what did your Sister Macintosh say when you went to her with your entertainment suggestion?'

Daisy was cautious. 'I think she quite approved, but I can't always tell with her. She was going to present it to Matron, anyway, so we shall just have to wait and see.'

She was more than shivery about the whole thing now, wondering if she had been far too daring. After all, a nurse's prime function was to nurse people, wasn't it? not set herself up as the prospective singing star of the ward! But she hadn't meant just herself, anyway. Between them the staff might be able to work out a small entertainment show to brighten the patients' lives on a Saturday afternoon – or whenever Matron allowed them to do it.

It might never happen; but the next day she was called into Sister Macintosh's office and told that Matron thought it was a splendid idea, providing it didn't interfere with nursing duties.

'You're to be commended for your ingenuity, Daisy,' Sister said briskly. 'And you may put a notice on the board asking for any likely performer who is interested to contact you.'

'Oh, but I didn't intend to organise it all,' she began.

'Didn't you?' Sister gave one of her rare smiles. 'Well,

I'm sorry, Nurse Caldwell, but it looks as though you've just been elected.'

Elsie telephoned her when she got home from Oxford at the weekend and had said her tearful goodbyes to Joe.

'It all feels like a huge anticlimax sitting here with nothing to do,' she wailed. 'I'm as big as a house, and I already miss Joe terribly – and he's only been gone a few hours. I'd come and see you but I couldn't face the train, and I've done enough travelling for a while, so when can you come home for a visit?'

Daisy was suitably sympathetic considering her underlying excitement at how her idea had been received at the hospital. 'Oh Lord, not right now, I'm afraid. You'll never guess what's happened. We're starting up a kind of small hospital concert party to entertain the patients once a month, and I'm in charge. We're having meetings about it this weekend.'

'What?' Elsie said. She started to laugh and then sobered up as the familiar kick of the baby brought her up short. 'Well, I shouldn't be surprised, of course. You were always a bit of a bossy-boots, weren't you, sweetie?'

'Well, thank you! I didn't actually ask to be in charge, but it just happened to be my idea, and I'm landed with it now.'

She didn't say it had come to her while she was transporting patients from a Bristol bombing raid to Weston General. Elsie must know the kind of danger they were all in, but she still stubbornly refused to move.

'I know you'll do a wonderful job, darling. Take no notice of my scratchiness. It's just that I never thought nine months could be so long, that's all, especially when it's so hot.'

'Is it really that bad?' Daisy said quickly, unable to imagine it, and not wanting to do so anyway.

'Yes – and no – of course not. But it will all be worth it in the end, or so Mrs Woodley keeps telling me. The minute they put the baby in your arms, you're supposed to forget all that's gone before,' she said delicately. 'I'll believe that when it happens. For a midwife, she's disgustingly cheerful, but I suppose that's better than telling you about everything that could go wrong.'

'Nothing's going to go wrong,' Daisy said, aware of the apprehension in her sister's voice now. 'Good Lord, people have babies every day. They'd stop doing it if they thought it was that bad, wouldn't they?'

'Oh yes, champion philosopher who knows nothing about it!' Elsie said, laughing, and with her own secret thoughts on the subject.

'Well, look, I promise I'll come up for a night or two when I can,' Daisy said, relieved that she sounded more like her usual self now. 'Unless you've had any thoughts about coming to Weston to have the baby?'

'What, and frighten Teddy out of his wits? Not likely. I know Mrs Woodley well by now, and she's the one I want with me when the time comes. Besides, I couldn't face moving all my things anywhere at the moment, and I wouldn't want to leave Father here all on his own.'

'Oh, Elsie, that reminds me!' As her sister became more decisive, Daisy couldn't keep her curiosity at bay any longer. 'Has he told you anything about having dinner with Mary Yard?'

Twenty

To Daisy's relief it was decided to have a nurses' choir, rather than individual singers. At once time she might have felt peeved that she wasn't to be the star of the show, but now she was glad it was going to be a community activity. The hospital staff all had jobs to do, and they worked different shifts, so this way they could call on the core of the available nurses to form half a dozen songsters at each performance. The porters and other staff with various talents would provide the extra entertainment. It was going to work well.

'I think you're amazing, Daisy dear,' her sister Imogen told her with a laugh on the telephone, hearing her enthusiasm. 'You and Baz were always going to come up smiling, weren't you? And I'm not going to get all embarrassed over what I just said, because he got exactly what he wanted out of life, and we must never forget that. So good for you, sis!'

'Thanks,' Daisy said briefly. 'So how are things with you, and to what do we owe the honour of this phone call? Are you still in London?'

'For the time being,' Immy said cautiously; 'but once Elsie's had the baby I hope the service for Baz will go ahead fairly soon afterwards. And I'm saying no more than that.'

She didn't need to, though where the army would be sending troops now that the Germans had occupied France, Daisy didn't know. And since nothing was ever given away, it was like a blessed mystery story, she thought crossly.

'What's it like being in London now then?' she said instead.

'Noisy. The sirens go off every night, and even if nothing's actually happening here, there are always aircraft overhead, and the sound of the south-east raids and the ack-ack fire,' Immy said grimly. 'The RAF boys are doing a grand job, of course, and did I tell you there are a lot of Australian and New Zealand servicemen around now? Interesting types.'

'Types?'

Immy laughed self-consciously. 'That's the way some of the officers refer to them, especially the RAF ones. They have a language all their own, Daisy.'

Daisy felt her heart give a pang, because Cal had only just begun his RAF career and hadn't had much chance to pick up some of the special slang that was so delightfully RAF talk. Presumably Glenn Fraser would have done so by now, despite being a Canadian. She found herself wondering where he was now and, more importantly, if he was still safe. She had liked him a lot . . .

Her thoughts switched to why her sister seemed happy to talk about anything but the situation in London and where she might be posted next.

'Oh, by the way, Immy,' she said casually, 'I saw an old friend of yours in Bristol the last time I was there. At least, he said he was an old friend, though I thought he was rather a brash kind of fellow.'

'Oh? And what do you know about my taste in young men? Not that I've ever had a large following to choose from, darling!' Immy said with a smile.

'Well, I meant the gorgeous James, of course! But let me think. It was some Welsh name – Morgan something-or-other. He implied that you'd be sure to remember him. Was it Morgan Raine?'

'Yes, it was.' Immy's voice had suddenly gone flat, and she might have known Daisy would sense it, and never be able to leave it at that.

'*Well*? Who was he? I don't ever remember seeing him before. Did you have a secret admirer before you fell in love with James Church? And should he be told about this other man, I wonder?' she teased.

'He certainly should not,' Immy said sharply, 'because there's nothing to tell. I knew Morgan Raine long ago before Daddy had to sell out the shop to Preston's Emporium. He was going to do some leaflets for Elsie once, when she thought of doing some work at home. He's a newspaper reporter, and he's just someone I used to know.'

'Well, methinks the lady doth protest too much!'

'Nonsense. I'm not protesting at all—'

'And I never knew you had such an interesting past!' Daisy went on.

'Daisy, don't be silly. If you've met him, then you'll know he's good-looking and quite charming, but also rather too fond of the ladies, and I mean that in the plural. So if he makes any advances to you, I advise you to keep well away from him. I think you know what I mean. Now, if you don't mind, I'd prefer not to talk about him any longer, and in any case I'll have to go, darling.'

She hung up before Daisy could say any more; but not before an image of Morgan Raine's dark and dashing good looks had flashed into Immy's mind. Not before she unwillingly recalled the times they had shared on the hillside above Vicarage Street, when she had lain in his arms in the sweet grass and listened to his persuasive, seductive Welsh voice telling her that he loved her and wanted her and needed her . . .

Immy shivered, thanking God that she had found out before it was too late that he had also been sweet-talking another girl; before she had fallen completely for his charms and given in to him; before she had realised that it was no more than infatuation, and that her one true love was James, her best friend's brother, who had been there all along, only she had just been too blind to see it . . .

Daisy was intrigued more by the things Immy hadn't said than what she had, and one of these days she must remember to ask Elsie just what she knew about a newspaper reporter called Morgan Raine.

After she had assured her aunt and uncle that Immy was fine, and seemed to be enjoying her war, especially with these dark and infuriatingly hush-hush hints that she might be doing something exciting in the near future.

'Why does nobody ever tell us anything definite?' she complained.

'What would you have our people do?' Bert said. 'Announce to the Jerries that we're going to bomb Berlin every Sunday night, or that we're planning to put up defences all along the south coast so that they'll sneak in around Norfolk instead? It's important to have strategies in a war, Daisy, and one of them is to keep the enemy guessing.'

'The enemy, yes! But we're not the enemy.'

'You're not, and neither am I, but who knows who else might be listening and passing on information to the enemy? You have to be careful who you talk to these days. Careless talk costs lives and all that!'

Rose started laughing. 'For goodness' sake, Bert, you'll have our Daisy thinking there are spies around every corner. Though there might be, of course, and we can never be sure of strangers these days. You never know who you might be talking to in a queue at the butcher's, or on a train, since everyone seems free and easy in talking to people without proper introductions nowadays.'

'Even in hospital,' Daisy said solemnly. 'Perhaps old Mr Sage was wired up to a listening device somewhere in Berlin while we were taking him to Weston General! Or the boy with the broken leg has been passing messages on his plaster to anyone who wants to see what has been written on it.'

'All right, you two, I know when I'm being had,' Bert

said with a grin. 'So let's forget it. When is your first concert to be, Daisy?'

'On Saturday afternoon. We're holding it in the main ward, and not all the patients will be able to be there, especially those who are too ill to be moved, so we're going to make it a kind of roving show, and by the end of it we'll probably all be hoarse. I'm sure we'll never be ready, and rehearsals are so haphazard it will probably be an absolute shambles.'

There was far more organising involved than she had imagined, which was why it had been decided to hold it only once a month. Since she had now been given the grand title of producer of the show, she was getting butterflies in her stomach, just thinking about it.

'Nonsense, love,' Bert said loyally. 'In any case, think what a treat it will be for the patients. Instead of looking at four dreary walls, they'll have the chance to see our girl singing her heart out.'

Daisy laughed. 'And the rest of them! We do make a good sound when we're altogether, though, and Nurse Sims is wonderful on the piano. Actually, the real star is Bill Watts and his magic. He's done his act a few times on the children's ward, but I've only ever seen him pushing patients about on a trolley.'

'He's obviously a man of hidden talents,' Rose said. 'Well, I hope it will be a great success, Daisy, and I'm sure the patients will love it.'

She was very nervous when the day came, and it didn't help to settle any of them when they had an emergency admission and Bill Watts was summoned to take the elderly patient up to the ward just as the entertainment was about to begin.

Fortunately, his act was one of the last ones, and they breathed a sigh of relief when he appeared as the songsters were still in the middle of their repertoire. By then the more able patients had joined in every chorus of the well-known songs, and it was obvious that this was the highlight of their day. The roving show was an excellent idea, since it gave the patients a chance to think about something other than their ailments.

But Daisy was right, and by the time she got home that evening, she didn't have much voice left. 'I'm very thankful we don't have to do it again tomorrow,' she said huskily to Aunt Rose, 'and that tomorrow is Sunday, so I can have a bit of a rest.'

'After church, of course.'

Daisy groaned. 'Must I go? My throat really is quite sore, Aunt Rose.'

'Then it's a dose of honey and lemon for you, some Vick to rub in your throat, and one of Bert's old woolly socks around your neck when you go to bed.'

'I wonder that anyone would need to go to hospital when you're around,' Daisy said, her voice cracking. 'All they need is an Aunt Rose with her patent medicines.'

'And they work too,' Bert reminded her with a chuckle. 'You do as your auntie says, my love, and you'll be as right as ninepence in the morning.'

Daisy didn't doubt it, nor did she dare to dispute it. Sometimes they made her feel like a child again, but when you were feeling out of sorts, it was lovely to feel so cosseted. And after feeling so exhilarated at the success of the afternoon, and basking in the congratulations the nurses and patients had heaped on her and the other members of their show, it was probably just the after-effects giving her this deflated feeling.

Next morning, she knew it was more than that. Her throat felt raw and ragged, and she had a raging headache. It hurt when she opened her eyes, and she closed them again quickly. When Teddy came and jumped up and down on her bed at what felt like the crack of dawn, she winced at his energy.

'Get up, lazy-bones. We're all having breakfast,' he shouted.

'Get *off*,' she croaked. 'Tell Aunt Rose I don't want any breakfast and I'm staying in bed. I don't feel well.'

When he said nothing for a moment, she opened her eyes a fraction and through the slits of her lids she saw him staring at her.

'Are you going to die, like Baz?' he said finally.

'Of course I'm not going to die,' she said crossly, and then she saw that he really meant what he said. She was so rarely unwell, and never stayed in bed unnecessarily, and she could see the scared look in Teddy's eyes now. She caught hold of his hand.

'It's only a headache, Teddy, and I'll be fine in a little while. Go and tell Aunt Rose, will you, love?'

He slid off the bed, his face still troubled. She forced a smile to her lips.

'*Shoot!*' she said.

Minutes later Rose came into the bedroom. 'I've heard of some excuses for not going to church, Daisy, but I didn't think you'd resort to this one!'

'It's no excuse, honestly,' she replied weakly.

Rose felt her forehead and then her pulse.

'Probably a touch of flu. You're in the best place, and you're to stay there for a few days. Hot lemon drinks and aspirins will do the trick, and I'll let the hospital know in the morning.'

'You should have been a nurse,' Daisy murmured.

'Oh, I've done my bit. That, and applying common sense,' Rose said with a smile. 'Now, I'll bring the necessary medication up, and then you try and get some sleep. That's often the best medicine in these cases.'

She stayed in bed for five days, letting the world revolve around her. There was a war on, but she was so light-headed that it meant nothing to her. The house could have fallen down, and she'd have been perfectly content to fall with it, floating in that weird sense of not being quite there at all.

269

Rose and Bert saw to her every need, and Teddy played the little doctor on occasion, bringing her magazines that she couldn't read, and carefully carrying her bowl of chicken soup for dinner, which was all she felt like eating, and being told strictly not to stay in the bedroom too long in case he caught it too. Hearing the instructions, she began to feel like a leper, and she didn't care . . .

On the sixth day, she awoke with her head clear and her eyes unfuzzy. Her throat didn't hurt every time she swallowed, and she was aware of the world outside her window for the first time in days. She could hear the sound of birds singing, and the clatter of the milk lorry going along the road. Her brain was becoming active again, and she no longer felt like a very old lady. She was eighteen and alive. She was better.

'You're awake then,' Aunt Rose greeted her when she came into the room a little while later.

'And sitting up, and eager to get up,' Daisy told her.

'Not so fast, young lady. Your legs won't want to move that quickly after five days in bed. Take it one step at a time.'

But Daisy could tell from the relief in her voice that she was glad to see the improvement. And looking across at her reflection in the mirror on her dressing table, she could see that she looked pretty well back to normal, except for the haystack tangle of her hair.

'Can I have my comb, please?'

Rose laughed. 'Of course you can, love. It's the first thing a woman wants when she's been ill, isn't it?'

'Have I been very ill? I don't remember much.'

'Just a sharp bout of flu, but that can be quite nasty. Anyway, you're young and strong, and you quickly responded to treatment, as you professionals say.'

'I don't feel much like a professional right now,' Daisy said, tugging the comb through the knots in her hair. 'I was looking forward to going back to work on Monday and having praises heaped on me from the patients after the show. What a let-down!' she mocked herself.

'You'd better have these cards then,' Rose said, handing her the small pile of envelopes. 'Alice brought them round last night. She knew it was best not to come up and see you until you're quite better because of taking infection back to the hospital. She's a very sensible young woman. And there are two letters for you as well.'

Daisy opened the envelopes, touched that the cards came from staff and patients, and she recognised Elsie's handwriting on one of the envelopes. Her father had called every night, Rose told her, so she hadn't been forgotten while she was lying in her bed of pain.

The second letter had been forwarded from the hospital, and when she opened it her heart gave a giant leap on seeing the signature.

'Oh, my goodness,' she said softly.

'I hope it's not bad news,' Aunt Rose said, busily tidying the bedroom.

'No. It's from an old friend – well, just someone I met really, not exactly a friend . . .

She was babbling, and she clamped her lips together before Aunt Rose thought she was going mad, and quickly read the words Glenn Fraser had written:

> You may not even remember me, Daisy, but I've never forgotten you, and I very much hope our paths will cross again someday. It's taken me a heck of a time to know where to write to you, but I put my detective nose to work and finally remembered you were at a hospital in some place called Weston-super-Mare, so I hope this reaches you. And if it does, and you feel like writing back, I'd love to hear from you.
>
> Yours cordially,
> Glenn Fraser

His image was instantly in her mind, dashing and handsome, and she was remembering how they had danced together in a wartime dance hall in Folkestone, almost floating around the floor to a slow waltz tune. He had remembered her all this time, and whether or not it was the thrill of knowing that, or the knowledge that at last she could respond without the awful feeling of guilt because of Cal, she felt suddenly, wonderfully invigorated.

The feeling was momentous, as if she had finally come out of a long, dark tunnel, and she wasn't quite ready yet to share her feelings with anyone. She needed to be alone and no longer fussed over. There was only one really private place, and she asked her aunt if she could have a bath.

'Only if you allow me to supervise, Daisy. I'll be outside the door, in case you need me.'

'I'm sure it won't be necessary.' But Rose was adamant, and once she had revelled in the sheer luxury of warm water for ten minutes, she was glad to be helped into her clothes and to start feeling human again. And to start feeling more positive about life than she had in ages. There was something to look forward to after all. There was Glenn . . . and she was thankful that Aunt Rose kept any curiosity about the letter to herself.

'So what have I been missing?' she said, after a wobbly walk downstairs and into the parlour. Bert was working in the garden and Teddy was at school, but she had to put up with George's ecstatic and very slobbery welcome.

'Well, the war's still going on, and the RAF have successfully bombed Berlin. Hitler had been assured that our boys could never reach Berlin, so that must have been a severe blow to his pride. It's not all bad news.'

The way she said it alerted Daisy. 'So what was the bad news?'

Rose was as casual as she dared to be. 'London was bombed last weekend. Mr Churchill has praised our RAF

272

pilots as being the finest in the world and he is assured that we shall soon fight them off.'

Daisy was deflated at once, unable to stop wondering if Glenn had been involved. So much for peace of mind . . . but she had never believed in being negative, and everyone had to face up to these things. She swallowed her fears for Glenn and tried to sound objective.

'It still doesn't stop Hitler's planes dropping bombs on our cities, does it, Aunt Rose? And Immy's in London . . .'

'Now, you don't want to go worrying about Imogen. I'm sure she can take care of herself, and she has a job to do, the same as everybody else. You just worry about getting better.'

'I *am* better, and I have a job to go to as well.'

'Not yet you don't, Daisy. I spoke to Sister Macintosh while you were in the bath, and she says you're to stay home all next week so that you're fully recovered and won't be bringing any germs into the hospital. She's quite right.'

And when Aunt Rose got that determined look in her eyes, Daisy knew there was no moving her. She and Sister Macintosh were a perfect match for one another, she thought, so she might as well be resigned to it.

But long before the next week was over her energy had returned and she was anxious to be doing something again. Inactivity didn't suit her at all. Besides which, she was beginning to feel mildly incarcerated. The summer weather was good, and she wanted to go walking on the beach, which always revived her spirits, as soon as her legs felt capable of holding her up for any length of time. But she discovered that it was going to take a few more days before that happened.

The next week dragged, and the war news was depressing. Air raids were becoming more frequent everywhere now, and once she felt more normal again, Daisy felt completely useless to be twiddling her thumbs while the rest of the country seemed embroiled in either trying to win the war or barricading themselves against possible invasion.

She had already written back to Glenn, assuring him that of course she remembered him, and that she would love to exchange letters with him. She was tempted to sign it 'with love', but that would be going just too far – it was too soon. They could be on the brink of something wonderful, or this could just be the beginning of friendship. All the same, as she posted her letter, she knew how eagerly she would be waiting for his next one. She had read that first one a dozen times by now, and each time she did, it seemed that she could hear his voice saying the words in his delicious Canadian accent, and her heart beat faster when she remembered it.

By now Teddy was forever badgering her to play with him, and he was constantly getting on her nerves, and in the end she suggested that she should go and spend a few days with Elsie to keep her company.

'I promised that I would at some stage, and it must be lonely for her when Daddy's out at the shop all day, and again if he's called out at night. What do you think, Aunt Rose?'

'I'm not sure if you should. You're still convalescing, remember.'

'Oh, but I feel perfectly well now, and if I have to stay inactive for much longer, I shall probably go mad with boredom!'

'We wouldn't want that, would we?' Rose said drily, and they both knew this was her way of giving her assent.

Elsie was delighted to see her.

'I know Daddy will be relieved too. He's taking this second job very seriously, Daisy, and they say all little boys grow up wanting to be either engine-drivers or firemen, so I think he's in his element.'

'I bet he is, but it's dangerous work too. It's not just ordinary house fires these days, is it? I know those are awful for the people concerned,' she added hastily, 'but it must be far worse when you're called to deal with fires in the middle of an air raid and you never know where the next bomb is going to fall.'

'Well, you're a proper Job's comforter, aren't you? I thought you were here to cheer me up. I'm sure they know what to expect and what to do about it.'

Elsie wasn't sure she believed it herself, because none of them knew what to expect these days, and the air-raid sirens were an almost nightly occurrence now, even if no substantial damage had been done to the city as yet. But she had other things to think about beside German bombs.

For several days now she had had the most appalling stitch in her side and it wouldn't go away. The midwife said it was just the baby lying awkwardly, and she shouldn't pay too much attention to it. It would soon be over, anyway. Sometimes she could be cheerful to the point of infuriating Elsie. It wasn't *her* pain anyway, but she trusted her implicitly.

'Why don't you stay in the flat with me while you're here, instead of in your old room?' she asked Daisy. 'You can have Mary Yard's old bedroom, and we can have midnight talks if we feel like it.'

'Back to our schooldays, you mean, when we crept into one another's bedrooms for a gossip, desperately trying not to disturb the parents?' Daisy said with a grin. Though she wasn't ready to tell her anything about Glenn yet, because there wasn't anything yet to tell. It was still her sweet secret, something that belonged only to her.

The memory of those old times was so wonderfully emotive, so heartbreakingly taking them back to days that could never come again, when the family had all been together, whole and alive, and there had been no talk of wars and danger. Her throat caught with the magnitude of all that had happened since then.

'I'll do that,' she went on brightly, in answer to Elsie's

suggestion. 'And talking of Mary Yard, you still haven't told me what you know!'

Quentin came into the house just then, and the chance to quiz Elsie was gone; but Daisy wasn't an observer for nothing – a nurse always watched out for signs in the patient – and her father was showing clear signs of happiness that was possibly only partly due to his youngest daughter having come home for a few days. Well, well.

'It's good to see you, darling,' he greeted her. 'I'm on duty for the next few nights, so you two can get your little heads together and do your plotting without me around.'

Daisy laughed. 'I can't think what you mean, Daddy. When did we ever do any plotting, as you call it!' But she didn't look at Elsie as she said it.

Once darkness fell, it seemed as if the noise of aircraft went on incessantly. Elsie said knowledgeably that they were theirs, not Hitler's, and she'd soon know the difference if they had a raid. Everyone was an expert in the different engine sounds by now. Daisy brought up their bedtime cocoa and sat on the edge of Elsie's bed as her sister gave up trying to get comfortable lying down and sat gingerly on the edge of a chair.

'We can go down to the shelter if you feel nervous, Daisy.'

'Do you want to?'

'No. I hate it in there. I feel as if I'm in a prison, and it smells of earth and Lord knows what else. In any case I've got no intention of stating on his birth certificate that my baby was born in an air-raid shelter at the bottom of the garden, thank you very much!'

'It's not about to be, is it? There's still two or three weeks to go, isn't there?'

Elsie gave a crooked smile as the stitch in her side became far more than that, and enveloped her. 'That was the plan, but apparently babies don't always arrive according to plan.

When they decide they want to be born, there's no stopping them, Daisy—'

Her voice ended on a huge gasp, and she put down her cup of cocoa with shaking hands. In the gaslight, her face was white and pinched as she looked at her sister. Beneath Elsie's nightdress they saw the sudden gush of water on the floor.

'Oh God, Elsie . . .'

'I think you'd better telephone Mrs Woodley. Better still, run down the road and fetch her. It looks as though you're going to be in on the big event.'

'Are you sure you're not mistaken . . . ?'

Her reply was a small scream from Elsie as she clutched her stomach.

'I'm sure,' she gasped. 'I'm told it will take hours and hours, but it doesn't feel like it. You'd better go, Daisy, unless you want to deliver the baby yourself.'

Daisy fled, only stopping to grab the torch that was kept by the front door, and remembering to keep it partly covered as she raced along the road to the midwife's house. She hammered on the door. An upstairs window opened and a voice asked who was there.

'It's Daisy Caldwell, Mrs Woodley,' she gasped. 'Elsie thinks the baby's on its way. Can you come, please?'

'It's probably a false alarm, but I'd better take a look,' the woman said, while Daisy fumed at her easy manner. It was presumably meant to calm the patients down, but it didn't help Daisy's nerves, realising she might have to assist, or at least be on hand . . . and it wasn't what she had come home for.

She hopped up and down until the midwife appeared a few minutes later, fully dressed, her gas mask over one shoulder, her bag of tricks in the other hand. Her hair was a metal torment of curlers, and it might have looked comical if Daisy had felt like laughing. There were aircraft overhead now and searchlight beams picking them out, and right on cue, the air-raid siren sounded as they hurried back to the house, and the sound of retaliating gunfire shook the road.

'Don't let it bother you, Daisy. If the baby's on its way we'll be too busy in the next few hours to pay any attention to Adolph's fly-by-nights, and neither me nor your sister want to use the blessed air-raid shelter, but if you're desperate to do so, you'll have to leave us to get on with it. All right?'

'Yes,' Daisy mumbled, recognising the professional's technique of keeping her mind occupied as the harsh rumble of enemy aircraft was replaced by the scream of bombs, and then an almighty explosion as the night sky was lit up by flames. 'But I am a nurse, remember? I never desert a patient.'

'Good girl,' Mrs Woodley said.

It seemed as if they had only taken minutes to return to Elsie's bedroom, but once they saw her it was obvious that her baby was impatient to arrive in the world and that this was no false alarm. Mrs Woodley took charge at once.

'Daisy, boil a kettle and fetch me some clean towels. And Elsie, get back in bed unless you want the child to crack its skull on the floor the minute it's born.'

Daisy appreciated her brisk efficiency now. Elsie did as she was told, while she herself was a shivering bag of nerves. She knew it and couldn't stop it. She had been to Dunkirk and back. She had seen ghastly sights in the hospital. She had helped to lay out the dead. But she had never seen a baby born before, especially not one that was so close to her. It was an intimacy she had never sought.

'I'm sorry, Daisy,' she heard Elsie gasp when she had done as she was told. By now they were all trying to ignore the way the house was shaking with the shattering sounds of bombs hitting their targets and the bursts of gunfire that threatened to split the eardrums.

Daisy looked down at her sister, her face contorted with pain, her lovely red hair darkened with sweat. Elsie reached out to grasp her hand, and gripped it tight, and as she did so,

Daisy's fear fell away, and she saw only a patient in pain, whom she could help just by being there.

'It's all right, I'm here,' she said steadily. 'Grab me as hard as you like, and just think how thrilled Joe's going to be when he knows his baby's arrived. Just think how the two of you are going to show him off to the rest of us. You'll make us all jealous, because I'm sure he's going to be perfectly beautiful, and it won't be long now before we see him.'

Although she was prattling on, she did it in a slow, calm voice, knowing it would make Elsie feel calmer in return. She had spoken to patients in this way so many times before, though never to a woman about to give birth, nor to an older sister; but she knew how a soothing voice helped.

Mrs Woodley evidently saw her as a medical aide now, giving her asides in how much Elsie was dilated and how soon she could expect to push. Daisy didn't particularly want to hear it, and she concentrated instead on trying not to admit how numb her fingers were becoming as Elsie gripped and clung to her.

'Do we need the doctor?' she said anxiously as the hours passed, and Elsie gave a particularly anguished cry as the contractions went on and on.

'Bless you, no. This is going very nicely,' came the cheerful voice. 'It's a harsh birth, but a quick one, and you can prepare to push now, Elsie love.'

Daisy had never realised it was such a struggle to be born, nor that she would have to witness her sister's pain. She would surely never want to go through such agony again, not even for Joe . . . She was finding it hard not to cry herself, and Elsie was pushing for all she was worth now. The baby's head and shoulders had already emerged, and Daisy found it impossible not to look . . . and then there was a sudden slithering expulsion as the baby slid into the world, drawing air into its lungs and crying at once.

'Oh, that's the most beautiful sound in the world!' Elsie

gasped, and Daisy tore her eyes away from the miracle, and looked into her sister's shimmering eyes.

'It's a beautiful sight too, and so are you,' she said huskily.

'It's a girl,' Mrs Woodley said, not giving them a moment to get emotional, since there was still work to be done, as she called it. 'And I bet neither of you even noticed that the all-clear sounded half an hour ago.'

They hadn't. And once the birth was complete, she wrapped the baby in a towel and placed her in Elsie's arms, and went to make them a cup of tea, leaving the two of them alone.

'She's just perfect,' Daisy breathed, looking down at the tiny face and delicate features, and the shock of glorious red Caldwell hair. 'Joe will be so proud of you, Elsie. And Mother would be too.'

'I'm sure she still is,' Elsie said with a tremulous smile. 'My only regret is that she'll never see her – and that Joe wasn't here with me. I was proud of you too, Daisy. I couldn't have done so well without you.'

'I wasn't that brave. I was scared, if you must know.'

'Well, it didn't show. You're a real nurse, darling. But I never doubted that everything would be all right. Joe told me always to have faith, and so I did.'

She drew in her breath. 'That's what we'll call her, Daisy.'

'What?' Daisy said, not following her train of thought, and still bemused by the perfection of the new little life that was now part of all of them, trying to imagine her father's face when he came home from his fire-watching to discover that their family had now expanded by one.

'We were too superstitious to think of a name, but I'm going to call her Faith, because that's something we all need these days.'

As if by magical, silent approval, the baby opened her eyes. They were vacantly blue right now, although the

280

midwife had told them they would almost certainly change to the glowing Caldwell brown. Daisy leaned forward and kissed the baby's satiny cheek, tasting her skin and feeling her sweet breath, as light as thistledown. It touched her heart as nothing else had ever done. It was their hope, and their future.

'Welcome to our world, Faith,' she whispered.